Romancing
DAPHNE

OTHER BOOKS AND AUDIO BOOKS
BY SARAH M. EDEN

THE LANCASTER FAMILY
Seeking Persephone
Courting Miss Lancaster

THE JONQUIL FAMILY
The Kiss of a Stranger
Friends and Foes
Drops of Gold
As You Are
A Fine Gentleman

STAND-ALONE NOVELS
Glimmer of Hope
An Unlikely Match
For Elise

Romancing DAPHNE

A Regency Romance

SARAH M. EDEN

Covenant Communications, Inc.

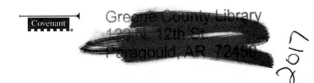

Cover image: *An 18th Century Woman* © Laura Kate Bradley, courtesy arcangel.com

Cover design copyright © 2017 by Covenant Communications, Inc.

Author photo © 2017 Annalisa Rosenvall

Published by Covenant Communications, Inc.
American Fork, Utah

Printed in the United States of America
First Printing: June 2017

23 22 21 20 19 18 17   10 9 8 7 6 5 4 3 2 1

ISBN 978-1-52440-296-9

To Jewel,

who read every incarnation of this story and expertly helped me decide what to keep, what to change, and what to pretend I never wrote in the first place

Acknowledgments

I COULD NOT POSSIBLY HAVE written a character possessing Daphne Lancaster's particular expertise with any degree of accuracy without some tremendously helpful resources:

Chemist and Druggist and *The Therapeutic Gazette*, two nineteenth-century British trade journals, which provided detailed information on the apothecary profession in the 1800s.

William Joseph Simmonite's 1865 guide to *Medical Botany*, which offered invaluable and incredibly precise information on the use of herbs for the treatment of disease and ailments in the nineteenth century.

Additionally, I wish to acknowledge with deepest gratitude:

Karen Adair, who keeps me on task and hopeful, who laughs with me and bemoans with me and who cheers me on when I need it the most.

Pam Howell and Bob Diforio, the greatest team an author could hope for.

Samantha Millburn, for always taking my writing to a whole new level. You are amazing!

My family, for putting up with all the chaos and encouraging me to tell these stories.

Chapter One

London, October 1806

Daphne Lancaster stood hidden in the shadows of her brother-in-law's terrace, spying on Society's first introduction to a young lady of unparalleled beauty. The belle of the ball that night was none other than her own older sister. Athena had always been inexpressibly stunning. No one, however, had ever lacked the words to describe how very plain Daphne was.

The first such comments had come from a Mrs. Carter when Daphne was six. "Such a lovely looking family, the Lancasters," Mrs. Carter had said to her sister. "Except for that little Daphne."

"Yes," had come the unwavering reply. "A little mouse of a thing. Has not a bit of her mother's beauty, poor girl. She'll not amount to much as far as looks, I'm afraid."

After overhearing that conversation, Daphne had spent an entire month attempting to overcome her unfortunate plainness. She had worn ribbons in her hair and had shined her own shoes twice a day. No matter the strength of her desire to run and play, she had kept still and quiet and, therefore, pristinely clean and well turned-out.

Some months later, the vicar's wife had told her how grateful she should be to not have her sisters' beauty, as a bit of plainness tended to keep young ladies from becoming overly pert. Surely a vicar's wife would know the truth of such a thing.

She hadn't bothered with the bows after that but had secretly hoped someone would tell her she'd grown into a lovely girl. No one ever had.

Now, at twelve, she'd learned to accept that she would not receive the attention she'd once longed for. She was too short, too plain, too shy, and too unnecessary.

Athena, though, was none of those things.

The Duke of Kielder's town house overflowed with fine gowns and glittering jewels. Voices slipped out through the open french doors, filling the night air. The crowd wove in and out amongst itself. Not a soul kept still.

Watching Athena's ball was the closest Daphne would come to being loved by Society. It wasn't the *ton's* notice she wished for, truly. Though she had never told a single soul, she dreamed and wished and hoped, deep in the most hidden bits of herself, for someone to fall utterly in love with her.

Do not be such a sentimental gudgeon, Daphne silently chided herself. She'd known all her life she would likely end up a spinster. *You aren't pretty, but you are practical. That is something.*

But watching Athena dazzle the gathering, the "something" Daphne had to offer felt far too much like "nothing."

She turned away, feeling her spirits drop with every passing moment. She leaned against the railing that ran the length of the terrace and lifted her face to the skies, sighing more dramatically than she ever allowed herself to.

"Now, what could possibly have inspired such a sorrowful sound?"

She stiffened. The voice was unfamiliar. Who was this man who had found her alone on the balcony? She turned warily toward him.

"Have you been banished to the nursery and thus find yourself longing to join the party?" he asked.

She had in fact been told to remain in her bedchamber. Her eyes settled on his face and seemed to stick there. He was very young, likely as young as Athena, who had only just turned nineteen. He had the most wonderfully brown eyes lit by a lantern very near where he stood. Daphne's eyes were brown as well but a pitiful, muddy brown. This stranger's glowed a shade closer to copper than dirt.

She stepped into the shadowed corner of the empty terrace, feeling overwhelmingly plain and conspicuous. No one had ventured out but this gentleman. If she slipped away, no one else would know she'd disobeyed Adam's orders about staying in her room.

"Do not fear, Little Sparrow, I'll not tattle." He offered her an almost commiserating smile. "Sometimes one simply must have a peek at all that one is missing." He motioned toward the window, just distant enough for the activity within to be unseen.

It seemed he understood her need to look, to see what she had only been able to vaguely hear and frustratingly imagine.

The young gentleman strode casually closer to where she stood, and Daphne slipped farther into her corner. She'd learned very young how to make herself appear smaller.

"I am assuming, Little Sparrow, that you are a relation of either the duke or the duchess, seeing as you appear to be a guest in this house." The gentleman's expression remained kind, though it grew a bit conspiratorial. Daphne felt her nervousness ease by degrees. "I have heard it whispered about that all the Lancaster family are named for Greek mythological characters. I assume, though, that you were not christened Medusa."

Daphne shook her head, recognizing that he was teasing her. It was a very unfamiliar experience.

"You do smile after all." His brilliant eyes softened as he spoke. "A pretty young lady such as yourself ought to smile."

A pretty young lady. Had he truly called her pretty? No one ever had before—not her father nor any of her siblings. Even her dear Adam, who'd become closer to her than she imagined any brother-in-law ever had to his wife's sister, had never said as much. Though none of them had ever spoken unkindly or unflatteringly of her appearance, Daphne couldn't remember any of them calling her pretty.

"Now, in exchange for allowing me to see that smile, which I am beginning to suspect is a rare sight, I shall provide you with what I am certain will prove a crucial piece of information."

Her eyes had not left his face. She simply could not look away. Perhaps he would remain and talk with her for a while longer. If she smiled again, he might tell her once more that she was pretty. If she were really fortunate, he would call her Little Sparrow again. Though she could not say why, she very much liked the name he had fashioned for her.

"The Duke of Kielder is even now making his way toward the very window through which you have been spying on the ball," the young gentleman told Daphne. "If it is *his* orders you are defying, you would be well advised to escape before His Dastardliness discovers your villainy. He does have a remarkably sinister reputation, as you are no doubt aware."

Daphne nodded. She knew of Adam's reputation and that he had earned every ounce of it. She further knew that he had a kind and caring heart beneath it all. He would not, however, be happy to find her on the terrace, at odds with his instructions. He was very accustomed to being obeyed in everything.

"Fly away, Little Sparrow," the young gentleman instructed.

"Please do not tell the duke I am out here." Her words did not reach above a whisper—they seldom did.

"You are not actually in danger, are you?" Genuine concern touched his words.

"No, but he will be very put out with me."

"I give you my word not to reveal your secret. And I assure you, a promise from James Tilburn" —a tip of his head told her the name was his own—"is as good as gold."

She sensed that about him—that he could be trusted. "Thank you, sir."

"You are quite welcome." He offered the very briefest of bows and one final smile before slowly making his way back toward the center of the terrace.

Daphne watched him for one drawn-out moment. *James Tilburn.* She committed the name to memory. James Tilburn, who thought her pretty and did not readily overlook her. James Tilburn, who called her Little Sparrow and spoke kindly to a young lady most dismissed on first glance.

He would not give her another thought. Indeed, he had probably already forgotten her. She, however, knew she would forever cherish the memory of him.

Daphne slipped into the empty book room and up the back staircase to her bedchamber, lost in her thoughts. She would likely find her mind wandering to him again and again over the days and weeks that stretched ahead of her. Perhaps she would see him again or hear of him in the passing comments of those around her.

"Someday," she told herself, "I should very much like to marry a gentleman exactly like James Tilburn."

James delayed his return to the ballroom as long as possible. At only eighteen years of age, he fit absolutely nowhere. He was too young to be a suitor, *far* too young to keep company with the matrons and seasoned gentlemen, and too old to be left at home, where he would much rather be.

His father, the Earl of Techney, had very strong opinions on the duties of his heir—attending Society's most anticipated functions, studying at Oxford and *not* Cambridge, belonging to any gentlemen's club that would accept an applicant from a family only two generations deep in the peerage, driving to an inch, being handy with his fives and deadly with a length of steel. Lord Techney permitted his son no say in his schedule nor his future.

Inside the Falstone House ballroom, the current set came to a close. James quickly glanced at the tiny, dark-haired girl he'd found spying on the balcony. She slipped nearly silently into an adjacent room, no doubt returning to the nursery. He hoped the poor child would escape the wrath of her host. How closely related was she to the Dangerous Duke? If she was forced into his company often, it was really no wonder she seemed so painfully shy. He felt certain very few people had been treated to the sight of her adorable dimpled smile.

He resignedly stepped back into the thick of the crowd. There were times when he wholeheartedly wished he could disappear as easily as that quiet little girl had, because he very much feared that eventually his father would find a way to control him completely.

Chapter Two

London
April, six years later

"You wished to see me, Father." James stood in the doorway of his father's library, no idea why he'd been summoned. Father never requested his presence unless he required James to do something inconvenient or unpleasant.

"Sit, Tilburn." Father always addressed him by his courtesy title and never with any degree of paternal affection. The man twisted his signet ring around his smallest finger. James recognized that smug gesture. Something had Father feeling exceptionally satisfied with himself. That was not a good omen.

Father's mouth turned up in a pleased smile. "The Duke of Kielder summoned me to his home this afternoon."

James's lungs seized. No man in the entire kingdom inspired the level of heart-stopping fear His Grace did. His presence at any event brought Society to an awe-inspired halt. The mere mention of his name left gentlemen, old and young alike, quaking in their shoes. A summons from the *Dangerous Duke* was not generally considered a fortunate turn of events.

Father continued spinning his signet ring, his face alight with eager anticipation. "His Grace finds our family quite impressive."

James doubted that very much. No one with His Grace's standing could possibly be in awe of the family of a lesser-known earl whose great-grandfather had been nothing more significant than a minor land owner in an insignificant corner of Lancashire.

"His Grace spoke highly of us—of *you*, as a matter of fact—though I am certain you have no comprehension of how significant that is." Father leaned over his desk, capturing James in a look of budding excitement.

"This is your opportunity, Tilburn. You've captured the notice of a man who holds all of Society in the palm of his hand. His approval can raise even the lowliest of the *ton* to places of influence and significance."

James cared very little for the shallow and ever-changing opinions of Society's *crème de la crème*. He came to London every Season and took part, to an extent, in the social whirl. But his focus had ever been on cultivating his place in political circles. One day when he assumed his father's title, he wished to undertake his Parliamentary duties with some degree of competency. That he had found his footing, however comparatively humble, amongst some members of the *ton* and had received invitations to a few events was nice but not crucial to his happiness.

"His Grace made a suggestion," Father added, blind to James's lack of enthusiasm, "and I, of course, accepted on your behalf."

A lump of apprehension began to form in James's stomach. "What precisely did he suggest?"

"He spoke of his sister-in-law, the quiet one whose name no one can ever recall."

James certainly couldn't put a name to the young lady. Try as he might, he couldn't even picture her.

"She possesses a dowry of £20,000 and is connected to the best families in the land," Father said.

"How very fortunate for her." James could think of nothing else to say. Why in heaven's name was Father discussing the social cache of a lady so wholly unconnected with them?

"His Grace suggested you might show the girl a bit of attention."

An odd request, to be sure. "I don't understand."

"You seldom do," Father drawled. "The chit has made her bows and will be launched into Society shortly. Unlike the older sister, *this* sister has raised no anticipation nor eagerness. By all accounts, she is rather plain and ill at ease in the company of others. Her connections will prevent complete failure, but her shortcomings will certainly make marrying the girl off more difficult for His Grace than he would prefer. He is looking to ease her into her debut by asking you to call on her, court her."

"He wants me to *court* her?" Surely the duke had meant no such thing.

Eagerness entered Father's eyes. He had no doubt already begun calculating the good this would do for the standing of the Tilburn family. His heir would be seen going about with the Duke of Kielder. Father would likely find a way to be included himself. Even the tiny climbing boys working for chimney sweeps throughout London couldn't boast the upward aspirations of the Earl of Techney.

James couldn't like the idea of this nameless, faceless young lady being a means to Father's social ends any more than he liked the unfeeling way Father and the duke had apparently spoken of her. But how to wiggle out of it when he knew climbing the ladder of Society was so important to Father?

"You said this was a suggestion, not an edict?"

"His Grace does not make 'suggestions.'" Father's pointed look only confirmed what James had heard about the Dangerous Duke. "He wishes you to be part of her entry into this Season, and you will. Kielder"—Father assumed a great deal addressing the duke so informally. James doubted His Grace had given him leave to do so—"is likely growing quite determined to prevent disaster. His invitation has given you a rare opportunity, has given *this family* an opportunity, and you will take advantage of it."

No. He shook his head at the absurdity of it. Father must have misunderstood. "The duke certainly might wish to guarantee she has dance partners at the next ball or that someone will drop into their box at the theater, but why would he risk even the appearance of a suitor who would inevitably not come up to scratch?"

Father leaned his elbows on the desk. "I do not believe he *would* risk that. If you are cognizant of the opportunity he has laid before you and mean to earnestly pursue the girl, His Grace, I am certain, expects you to 'come up to scratch.' However, if you do not intend to accept the entirety of his offer and mean only to ease her way in Society a little with your friendship and attentions, he will require you to be very circumspect and not raise any expectations."

"That is a fine line to walk." Too fine to suit him.

Father nodded firmly. "But walk it you will. This family has hovered long enough in the shadow of obscurity. The duke and I have served in Parliament together his entire adult life. We have both come to Town every Season. Yet he has never once done anything more than vaguely acknowledge my existence."

James and His Grace had spoken on several occasions regarding matters of government and international upheaval. Their political leanings were similar, if not truly identical. He wouldn't call them friends by any stretch of the imagination, but neither were they complete strangers. If Father had failed to make any kind of impression on the duke, that was not James's fault.

"It is unfortunate your ambitions have not proven fruitful, Father. I am further sorry the girl is beginning her debut under such a cloud of low expectations, but I do not wish to take up the task laid out for me. That is a role far too fraught with pitfalls for my taste." James rose to his feet.

Father remained calm, collected. "Kielder is expecting you to make an appearance at tea tomorrow during Her Grace's first at-home of the Season."

"You shall simply have to inform His Grace that you were presumptive in your assurances." James offered a dip of his head before moving toward the door.

"You would truly turn your back on this opportunity?" Father's shock could scarcely have been more apparent in his tone. "Why on earth would you do such a harebrained thing?"

James kept his place a few paces from the doorway but turned to face his sire. "You are asking me to lie. That is something I refuse to do, even for you."

"I asked nothing of the sort."

"You did, in fact." The precise word may not have been spoken, but a lie it would be. "You've asked me to call on this young lady, whom I've never met and can't even picture in my mind, and pretend she has captured my attention. Every moment I spent with her would be based on an untruth."

Father released a short, annoyed sigh. "Well, certainly, if you showed up on her doorstep professing an undying love for her, that she was the answer to all your most earnest prayers." Father rose as he spoke and crossed nearly to where James stood. "I am not asking you to do that. Call on her, Tilburn. Make her acquaintance. Treat her to a ride in the park, or tip your hat to her if you see her out shopping or taking ices. These are not lies; these are social niceties."

While Father had a point, the undertaking still felt less than honest. "Those are niceties I would never have presumed to undertake nor so much as think of." How could he articulate his discomfort when he himself couldn't quite put his finger on it? "We are not connected to that family. They are astonishingly above our touch."

"And yet the duke has seen fit to close that gap. He has gone so far as to open the door for you to not merely join his circle but, should you seize his invitation, join his family."

He leaned against the wall near the door, Father standing but a few feet from him. "I cannot like this."

"I am not insisting you marry Kielder's sister-in-law; he isn't truly insisting upon it either. He has created the possibility. Even the very smallest fulfillment of his request would be little more than being a friend to some-one who is sorely in need of one. That is a fine thing to do, is it not?"

It was an unusually thoughtful sentiment from Father, who gener-ally overlooked those he felt deserved to be neglected.

"Surely you are enough of a gentleman that you would not turn your back on a lady in distress."

How could he argue with that? And yet he wavered. "Something about this still feels wrong."

Father crossed to the sideboard, unstopping a decanter of sherry. "What the Duke of Kielder has declared right is not for us to deem wrong."

"Are you certain you are not confusing His Grace with the Almighty?"

"I do know the difference, Tilburn. One possesses endless power, holds the fate of nations in his hand, and is universally feared by saint and sinner alike. The other is—"

"The Almighty," James drawled. He knew the quip well, having heard similar versions for years. "You and the duke may not have qualms about this arrangement, but what about Miss Lancaster? Does she not deserve some say in the scheme?"

Father poured himself a bit of the amber-colored liquor. "She cannot be ignorant of how Society works and must realize how ill-suited she is to the task at hand. Her brother-in-law has, no doubt, enlisted the aid of many young people to act as friend to her. His rallying of the troops will not be done without her knowledge."

"You make her sound coldheartedly calculating." James didn't at all like the picture his father painted.

"Who on Society's upper rungs isn't?" Father shrugged as he took a drink. "We may or may not like it, but this is the way of things. If we wish to walk in exalted circles, we must know how the game is played."

James shook his head. "I don't care to play that game."

Father walked to the tall window, his glass yet in his hand. "I don't care for it myself." James had never heard his father express such a sentiment. "But you cannot comprehend the difficulties I have passed through because our family lacks standing. Some things, important things, can only be accomplished with the right connections. Those in a position of wealth and influence can open locked doors."

"What doors of any importance have truly been closed to us, Father?" This was an old complaint, one James had heard throughout his child-hood. He'd actually fully believed it until coming to Town and seeing the truth of things for himself. "We may not be regularly called to attend the Queen's drawing rooms nor invited to the most exclusive balls and entertainments, but we have not been denied membership at our club. We receive more invitations during the Season than we can possibly accept. With a seat in Lords, our family has the opportunity to have a say in the future of the kingdom." Of course, Father very seldom attended Lords, the very reason James felt the necessity of making the acquaintance of party leaders and policy makers. Someday the neglected Techney seat would be his own. "These are not insignificant, Father."

But his father had already begun shaking his head. "You are not here often enough nor were you old enough to remember the very real limitations of our position."

"We are not royalty," James reminded him. "Of course our standing has limits."

"Your mother comes from the gentry," Father said.

"Yes, I know. A very respectable family."

Father took another drink. "Respectable, yes, but in the eyes of the *ton*, nearly irrelevant. She was not raised in Society. She has no connections there. Her first two Seasons in Town came after our marriage. She hadn't so much as a friend among any of the ladies in the upper crust. She held at-homes that no one attended. She never received vouchers for Almack's. Though I was heir apparent to an earl, I hadn't the standing to ease her way."

James's heart ached at the thought of his quiet, sensitive mother enduring such humiliation. She took difficulties very much to heart, easily wounded and hurt.

Father drained the contents of his cup. "She avoids London as though the plague yet raged here." He shook his head. "I've never been able to convince her to return, though I cannot blame her. Society's proverbial door is closed to her, and neither you nor I have the ability to open it."

"Mother has not been to Town since before I began coming, and that's been six years." James had always assumed she simply didn't care to leave home.

"She has not been to Town in twenty years, Tilburn. The very suggestion brings her to tears." Father set his empty cup on the windowsill, his gaze on the cobblestone street below.

"I always assumed she did not come because her health is so often poor."

"Do not be a simpleton," Father said. "Her unreliable health ought to have propelled her to town. Here, she would have access to the best physicians, the best care, and yet she stays away. Why do you suppose that is, Tilburn?"

James had long ago learned to recognize when his father was posing a rhetorical question. He no longer wasted his breath attempting to answer.

"She cannot bear the rejection or the loneliness. I have attempted to convince her to come. What have you, her oldest son, done to ease her way?"

"What could I have done? I didn't know any of this."

Father held him with a steely gaze. "And now that you do know? To have the right friend, even *one* friend of influence, would make all the difference in the world."

James paced away, his mind full of revelations and possibilities and questions. "The duke would smooth the way for her?" No. That didn't sound right. Everyone knew the duke rather despised people.

"Not the duke, but the duchess. She herself comes from humble origins but made a name for herself among the *ton*. She would be unlikely to look down on your mother for having married above herself. Her Grace could whisper a word or two in the right ears, and your mother would have the allies she needs."

James leaned against the tall back of the chair he'd sat in earlier. He'd not given a second thought to his mother's isolation in the country. She'd always insisted that she had no desire to go to Town, and he'd taken her at her word. Had she really avoided it all these years out of humiliation, for want of friends? She must have longed to join him when he'd made his annual trip to London. She had needed competent physicians. If only he'd known, he might have done something.

But what could he have done? His connections were not only mostly political but mostly male, though he did receive invitations to a good number of balls and soirees, being an unmarried heir to a title with a small but respectable fortune awaiting him. Enough of the matchmaking mamas in Town viewed him as a relatively good prospect for their daughters, provided someone of greater significance didn't come around. But he didn't think he was enough in demand to warrant invitations being extended to his mother for teas and ladies' entertainments.

You haven't the ability to unlock those doors.

"The duke has given you the opportunity to help your mother, to give her a taste of Society, a friend or two. In London, she could receive a doctor's care. You might improve her entire life, and yet you refuse because it would be uncomfortable." Father's reprimand hit its mark. "Are you truly so unfeeling?"

With something of a sinking feeling, James realized his father was more right than he'd thought. Here was an opportunity to do something for his family, and he was refusing. Surely he could undertake something so simple as being a friend to a young lady. The duke had suggested a courtship but did not appear to be actually requiring one.

"Must I pretend I am calling of my own volition?" The hint of dishonesty was the only part of the arrangement that truly bothered him. He would be very circumspect in his attentions so no one seeing him would believe him truly courting her. But to feign a connection between them when none existed was not precisely aboveboard.

"You cannot arrive at their home declaring you have come only because the duke forced you to do so." Father shook his head, a scold clear in the gesture. "While that may be the truth, it is hardly a gentlemanly sentiment to throw at a young lady."

James allowed a smile. Though the conversation hadn't truly been a friendly one—they never were—it had been an improvement over most. "I don't know that I would have explained things in quite those words."

"I should hope not." Father absentmindedly tipped his empty glass back and forth. "You needn't pretend the two of you are the very closest of friends. Find a happy compromise."

For a moment, his determination wavered. But then he thought of Mother, alone in Lancashire. Not even Bennett, James's younger brother, remained at home to keep her company, having his own admittedly dilapidated estate. With the right connections, Mother might one day come to Town rather than remain behind on her own. She might at last regain her health.

"If I am careful, I could likely manage to walk that line," James said.

Father began spinning his signet ring once more. He dropped a firm hand on James's shoulder. "A wise course, Tilburn. Kielder's sister-in-law will benefit from your assistance. You'll have a fine set of new acquaintances. Your mother may even, in time, benefit from these efforts you are making."

James nodded. Spending a little time with someone he hardly knew wasn't much to ask, really. And if the duke and his sister-in-law both knew the reason for James's attention, then he wasn't deceiving them.

This will work out fine. Just fine.
He hoped.

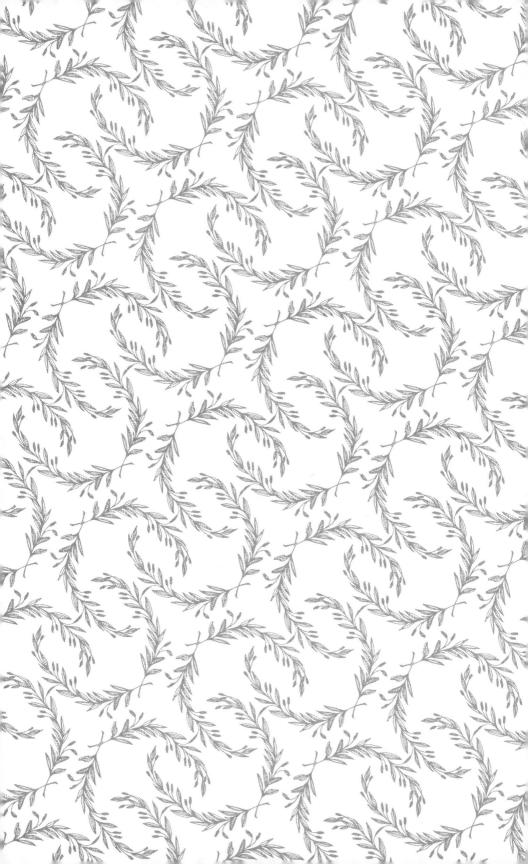

Chapter Three

Daphne sat at her dressing table eyeing her formidable brother-in-law in the mirror. "I fully intend to petition the House of Lords and have this particular form of torture outlawed."

Adam merely shrugged. "Most of them would not comprehend a word you said."

She smiled in spite of herself. Adam had on more than one occasion denounced the Upper House as "a collection of molded jellies piled atop one another without so much as a thought between them all."

"I will speak in short, simple sentences," she said. "That should increase their chances of grasping the issue at hand."

"Your sister was so eager for a Season she resorted to underhanded schemes and the employment of diversionary tactics." Adam looked no more happy about that bit of history than he had six years earlier when it had originally played out.

"Circumstances were different for Athena." Daphne's gaze drifted back to her own reflection—her plain, short, unexceptional reflection. "For one thing, she was older than I am. Further, she takes great enjoyment in the social whirl. Also, she had Harry."

"She did not know she had Harry," Adam countered.

"She did not know she had Harry in the way she had Harry, but she still had him."

"Splitting hairs will do you no good, Daphne." Adam came and stood beside her mirror, looking at her directly rather than reflection to reflection. Though she did not think his badly scarred face truly bothered him, she had noticed he seldom looked in mirrors. "Like it or not, you are to have a Season."

"But I do not wish to have one." She preferred the quiet of home and the company of those who understood her reticence and accepted her as she was. "I have made my bows. Can we not declare that sufficient pain and suffering and return to Falstone Castle?"

"This is Society. No amount of pain and suffering will ever prove sufficient."

"How comforting." She turned in her chair and looked directly at him. "You know I hate these things every bit as much as you do. I am doomed to end my debut in failure."

"If Society doesn't take to you, Daphne, it will be no failure on your part. You are well-spoken and intelligent and—"

"When was the last time a gentleman at your club slapped his crony on the shoulder and said 'Perchance, have you met London's newest diamond? Every gentleman in Town is clamoring to win her regard because she is so *well-spoken and intelligent*.'" Daphne ended in a withering tone.

"I doubt 90 percent of the gentlemen in London could spell the word *perchance*, let alone use it correctly in a sentence."

She let her disenchantment show. "And these are the gems with whom Persephone wishes me to spend the next few months?"

Adam was clearly not willing to debate. He stood mutely, waiting.

"Why could we not spend the afternoon in our usual way?" Daphne tried a different approach. "Would not an hour spent in your book room discussing the issues of the day or simply reading quietly be a more pleasant use of our time?"

She had begun spending every afternoon with Adam shortly after coming to live with her sister and brother-in-law years earlier. Persephone, however, insisted that Daphne begin making calls and receiving callers as the other ladies of the *ton* did. Not only was Daphne to be forced into social interactions, something she severely disliked, but she was also to be denied her afternoons with Adam, something she treasured.

"You know better than to expect me to contradict your sister." He was unwaveringly devoted to his wife.

There would be no avoiding her obligations. She took a fortifying breath—a tactic Adam himself had taught her when she was young and often too shy to leave the house.

"I suppose I must report to the drawing room for Persephone's at-home." She stepped toward the door. "Shall I provide you with a detailed recounting afterward?"

"Actually"—he caught up to her and guided her into the corridor— "I will be joining you."

"*You* are attending an at-home? Has someone informed the *Times*? This could be the lead story." Though she teased him, Adam's presence at tea was entirely unprecedented.

"One remark like that and I will have you locked inside Almack's and force you to listen to Lady Jersey prattle for hours on end until you apologize in abject humiliation, you impudent child."

Daphne smiled inwardly. Adam did have a flare for colorful threats.

Persephone was standing at the center of the drawing room when Daphne and Adam arrived, supervising the setting out of tea and finger foods for the guests who were anticipated.

"Adam, are you joining us this afternoon?" Persephone laughed, obviously convinced her husband had no intention of remaining.

"I am," he said.

The look of surprise on Persephone's face was very nearly comical. "What, may I ask, has brought on this unexpected change? I doubt you have suddenly grown fond of Society."

"I would like nothing better than to see the lot of them fall into the Thames and never be heard from again."

Persephone's brow pulled down. "Are you planning to abscond with them, here, this afternoon, and deliver them to their watery graves? Because I warn you, there will be no kidnapping during my at-home, Adam Boyce."

"I won't abduct or shoot any of your guests. Beyond that, I make no promises."

With a grace Daphne had never possessed, Persephone glided to Adam's side and slipped her hand in his, pulling him to a nearby sofa. She sat close to his side, a smile touching her face. Daphne enjoyed watching the two of them together. To be so loved by another person. She had wanted that all her life.

She'd been but twelve years old when James Tilburn had captured her heart. She always thought of him as James Tilburn, both names together. He, however, likely had no recollection of that meeting or of the timid girl who had been so touched by his kindness. She saw him about Town occasionally but never managed the courage to speak with him beyond the polite greetings customarily exchanged amongst very distant acquaintances.

"I have a feeling you have concocted some sort of plan, Adam," Persephone said. "You simply must tell me what it is."

"Not a plan, dear." He held his wife's hand in both of his.

"Then why remain? You seldom do."

"Because today I have"—his gaze flicked briefly to Daphne—"invited a guest."

A guest?

"And who is this guest?" Persephone's curiosity had clearly been piqued.

"Do not press for information, as I have no intention of offering any."

Daphne could see Persephone intended to do just that, and she silently encouraged her sister. Whom could he possibly have invited? Adam could not abide the company of anyone outside their intimate circle of family and close friends.

"Lady Genevieve," the butler announced from the door of the drawing room.

Persephone shot Adam a questioning look. "Your guest?" she whispered.

"That old bat had better not even be invited to my funeral," Adam grumbled.

"Behave," Persephone scolded as she rose to her feet and moved to greet the first arrival of the afternoon.

Adam stood as well, though no one could possibly interpret his expression as one of pleasure. Lady Genevieve appeared appropriately alarmed at his presence and general aura. She quickly found a seat far enough from Adam to apparently feel safe once more. He offered a bow and a mumbled greeting before selecting a chair beneath the tall windows as far as possible from the designated gathering area without actually leaving the room.

Persephone sat at the tea service, as was expected of a hostess. Daphne sat beside her, knowing she would be required to help serve the guests.

Why could Persephone not have left well enough alone? Daphne wanted no part in any of this. A future as an elderly, maidenly aunt appealed far more than being paraded about Town in the hope that somebody of reasonable intelligence, conversation, and hygiene took notice of her.

Lady Genevieve looked her over with an air of blatant curiosity. Daphne doubted she would ever grow accustomed to that. For eighteen years, she had been the Lancaster sister no one ever noticed.

"I understand you mean to attempt a Season, Miss Lancaster. I applaud your determination. You have never struck me as one who could make a splash in London society."

From his distant seat, Adam cleared his throat far too loudly for the act to have been unintentional. Lady Genevieve, obviously startled, glanced in his direction. Adam's piercing glare did not waver from their guest.

Lady Genevieve looked decidedly uncomfortable for a moment. "That is to say . . . I am so pleased you will be gracing Society with your presence."

Adam's lips silently formed the words *old bat* as his eyes drifted to the window. His offense on Daphne's behalf was touching, if unnecessary. Daphne knew all of London was not only shocked at her come-out but was also fully expecting her to fail rather spectacularly.

The presence of the Dangerous Duke had the happy effect of cutting short Lady Genevieve's visit. She stayed not a minute longer than the quarter-hour expected of her and spent the entirety of the call glancing uneasily in the direction of her host.

Looks ranging from apprehension to full-bodied fear seemed the order of the day. A great many guests paraded through the drawing room. Every single one stopped short upon spying Adam; a few even turned around and darted back out. Persephone barely concealed her amusement, letting her annoyance show more often. For her part, Daphne rather preferred the shorter visits.

Nearly the entire two-hour allotment passed without her brother-in-law giving the slightest indication that his expected guest had arrived. Each time someone new arrived, Daphne looked quickly in Adam's direction, wondering if his mystery acquaintance had at last come. Each time, he appeared no more pleased than before.

The ormolu clock chimed the half hour to an empty room. Daphne had nearly met her social obligation for the day.

"It seems your guest has chosen not to attend," Persephone said.

A bit of the tension Daphne felt eased at the possibility. Two hours of conversation and polite interaction had proven exhausting. She far preferred quiet solitude.

"He will come." Adam spoke without the least doubt.

"For heaven's sake, Adam, whom have you invited?" Persephone's eyes shone brightly. She obviously enjoyed the mystery.

Daphne sorely disliked surprises, especially those involving people with whom she was expected to interact.

"A gentleman," Adam said. "One whom I find, surprisingly, is not an idiot." For the infamous Duke of Kielder, that counted as a compliment.

Persephone nibbled at a watercress finger sandwich. "He sounds remarkable."

Daphne heard the distinct sound of a knock at the front door. She braced herself. Was this the gentleman Adam had invited? All of the guests that day had been female, married, and many years Daphne's senior. No other young ladies making their debuts had come, certainly no gentlemen. The house had been crawling with eager, unmarried suitors from the very first moment of Athena's come-out.

Adam turned toward the drawing room doors. "That, I believe, is he."

Daphne held her breath. Adam's guest had arrived, a gentleman, apparently, and one likely to be a stranger. Her heart pounded high in her throat at the thought. How she wished she had her sisters' courage. Even more than that, she wished she were not in London in the first place.

Footsteps sounded down the corridor. Daphne rose and turned toward the slightly ajar doors. She told herself repeatedly that she could face another caller. If an hour and a half of socializing had not done her in, another thirty minutes certainly would not.

The door slowly opened. The butler addressed Persephone, as was proper. "Lord Tilburn, Your Grace."

Daphne's mind emptied of all thoughts beyond that name. *Lord Tilburn*, James Tilburn's courtesy title. James Tilburn was at Falstone House. Six years of reading about him in the papers, of listening raptly whenever his name came up in conversation, of learning all she could of him and his character and, without warning, he was in her house. She had admired him in secret for a third of her life, and there he stood in the doorway of the drawing room.

He always dressed with care but would never be labeled a dandy. His manners were ever impeccable without being pretentious. She liked so much about him but didn't feel anything but trepidation at his arrival.

Her gaze met Adam's. *I will not survive this*, she silently implored, knowing her agitation must have shown in her expression. His mouth drew tight in a line of censure. Only when he looked at her precisely that way did she truly notice his badly scarred face. She'd grown so accustomed to the disfigurement over the years that she seldom actively noted it. But that expression, the one that always meant he expected more bravery from her than she was showing, pulled on his scars in a way that brought them to her attention once more, reminding her that he wasn't merely her beloved Adam but the Dangerous Duke, whose dictates were ironclad.

Defeat seeped into her. There would be no escape from this unexpected encounter, no opportunity to prepare herself to be in James Tilburn's company.

Adam drew their guest over to her. "Daphne, may I make known to you Lord Tilburn of Techney Manor in Lancashire."

She managed to keep her calm long enough to execute a creditable curtsy. *Good heavens. James Tilburn.* If she'd known he was expected, she might have chosen a prettier gown or had her maid spend a few extra moments on her hair. She knew, though, that had she been privy to Adam's plan, she likely would have called upon every imaginable excuse to avoid the encounter. Dreaming of his presence was not nearly as unnerving as being with him.

James Tilburn offered a very correct bow. "I believe I may have met Miss Lancaster in your company on a previous occasion or two."

His words surprised her. Did he in fact remember their meeting at Gunther's toward the end of the previous Season? Very few words had been exchanged, but he had inquired after her enjoyment of the various diversions London offered and had expressed his pleasure at hearing she had spent an enjoyable few weeks in Town. He had seen *her*, despite the presence of her graceful older sister and her beautiful younger sister, just as he had on the terrace years earlier.

"Tea, Lord Tilburn?" Persephone asked, smoothly guiding him to a seat near the recently replenished tray of offerings.

Daphne glanced at Adam. He stepped close enough for a whispered exchange. "If you faint, I will publicly and irrevocably disown you."

"Adam, how could you do this without telling me?" She kept her voice low enough to avoid being overheard.

"And give you a chance to run away?" Adam executed the slightest lift of one eyebrow. "I know you well enough to realize this frightens you. However, I expect you to summon the courage to grasp this opportunity."

"Opportunity?" Just how much of her feelings did Adam understand? A horrible thought occurred to her. "You didn't force him to come, did you?"

"No. I simply issued an invitation." He looked at her, his expression stern but kind. "But I will force you over there. I have endured an hour and a half of worthless prattle waiting for this, all for your benefit, and I do not intend to waste my sacrifice."

"Did you 'invite' him to do more than merely call on us?" Her stomach dropped at the possibility.

"One call, Daphne. One afternoon's tea. I suggested nothing beyond."

The relief she felt was quickly mired by an unexpected sense of strain. He had come for this one single visit. If he enjoyed the visit even the smallest bit, perhaps he would return. If not, however, this might very well be her only opportunity to enjoy his company.

"What if I fall apart?" She had not yet calmed from the initial sight of James Tilburn standing in her home.

"I suggest you don't, as I refuse to piece you back together."

Had he any idea how close she was in that moment to simply crumbling? "He does not seem the type of gentleman in whose presence I need to feel nervous." She spoke as much to herself as to Adam.

"I would not have invited the whelp if I'd thought otherwise. Still, I will shoot him dead if he tries anything untoward or ungentlemanly." With that declaration, Adam returned to his isolated chair.

"You promised Persephone you wouldn't shoot anyone."

"I'll run him through, then. That would be more satisfying anyway." Adam shooed her away.

Doing her best to appear poised, Daphne retook the seat she had occupied all afternoon.

"Lancashire is a lovely county," Persephone was saying. "We have passed through many times on our way to Shropshire."

"I am rather partial to Lancashire myself," their guest said. "I have lived there my entire life."

Daphne covertly watched him, remembering once more the first time she'd seen him and how struck she'd been by him. He would not elicit sighs and swoons from all the ladies, perhaps, but no one could honestly say that he was not handsome. And there was a kindness in his face she had always appreciated.

"You must miss home when you are in Town for the Season." Persephone's conversational skills far surpassed Daphne's. She had a knack for putting her guests at ease.

"There is a lot I miss about home." He smiled fondly.

For the briefest moment, his gaze met Daphne's. A shiver slid through her at the unexpected connection.

She summoned what courage she could, pulling forth the rote phrases she'd learned to summon when called upon to speak to someone who made her nervous. "How pleased we are to have you call on us."

His eyes darted about the room a moment, no longer looking at her. "I am afraid I do not make many social calls, something I am trying to be better about." He spoke in a voice of distraction, looking around once more at the conspicuously empty room.

Was that the reason for his continued discomfort? Her lack of callers? Quite a few people had come and gone during the first part of the at-home. Were she a great beauty or more at ease in Society, the house might have been overflowing with callers for the entire two hours. Heat spread slowly over her face, something he likely couldn't help but notice.

"I believe a great many gentlemen take quite the opposite approach to yours," Persephone said, handing him a cup of hot tea. "Rather than decide to make *more* social calls, they do their utmost to make far fewer."

"It is a miracle any gentlemen are ever seen socially," he answered.

Persephone smiled. "Indeed."

Daphne sat miserably mute in her chair. James Tilburn had come to call only to find an echoing cavern of a drawing room. He must think her the most pathetic of figures. Though Adam had denied as much, she fully suspected he had in some way forced the visit.

Persephone kept their visitor engaged in conversation. Every possible comment that came to mind, Daphne quickly dismissed as inane or unforgivably doltish. The few times she thought of a remark that might have reflected well on her, she spent too long convincing herself to speak and the opportunity passed.

The allotted time for visiting came to an end without her speaking more than a half dozen times, few of those remarks constituting more than a word or two. James Tilburn rose, making the expected farewells.

Daphne's heart sank to the very soles of her feet. Her one opportunity to make the acquaintance of a gentleman she had admired so long from afar and she'd made a mull of it, just as she likely would her entire debut. Why could she not have been blessed with even an ounce of her sisters' social graces?

She curtseyed in response to James Tilburn's bow. "Thank you for calling on us, Lord Tilburn." Another phrase she'd memorized before embarking on her come-out. Greetings and farewells occurred so frequently that they needed to come from a place of habit rather than thought.

He replied with "A pleasure," a phrase so common Daphne suspected he too spoke from memory.

She looked over at Adam as James Tilburn made his way to the drawing room door. She was sinking in her own misery. How was it she managed to fail at every single social encounter? Adam gave her his "screw your courage to the sticking place" look.

At the door, James Tilburn turned back. He looked from Adam to Persephone. "I will confess I am not at all certain who is the proper one to ask, but I wondered if I might be permitted to take Miss Lancaster for a drive tomorrow in the park."

All the blood seemed to drain from her face before rushing back with force. Her heart pounded so hard in her ears she could hardly make out Persephone's response. Permission was granted and a time arranged.

"Until tomorrow, then, Miss Lancaster." James Tilburn bowed at the door.

Daphne had never before been invited to take a drive and, not having ever expected to receive such an invitation, hadn't a ready response. She muttered something even she didn't understand and managed a creditable curtsy.

A moment or two passed in silence. Likely Adam and Persephone were as shocked as she was. The couple stepped from the room, walking arm in arm. Persephone gave her a broad and happy smile. Adam simply nodded, looking both surprised and intrigued.

Chapter Four

JAMES ARRIVED AT THE DUKE of Kielder's residence for the second time in as many days. His horses whinnied in irritation from the street behind him. He completely empathized. An afternoon drive with a complete stranger was hardly on his list of preferred excursions. He'd asked permission at the very last moment the day before only after realizing he'd done very little toward truly making Miss Lancaster's acquaintance. Indeed, he'd spoken hardly a word to her.

The Falstone House butler took James's card, his very disinterested and professional demeanor only adding to the intimidation one felt at the stately residence. Resisting the urge to tug at his suddenly tight cravat, James indicated he had come to take Miss Lancaster for a ride and added rather hastily that he was expected.

Hat in his hands, he followed the silent servant inside and up a flight of stairs. His nervousness mounted as he reached the open drawing room doors. He was not to have any kind of reprieve. His Grace sat in a chair inside, watching as James stepped into the room.

"Good afternoon, Your Grace."

"Sit." The duke motioned to an empty chair with a quick flick of his hand. "You are taking Daphne for a ride in Hyde Park this afternoon."

James nodded. His Grace did not look particularly pleased by the arrangement, though he hadn't vocally objected the day before. He, in fact, had set this entire thing in motion.

"If you overturn your carriage with her in it, I will shoot you dead." The duke made this pronouncement without a hint of hesitation and with every appearance of sincerity. "Dead," he repeated with emphasis.

"I will endeavor to drive carefully, I assure you." James had no intention of earning the ire of the Dangerous Duke.

"See that you do." His Grace's posture changed not a bit, but his gaze grew infinitely more cutting. James kept himself still, determined not to squirm despite his growing discomfort. "And know this"—not a hint of friendliness touched his voice—"if I hear you have hurt her in any way, I will personally cut your liver out with a spoon, instruct my chef to prepare it with onions, and will enjoy eating it immensely. And *then* I will kill you."

"I was raised to be a gentleman and have every intention of living up to that ideal."

The duke raised an eyebrow. That was all the change his expression underwent, but the effect was chilling. His web of scars tugged at his features, rendering the already frightening gentleman terrifying. James had never fully believed the rumors surrounding the Duke of Kielder, but the sight sent a ripple of unease through him. For the first time, he began to believe His Grace might truly be capable of all his reputation credited him with.

"I assure you, Your Grace, your sister-in-law will come to no harm at my hands." He tried to sound and look convincing. The weight of the duke's glare made him terribly uneasy.

"You will find I do not put much store by the word of a gentleman with whom I am not well acquainted. I require proof of his reliability."

It was a warning, if James had ever heard one. The duke would be watching him. Not a particularly comforting thought. And a confusing one at that. Had not the duke asked James to call on his sister-in-law? Father said His Grace had gone so far as to suggest James court the young lady. Why, then, did the duke act as though he distrusted James as much as he would a shifty-eyed snatch-thief?

"I will see if Daphne still wishes to go driving with you." His Grace gave no indication that he expected Miss Lancaster to do anything but give James the cut direct or, if she was feeling particularly good-natured, cordially invite him to take himself off.

His Grace's departure did not relieve the tension. James rose and crossed the room, fighting the urge to pace—or flee. The duke had more or less forced him to call on Miss Lancaster, yet he could scarcely have been less welcoming. And when he'd called the day before, no one else had been visiting. He'd fully expected to walk into a room full of people making a good show of being Miss Lancaster's particular friends. Something was odd in the arrangement, but he could not put his finger on just what.

"I hope you realize the duke is not being dramatic when he makes these threats. He means every word."

James spun around at the sound of a young lady's voice. In a tall-backed armchair near the fireplace sat a young lady with golden ringlets and an angelic face. She could not have been more than fifteen or sixteen years old. Her startlingly green eyes twinkled with unmistakable mischief. The girl, no doubt, was a handful.

"I am Artemis." She smiled amusedly—apparently his confusion showed. "Daphne's younger sister."

"Miss Artemis." He offered a small bow.

"Are you going to marry her?" She certainly didn't want for nerve.

He managed to speak through his shock. "I am utterly unacquainted with your sister."

Miss Artemis shrugged. "There is not much to know. She is quiet and bookish and terribly boring." She sighed quite dramatically, leaning back in her chair. "Sometimes I marvel that we are at all related."

James had no idea what to say to that. Agreement would be ungentlemanly toward Miss Lancaster, but arguing with Miss Artemis was not acceptable either. No response proved necessary. Miss Artemis kept talking without his input.

"Our older sister Athena was a smashing success when she had her debut. Falstone House was simply crawling with gentlemen from the very first day, and she has hordes of friends every time she comes to Town. Persephone is welcomed simply *everywhere*. I don't imagine Daphne will convince very many gentlemen to call on her more than twice." Artemis shook her head. "This is your second time, so I suppose you won't be back again."

"I can think of no reason not to return." In reality, he could think of plenty but knew himself committed to being a friend for the remainder of his time in London. Miss Artemis seemed unaware of her brother-in-law's machinations. James had no intention of being the one to inform her.

He heard footsteps approaching in the corridor. Miss Artemis tucked her legs up onto the chair, indicating with a finger to her lips that she wished him to say nothing of her presence there. He looked about and realized just how he'd missed her upon first arriving. The position of her chair completely hid her from the rest of the room.

"Guard your liver with your life," Miss Artemis whispered. "Adam is particularly fond of *foie gras*."

"Which of *your* organs would the duke harvest if he found you here?"

Miss Artemis grinned. "All of them."

Yes, the youngest Miss Lancaster was definitely a handful. Not wishing to get the girl in trouble nor wanting to attempt an explanation of their very private tête-à-tête, James moved closer to the door.

Miss Daphne Lancaster stepped inside an instant later. She could hardly have proven more of a contrast to her sister—dark hair, dark eyes, and entirely subdued. Her expression remained passive, no hint as to her feelings. Miss Artemis had described her sister as "terribly boring." James could not say how accurate the evaluation was.

Seeing Miss Lancaster dressed for a carriage ride, James assumed she had not, as the duke had predicted, decided to toss him out on his ear. "Shall we, Miss Lancaster?"

She nodded. That was all the conversation he was to receive, apparently. Perhaps she meant to save all hints of gratitude for the efforts he was making until they were out of the house.

He offered his arm and led her from the drawing room to the front door. The Duke of Kielder stood in the entryway, his expression black and foreboding. That threatening eyebrow of his had lowered, though it made him only slightly less intimidating.

"Not a scratch, Tilburn."

James dipped his head but did not manage a reply. He was doing a favor for this family, after all. Why, then, did they all seem so put out with him? Even a potentially homicidal guardian ought to lower his weapons for a ready-made friend he himself had acquired for his ward.

"Fanny." At the duke's command, a maid stepped to the door wearing an unprepossessing outer coat, obviously intending to spend time out of doors. "I expect a detailed accounting of all Lord Tilburn's actions, especially those of which I would not approve."

"Yes, Your Grace." The maid curtsied, gave James a look of warning, and, head held triumphantly high, led the way out the door and to the waiting carriage.

A detailed report. He hadn't expected that. It certainly was not the first time he'd taken a young lady for a ride in the park, but it was likely to be, by far, the most uncomfortable of such outings he had ever undertaken.

Chapter Five

DAPHNE SLOWLY RELEASED A BREATH, willing the tension to ease from her shoulders. She would never forgive herself if she ruined this once-in-a-lifetime opportunity by being too nervous to enjoy even a moment of it. Perhaps if she thought of him as *James* instead of both names together, he would seem less intimidating, different somehow from the imaginary gentleman she'd thought of so often during the past half dozen years.

He broke the silence between them. "Has your sojourn in London been pleasant thus far?"

Her voice stuck in her throat a moment when she turned to look at him. His eyes focused ahead as he carefully drove the carriage toward the park. Even in profile, she thought him the handsomest man of her acquaintance.

Stop being a gudgeon, she told herself. What a ridiculous person she must seem, entirely unable to speak a coherent sentence. Was it any wonder she'd sunk under the weight of her come-out?

"The warmer weather of Town is . . . is a welcome change after the long winters of Northumberland," she said.

Had her very first sentence really been a comment on the weather, and a broken, inarticulate one at that? He was bound to think her an imbecile now.

"Lancashire is not particularly warm during the winter months either."

He hadn't laughed at her. That was encouraging.

"You seem to prefer Lancashire to London." That was a better topic of discussion. He would at the very least realize she had paid attention during their conversation the day before. And the comment had emerged whole. That was an accomplishment.

A moment passed before he replied, his attention focused on maneuvering the carriage around a cart on one side of the street and a carriage moving in the opposite direction on the other. The vendor who tended the cart watched them rather closely as they passed. A touch too closely, in fact.

"My mother's health has been poor for many years," he said when they had successfully passed the obstacles. "I worry for her when I am away. Likewise, my brother remains on his estate a great deal of the time—also in Lancashire—and I sorely miss his company while I am in Town."

A note of longing threaded through his words. Daphne glanced at him as they continued at a subdued pace. She understood loneliness. Perhaps he would appreciate knowing she did. She was not, however, ready to confess that she felt alone most of the time. Her father had begun rejecting her company when she was still very young. She had tried again and again to convince him to allow her a space in his life, but to no avail. One did not endure such personal and repeated dismissals without a great many scars. She would not, however, speak of that. His opinion of her would be rendered decidedly low if he knew her own father had not cared overly much for her. An accounting of her siblings was a far safer topic.

"My sister Athena and her family do not come to—They do not travel from their home often," she said, "and I miss my brothers as well."

"I did not realize you had brothers." James glanced briefly at her before returning his attention to the increasingly busy street.

She nodded. "Linus is in the navy."

He looked over at her once more, his gaze lingering.

She had to turn her gaze away, uncomfortable with the scrutiny. He would probably like her better if he did not study her overly much.

"You said you had brother*s*. How many others are there?" he asked.

"One other: Evander. He—" Her throat closed up a touch. Speaking of her siblings had not proven a harmless subject after all. Thoughts of Evander did not always affect her as they had in the first few years after Trafalgar. What a time for her emotions to take hold once more. She prayed her voice would remain level. "He was killed at the Battle of Trafalgar." Her voice broke as she forced out the word *killed*.

Evander had meant the world to her. Of all the members of her family, only he had never been too busy to notice a lonely child desperate for affection. After leaving for the navy, he had regularly sent her letters in addition to those addressed to the family as a whole. She had lived for those letters. She would read them again and again until the creases wore through. He had been her reassurance that she mattered to someone. His death had torn her to pieces, fragments of which remained unhealed and broken still.

"I am sorry for your loss," James said.

Dear heavens, she was very nearly crying in front of James Tilburn. What a ridiculous impression she must have been making. Not only could she not seem to produce an unbroken sentence, but she was turning into a watering pot too. "Forgive me." She blinked away a tear threatening to form in her eyes. "I do not always grow so emotional when speaking of him."

"I assure you, Miss Lancaster, there is nothing to forgive. Were I, heaven forbid, to lose my brother, I doubt I would ever fully recover."

James carefully tooled his way into the mad crush of carriages and horses descending on Hyde Park. The outing had not yet proven disastrous. She was keeping up her end of a conversation. He did not seem utterly bored with her. A smile tugged at Daphne's lips even as she felt warmth creep into her cheeks.

She had worried for hours on end over the reason for James's call the day before. Adam, she feared, had forced the call despite insisting he'd merely suggested it. But James didn't act like someone being bullied into spending time with a young lady. He'd asked her to take a ride with him without any noticeable prodding from her brother-in-law. She had reason to hope James enjoyed her company.

"Hyde Park is busy this afternoon," he said. "A sure sign the Season has truly begun."

Daphne nodded, glancing around at the others who had ventured out for the promenade. "I have never been at the park during the fashionable hour. My sister and brother-in-law prefer to avoid crowds."

"I cannot say I blame them. With the Season in full swing, the madness of this undertaking boggles the mind."

Daphne would gladly endure even the most crowded days in the park simply to sit beside James Tilburn as she was. She'd wanted for so long to know him better. "Do you often come for the promenade?"

He nodded. "Often enough to know that this is Mrs. Bower and her daughter approaching in their carriage. Have you met them?"

Daphne's pulse quickened dreadfully, as it always did at the prospect of meeting new people. "I have not."

"I would be happy to make the introduction, if you would like. This is also Miss Bower's first Season, and I believe the two of you are of an age."

Her first inclination was a quick and decided refusal. But that would make her even more ridiculous than she likely seemed, having admitted to never before entering Hyde Park during the daily crush. "Yes, please," she managed with some degree of believability.

He brought the carriage to a very gentle stop. The approaching carriage did the same. A matron in a bonnet with so wide a brim as to cover her face entirely sat on the far end. Closer to James's carriage sat a young lady who looked shockingly like two of Daphne's sisters: flawless complexion, beautiful golden curls, and a figure that would have inspired even the pickiest of sculptors. How horribly dowdy Daphne must have appeared in comparison, with her drab-brown hair and alarmingly colorless complexion. She had a figure, but only just.

"Miss Lancaster," James began the introductions, "may I make known to you Mrs. Bower and Miss Bower."

"A pleasure to meet you," she offered.

"Mrs. Bower, Miss Bower, may I present Miss Lancaster, sister of the Duchess of Kielder."

That never failed to both impress and terrify people. Miss Bower's eyes widened, though in a way that somehow only made her more pretty. Her mother's may very well have done the same, but her face was not visible.

"Lord Tilburn," Mrs. Bower said, "I did not realize you were at all connected to Her Grace's family."

"The duke and I belong to the same political party and the same club," he said. "Now that Miss Lancaster has made her bows, I am pleased to be given the opportunity of knowing her better."

Daphne recognized it for the polite explanation it was but cherished it just the same. She hoped he really was pleased at the acquaintance. She herself was elated.

The same scenario repeated a few times. Some of the individuals they spoke with were already known to her; others were new acquaintances. Some of her trepidation over the coming Season abated over the course of their ride. She would recognize a few faces in the crowd, at least.

They had completed half a circuit of the park when a rider on horseback slipped into her line of vision, keeping pace with James's carriage. Though she did not see the rider's face, Daphne felt certain she knew him. She attempted to watch the stranger surreptitiously.

"I did not wish to alarm you," James said, "but that man has been following us for some time, hovering nearby every time we have paused to greet someone."

The man in question looked very briefly in their direction. That fleeting glimpse was enough to identify him.

"Good heavens," Daphne whispered. Her face heated in an instant. She might as well confess. "That is Johnny from the stables."

"One of your stable hands?"

"Yes."

"And does the man on the horse just ahead of us look familiar as well?" James asked. "He has done a remarkable job of following us, considering he is in front and not behind."

Though she could not see who was riding, Daphne knew the horse. Fanny's barely veiled look of guilt told Daphne her growing suspicions were entirely accurate.

"How many others are there?" Daphne asked under her breath.

Fanny hesitated. Slowly she raised both hands.

"Seven?" Daphne's shock added unintended volume to her words.

She turned her face forward, keeping her expression neutral by sheer willpower. Adam was having them followed? A maid in the carriage was to be expected if a young lady did not have a mother or sister or companion with her, but to commission the entire stable staff to keep an eye on them was the outside of enough. She began calculating in her head. The two mounted men. She suspected the "vendor" they'd passed earlier was likewise a spy Adam had sent. Four others lingered somewhere in the vicinity.

"This is a decidedly new experience for me," James said. "I have driven out with young ladies on any number of occasions but have never once been stalked."

Humiliation closed swiftly in on Daphne. She refused to break down in front of him twice in the course of a single carriage ride. Yet her embarrassment threatened to overcome every effort to conceal it.

"I am sorry," she managed to say.

An awkward and heavy silence fell between them.

The tiny tiger perched on the back of the carriage in front of them glanced back at them a few times. By the second look, Daphne recognized the Falstone House knife boy.

"A flower for your lady?"

Daphne turned at the sound of a voice thick with a lower-class London accent. A girl, probably only a year or two younger than herself, held up an assortment of nosegays as she kept pace with the slow-moving carriage. Hyde Park traffic never was likely to set any speed records during the busiest times of the Season.

"As much as I would like to give the lady a flower," James said, "I do not dare allow my horses the opportunity to run off with us by giving them less than all my attention."

The girl nodded in approval. Daphne very nearly rolled her eyes. No sooner had the flower seller slid back from the carriage than James turned questioning eyes to Daphne.

She sighed. "She is a chambermaid at Falstone House."

"If my calculations are correct, we have identified all but two of your brother-in-law's henchmen." His teasing tone fell just the slightest bit flat, as though he were earnestly attempting to find the situation humorous. "Perhaps one of them was hiding beneath Mrs. Bower's bonnet."

If she hadn't been absolutely mortified, she likely would have laughed at the very amusing observation.

The remainder of the ride passed in relative silence. They stopped a small number of times, James making introductions and striking up quick, innocuous conversations with the people he knew. But between visits, he kept quiet. Daphne's face never fully cooled.

They returned to Falstone House, an entire entourage of mounted groomsmen arriving at the same time they did. James assisted her from the carriage and walked with her to the door. His stiff posture and stoic silence starkly contrasted his earlier easy demeanor.

Adam and Persephone were both sitting in the drawing room when James escorted her there. "I have returned Miss Lancaster unharmed, as requested," he said.

Adam's gaze turned to Fanny standing just behind them. His look of inquiry received an "I've nothin' to report, Your Grace" from the maid.

"You're free to go," Adam said, looking entirely unrepentant about receiving a report on James's actions with him still in the room.

James bowed civilly. "Miss Lancaster, it has been a pleasure."

She stood still, not moving from the spot. He no longer smiled at her. His manner had become distant, formal.

"Thank you." Her words hardly broke a whisper.

James left with little beyond the barest words of farewell.

"Did you have a nice ride?" Persephone asked after he was gone.

The last thing she wanted was to rehash the disaster that had been her one and only drive with a gentleman at the fashionable hour. "It began well." To offer anything more positive than that would not have been entirely honest— quite dishonest, in fact.

"What did Tilburn do?" Adam's lips pursed in the way they did when- ever his cousin George came up in conversation. He thoroughly disliked his cousin. Apparently he felt similarly about Lord Tilburn.

"He was a perfect gentleman, and very tolerant, as I am certain your army of spies will assure you once they make their various reports." Daphne sat in a nearby chair, striking a very unladylike, slumped posture. She'd imagined so many times driving out with James Tilburn, but never in all her imaginings had the outing ended so disappointingly.

"Spies?" Adam managed to sound almost as if he didn't know what she was talking about.

"Over the course of the ride, we crossed paths with a veritable horde of staff from this house, all under instructions to follow Lord Tilburn's carriage."

Persephone turned to her husband. "You had them followed?"

"Merely precautionary." Adam's unshakable confidence seldom grated on Daphne the way it did in that moment.

"You do not trust Lord Tilburn?" Persephone asked.

"I did not say that."

"Then you do not trust *me*," Daphne surmised.

"I most certainly did not say that."

Persephone seemed genuinely confused. "Then why the armed guard?"

"Only two of them were actually armed."

Daphne dropped her head into her open palm. An armed guard. Was it not clear to him how slim her chances were of enjoying any degree of social success? A strikingly beautiful young lady or one who conversed eas- ily or possessed obvious accomplishments might be worth enduring such treatment. The gentlemen of Society would never make such an effort for a plain, quiet girl who could claim little talent beyond a knowledge of home remedies and the ability to go unnoticed for hours on end.

"Oh, my dear Adam." A laugh touched Persephone's words. How could she, Daphne's own sister, find this amusing? "Were you attempting to test his mettle?"

"Only offering a friendly warning."

"*Friendly?*" That brought Persephone's laugh entirely to the surface.

Daphne didn't find the conversation funny in the least, though it did explain something she'd wondered about. "You meant for Lord Tilburn to realize the extent of your ability to keep an eye on him?"

"Believe me, Daphne, if I had wanted my efforts to go unnoticed, they would have."

She shook her head and could not for a moment formulate a response. He'd embarrassed her on purpose. He'd likely driven James away and still remained entirely unrepentant about it. "You realize, don't you, he'll probably never come back."

Adam crossed his arms in front of him, his stance of choice when feeling particularly impatient. "If he is such a lily-livered, kitten-hearted coward, he is hardly worth your time."

Daphne returned Adam's look of annoyance with a dry look of her own. "So I should turn my attention to the dozens of eager gentlemen waiting to take his place?"

"You have admitted defeat before the Season has even begun. There will be dozens of gentlemen, though you obviously believe otherwise," Persephone insisted.

Adam's expression only grew more cloudy.

"How many gentlemen do you know, Persephone, who would endure this kind of treatment?"

"I can think of one—he married our sister." Persephone gave her a pointed look.

"Harry is the universal exception to every rule," Daphne said. "And he wasn't Athena's only option."

Persephone was undeterred. "Then let me suggest you wait and see if Lord Tilburn is every bit as exceptional as our dear Harry. If he comes back despite your well-meaning guardian's tactics, that would be a very good sign. And I would, once again, insist you not decide before your Season even begins that you are going to be an abysmal failure."

Daphne nodded, recognizing her sister's wisdom. They'd taken that approach often during the years they'd gone without the luxury of funds to cover even some of their most basic needs. "No use borrowing trouble" had been Daphne's favorite version of their oft-repeated family motto. If a childhood spent in poverty had taught her anything, it was the sustaining power of seemingly naive optimism.

So long as there remained a chance that James would come back, Daphne would allow herself to hope that tiny bit.

And tiny it was, indeed. For James had shown no inclination to return.

Chapter Six

"THE DUKE HAD ME FOLLOWED. And I am convinced his minions were armed." The drive he'd taken with Miss Lancaster the day before remained uncomfortably fresh in his mind. "Those are not the actions of a gentleman who invited another to call on his sister-in-law, let alone court her."

Father sipped at his favorite sherry, not appearing terribly concerned. "One must bear in mind His Grace's reputation."

"He threatened to eat my liver."

"No one would actually eat another person's organs," Father said.

James couldn't be so certain. He sank back in his chair. He hadn't been enamored of this plan when Father had first presented it, and his discomfort had only grown. "You are certain His Grace wished for me to befriend Miss Lancaster?"

Father nodded, setting aside his half-emptied glass. "He was quite specific."

That pulled the foundation out from under one of James's theories regarding the duke's behavior. Why, then, had he been made to feel so unwelcome? He was not so foolish as to need further proof he ought not return.

"I've called on Miss Lancaster and taken her for a ride in the park. I made introductions to every person we passed of whom I thought the duchess wouldn't disapprove. Miss Lancaster will know a great many people when she next ventures out in Society. Surely that satisfies my obligation." Simply saying as much out loud proved calming, reassuring.

"I trust you are not so thickheaded as that," Father said. Their previous conversation had been blessedly thinner on insults than usual. Today's interaction seemed likely to run closer to normal. "A gentleman would do what you have even for a lady he had little interest in," Father said. "You are supposed to be giving the impression she is an enjoyable companion, someone of whom Society ought to take notice." He shook his head, brow creased in thought. "Deserting the field now would only add weight to the arguments against her social desirability."

James rubbed at the ache pounding in his temples. "I didn't realize I was volunteering to single-handedly make her debut a success."

"Single-handedly?" Father raised his glass to his lips once more, shooting James a quizzical look.

"Both times I called at Falstone House, no one else was there. Not a single soul beyond the family and staff." James hadn't yet made sense of that. "Honestly, I had expected a crowd of people all enlisted in the cause."

"His Grace was quite specific regarding *when* you were to call that first time," Father said after a long moment's silence. "I am certain he did the same with the other young people so as to keep a constant flow of visitors coming into the house."

"But if the point is to show the *ton* that Miss Lancaster is enjoying immediate success, what would be the point of visitors no one else sees? I doubt anyone beyond the staff knew of my arrival there on either occasion."

Father huffed. "Sometimes I despair of you ever becoming a gentleman of sense."

Yes. Here was the Father to whom James was accustomed. The coconspirator role had been rather ill-fitting from the beginning.

"How do you think word of anything gets around Town, Tilburn? Servants spread news more reliably than the *Times*."

James didn't know if it was his father's criticism pricking at his pride or his own unease over their current endeavor that propelled him to argue with Father's logic. "I can't picture the Falstone staff gossiping. The duke would likely cut their tongues out if he caught them at it."

"It is not the servants you should be concerned with," Father said. "The duke will not take kindly to you breaking your agreement with him."

"*Your* agreement." James was not the one who had started this ordeal.

"To which you are now party."

I am, indeed. His participation in the charade was as good as agreement to Father and His Grace's scheme. He had rather committed himself to continue.

Father tipped back the last drop of sherry in his glass. "What do you plan to do next?"

James wasn't at all sure. "Calling on her again in her home might be easily misinterpreted as a sign of serious intentions."

Father didn't look overly worried, nor did he seem eager to offer advice.

James searched his mind for some idea of his next step. "I have heard that the family is planning to attend the theater tomorrow evening. I thought I would look in at their box during the first intermission."

Father nodded his approval. "Public enough to help the girl out but commonplace enough to not commit yourself."

And early enough I can do my duty and be off before it grows too late. He meant to spend the evening with a few political chums and a handful of gentlemen he'd known at school. A night spent at his club with friends certainly sounded more pleasant than an evening watching the duke formulate new and creative ways to kill him.

James approached the Kielder theater box the next night to find something of a crowd.

At last. The handful of the others His Grace had cajoled into acting as a friend to Miss Lancaster were finally making an appearance. They had not, however, actually entered the box. Odd, that.

Mr. Hartford, a gentleman near James's age, with whom he had a passing acquaintance, both having been at Oxford at the same time, stood at the back of the pack.

"Is there a reason we are all gathered out here?" James asked.

Mr. Hartford fussed with his gloves. "Because going in the box no longer seems like a wise thing to do."

"Why is that?"

"Mr. Bartram went in first, and His Grace instructed the usher to throw him out."

James didn't envy Mr. Bartram that experience. "That was likely a bit embarrassing."

"You misunderstand. Mr. Bartram was not to be asked to leave; he was to be thrown out. Literally thrown. Off the balcony."

Miss Artemis Lancaster's earlier warning rang in his ears. *The duke is not being dramatic when he makes these threats.* And yet James doubted even the Duke of Kielder would throw a man to his death.

"I will assume Mr. Bartram left on his own."

Hartford nodded, even as he tugged at his cravat. "Now nobody knows quite what to do. If anyone dares step inside, we might find ourselves in broken heaps on the floor below."

"Then why not leave?"

"Mrs. Bower pointed out that coming this far and *not* making an appearance might be seen by His Grace as a slight to Miss Lancaster, and that could be disastrous as well."

Perhaps the necessity of enlisting James's aid in Miss Lancaster's Season had, in reality, been less about the young lady's social struggles as it was about His Grace's tendency to send any potential friends or suitors fleeing in fear for their lives.

James was not, however, in a position to make a very welcome run for the hills. He'd committed himself, and His Grace knew it.

He wove his way through the gathering of quaking individuals all the way to the door of the box and, to the obvious astonishment of those onlookers, stepped inside.

"Good evening, Your Grace, Your Grace." He made the appropriate bows and received the expected responses. "I saw your family was in attendance tonight and thought I would drop in."

"We are so pleased you did, Lord Tilburn," the duchess said with her usual grace.

"No, we're not," the duke said with his usual testiness.

James allowed his gaze to drift to Miss Lancaster. He knew the moment she realized he was watching her. Color stole over her cheeks—not the practiced blushing so many young ladies in Society had perfected but the fiery, spotty color of one truly embarrassed by something. Despite his continued discomfort at being cajoled into pretending a friendship with her, James couldn't help feeling bad for putting her to the blush.

He offered a smile and an inclination of his head. She only blushed more deeply. To her credit, she didn't turn and hide nor melt into a heap of embarrassment. She kept her place and offered a "Good evening."

"And a good evening to you."

The duke shot them all a look of unfettered annoyance. "I believe we have thoroughly established that the evening is a good one. Let us move past the polite posturing and on to the meaningless conversation."

Miss Lancaster's color heightened significantly. It seemed the poor young lady needed rescuing from her brother-in-law as well as Society.

James could certainly do that much. Father regularly intimidated Mother into fitful fretting. And Bennett was forever being tormented by their father as well. James had often been thrown into the role of rescuing knight. He was convinced he spent more time fixing his family's various problems than he spent eating or sleeping. He stepped past the duke and duchess and made his way to Miss Lancaster's side.

"How have you enjoyed the opera?" She spoke quietly without looking up at him.

James opted to act as though she were entirely at ease with him, the ideal person with whom to have an unexceptional chat. That was his part, after all. "I confess the performers themselves seem a bit bored with the show, which makes it that much harder for the audience to not be, especially those of us who have no idea what any of them are saying."

"Do you mean to tell me you aren't proficient in Italian?" Her tone was light, with no hint of criticism.

"I don't even know enough to be considered dismal at the language," James said.

The tiniest hint of a smile touched her face. James didn't think he'd ever seen her truly smile. The realization made him worry. Was she mistreated, punished for her social disappointments? He hoped not. He sat in the vacant chair next to hers.

"I am afraid, Lord Tilburn, I cannot say much more for my own abilities with Italian." Her words carried that ever-present nervous quiver at the back of her voice. In a flash of clarity, James understood something about her. Miss Lancaster was shy, painfully so, if he didn't miss his mark. Little wonder, then, they'd felt the need to coerce someone into calling on her. Still, she pressed on. "My lack of proficiency has led me to spend my evenings at the opera imagining my own translation of what is said between the performers."

"Invent it as the evening plods along?" It was a very entertaining solution to the situation. "And what has this evening's selection been about, according to your translation?"

"Well." Her brow furrowed as she recounted in mock-serious tones. "The larger man with the dark hair, he is on a quest to ascertain the whereabouts of a misplaced Cornish pasty."

So unexpected was the remark that James laughed right out loud with enough volume to draw the attention of the nearby boxes as well as that of the duke and duchess. He bit his lips closed and held back the remainder of his laugh. "A Cornish pasty?" he repeated once his voice was under control again.

"Not just any Cornish pasty. The most delicious Cornish pasty ever created, hence all of the weeping at the end of act 1."

He didn't fight his grin. "Those Italians do take their pasties very seriously."

"Indeed," she said with that same small suggestion of a smile he'd seen earlier.

This was a side of her he'd not expected. If only Society were shown even a glimpse of it, she wouldn't want for attention. But the timidity he sensed in her likely prevented that. Thus the need for securing ready-made friends to keep her company.

"How have you been since last we met?" He wished her to feel enough at ease to continue in lighthearted conversation.

"I have been well, thank you." Her voice grew slightly steadier. "We received word that my brother is to arrive in London next week. I find myself suddenly less miserable at the prospect of remaining here."

"I believe you said your brother was a navy man." He had to think a moment to recall the man's name. "Linus."

Again the smallest suggestion of a smile, accompanied by an unmistakable glimmer of gratitude in her eyes. "You remembered."

"You sound surprised."

Her color heightened again. "Not many people pay much heed to what I say."

James knew enough arrogant poppinjays to fully believe she didn't exaggerate. Too many in Society were too full of their own importance. "It seems to me, Miss Lancaster, not many of those you regularly converse with are terribly bright."

"One of those people *is* only fifteen," she confessed in a tone of exaggerated seriousness. "And she is my sister, which I am certain doesn't help in the least."

"Younger siblings are positively unbearable," he said with a grin.

"I don't know whether to wholeheartedly agree with you or be offended. I am both an older and a younger sibling, you realize."

When Miss Lancaster rallied her courage enough to speak, her conversation was quite enjoyable. Perhaps the duke's plan wasn't so preposterous after all. If a few more people were given the chance to know her, she would likely have a relatively successful Season. James began to feel a bit more enthusiastic about this latest rescue. He didn't mean to set himself up as a suitor nor as the young lady's very dearest friend, but he could at least help ease her way a bit.

"Did you know, Miss Lancaster, there is quite a crowd gathered just outside this box?"

Some of her color dropped off as her gaze darted to the back of the box. "Why is that, do you suppose?"

He leaned closer and lowered his voice conspiratorially. "I asked that very question and was told they came to call on you and your family but, having heard that one of their ranks was nearly tossed to his untimely death, are now huddled in paralyzing fear in the corridor."

She leaned a bit closer as well. "They wished to see me? Truly?" Hope warred with doubt in her expression.

"Truly. I spied Mr. Hartford and the Bowers, whom you met during our drive. I saw any number of other young ladies and gentlemen of the *ton*."

"That is unexpected," she said.

"Perhaps in time the *ton* will rediscover its collective courage."

She smiled once more. "Adam is convinced they don't have any."

"You—"

"Lean in any closer, Tilburn, and I will personally hang you from this balcony by your feet." The duke sounded utterly serious.

"That will not be necessary." James stood once more. "I do need to be on my way." He sketched the briefest of bows. "A pleasure to see you again, Your Grace. Your Grace. Miss Lancaster."

Miss Lancaster smiled quite prettily, the color still high on her cheeks. He hoped he'd brought her a moment of reprieve from the pressures of Society. He could not quite imagine how difficult the social whirl must be for one who was truly bashful.

He offered her a smile in return. She blushed ever deeper.

As he stepped out of the box and into the corridor, the crowd of nervous theatergoers eyed him with a mixture of awe and incredulity. He could hear more than a few of their whispers.

"The duke didn't toss Lord Tilburn to his death. That is a good sign."

"If Lord Tilburn is welcome in the Kielder box, surely someone of my station will be."

Father would have pointed out that comments such as that one supported his argument that their family severely lacked standing. James had

never overly cared for such things. The Tilburns were far from social pari-
ahs. That was good enough for him.

"I am certainly not going to be left standing out here like a goose,"
someone else declared as she pushed her way into the box.

Poor Miss Lancaster. James doubted she would appreciate the sudden
incursion. He reached the outer portico of the Theatre Royal and buttoned
his coat against the downpour. The evening had gone well, he thought. He'd
kept his word to his father and His Grace. He'd enjoyed a friendly conversation with Miss Lancaster. And he'd managed it all without raising any expectations.

He might just navigate his way through these shark-infested waters
after all.

Chapter Seven

DAPHNE REMEMBERED WITH PERFECT CLARITY the night Athena had attended her first ball six years earlier. Her sister had overflowed with excitement. Facing her own first foray, Daphne felt nearly certain she was going to be sick.

Persephone, who had been mingling amongst the other guests during the quarter of an hour since their family's arrival, returned and took a seat beside the one Daphne occupied. "Your worries over being a wallflower appear to be all for naught, dearest. No fewer than a dozen gentlemen told me in no uncertain terms that they are quite anxious to dance with you."

As that was highly unlikely, Daphne simply offered her sister the doubt-filled look her words deserved.

"I am perfectly serious, I assure you." Persephone put her arm around Daphne's shoulders. "I realize your first week of the Season was less than spectacular, but I do believe that was Adam's fault. He rather frightens people, you realize."

Adam stood beside and a bit behind her chair. Though he stood in utter silence, Daphne swore she detected a growl.

"Did he have to wear his sword?" she asked her sister in a whisper.

Persephone nodded without hesitation. "He wore it throughout Athena's Season. And though I love our sister dearly, I readily admit he likes you far better than he does her." Her grin was unmistakably conspiratorial. "These next few months might prove a bit tense for the residents of London."

"That doesn't bode well." Her success was in question as it was.

"I thought after Adam's dispatch of Mr. Bartram at the theater a few nights ago that no one would dare so much as offer any of us a good day." Persephone moved her hands to her lap once more, but her earnest gaze stayed on Daphne's face. "But then Lord Tilburn arrived like a rescuing knight. If not for his willingness to brave Adam's wrath, I don't think a single soul would have stepped inside."

"Adam glared them all back out as it was," Daphne reminded her.

"Yes, he did." Persephone's eyes slid to Adam, something secretively warm in her expression. Persephone enjoyed that aspect of her husband's character, Daphne was certain of it. Though she loved Adam dearly, she herself couldn't imagine being married to someone who tended more toward the frightening than the tender.

"Ah, here comes Mr. Vernon," Persephone said to Adam. "Please don't threaten him. He's only a pup."

Daphne watched Mr. Vernon's approach with growing trepidation. She knew how to dance; Persephone had seen to that. But she was not a very good dancer. Hers was not an overly critical evaluation of herself; grace simply wasn't one of her strengths. She knew that. She accepted it. And until that moment, she hadn't been the least bit bothered by it.

Mr. Vernon arrived looking almost as ill at ease as Daphne felt. "Good evening, again, Your Grace." He made a quick bow to Persephone. His eyes grew wide when they fell on Adam. Daphne didn't dare look at her brother-in-law for fear she would either laugh in amusement or melt into a puddle of embarrassment—both felt entirely likely in that moment.

"Adam," Persephone said. "Have you made the acquaintance of Mr. Vernon, younger son of the Viscount Dourland?"

"I am aware of his existence," Adam said.

A bow punctuated by almost violent trembling was all the response Mr. Vernon seemed capable of making.

"How old are you?" Adam demanded, ever the epitome of social graces.

Mr. Vernon cleared his throat. "Nineteen." The poor man's voice actually cracked.

"This one isn't even housebroken, Persephone," he muttered.

"Would you rather your sister-in-law be escorted to the dance floor by a man of great worldly experience?" Persephone asked. "Because I do believe Lord Byron is expected here this evening."

"If that impudent mutt comes within a ballroom's length of Daphne, I will see to it he is never able to hold a quill again. Then we'll see how many more volumes of his poetic drivel he can foist on an unsuspecting public."

Mr. Vernon took a step backward.

"There are a great many people who enjoy his drivel," Persephone said, apparently oblivious to the flight of Daphne's only prospect of the evening.

"There are also a great many people who think I will stand idly by while presumptuous muttonheads make fools of themselves."

Mr. Vernon fled entirely.

Adam, however, wasn't finished. "I believe we have endured enough of Society for one Season."

"It has been one week, Adam," Persephone said. "And you agreed to this."

"I am the Duke of Kielder. It is my prerogative to change my mind."

Persephone stood slowly, her eyebrow arching in a perfect imitation of Adam's most famous facial expression. "Well, I am the *Duchess* of Kielder, and it is my prerogative to change it back."

"That would require a great deal of convincing," Adam said.

"Is that a challenge?" Persephone tipped her head saucily.

"Would you like it to be?"

"Do you two never stop flirting?" Daphne muttered.

"Hush, Daphne," her sister answered. "I will change his opinion yet."

"You might convince me to remain, but you will never convince me to be happy about it."

Persephone shrugged one shoulder. "That is good enough for me."

"You, there." Adam eyed a gentleman standing surprisingly nearby. "You had better be deaf, for I do not abide eavesdroppers."

The gentleman turned an unearthly shade of pale, his mouth flapping about. "I—er—I—What was that? I don't hear well." The last sentence was muttered too mechanically and too much like a question to have been anything but a desperate attempt to comply with the Dangerous Duke's command. He ran off quickly.

Adam's hard glare darted about, catching every person within thirty feet of them. They scurried away faster than rats off a sinking ship.

A sinking ship. That is not quite the way I would like to think of myself.

"Oh, Adam." Persephone sighed. "Must you frighten everyone away?"

"Only those I find unbearable."

"But that, dear, is everyone."

"And that, dear, is not my fault."

Persephone took Daphne's hands. "He will not send them all running, Daphne. I will see to it."

"In all honesty, I'm not certain I don't *prefer* that they all run off." She didn't want to be a diamond or a failure but something quietly in between.

Persephone shook her head. "That is Adam's influence. I fear sometimes you have spent too much of the past six years with him. He has rendered you so very reticent."

Had not even Persephone seen the person she was all her life? "He did not change me. He accepted me just as I am."

"And somewhere, Daphne, there is another gentleman who will do the same." Persephone spoke with such confidence. "We simply have to find him."

While she didn't intend to spill all of her secrets to her sister, Daphne had been attempting to find a certain very accepting gentleman all night. Her eyes had never stopped searching for James Tilburn. He hadn't objected to her bashfulness all those years ago. He didn't seem bothered by it now.

She turned her head in the direction of approaching footsteps only to be disappointed once more. Mr. Handle, who had made an extremely abbreviated appearance at the Kielder theater box, stepped up to where she sat.

"Mr. Handle," Persephone greeted quite pleasantly. "A pleasure to see you again."

He made a very proper bow. "The pleasure is entirely mine, Your Grace."

"That it is," Adam muttered.

She loved her brother-in-law dearly and agreed with his general opinion of social gatherings, but if she was to be forced into enduring them, Adam might at least give her a chance to be remembered fondly by the other attendees, or at the very least with something other than fear and trembling.

"Your Grace." Mr. Handle's voice shook as he addressed Adam. "Might I be permitted to stand up with Miss Lancaster for the next set?"

"No."

Daphne very nearly smiled at Adam's gruff and immediate response, as exasperating as it was. Persephone was clearly less amused.

"I give you full credit for bravery," Adam added. "And I will temporarily consider you more intelligent than most of your contemporaries if you manage to summon the presence of mind to move along before my patience with you inevitably deteriorates."

"Yes, Your Grace." Mr. Handle made several bows in quick succession as he backed frantically away.

Persephone pushed out a frustrated puff of air even as Daphne breathed a slightly disappointed one. The thought of standing with anyone was a daunting one, but she knew perfectly well that doing so was a crucial measurement of a lady's social success. She had hoped to stand up with at least one gentleman over the course of the evening so any curious onlookers would have reason to declare her something of a success.

Persephone stood with palpable dignity. "Let us go make our farewells to Lord and Lady Debenham."

"We are leaving?" Daphne's stomach dropped.

"If Adam will not permit anyone to stand up with you, there is little point in remaining." Persephone gave her husband a look of reprimand.

He showed no signs of feeling guilt-ridden.

"But—" Daphne rallied her determination. "But Adam would allow me to stand up with Lord Tilburn if he asked. Surely."

"Lord Tilburn?" Persephone asked the question in a hinting manner, having apparently found significance in Daphne's words. Daphne was actually surprised her sister hadn't already discovered her preference for James. Adam, it seemed, had pieced that secret together ages ago. Why else would he have issued an invitation to call upon her to James and only to James?

"I imagine he would," Persephone said after a moment. "Perhaps we could stay a bit longer and see for ourselves."

Adam had already taken a step toward the door, clearly intent on making his usual early exit. "Tilburn isn't here."

"He might yet come," Persephone said.

"I do not stand about in ballrooms waiting for someone to afflict me with their company." Adam held his arm out for Persephone, clearly confident his declaration would not be met with any objections.

Persephone's expression softened as she slipped her arm through his. "I believe we have pushed our duke to the edge of his endurance, Daphne. We had best go before he decides to utilize his sword for more than *visual* intimidation."

She didn't argue. She never did. But as they made their way through the pressing crowd, offered farewells to their host and hostess, and finally stepped out of the ballroom, she kept her eyes open, searching for James.

She didn't know what to make of his absence. He had shown her rather particular attention. Had she been wrong to hope he did so because he enjoyed her company?

Whatever the reason he'd stayed away, she'd missed seeing him there. She did her utmost not to worry that he'd deserted the field after having only barely stepped foot there.

Chapter Eight

FATHER SUMMONED JAMES TO HIS library for the third time in a week. James was not generally a superstitious person, but he couldn't help a feeling of foreboding. Father sat at his desk spinning that blasted signet ring. His eyes shone with anticipation. What was he plotting this time?

"Good afternoon, Father," James said, hoping he sounded more self-assured than he felt. "I received your missive. What was your pressing matter of discussion?"

"You did not attend the Debenhams' ball last evening." It was a demand for an explanation. James knew there was no point ignoring it.

"No, I did not." He had spent the night with a gathering of gentlemen at his club debating matters of Parliament, a far preferable pursuit than a ball.

"Kielder's sister-in-law was there." Father made the announcement as though James had neglected a direct summons from the Prince Regent rather than simply forgoing one in an unending line of balls.

Father took a deliberate breath. He slowly spread his fingers out on his desktop. "You agreed to pay her particular attention."

"And so I have. I called during an at-home. I took her for a ride in Hyde Park. After I spent a few moments in their box at the theater, she had any number of others do the same." He hadn't broken his word to any of them.

"All of Town is quaking over Kielder's mood last evening. He apparently insisted one of the young gentlemen there feign a loss of hearing or risk being run through." Why did Father sound so pleased by the reports? "He ordered Devereaux's heir presumptive to take himself off. He glared poor Mrs. Bower into a very unflattering bout of weeping. The social casualties last evening were staggering."

And Father was scolding him for not attending the figurative beheading of the upper classes?

"You were supposed to be there, Tilburn, making your case."

"Making my case?" That was exactly the sort of entanglement he'd been trying to avoid. "It seems you and I have very different ideas of what I—"

"Fortunately, I have already taken pains to make recompense on your behalf."

James's entire frame froze on the spot. "What did you do?"

"I sent her flowers along with your apology for not being present at the ball." If the spinning signet ring was any indication, Father was quite satisfied with his efforts.

Flowers. And a missive. "She will think I am courting her."

"Aren't you?" The question was offered in too self-satisfied a tone to be anything but rhetorical.

"Of course not." James jumped to his feet. "I befriended Miss Lancaster as a favor to you because you made an ill-conceived promise to the most dangerous man in the kingdom. *Only* befriended her. We were quite specific on that matter."

"You agreed," Father replied.

"But not to *this*." Panic was quickly setting in. "I said I would stand up with the young lady on a few occasions, call at her home once or twice. You are speaking of courtship."

"We have always been speaking of courtship, Tilburn."

James choked back the immediate, very vocal objection he felt. He needed to proceed carefully. Once determined on a path, Father was difficult to dissuade. And James was already in far deeper than he'd ever expected to be.

"His Grace welcomed you, something the rest of Town has little expectation of. You have the advantage of acquaintance. You need only woo her, talk sweet to her, whatever you must. You could emerge triumphant."

Father could plot and plan all he liked, but James would not stand idly by and watch it happen. Miss Lancaster was a sweet-natured and lovely young lady. She didn't deserve to be tossed out like an eel pie past its peak of freshness.

"I have no intention of courting the girl," he insisted. "You have not the legal ability to contract a betrothal for me, nor will I allow you to trap me into undertaking one."

"Trap you?"

"You talked me into this mess in the first place," James reminded him. "Now you have sent her flowers on my behalf. This feels far more like a trap than a tender moment of father and son togetherness."

Father's mouth pulled into a tight line. "I will not allow this opportunity to slip away. I will do what I must for the good of this family."

The good of this family. That only ever meant the furthering of his own ambitions.

"I cannot like this, Father. I was invited to act as her friend *only*. I will not impose upon her further."

Father didn't take even an instant to contemplate James's objection but immediately offered his counterargument. "A courtship from a gentleman who is already a friend is not an imposition."

"It is when that courtship was enacted on false pretenses." He was firm on this point. To continue on the path Father was laying out would be dishonest. James would not do that. "I have fulfilled my agreement. I will do no more."

"Do you not care at all for your name? Your station?"

James despaired of making his father understand the importance of choosing the ethical path even if doing so meant personal inconvenience. His sire seldom bothered to ponder whether or not he *should* behave in a certain way, preferring instead to be guided by the simpler argument of whether or not he *could*.

"Our station in life is sufficient for me," James said.

Father's gaze narrowed. "That is a very selfish stance, Tilburn."

"I do not see it that way." He rose, then sketched a quick bow. "Good day—"

"Shall I tell your mother you no longer concern yourself with her well-being?" Father sat perfectly still. "You know as well as I do how much she depends upon you."

This scheme had been concocted in part to bring Mother to London with the promise of the duchess's friendship and support. James couldn't say his efforts had guaranteed that, but he felt certain Her Grace would at least acknowledge Mother. He needn't perpetuate a lie to garner further favor.

"No," James said firmly. "I will not take this further."

"Then I must." Father's confidence remained unshaken. "You subsist upon the income provided you by the estate, do you not?"

Apprehension inched over him. "You know that I do."

"This estate need not support anyone who does not act in its best interest." Father pegged James with a firm and painfully patient gaze.

"You cannot disown your heir. My coveted Oxford education taught me that much." Father's devotion to that institute of learning bordered on religious.

"Not ultimately, but I have complete control over your income during my lifetime," Father answered.

"You would threaten to cut me off if I do not acquiesce? You would subject your son and heir to penury in order to have your way?"

"You force my hand." The words emerged slowly. "I have the betterment of generations of this family in mind, and you can think of nothing but your own willfulness. If you will not do what is best, I must see to it that you are made to. If that requires that I take away your financial support, I will do it, however much it pains me."

James didn't imagine anything about the undertaking would truly pain Father other than the embarrassment of a penniless heir. And yet there had been moments in the past week when Father had seemed to soften the tiniest bit. Perhaps it had all been a ruse, a ruse he had been fooled by.

"What say you, Tilburn?"

"It seems I am to live in poverty."

Father's brow creased in deep confusion. "What of your pride?"

James squared his shoulders. He would not be forced into this. "Deceiving an innocent young lady by undertaking a feigned courtship, choosing a bride based on my father's ambitions, making a liar of myself for the sake of social standing does not, in my mind, equate with taking pride in oneself."

"Do you dare presume to lecture me, boy?"

James took a calming breath. He had long ago promised himself to always treat his father with the respect he himself wished he received from his sire. Though he often fell short of the mark, he was determined to try.

"I do not wish to give offense." He kept his voice level. "But I will not yield on this matter, even if doing so casts me into difficult straits."

Father was unshaken. "I control more than *your* income, you realize. Bennett quite appreciates his quarterly allowance."

James's younger brother more than merely appreciated the income he received from their father; he required it.

"How would he live if he were cut off?" Father spoke more quickly, more forcefully, apparently realizing he had struck a nerve. "Bennett has far more to lose than you do should he find himself short on funds."

Their maternal grandmother had bequeathed to Bennett a small estate in Lancashire. The bequest had come as a lifeline only a year earlier when Bennett had grown desperate to escape the tyranny of their father's household. He had sunk every ounce of his strength and every penny he had into turning the rundown estate into a livable bit of property. That land meant the world to him, and without the quarterly allowance he received from the Techney estate, he hadn't the means to keep his inheritance. It was not yet self-sustaining. He would lose everything.

"You would take away Bennett's income?"

"I will not allow you to throw away the future of this family." Determination had turned Father's expression hard and unyielding. "If you will not act in their best interests, then I must."

James didn't move, his mind spinning. How could he deprive his brother of the one thing they had both longed for all their lives: freedom? Losing Halford Grange would destroy Bennett.

"You choose, Tilburn. You can defy me and strip your brother of his land and future, or you can accept the good fortune that has been laid in your hands and do the right thing by your posterity."

"I cannot—"

"I control your mother's pin money as well." Father's piercing gaze didn't waver in the least.

"You would punish your own wife?" Just how far was Father willing to go?

"I am doing nothing of the sort. You are tying my hands by refusing to do what is best for your relations."

James couldn't breathe. How had he found himself in such a position? Holding his ground, refusing to bow to his father's dictates would destroy his mother and brother, rob them of their incomes and contentment. Bowing to his father's demands would save Bennett's land and Mother's income and grant her entry into the Society of which she'd once dreamed of being a part. But giving them those concessions meant feigning an interest in a young lady who did not deserve his deception, who, if his assessment of her character was accurate, would be hurt quite personally by such ill treatment.

He needed to think, to find a way around this dilemma.

"You cannot expect me to make such a decision without so much as a moment to think it through."

"I foolishly expected you to act rationally from the beginning." Much of Father's anger had dissipated, replaced by a calm James found even more unsettling. Father had made his decision; he would not be dissuaded from his threats. He would follow through, even if it meant making every person in his family miserable for the rest of their lives.

James was too upended to even pace. He could only stand there, frozen and mute, desperately thinking. Only one thing was truly clear: he could not allow the people he cared for to be hurt by Father's selfishness.

He *had* already decided to continue being a friend to Miss Lancaster— although pretending a sincere interest in courting her was hardly the act of a friend. What he knew of her, he liked. That aspect of their acquaintance would not be a lie. There was the very real possibility that she wouldn't accept his suit and an even greater possibility that the duke, should he discover James had not taken on the role of suitor with any degree of willingness, would simply challenge him to pistols at dawn, shoot him through the heart, and leave his carcass for the various wild beasts to devour.

How did this happen? He made a quick circuit of the room, trying to formulate some kind of plan. He could continue calling on her but keep his efforts as circumspect as possible, perhaps even helping the causes of any number of her other suitors. Father might be in a position to force James into a courtship, but he would never be able to force Miss Lancaster to accept.

That was his answer: continue his efforts without truly working to convince Miss Lancaster. She would choose someone else in the end. He could do that, and she wouldn't be hurt by Father's schemes. Neither would Mother or Bennett.

"I will have it in writing," James said.

"You will have *what* in writing?"

"Your promise that should I pay suit to Miss Lancaster as you require, you will never deny nor diminish Bennett's quarterly allowance nor will you deprive Mother of her expected pin money. And that you will never force Bennett into a courtship the way you are forcing me."

Father raised an eyebrow in obvious surprise. "My word should be more than enough—"

"It is not remotely enough," James said. "If I am to bow this much to your demands, I will protect my family from you."

"*You* will protect the family from *me*? I, who am doing this for them?" Father shook his head, though whether in amusement or denial, James couldn't say. "You are quite mistaken, my boy. It is I who am protecting them from your selfishness. None of these threats would have been necessary if you had been thinking at all of their well-being from the beginning."

He doubted he would ever see eye to eye with his father on the matter of what constituted the best interests of the family. There was little point arguing with him.

"Have your solicitor draft a binding document with my required commitments from you." James spoke as his heart dropped further into the coldest recesses of his soul. Even with a plan in place to protect him from an unwanted marriage and his firm commitment not to impose on Miss Lancaster if he could at all help it, he did not like the future that now lay before him one bit. "Then, and only then, will I so much as speak to Miss Lancaster again."

"I will have the document ready by day's end." Father spun his signet ring about his finger quickly, eagerly.

Without a word of parting, James left the library. He was likely the only gentleman in the entire kingdom who desperately hoped a young lady with enviable connections, social standing second to none, and a fortune of £20,000 would meet his efforts at courtship with complete and utter rejection.

Chapter Nine

DAPHNE SAT IN HER USUAL spot in Adam's book room. He occupied a nearby armchair. Their daily time together had of necessity grown more rare with the start of the Season. She took tremendous comfort in the fact that he had seemed as grateful for her presence that afternoon as she had been for the opportunity to spend time with him again. How often she had pleaded with her father for a small space beside him while he'd worked or for a moment of his attention. For years, he'd turned her away, until she'd eventually stopped asking.

At twelve years old, she had taken trembling steps into this very book room and posed to Adam the same question she had to her father so many times. Years of rejection had echoed painfully in her heart and mind as she'd waited for his answer. He had nodded and motioned her to the same sofa she sat on now. For six years, she had spent time with him nearly every day. He had welcomed her, something for which she would be forever grateful.

"Talk of hostilities with the former colonies grows more specific by the day." Adam often spoke to her of the matters before Parliament. "A great many in both Lords and Commons feel any difficulties across the ocean would be easily put to rest, as ours is the superior naval power."

"As I understand it, that was the argument thirty-five years ago, and we all know the outcome of those hostilities," she said. "And at that time, we weren't already fighting a war nearer home as we are now. Parliament would do well to proceed with caution."

He nodded. "If even a fraction of those in a position of influence had your intelligence, this country would be in far better condition."

A knock echoed off the slightly ajar book room door. Daphne and Adam both turned in that direction. The butler stepped inside, a vase of bright flowers in his hand.

He addressed Adam, as was proper. "This has arrived, Your Grace, for Miss Lancaster."

Daphne eyed the bouquet in disbelief. Athena had received countless floral tributes during her Season. After hostessing a ball or gathering, guests often sent flowers to Persephone. But Daphne had never received a single flower—not from Adam or Harry or either of her own brothers.

"You are certain they were sent to me?" she asked the butler.

"Quite certain, Miss Lancaster." He set the vase on the end table directly beside the sofa, then, with a bow, stepped from the room again.

She pulled a small sealed note from amongst the blooms. Did a lady generally wait until she was in the privacy of her own bedchamber to read the accompanying message? Asking Adam would do no good. He wasn't likely to know how she was meant to act in such a situation.

She attempted to appear quite casual as she eyed the as-yet-unopened note. Who could the flowers be from? Why were they sent? Adam would not have thought to do so, having referred to the offerings from Athena's many admirers as "ridiculous" on multiple occasions.

"Holding a note and not reading it seems a waste of effort," Adam said.

"Are you eager to know who sent the flowers?" She tried for a teasing tone, hoping to hide her growing impatience.

"I only want to know if I need to squelch anyone's presumptuousness."

"Adam, we talked about this. You promised—"

He sighed, the sound full of exasperated acceptance. "I agreed to be less surly in public. I made no promise about my own book room."

Daphne's heart leaped as she slowly, carefully opened the note. Her eyes dropped first to the signature at the bottom of the note. "Ld Tilburn." The flowers were from James. She kept her expression calm, not wishing to give Adam further reason to find flowers and those who sent and received them as ludicrous.

She eagerly read the note.

Miss Lancaster,

I must abjectly apologize for my absence last evening at the Debenhams' ball. Though I had hoped to see you again, I was detained. I pray these flowers will serve as an adequate expression of my dismay at being denied your company.

Yours, etc.

Ld Tilburn

It was a far more earnest note than she would have expected. He had always been friendly, but this note felt . . . different from that somehow. It felt like something a gentleman would write to a lady with whom he had a much closer connection than they had. The wording as well as the sentiment felt mismatched to the sender.

"You appear deep in thought."

When had Persephone come inside the book room? Daphne's face heated as it always did at the slightest embarrassment. Her sister, however, did not appear disapproving nor censuring. If anything, she looked amused.

Daphne held her treasured note up but offered no spoken explanation.

"Am I to assume, then, this lovely bouquet is for you?"

Daphne nodded.

"Sent by a young gentleman whose absence you mourned last night?"

Daphne eyed Adam. She saw no surge of disapproval or irritation. He seemed legitimately curious. "What did the lordling have to say?"

She ignored the word he chose in reference to James. "He said he was sorry to have missed the ball."

Persephone joined her on the small sofa. "I am pleased to hear he is being so attentive."

"Except, it—The tone of the note is odd."

"Perhaps your cautious nature is forcing you to doubt things you do not need to doubt."

She held the card out to her sister. "Tell me your impression of it."

Persephone made a quick perusal of the very brief note. "It does seem a bit more ardent than is usual for Lord Tilburn."

"Is he being brash?" Adam demanded.

"No, dearest," Persephone was quick to say. "Nothing in his note is the least bit untoward." She looked over the note once more. "Perhaps word of your unending grumpiness reached the poor gentleman and he felt the more abject his apology, the more likely he was to not be drawn and quartered." She tipped her head and caught her husband's eye once more. "I have warned you about making too grand a show of your disapproval."

"I am what I am," Adam said.

Persephone's gaze turned warm as it so often did when focused on him. "Yes, you are."

"Besides, my afternoons with Daphne, a rare enough occasion of late, were interrupted by these flowers and that note. I have every right to be grumpy."

Her father had turned down her company. Adam grew sullen when denied it. Was it any wonder she loved her brother-in-law as much as she did?

"Do you like Lord Tilburn?" Daphne asked them both.

"What I have learned of him these past five days, I like," Persephone said. "He seems very kind and amiable, and his obvious preference for you certainly raises his worth in my eyes."

Obvious preference. Another smile broke through her usual reserve as a wistful thought occurred to her. "I wish Harry were here this Season."

"Harry?" Persephone lightly laughed. "He would tease you mercilessly."

"True. But he would offer an honest opinion on Lord Tilburn. I should like to have a gentleman's viewpoint."

"Is mine not sufficient?" A hint of a smile tugged at Adam's scars.

"You think everyone ever born is an imbecile," she reminded him.

Persephone's expression grew more amused. "Harry is so run ragged by his mischievous children that he might very well be too short on energy to sort all of us out as well as his growing brood."

A memory of Harry and Athena's second oldest escaping the nursery wearing not so much as a nappie during their last visit to Falstone Castle drove home the truth of Persephone's words. "And with Athena so near another confinement, he likely would be distracted by that as well."

"It is a miracle we get any coherent thoughts out of Harry these days," Persephone said. "Though he does smile a great deal."

"When has Harry ever *not* smiled?" He was the happiest person of Daphne's acquaintance. "You do not find anything suspicious in Lord Tilburn's flowers or note?" How she wanted to believe the sincerity of her very first floral offering. "Do you think he meant those ardent words?"

"Do you think he did not?" Persephone watched her pointedly. "I have no reason to doubt that he is being genuine. Have you?"

She couldn't say that she did. Her experience with suitors and attentions was nonexistent. She simply didn't know what to think.

"Lord Techney is an imbecile." Adam made his entrance into the sitting room the next afternoon with his usual lack of subtlety.

Daphne and Persephone exchanged looks, but both managed not to laugh out loud.

Persephone rose and crossed to where Adam stood and wrapped her arms around him.

"This is a change," he said. "At the Debenhams' ball, you did nothing but scold me."

"At the Debenhams' ball, you were being difficult." Persephone sighed as she leaned into him.

Adam held her but with a look of confusion directed toward Daphne. She shrugged, not knowing the reason for the unusually thorough display of affection.

"Are you unwell, Persephone?"

She shook her head.

"Are you certain? No one has upset you or been unkind?"

"No."

"Insulting? Impertinent? Anything at all?"

Adam's kind treatment of her sister was the first thing that had endeared him to Daphne.

"I am well." Persephone kept her arms around him. "You have simply been gone all day, and I have missed you."

"Unfortunately, the House of Lords is in constant need of adult supervision." Adam kissed the top of her head—a display to which Artemis would have vehemently and vocally objected. Daphne never felt the discomfort her younger sister did. She found her sister's happiness reassuring.

"So why is Lord Techney an imbecile?" Persephone led Adam to the sofa facing the one on which Daphne sat.

"There are far too many reasons to list them all."

"The most pertinent, then." Persephone sat tucked under Adam's arm.

Daphne couldn't look away. She had often imagined herself being held that way, with such tenderness and care.

"He has invited us to have dinner with his family." Adam could not have looked less pleased if he'd been invited to be the guest of honor at a hanging.

Daphne likely looked almost as horrified but for entirely different reasons. Dinner with James's family seemed like a much larger step in the direction of courtship than she'd expected. He had sent her flowers along with a very personal note, but she still couldn't help thinking he acted more like a friendly acquaintance when they were together than he did a suitor.

"When is this dinner party?" Persephone asked.

"Three days, Persephone. The Almighty took seven days to create the world; we have three to prepare for the end of it."

Persephone shook her head, though whether at his exaggerated objections or Lord Techney's invitation, Daphne wasn't sure. "What could have inspired Lord Techney to invite us to a family dinner? Certainly your reputation would be enough to convince him of the inadvisable nature of such a thing."

"You were apparently not listening when I explained that Lord Techney is an idiot."

"An *imbecile*, dear," Persephone corrected. "A dinner party, though poorly thought through when the invitation is directed toward the Dangerous Duke, isn't entirely an unreasonable thing. I assume there is some other bit of logic behind your dismissal of poor Lord Techney's mental acuity."

"He delivered the invitation to me at Lords, despite having not spent more than a moment there on any given day these past weeks and not often before that." Adam's censure was apparent. "We are on the brink of war with the Former Colonies, whilst already deep into war on the continent, and are seeing rioting in the north and in the midlands. A gentleman with any degree of responsibility would have done everything in his power to take up his duties in Lords this session. Techney, however, feels his duty there does not extend beyond irritating people with presumptuous invitations."

Did Adam intend to refuse the invitation? Daphne could not say how exactly she felt about that possibility.

"And," Adam continued, "Linus makes port the morning of this dinner and will arrive in London the next day. We cannot very well welcome him back into the bosom of his family"—Adam's sarcastic tone brought a smile to Persephone's face and very nearly to Daphne's as well—"if that family is off prancing about London."

"I would give a year's pin money to see you prance, Adam."

He laughed, something only Persephone had ever managed to make him do.

"This is one invitation, dearest," Persephone said, "and one to a single dinner being held before Linus can possibly reach Town. You cannot use him as an excuse to avoid it."

"When have I ever required an excuse to avoid anything I didn't wish to do?"

Persephone only smiled. "The solution to this difficulty is quite simple. I will accompany Daphne to the dinner party, and you can sulk here at Falstone House."

"You will be spending much of the Season at balls and musicales whilst I am home, and you wish to add another evening apart to our already ridiculous schedule of them. This is your perfect solution?" He eyed Persephone with patent disapproval.

"Then you shall simply have to come to the dinner with us."

"How fortunate for me," he drawled.

"Do you mean to accept the invitation, then?" Daphne asked.

The flash of surprise that crossed both Adam's and Persephone's faces clearly indicated they had forgotten her presence in the room. That happened far more often than it ought.

"I believe we should," Persephone said. "Lord Tilburn has been attentive. His father clearly wishes to deepen the connection. An intimate dinner party would be the best opportunity for us to come to know Lord Tilburn better."

"That is likely their purpose, after all." Daphne tried to convince herself that she was living the smallest fulfillment of her hopes where James was concerned. She wanted to believe it. She truly did. She also didn't want to be disappointed if nothing came of these dreams.

Persephone pulled away from Adam and leaned toward Daphne, her brow pulled with concern. "What is it that has you so worried, dearest?"

"What if—" Personal confessions never had come easily to her. And yet this undertaking was so new and unfamiliar that she needed some guidance. "What if he comes to know me, then decides he doesn't care for what he has found?"

"Then the whelp is a fool," Adam declared.

Persephone stopped him with a gentle hand on his leg without ever looking away from Daphne. "You always have been wont to worry. But being courted—and I *do* believe this is the beginning of exactly that— ought to be a wonderful and enjoyable experience. Please try to simply enjoy it. Allow Adam and me to worry and watch."

"And I most certainly will be watching him, Daphne," Adam declared in his very sternest duke voice. "I offered my approval of his first visit to this house, but I made no promise beyond. I will keep a very close eye on Lord Tilburn, make no mistake about that."

Chapter Ten

"This is lunacy, James. Utter lunacy."

James walked beside his brother as they made their way from his London rooms toward Techney House. Bennett had arrived unexpectedly in Town only that morning.

"I have never once heard you mention this Miss Lancaster, and then word arrives from Father announcing that you are courting her? It is madness."

James completely agreed, but giving voice to that opinion would not be helpful. He straightened his cuffs, attempting to appear at ease despite the weight in his chest and the oppressive heat of the late-summer day. The heavy clouds did little to improve conditions.

"I am certain all will work out fine in the end." He'd been telling himself that ever since signing his deal with the devil the night before.

"By whose estimation?" Bennett demanded. "Mother wept when she read Father's letter, and not tears of joy. I would certainly never advocate you marrying someone I know you do not love. Lands, I doubt you even care for her. You could not have known her before this Season."

"I am sure I have met her in the past," James said. "She looked familiar."

"*She looked familiar?*" Bennett laughed humorlessly. "What kind of a beginning is that to a courtship?" He grasped James's arm, stopping their forward progress. "Did she trap you into this? Trick you into compromising her?"

"No." Miss Lancaster wasn't the type to do anything so underhanded. "Father was more than a little presumptuous in what he wrote in that letter." And even more presumptuous in his timing. For Bennett to have received the letter and come to Town, arriving less than twenty-four hours after James himself had been forced to agree to the courtship, Father had to have sent the letter several days ago. "A betrothal between us is not a foregone conclusion. I would wager Miss Lancaster would be shocked to hear that any kind of future between us is being discussed at all."

Bennett did not look relieved. "You have never been one to act rashly, and such a swift courtship is inarguably rash." He shook his head as they turned a corner. "I'd sooner expect the Duke of Kielder to run you through than allow you to compromise his sister-in-law." Bennett's voice suddenly dropped in volume. "Did the Dangerous Duke force your hand?"

"No." There'd been no true force from anyone but Father. Despite having been the one to first propose a courtship between James and Miss Lancaster, His Grace watched James with suspicion. "No, he didn't."

James could see Bennett's posture stiffen. Realization, it seemed, was dawning. "Father is forcing you, isn't he?"

He didn't answer. He knew he didn't have to.

They turned onto the street where the family home sat. It was not the most fashionable address, something Father no doubt wished to rectify by means of his heir's marriage. If there was any justice or mercy in the world, James would yet find a way to avoid that heart-wrenching conclusion to his father's schemes. Neither he nor Miss Lancaster ought to be doomed to a loveless marriage.

"What is he holding over your head this time?" Bennett asked.

"Does it matter?"

"Of course it matters what Father used to entrap you. This is your entire life, James. Your future, your children. Marriage is final, irrevocable. Deuce take it, it blasted well better be worth it."

Backing out of the courtship would have cost Bennett his land and, with it, his very future. James had placed in the keeping of the Bank of England one copy of Father's sworn and signed promise to never deprive Bennett or Mother of their incomes or to ever force Bennett's hand in marriage. He kept another copy in his portable writing desk. Father's scheming and planning would stop with him.

"It was worth it," he whispered.

"You're not going to tell me what it was?"

And allow Bennett to feel guilty about the entire debacle? "No, I'm not."

James could see disappointment in his brother's eyes.

Bennett waited only a moment to light into him. "What happened to 'the bird slipping from its cage,' James? You have talked all these years about fighting for our freedom, of not letting Father take control of our lives. How could you let him win like this?"

"If I could have found a way around this, I would have." James did an admirable job of maintaining his calm in the face of his brother's onslaught. "Until and unless I stumble upon something miraculous that disentangles me, I have no choice, Ben. No choice."

They were within sight of Techney House. A traveling carriage sat out front, servants rushing back and forth.

"Mother must have arrived," Bennett said.

"Mother?" James could not have been more shocked. "*Our* mother?"

Bennett gave him a look of annoyed impatience. "Her oldest son has, according to the post, quite suddenly undertaken a serious courtship with a young lady none of us has ever met. Of course Mother came to Town."

Mother feared London. She had for decades. His promise to Father had brought her to Town. He could not allow her to be miserable here once again.

They hurried up the front steps. The chaos in the entryway spoke volumes of everyone's unfamiliarity with the arrival of the mistress of the house. Trunks sat stacked whilst footmen looked to the butler in obvious confusion. A maid hovered near the doorway, her brow knit as she listened to a chain of garbled instructions from the housekeeper.

"Were you not warned of Lady Techney's arrival?" James asked the harried housekeeper.

"We were not, Lord Tilburn," she said, apology and pleading coupled in her tone and expression. "I am afraid she isn't seeing us at our best."

Had Mother ever been in residence with Mrs. Green as the housekeeper? James didn't think she had. No wonder the poor woman was beside herself.

"I am certain you have kept the mistress's chambers tidied."

Mrs. Green pulled herself up quite proudly. "Of course I have."

"And your menus are always beyond reproach," James added. "The secret to pleasing Lady Techney is a comfortable, quiet room and soft bread with her dinner. She is excessively fond of bread."

Mrs. Green's expression turned very thoughtful. "Cook is a genius with breads of every kind."

James agreed with a nod. "And we've already established that you take prodigiously good care of the bedchambers. I believe, Mrs. Green, you have nothing to fear in pleasing your mistress."

A flicker of relief passed across Mrs. Green's face before she straightened her shoulders once more. Her air of command firmly in place again, she instructed the quaking maids on their duties. In the meantime, the butler seized control of the situation and the traveling trunks were on their way to the appropriate chambers.

James kept his further concerns to himself. The already shaken staff hardly needed to see that his faith in them was wavering. All was running smoothly for the moment. He would wait to explain the necessity of having a footman ready to send for a physician or apothecary at all hours.

Mother could settle in while James readied himself to explain to her his intention to pay particular attention to a young lady entirely unknown to her. Somehow he would soothe her fears as he always did. He would act as a buffer between his parents, keeping their unhappy relationship from souring further. Somehow he would prevent Bennett and Father from coming to blows. And in the midst of it all, he would attempt to unsuccessfully court an innocent and unsuspecting young lady.

He rather hated himself for that last part.

He knocked lightly on Mother's bedchamber door. Her lady's maid opened it a moment later. "Good afternoon, Jenny. I've come to bid my mother welcome."

Jenny nodded, pulling the door open. James stepped inside. Mother sat with her feet up on the room's fainting couch. Her coloring was poor, even more so than usual. She looked up as he stepped nearer.

She held her hands out to him. He took them, then sat beside her on the couch.

"Oh, James. What a journey I had. Never have I been so thrown about in all my life."

"I am sorry, Mother." James didn't at all like the redness he saw in her eyes. "You are not feverish, are you?"

"No," she answered. "But I am exhausted. The puppy did not at all care for the carriage ride."

"Puppy?"

She sighed and leaned her head against his shoulder. "I have taken in a puppy."

Again? James had spent the better part of a fortnight searching out a home for the last pup Mother had saved from some horrific fate or other.

"He is a little terrier," Mother continued. "The most adorable little puppy and so very well behaved. He does jump about a lot and likes to chew on things he really rather shouldn't. And when he gets it in his head to bark, nothing can dissuade him from it. But otherwise, he is perfectly lovely."

"A terrier, you say?" *He sounds far more like a terror.*

"Mrs. Allen threatened to have my little pup banished to the stables. All he'd done was chew up a leg on one of the dining room chairs. Only one leg on one chair."

Mrs. Allen was the long-suffering housekeeper at the family's country estate. She had endured a long line of Mother's destructive puppies.

"I was quite distraught," Mother said. "My poor little puppy would have been so very lonely in the stables, and Mrs. Allen would not listen to my pleadings. You were not there to talk to her. She only listens to you."

"I was here in Town, Mother."

"I know, dearest. And I do not fault you for that. You are a young gentleman with social obligations. I am so happy you have found your footing in London Society. Not everyone does, you know."

Father's account of her disastrous attempt to find her own footing returned with force to his memory. "I do know, Mother. I know."

"My little pup has been such a comfort this past week as I have endured a sore throat. I simply couldn't bear to leave him behind, so he has made the journey here. I do hope he takes to Town and isn't too miserable. But I know you will know precisely what is to be done."

James nodded. He'd deal with the puppy eventually. The sore throat was the more pressing matter. Mother's health had always been uncertain, her throat being particularly vulnerable. He would speak with an apothecary. Cook could be counted upon to provide a warm posset. As always, James would see that all was well.

"This journey must have taken a toll on your strength," he said. "I am certain Jenny will have a bath drawn at once, then you can rest for the remainder of the afternoon."

Jenny made a quick curtsy and left to draw the bath. Alone at last, James struck at the topic he knew he must broach with his very sensitive mother.

"Bennett told me why you have come," he said. "I wish you had spared yourself the effort, Mother. I would not see you ill for the world."

"And I would not see you unhappy for the world," Mother answered. "I needed to see for myself that you are making a wise choice in courting this young lady. I need to know you are happy."

"Father was a bit hasty in his letter," James said. "There is no understanding between Miss Lancaster and myself, no determined course for our future. I am coming to know her, and Father, in his eagerness for a beneficial match, has chosen to interpret that as something just shy of a betrothal."

He left unspoken his obligation to move in that direction. Mother worried greatly over even the smallest of things. He had learned long ago not to burden her with his troubles.

"Your father said he meant to invite her family to take dinner with us," Mother said.

It was the first James had heard of this plan. "I shall have to ask Father about that," he muttered.

"How did you meet this Miss Lancaster?" Mother asked. "You haven't mentioned her before."

"I have a very slight acquaintance with her brother-in-law." James intended to do his utmost not to be any less forthright than was necessary. "I had met her briefly on a few occasions before. This is her first Season and the first time I have spent any length of time with her."

Mother's brow drew inward. "Do you like her?"

"I do." He knew the moment he spoke the words that they were true. He did like Miss Lancaster. He didn't *love* her, nor did he truly wish to marry her, but he most definitely liked her. "I believe you will like her as well."

Mother's concern only seemed to grow. "I do not know that she will take much notice of me. Your father said her sister is a duchess. Duchesses do not care for unimportant people."

"They will all be very kind to you." James prayed that proved true. He held out no hope of civility from His Grace, but what he knew of Miss Lancaster told him he could depend upon her kindness. "Rest now, Mother."

"Will you check on my puppy?"

He nodded his agreement.

"And see if the housekeeper can tell us of a reliable physician?"

He nodded again.

"And where the nearest apothecary can be found?"

"Of course, Mother." He pulled a light throw from the back of the couch, settling it over her as she lay down once more. "I will see to it all."

She reached up a frail hand and lightly touched his face. "You'll make everything right. You always do."

So he did. Mother's well-being and Bennett's future had always been his responsibility. For years, he'd held them all together. He had dedicated himself to caring for his family, to sacrificing for their happiness. That was forever the role he fulfilled, and it was an often lonely one.

Chapter Eleven

"ARE YOU SIMPLY DYING, DAPHNE?" Artemis seemed to hope the answer was yes. "Here you are, being whisked across Town"—she made a sweeping gesture, filling almost the entire interior of the carriage—"to meet the mother of"—a hand pressed to her heart even as she sighed—"your dashing hero." Her look turned very commiserating. "The hero's mother is *always* a dragon, you realize."

Daphne rested her forehead against her upturned hand. Artemis was on her third round of tragic predictions.

"She will be positively horrid and make you excessively miserable." Artemis's eyes pulled wide with excitement. "She might even demand that you be thrown from the house and the doors locked."

"That is quite enough, Artemis." Persephone generally had a large store of patience when dealing with the youngest of the Lancasters, but she had apparently reached the end of her endurance this time.

"But Daphne will be a tragic heroine. Those are the very best kind. They suffer and pine away in destitution, and some don't even survive. I would be a tremendous tragic heroine. I would suffer with dignity only to faint dead away and quite possibly never revive." Artemis made a habit of announcing herself on the verge of expiring. Did she even realize how many times she had, by her own declaration, narrowly escaped death in her fifteen years? "It would be heartbreaking."

"But not unforeseen." Adam made the comment under his breath, though Daphne overheard. Artemis might have as well had she not been occupied with positioning herself in a dramatic pose of ultimate suffering on the opposite side of the carriage.

"Artemis." Persephone attempted to gain the girl's attention. "Artemis."

She looked up at last.

"Do attempt to act mature enough to warrant the invitation you have received," Persephone said, a rare show of correction on her part. A bond existed between the oldest and youngest Lancaster sisters that none of the others shared. Daphne certainly had never been the favorite that Artemis was. "Lady Techney did not have to include you."

Artemis pulled out her brilliant smile. "I know how to behave in public."

"Adam knows how to dance the minuet," Persephone pointed out. "That doesn't mean he actually does."

"I also don't attend dinner parties," Adam grumbled. "But here I am."

Daphne sincerely hoped he meant to be at least a little cooperative. She wanted to make a good impression on James and his family. If Adam spent the entire dinner glaring everyone into terrified silence, the whole evening would be for naught.

The landau pulled to a stop at Techney House. A lump formed in Daphne's throat. *The hero's mother is always a dragon.* Daphne usually dismissed Artemis's dramatic declarations. That particular observation hit too close to the mark though. She wanted to believe James Tilburn's mother was as kind and caring as he.

They were handed out of the carriage in succession, and when Daphne emerged, she glanced up at the house's façade with a growing sense of trepidation. Falstone Castle was far bigger and more imposing than Techney House, built almost entirely of stone, isolated in the midst of a thick, planted forest inhabited by a pack of formidable feral dogs. Yet the castle felt far more warm and inviting than this grand house did. Techney House felt empty in a way not at all physical.

The Techney butler received them with the correct degree of propriety. Not a single fault could be found with the entryway nor the state of the floors. Even the flowers on the narrow table were fresh and flawlessly arranged. The orderliness of it was reassuring, even as the perfection proved quite the opposite.

During her morning calls with Persephone, a social expectation her sister had seldom permitted her to skip, Daphne had more than once overheard comments questioning James's motivations. Why, people had asked behind their hands, would a gentleman suddenly take up a whirlwind courtship with a girl so wholly unconnected with his family? Her dowry had come up often in those discussions, as had the likelihood of her acerbic guardian forcing the match to rid his hands of her.

She had borne the curious looks and whispered evaluations with the stoic endurance Adam had taught her more than half a decade earlier. In her heart, however, she couldn't help but worry a little.

James stepped out onto the first-floor landing, and Daphne's heart leapt at the sight of his familiar copper eyes.

"Forgive me, Your Grace. Your Grace." He sketched a brief bow, his tone indicating a degree of anxiety that caught Daphne's attention. "I had intended to greet you upon your arrival"—his gaze encompassed all four of them—"but my mother has been unwell. At the time your carriage was announced, I was attempting to comfort her."

Was his mother often unwell? Perhaps that was the reason she, according to a great many comments made during their at-home earlier in the day, had not come to Town in at least twenty years.

"I hope Lady Techney recovers quickly," Persephone answered on everyone's behalf.

"As do I," he said, again seeming to address them as a whole. "If you will follow Billingsley to the drawing room, my father and brother are waiting there."

Adam offered Persephone his arm, ever the perfect gentleman where his wife was concerned. They followed the path the butler took. Artemis kept close on their heels.

"Good evening, Miss Artemis," James said as she passed and received a very undramatic curtsy in return.

Daphne did her utmost not to wring her hands, all the while fearing their shaking was noticeable. Seeing James always set her stomach fluttering, simultaneously pleasing and unnerving her. It had always been this way, ever since that night on Adam's balcony.

"Miss Lancaster." He smiled a little awkwardly.

"Lord Tilburn." Daphne was proud of the steadiness of her voice—not a hint of her nervousness had entered it. "I hope your mother is not seriously unwell."

"She is not in any danger." James's worried, tense expression belied his confident words. "I fear, though, she is very uncomfortable."

Artemis had not stepped entirely out of hearing range and, true to form, inserted herself in their conversation without invitation. "If your mother is

ill, you must have Daphne recommend a tisane. It is her defining talent, you
know."

Did she have to point out one of Daphne's oddities so early in the
evening? The ability to recall herbal remedies was hardly a lauded accomplishment. James would think her strange, indeed.

"Have you a knack for such things?" Did he ask out of genuine curiosity or merely a desire to be polite?

"Oh yes," Artemis said. "Even the apothecary we use at Falstone Castle
cedes to Daphne's expertise. She is an herbal genius."

James walked with them down the corridor. "Does your sister exaggerate, or is this truly something you have studied?"

She heard no mockery in his tone nor saw dismissal in his expression.
Others who heard of her interest in herbology responded with everything
from disapproval to hurtful amusement.

"I have studied it," she said. "Though I cannot say I would deem
myself a genius."

The look of concern that yet remained on James's face echoed many
such moments in her own life. How often she had worried over the health
of her family members. Having the ability to help them with the knowledge she'd gained had always been a comfort.

"Perhaps if you told me, at least in general terms, what is ailing your
mother, I could suggest something."

"You would do that for a woman you've never met?"

"Certainly." Why did that seem to surprise him so much? "If she is
unwell and I can help, I would like to."

James's brow furrowed. Daphne felt suddenly very unsure. Did he
disapprove of her forwardness in placing herself in the midst of his difficulties? They were not, after all, very well acquainted yet. She fumbled
a moment in her mind, seeking a means of salvaging the situation. "Of
course, if your mother would feel uncomfortable or if I have overstepped
myself—"

But he shook his head without hesitation. "Not at all. I am only unaccustomed to offers of help, I suppose."

"You are often left to fend for yourself?"

"I am often left to solve everyone's problems on my own."

Adam could be like that as well—independent to the point of isolation. Persephone had a talent for undermining his hardheaded insistence
on doing things himself.

"I would like to help if you will let me," Daphne said.

"There is nothing specifically the matter with her," James answered. "She simply feels unwell in general and, as a result, has not slept as she ought."

Daphne nodded. One needed rest during an illness, and yet the misery that accompanied it often made sleeping difficult. "Do you think she is more in need of an invigorating tonic or something to help her sleep?"

"I believe she needs sleep more than anything else."

They had very nearly reached the drawing room.

"I know of several tisanes she might take. I will write a few of them down so your cook can choose the one she has the ingredients for."

"You know several by memory? A lady of hidden talents." His lightened tone did her heart good. Perhaps she had eased some of his worry.

"If she is still unwell tomorrow or is bothered by new symptoms, I hope you will send word to Falstone House. I likely know of something that can help."

Then James Tilburn smiled at her, the very same smile he'd offered to a twelve-year-old girl hiding in the shadows of a balcony. It was soft and caring and infinitely charming. "That is very good of you," he said. "Thank you."

Her heart fairly sang at the realization that he hadn't brushed aside her offer. As a girl, her attempts to help the family had been met with insistence that she was too young or too incapable of making a difference. Even after she'd proven herself more than adept at tisanes and herbal remedies, the family had been hesitant to come to her when ill. And now, though she was quite grown up, they still tended to dismiss her suggestions or tell her not to trouble herself. James had done neither.

They stepped inside the drawing room. Daphne vaguely noted the other occupants. James's company was too distracting.

"Allow me to introduce you to my father and brother." James stepped with her in the direction of their gathered family members.

Daphne felt a moment's concern—introductions always made her uncomfortable. But James was with her. She trusted him.

Chapter Twelve

WHEN JAMES HAD FIRST CALLED at Falstone House, he'd expected Daphne Lancaster to be grasping and pampered, a young lady who could have any gentleman for the taking at a mere snap of her guardian's fingers. He'd quickly discovered otherwise. She was quiet and vulnerable and fragile. She was also, he had realized during their short walk to the drawing room, good-hearted.

She had offered, without hesitation or any degree of pretense, to help his mother. She had listened to his confessions about being the paste keeping his family together—a confession he'd not intended to make—with sincere concern and interest.

She'd proven entirely unspoiled and inherently likable. That made the ruse he was enacting all the more despicable.

He led Miss Lancaster across the drawing room. The Duchess of Kielder appeared to be listening to whatever Father had chosen to expostulate on, though James could not guarantee the accuracy of that evaluation. The duchess's social mask was far more polished than Miss Artemis's, who looked unmistakably bored and inattentive at her sister's side.

The duke never had bothered to hide his annoyance with people. He didn't do so in that moment either.

Does Father have any idea how little His Grace cares for his company?

James guided Miss Lancaster to where Ben stood a little apart from the rest of the group. "Miss Lancaster, may I present my brother, Mr. Bennett Tilburn."

"I am pleased to meet you, Mr. Tilburn."

"Miss Lancaster." Ben dipped his head but only the smallest bit. "Welcome."

His distinct lack of enthusiasm could not have been more apparent. The show of incivility was uncalled for. Miss Lancaster looked a touch confused, and though the high color in her cheeks remained, the rest of her countenance turned a bit pale.

James skewered his brother with a look of warning. No matter the injustice of the situation, mistreating Miss Lancaster would help nothing.

"Please forgive my brother's lack of manners, Miss Lancaster. Our riding master regularly tossed him from his pony during childhood, and I'm afraid the experience had a profound impact on his mental capacity."

"How tragic." Miss Lancaster managed a tone of near sincerity with just the right amount of irony. She had grasped James's intent quickly. "Reliable help has always been difficult to come by."

James nodded gravely.

"Are you still afraid of ponies?" she asked Ben.

The slightest twitch tugged at his brother's lips.

"Sweets generally stave off any truly juvenile behavior, Miss Lancaster," James said, enjoying watching the obvious struggle required for Ben to not be entertained by their humor. "I have also found naps are very efficacious."

"That works with my four-year-old nephew as well."

A smile finally broke across Ben's face. "Enough, you two. You win." Ben executed a very respectful and proper bow, then spoke to Miss Lancaster. "I apologize for the incivility of my initial response to our introduction. I can offer no excuse beyond my own weariness. Life has been tumultuous here as we have prepared for this dinner party a scant three days after arriving in Town."

"*Tumultuous* is a rather large word for a person who was dropped on his head," Miss Lancaster observed.

James laughed out loud at the unexpected parry. Ben, he noticed, smiled ever broader. Miss Lancaster's eyes shifted between the two of them, and her frequent blush returned.

"I hope I have not offended you, Mr. Tilburn," she said.

"On the contrary," Ben replied. "I am rather enjoying hearing James laugh—he seldom does."

"Ah, but I know any number of people at the opera earlier this week who would disagree with you." A twinkle of mischief lit her eyes. James would not have thought that possible during their very first encounter. She'd sat so still and quiet in her sister's drawing room.

"Was it a humorous production, then?" Ben asked.

"It was when Miss Lancaster translated it."

She bit back a smile.

"I'm sorry to have missed that," Ben said. "A bit of joviality could only improve an opera."

"I take it you do not care for opera?" Miss Lancaster asked.

Ben shook his head.

"I think my brother far prefers a country-fair offering of 'Punch and Judy,'" James said.

She assumed a look of overdone sympathy. "That seems fitting." She motioned quickly to Ben before tapping her temple as she shook her head. "*Considering.*"

Ben's chuckle joined James's, and the tension that had built between them since Ben's arrival in London evaporated.

"I like you, Miss Lancaster," Ben said with a grin.

The poor lady blushed again, but she didn't try to slip away nor hide as one might have expected of someone so timid and easily embarrassed. That was an argument decidedly in her favor. Timid, she might be, but Miss Daphne Lancaster had steel in her.

"Tilburn. Bennett." Father's voice interrupted their brief moment of revelry. He had crossed the room and stood near at hand, the air of confident contentment he always wore in public firmly in place. "I certainly hope I taught you to behave in a more civilized fashion before guests. Miss Lancaster will think you had a poor upbringing."

Miss Lancaster grew quiet, though her eyes retained a bit of their earlier playfulness. Father's imposing presence had never failed to drain Mother of every ounce of animation. James hated seeing it happen to yet another lady.

"Has our lack of civility shocked you beyond bearing?" James asked her, keeping his tone light and teasing.

She answered in kind. "I will no doubt spend every moment of tomorrow's morning calls spreading gossip about how ill-mannered the Tilburn brothers are. It will be quite the scandal."

The Duchess of Kielder had come near the group as well. Her husband and youngest sister remained across the room, deeply discussing something. Her Grace eyed James, Ben, and Miss Lancaster with an irrefutable degree of confusion.

"You must forgive my brother and me, Your Grace," James said. "I fear we have been a poor influence on your sister."

The duchess did not immediately reply but continued to study them a moment. Her eyes rested longest on her sister. "On the contrary," she finally said. "The three of you seem to be enjoying each other's company."

"We are." James found he truly meant it. Miss Lancaster had proven herself a diverting addition to their conversation.

Her Grace's gaze held an analyzing quality that left him more than a touch uneasy. He looked away only to find Ben regarding Miss Lancaster and him in much the same way.

Billingsley announced dinner as if cued by a burst of divine intervention.

"And I am most honored to walk Her Grace in to dinner." Father made a bow.

The duke's already stern demeanor turned even more icy. "No one other than myself ever walks Her Grace in to dinner when I am present."

"But . . . but formality dictates—"

"I said *ever*. There should be no further words coming out of your mouth."

If James hadn't been certain doing so would only cause more difficulty, he would have applauded.

Father recovered quickly. "Then I shall be pleased to escort Miss Lancaster—"

"Lord Tilburn will be afforded that honor," the duke declared. "And before you make the next impertinent leap, Mr. Tilburn may escort the youngest Miss Lancaster."

Ben did the wise thing and nodded without objection. His eyes met James's for the briefest of moments. The duke's ease in dealing with their usually difficult and overbearing father had not escaped Ben's notice.

Father's expression of pleased contentment seemed a little strained. "And with whom am I to walk in to dinner?"

"Your guest list is no concern of mine." The duke offered his arm to his wife and turned without comment toward the door. Father stood on the spot, dumbfounded.

"Adam is accustomed to having his way," Miss Lancaster said quietly. Her eyes held an unmistakable apology. Little did she know just how well James understood the strain of difficult relations.

"My father is as well. The two of them in the same house for the next few hours ought to be entertaining at the least."

Amusement replaced some of the embarrassment in her expression. "Perhaps they will annoy each other into silence. That would be an unforeseen benefit."

"Indeed." He offered her his arm.

"Do you promise not to hold my relatives' actions against me?" Her lightheartedness hadn't entirely disappeared. James was grateful for that—it gave him one less person whose problem he needed to fix.

"Only if you will make the same promise to me."

"It seems we are to be coconspirators, Lord Tilburn," she said, "bonded together by our mutual lack of Italian and the need to overlook one another's embarrassing family members."

"I do believe we could start our own very exclusive club only to find most of London is in similar straits, at least as concerns their relatives."

She offered a timid smile, nothing earth-shattering nor transformative but sweet and lovely just the same. She would never be declared a diamond nor a breathtaking beauty, but she was pretty.

And she'd surprised him with her show of wit that evening. That she had the strength of character to hold up even in embarrassing and difficult situations was endearing. But liking her even that little bit more made the ruse of his deception that much harder to justify and the pain his dishonesty would cause that much more unfair.

"Oh, but, Daphne, he was looking at you in *such a way!*" Artemis flopped down on her back on Daphne's bed, both hands pressed to her heart. "He thoroughly likes you. I am certain of it."

The door of their shared dressing room had opened not long after Daphne had retired for the night. Artemis's dancing, spinning entrance had quickly given way to an excessively emotive discussion—on Artemis's part—of James's hypothetical feelings for her. Under normal circumstances, Daphne would have shooed her from her bedchamber. James's feelings, however, were too much of a mystery and far too important to forgo the opportunity to hear another opinion.

"*Likes*, however, is a far cry from *loves*," Daphne pointed out.

"Not so very far." Artemis spoke as though from great experience. Still lying on her back, she held her hands up, counting off on her fingers. "'Notices' comes first, followed by 'is interested in.' Then comes 'likes.' Then

'thoroughly likes.' Next is 'desperately likes.' Then the only step left is 'loves.'"
Artemis clasped her hands together and allowed them to sink back down
against her heart. She sighed rather too loudly. "You are only two steps from
'loves,' Daphne."

"And you obtained this information from where? A novel?" Daphne
knew enough of Artemis's reading habits and daydreaming tendencies to
put very little faith in her declarations of expertise.

Artemis turned on her side, propping herself up on her elbow and looking at Daphne with absolute conviction. "Novels are the very best place to
look for this sort of thing. The heroines are always finding themselves the
object of affection from a dashing hero."

"Aren't these the same heroines you declared do not always survive
their amorous adventures?"

"Only the truly tragic ones."

Daphne leaned back against the pillows piled at the head of her bed.
"I believe you said only this morning that I was poised to be a tragic
heroine."

Artemis crinkled her nose. "Persephone is proving far more tragic. She
hardly ate a morsel at dinner, seldom spoke, and it was she, not Adam, who
wished to leave the dinner early." Artemis executed another highly dramatic
drop onto her back. "'Tis a shame those closest to the tragic heroine always
suffer as well. And they are far less likely to survive all the way to the final
page."

"You are not fooling me in the least. You were more anxious than
anyone to leave the dinner this evening."

"Only because everyone treated me like a child." Artemis's pout lasted
only a moment before a flash of something resembling an epiphany
crossed her features. That look had always preceded a disastrous plan of
some kind or another. Daphne braced herself for her sister's next words.
"If you would only hurry and get married, I could have my come-out, and
then I would not be looked at like I'd only just arrived from the nursery."

"You say that as if getting oneself married were as simple as selecting fabric at a dressmakers."

Artemis shifted to a seated position, her eyes growing larger with
obvious excitement. "But you are a mere two steps from 'love.' A little
effort and you could get there quickly."

Daphne shook her head. "These schemes you are hatching will do you
no good. For one thing, Lord Tilburn and I have been acquainted for only

a couple of weeks, hardly enough time to be scheming as deeply as you are. For another thing, you are only fifteen. Adam will not agree to a come-out while you are still so young."

A dismissive wave of the hand clearly communicated Artemis's feelings about Daphne's logic. "Adam has been desperate to be rid of the lot of us for years."

Obviously Artemis did not know their brother-in-law very well. Though he often grumbled about his responsibilities as a guardian, he cared more for them than he let on.

Daphne had been rather afraid of her formidable brother-in-law when she'd first come to live with him. She had taken solace in the assumption that she would be as overlooked in his home as she had been in her own. Her family loved her—she didn't doubt that—but when she was little, she often went days at a time without any of them paying her much heed. Only Evander, her oldest brother, had regularly thought to check on her when the silence had stretched out.

Adam, however, had surprised her. He had noticed when she was particularly withdrawn. He had never permitted long periods of self-pity. He had welcomed her company, had even sought it out. In his home, she no longer felt so disposable.

"We could do this, Daphne. Two steps is not so very large a leap." Artemis's thoughts had not strayed far. "Lord and Lady Techney certainly would not have invited us to dine with their family if Lord Tilburn weren't at least leaning in the direction of an earnest courtship."

Good heavens, the girl looked ready to burst with excitement. The last thing Daphne wanted was to be Artemis's latest project.

"Persephone's abigail could fix up your hair—your Eliza prefers styles that are far too simple. And you could borrow that paisley shawl I pestered Adam into buying me—"

"I appreciate your offer of help"—the white lie seemed entirely necessary—"but I would far prefer to leave things as they are."

"You mean you would prefer to not draw attention to yourself." Artemis clearly disapproved of that notion. "If Lord Tilburn doesn't notice you, how can you expect him to ever move past 'liking' you? There is a reason gentlemen do not fall in love with the furniture."

The comparison was not particularly flattering. Daphne wanted to believe she had made more of an impression that evening than Artemis insinuated. She had forced herself to join in the conversation with the Tilburn brothers. After her initial moment of timidity, she had found them remarkably easy to talk with. Lord Techney, however, was not. His visage never wavered from stern, his tone of voice always a mixture of overdone civility and arrogance. She had overcome her discomfort with Adam once upon a time and hoped the same would occur with James's father.

Artemis rose from the bed and leaned against the bedpost in a pose that would not have been out of place in a painting of some epic tragedy. "When Lord Tilburn begins to grow bored with you and you realize that leaving things as they are is not enough to make you stand out in the crowd, I will be more than happy to help." She sighed rather loudly. "I will be in the nursery, pining away and suffering."

Daphne shook her head as Artemis left the bedchamber. She would have far preferred to have Persephone offer advice. Their oldest sister, however, had seemed a touch worn out that evening. Daphne didn't want to bother her if she was unwell.

She blew out the candle and settled in under her blankets. Though she wanted to entirely discount Artemis's warnings, Daphne found the words would not leave her thoughts.

When Lord Tilburn grows bored with you . . .

Not enough to make you stand out in the crowd . . .

Daphne never had stood out, never had garnered notice. The smallest of knots began to form in her stomach. James didn't overlook her as nearly everyone else did. He had noticed her as a child and again now that she was grown. He did not so readily dismiss her from his thoughts. Not yet, at least.

"All will be well," she told herself. But deep inside, a hint of doubt remained.

Chapter Thirteen

JAMES COULD SENSE A PENDING disaster from the moment they arrived at Falstone House. Her Grace had invited his family to a small gathering but two days after the family dinner. Mother had spent the short carriage ride in noticeable discomfort. Ben had spent it in utter silence. Father's expression bordered on giddy. This farcical courtship was supposed to have been undertaken for the sake of the entire family. Only Father appeared remotely happy about any of it.

They were ushered inside by a very correct butler and greeted civilly, if briefly, by the Duchess of Kielder. The Dangerous Duke eyed James with what could only be termed disapproval.

James saw his mother seated comfortably at just the right distance from the very low-burning fire, which also fortuitously happened to be outside of the conversational circles of any of the other guests. That, as much as the warmth, would secure Mother's comfort to the greatest degree possible.

"Is there anything I can get for you, Mother? Anything you need?"

"No. We are here and must simply make the best of whatever treatment we are subjected to." Mother's eyes darted about as if expecting an ax-wielding murderer to jump out at any moment. "We must make every effort to put our best foot forward."

And by *we*, Mother meant *you*. James knew she did not mean to burden him, but so many responsibilities invariably fell on his shoulders. He offered a bow of acknowledgment and turned to face the room. He would mingle with the other guests and do his duty by Miss Lancaster, but someone ought to stay near Mother to see to it she held up under the weight of her fears.

He spotted Ben not too far distant speaking to Miss Lancaster. Theirs appeared to be quite an involved conversation considering it could not have been going on for more than a few minutes.

He would begin there. Miss Lancaster must be given at least a moment of his attention—just as soon as he saw to Mother.

"Miss Lancaster," he greeted as he reached them. "Forgive the interruption. Might I steal Ben away a moment?"

That touch of pink he so often saw colored her cheeks once more. "If you promise not to drop him on his head. The poor man is only just beginning to make sensible conversation."

James smiled at the teasing remark. He noticed Ben did as well. For a man who had been quite firmly set against Miss Lancaster, Ben had grown noticeably friendlier to her. Somehow the timid Miss Lancaster was making friends. His first conversation about her with Father as well as his earliest interactions with her had very nearly convinced him she needed to be guided through Society with kid gloves. He was pleased to be wrong.

He pulled Ben a bit away. "Will you sit with Mother a moment?"

Ben nodded his agreement but only after a backward glance in Miss Lancaster's direction. Why did he have such a sudden interest in the young lady?

"What were you and Miss Lancaster speaking of?" James asked.

"Agriculture."

Agriculture? "I thought you a better conversationalist than that. I no longer wonder at how very unattached you are."

"*She* initiated the discussion," Ben said. "She asked how far distant my estate was, and when I told her I lived in northeastern Lancashire, she surmised that I likely raise sheep."

A very insightful conclusion, to be sure.

"We were discussing the benefits of raising sheep for wool versus meat."

"And does that not strike you as an odd topic of conversation with a young lady at a high-society soiree?"

Ben didn't seem the least put off the topic. "She said her brother-in-law turned around his estate, which had been in a state of ruin for decades, in only six years, and his primary commodity is sheep."

James could see the interest in his brother's eyes. Ben had been attempting to turn a profit at his estate but had done so with very little direction and absolutely no experience. He felt his own heart thud a bit with hopeful anticipation. "And Miss Lancaster said her brother-in-law found success with sheep?"

Ben nodded, a distant expression on his face. "I wish I knew Mr. Windover. I would write and ask him precisely what he did."

James did not know the gentleman either. How frustrating to be so close to a means of assisting his brother and yet be entirely unable to do so.

"I will sit with Mother, as you requested," Ben said, a warning in his tone. "You, brother, have a crisis to avert." He motioned subtly with a nod of his head just over James's shoulder.

James looked back and watched in growing alarm as his father approached the formidable Duke of Kielder. That would not end well. He moved as swiftly as decorum would allow, reaching the duke just as his father did.

"Well met, Kielder," Father greeted quite as if they were old chums.

Several other guests turned, shocked. Worried expressions landed on the two of them. His Grace eyed Father much as one would a small child wiping his sweets-stained hands all over one's best pair of breeches.

James recognized the faux pax, even if Father didn't. "You assume a great deal in your casual greeting, sir," James said under his breath. He didn't wish to publicly scold his sire but couldn't help feeling the situation would only grow worse if he didn't do something.

"Nonsense, my boy. Two evenings spent with our families in company with one another has made the two of us friends."

Oh, good heavens. Several nearby guests were openly staring.

"I do not have friends," the duke said calmly. "Those who believe otherwise are delusional." He shot a glare at those eavesdropping on the uncomfortable encounter, sending every last one of them scurrying away, excepting James and his father.

"I understand," Father said, giving the duke a conspiratorial look. "You wish to keep the connection between our families something of a secret until things are more settled. You needn't worry on that account. I'll not make anything public until the boy, here, comes up to scratch. And he will. I can promise you that, Your Grace."

If it were possible to die of horrified embarrassment, James would have in that moment.

The duke's gaze was captured by something a bit off to the side. "It seems I have an annoyance to deal with." His eyes darted to Father. "*Another* one. You"—he skewered Father with a look—"stay here. And you"—his gaze moved to James—"walk with me."

One did not ignore a dictate from the Dastardly Duke. One also did not annoy him with impunity. Once again James was left to protect his family from the stupidity of his father. He walked beside the duke, growing ever more unnerved as he watched the gathered attendees part at his approach with expressions bordering on terrified.

"I am sorry for my father's presumptuousness," he said. "He is—"

"I know full well what your father is." Clearly the duke didn't consider the acquaintance a pleasant one. "You are the one I am still attempting to sort out."

James's liver shouted out for help in that moment, the duke's well-remembered promise about eating that vital organ still fresh in James's mind.

A small cluster of guests didn't move out of the duke's path as quickly as the others. His Grace eyed them only a fraction of a moment, long enough for his message to be clear. They scurried away with the speed of birds on the wind.

"How are you at fisticuffs?" the duke asked.

After a momentary sputter, James managed a reply. "I've never bested Gentleman Jackson. I have never come close, truth be told, though he says I've improved a great deal over the past few years."

"An honest answer. How refreshing."

It was perhaps the most honest thing he'd said to any member of the duke's family over the past fortnight. "Are my abysmal skills in that arena about to be called upon?"

"Most gentlemen would have posed that question in terrified tones rather than merely curious ones," the duke said.

"I am acting under the assumption that if you intended to beat me to a mangled pulp," James said, "you would simply do so without taking the time to warn me first." That seemed more the duke's style.

His Grace made a brief sound of pondering. "That is a far more intelligent observation than most gentlemen ever manage. I find, despite all of my expectations to the contrary, you are not entirely unbearable." They had reached the far side of the drawing room. The duke motioned ahead of them. "Mr. Finley has been monopolizing my sister-in-law's attention for a full five minutes, something she doesn't appear to appreciate. I suggest we dispatch him with all due haste."

"And you wish me to employ my pathetic boxing skills?"

"Would you if I asked?"

Knowing the duke preferred an honest answer, James gave him one. "I cannot like the thought of anyone being permitted to disconcert Miss Lancaster. What I know of her tells me she is worthy of far better treatment. Though I am not in a position to take up her cause, I will certainly aid you in doing so, though a bout with my fists is more likely to break my nose than save the day."

The duke nodded in what might have been hesitant approval. "Then, Tilburn, let me show you how it is done."

He approached Mr. Finley from behind, slowly, silently.

"My cronies and I have heard sums exceeding £35,000," Mr. Finley was saying to Miss Lancaster. "Your brother-in-law has all of London terrified to so much as speak to you and yet, if rumor is to be believed, wishes to have you married off by Season's end, necessitating an increase in your dowry. If such is true, I should very much like to know. Any number of us would make a go of it for that amount of money."

What a pompous, insufferable jackanapes. To say such a thing *to* a young lady was absolutely unforgivable.

"If another rumor is to be believed," His Grace spoke to Mr. Finley with a chilling degree of calm, "I am capable of killing you in six different ways from my current position."

Mr. Finley turned around slowly, his eyes wide with terror.

"Would you care to test the veracity of that bit of gossip?" the duke asked.

Mr. Finley shook his head vehemently.

"Then know this: should you ever speak to Miss Lancaster again, I will see to it you are very personally acquainted with the reasons why all of London is afraid to address her without my express approval."

Though the threats were not leveled at him, James acutely felt their ferocity. Looking around at the pale faces in the crowd, he knew he was not the only one. Mr. Finley literally ran from the room, something James didn't think he'd ever seen happen at a soiree. The rest of the gathering gave the duke, James, and Miss Lancaster a very wide berth.

"Daphne." The duke motioned her to his side.

James did not at all like the redness that had crept in about her eyes. The poor lady looked on the verge of tears.

"You know the rules," His Grace said.

She nodded. "No crying," she whispered.

James was worried anew for her. Mr. Finley had treated her quite poorly. If she felt the need to cry, she ought to be permitted that release.

"Now, Tilburn, here is where you come in." His Grace never spoke with anything less than absolute confidence. "Take Daphne for a turn about the room, several if necessary. And do not under any circumstances allow her to be annoyed by any of the guests until she has recovered sufficiently to be equal to enduring them."

"It would be my pleasure, Your Grace." James would even shield her from the duke himself if need be. "Shall we, Miss Lancaster?" He held his arm out to her. She accepted it without so much as glancing up at him and allowed herself to be led away.

"I see your mother is well enough to join us this afternoon, Lord Tilburn," she said after they had wandered a bit. "I hope she is recovered from her illness of a few evenings ago."

"She is much improved, thank you," James answered.

"That must be relieving." Miss Lancaster's blush heightened as she spoke. Her witty conversation of two evenings before seemed to have deserted her, owing, no doubt, to the added company of a great many people. He needed to remember she was timid and would likely benefit from quieter attentions and conversation.

"I had been told this evening's gathering was meant to welcome your brother home," he said. "I have not yet spied anyone in a navy uniform. Is he in civilian dress this evening?"

"Linus's ship has not yet made port. It seems they hit a patch of bad weather and are behind schedule."

"I am sorry to hear that." They continued their slow circuit of the room. "I know you were looking forward to seeing him again."

"Adam has promised Persephone that he will commandeer a ship himself and go fetch Linus from the middle of the ocean if need be." The smallest hint of a smile returned to Miss Lancaster's expression. "She has always been like a mother to all of us. She worries terribly when any of us are away."

"Your description casts me in the role of mother to my family," he said. "*I* worry about *them* when I am away."

Miss Lancaster turned her attention to the small reticule hanging from her wrist. She pulled a slip of paper out. "I've written down recipes for three different tisanes that are very soothing on a sore throat." She held the paper out to him. "If Lady Techney is still feeling a little unwell, she might find any one of these helpful."

James took the paper, grateful for her thoughtfulness. "The tonic you provided to Cook the night of the dinner has proven exceptionally helpful. I do not believe Mother has slept so well in years."

Out of the corner of his eye, James saw the duchess watching them with concerned curiosity. From the other side of the room, Ben and Mother did the same. Father stood beneath the tall windows looking utterly pleased with himself. James didn't dare search out the duke's expression.

"I realize my brother-in-law is very demanding," Miss Lancaster said after the silence between them had stretched out. "You needn't continue walking about with me if you would rather not."

The cowardly part of him was tempted to accept her offered escape. But Mr. Finley's unkindness sat too fresh in his mind. He would not treat her ill as well. "I have had the misfortune of knowing Mr. Finley for several years."

"Have you?" she asked quietly.

"He has always been something of a lackwit."

That brought a touch of a smile back to her pale face. "I know I shouldn't allow his comments to wound me, but there is something so belittling about knowing people talk about me that way, as though I were so burdensome and worthless that Adam had to raise extra funds just to rid himself of me."

He set his hand atop hers, where it rested on his arm. "No one cares to be treated like a commodity, worthless or otherwise."

"Does your family treat you that way?" she asked.

"My father certainly does." He was making confessions to Miss Lancaster he hadn't to anyone else. Even with her reticence and his discomfort over their situation, he found her an easy person to talk with. "I am the heir, you must understand. He feels the future of our entire family depends on me toeing the line and doing as he commands."

"That belief is not an uncommon one," she said. "It has been instilled in the aristocracy for generations. My grandfather was a baron who was raised by a baron who was raised by a baron." She moved her hand in circles, indicating the pattern continued on beyond even those generations. "Persephone heard Grandfather's lecture on the topic of family name and pride anytime she suggested she should find employment to support our family."

Father would have apoplexy if James ever hinted at taking a position for pay. "My grandfather was the first Earl of Techney. My relations needed only one generation to become insufferably obsessed with family pride."

Far from being shocked or dismissive, Miss Lancaster simply nodded her understanding. "Perhaps your grandfather feared being rejected as an upstart, so he clung ever more fiercely to those dictates."

James hadn't ever thought of it in those terms. Perhaps Father's father had been just as persistent and unfeeling on these matters as Father was. He could almost feel sorry for the young man Father had once been.

"Are you suggesting I ought to be patient with my father?" He made certain his tone held no censure, as he meant the comment as a self-recrimination and not a scold.

"I suppose I am simply accustomed to looking for reasons why people do the things they do. It helps me think better of them."

"Are you this forbearing with your brother-in-law?" He was likely a difficult person to think the best of.

"Adam is not a bad person. He is simply very accustomed to being obeyed." She spoke of the fearsome duke with a very real fondness in her voice and a smile in her eyes.

What kind of a young lady must she be to see good even in a man whose well-earned reputation set the entire kingdom to trembling?

"Your mother appears ill at ease," she said.

"She grows anxious over social gatherings," he explained. "I suppose she has been away from Society too long." While the explanation was not a full one, it was honest as far as it went. Telling her all of his mother's insecurities felt too much like a betrayal. The duchess had just taken a seat beside Mother. "Your sister is kind to sit by her, even if only for a moment."

"She need not fear ill-treatment whilst she is a guest of the Duchess of Kielder."

James watched from a distance as the two ladies interacted. Her Grace said something. Mother nodded. Another comment from the duchess brought a look of palpable relief to Mother's face. A moment later, Mother was the one speaking. She still appeared uncomfortable, but the borderline panic that had been there upon their arrival at Falstone House had eased.

"Would your mother be overset if we paused a moment to speak with her?" Miss Lancaster, though timid herself, intended to help alleviate his mother's worries.

"I believe she would appreciate that," he said.

There was a generosity in Miss Lancaster that could not be denied. And better still, this was the first conversation he'd had with anyone in years in which nothing was demanded of him and nothing required. He could easily grow very accustomed to that.

Chapter Fourteen

Daphne stepped inside Persephone's sitting room late in the morning a week after the gathering at Falstone House. During that time, James had come for an obligatory morning call and had spoken to her only briefly at the two social engagements they'd both attended. His interest seemed to have quickly waned, and Daphne was growing worried.

Artemis lounged on the window seat. She leaned her head against the glass, gazing out over the street below. "I do not understand why I am not permitted to go anywhere." She managed to sound as though she were being terribly ill-treated.

Did the girl never have a drama-free moment?

"You go any number of places," Persephone answered from her seat nearer the empty fireplace. She didn't look up from her stitching.

"But not to a ball. You are all going tonight without me, and it is horridly unfair."

Daphne remained near the door. Neither of her sisters had seen her yet.

"When you are old enough for your come-out, we will run you every bit as ragged as you please."

With a sigh, Artemis seemed to resign herself. Now was the time for Daphne to speak up.

"May I speak with you a moment, Persephone?" she asked.

"Of course." Persephone motioned her over. "What is on your mind?"

I cannot believe I am doing this. "I want to try doing something different with my appearance. I am not certain just what, but something more . . . pretty."

Persephone didn't laugh as Daphne had worried she might.

Artemis spun so fast on her cushion that Daphne half expected her to tumble to the floor. In a flurry of fabric, the girl rushed to her side, hands waving in unfettered excitement. "I knew it! I just knew you'd blend into the walls. I was so very, very certain of it."

"Hush, Artemis." Persephone's gaze never wavered from Daphne. "What is it you're wanting to do?"

Daphne didn't like how doubtful her sister sounded. Still, she needed to do something. "Not anything drastic," she said. "I only want a little change, something simple I could try."

"Oh, but there is nothing simple about it." Artemis took hold of her arms just above the elbow, her gaze boring into Daphne's. "A complete and utter change is absolutely necessary. A new wardrobe, a new coiffure, perhaps a touch of rouge."

"Artemis Psyche Lancaster!" Persephone actually sounded shocked. Artemis's antics seldom surprised any of them. "If you are so much as considering using face paints, I promise you that Adam and I will never let you out of this house—"

"Not for *me*, Persephone. For Daphne. She is the one with the complexion of snow."

Daphne slumped in her chair. This was exactly the reason she'd come to Persephone for assistance and not Artemis.

Persephone chose to ignore their youngest sister. "What if we tried a new hairstyle? Perhaps even a different cut. It need not be drastically different. Merely a touch more—"

"Flattering," Artemis said. "And fashionable."

Meaning Daphne's current style was *unflattering* and *unfashionable*. She preferred to think of it as practical. But practicality did not appear to be what a certain gentleman noticed in a young lady.

She generally wore her hair up in a simple knot at her neck. What precisely did Artemis have in mind? Certainly not the very short curls worn by some of the faster ladies of the *ton*. For one thing, Daphne's hair did not curl. For another, she had no desire to connect herself in any way to the more scandalous in Society.

"Artemis, would you go look forlornly out the window again, please, and leave us to talk in peace?"

Artemis obliged but only after a look of utmost annoyance.

"Daphne." Persephone possessed a knack for saying her name in such a way as to convey warning, firmness, and kind concern all in the space of two short syllables. "Why do you wish to undertake this change?"

"I have noticed other ladies wear different—"

"Daphne." It was a gentle scold. "I didn't ask about other ladies. I asked about *you*."

Persephone always had been persistent.

"I am trying to be brave," Daphne admitted. "The way I look now makes me blend in. I think I am ready to be noticed, at least a little."

Persephone took her hands and squeezed them eagerly. "I am so pleased to hear this. You are so worthy of being noticed. I have waited so long for you to realize that about yourself."

It wasn't quite the realization she'd had.

Within an hour, Daphne was seated in a straight-backed chair, bidding farewell to the coiffure she had worn for four years. Persephone had not eaten lunch. She nibbled at nothing more substantial than a piece of toast while watching her maid very carefully snip and pull at Daphne's hair.

"Taking off a little length will make a world of difference." Artemis had been giddy to the point of giggles throughout the process, insisting she not be left out of the fun.

Daphne cringed as the sound of snipping shears echoed loudly behind her. She hoped "a little length" did not translate into something drastic.

In the corner, her maid and Artemis's were busy altering two gowns of Artemis's she had somehow been convinced to accept as her own, both a touch more fashionable than anything she'd worn before. A paisley shawl of Persephone's lay waiting and ready on the dressing table.

"I cannot seem to convince her of the perfection of my yellow dress," Artemis bemoaned.

"The one with the square neckline? It is a little brighter than Daphne is accustomed to."

Daphne silently offered thanks for Persephone's logic and rational influence. She wanted to garner some notice from James, not make a fool of herself.

"How does that look, Your Grace?" the abigail asked, stepping back from Daphne, allowing her mistress to inspect the results of her handiwork.

Persephone studied Daphne without rising from her seat or moving closer. She had seemed far more inclined to remain stationary of late. The energetic, ever-busy Persephone had given way to a seemingly worn and tired lady.

Daphne worried about the change. How she hoped it was a temporary and inconsequential one.

"I like it very much," Persephone said. "It seems with some of the weight gone, her hair has a hint of a wave to it."

Truly? Daphne reached up, running her fingers along her hair. The abigail held up a hand mirror, allowing Daphne to see the results of their efforts. Her hair did have the slightest bit of a wave—not truly curly but not so painfully straight either.

"More important than my opinion, what do *you* think?" Persephone asked.

Daphne wasn't entirely certain. She'd never worn it any shorter than several inches down her back. The new length only came halfway between her chin and shoulders. "Are you certain it isn't too short?"

"Not at all." Persephone addressed her lady's maid. "If you will pile it higher on her head, as opposed to low where she has been wearing it, and with a few wisps left free to frame her face, I believe she will look vastly pretty."

Daphne wanted to believe her, but "vastly pretty" was not a phrase that had ever been used to describe her.

"Do not look so worried," Persephone said. "Not only will the coiffure be flattering, but I also firmly believe Adam would vehemently object to it. And that is a very good sign. You may recall that he was quite upset when you first eschewed your braids and began wearing your hair up."

Adam had stormed from the room in a rare taking the day she had debuted her new, more mature look. Persephone had explained his reaction as the result of his being unprepared for Daphne to grow up. So long as she still looked like a little girl, he could continue telling himself she was one.

Perhaps that was the true culprit behind Adam's disapproval of James— he saw a serious suitor as inarguable evidence of her inevitable maturation. In time, Adam would learn to accept the change and would see how perfectly everything had worked out. Of course, first she had to discover why James had stopped coming to visit her.

Daphne watched in the mirror as her new coiffure took shape. It was more bold than she was accustomed to, yet she could not deny it was more flattering.

"Do you think . . . do you think a gentleman would find my hair pretty worn this way?"

Persephone took her hand and squeezed it gently. "I do think so. But remember, dearest, if that particular gentleman notices you only for your coiffure, he is hardly worth *your* notice."

Daphne nodded. She understood Persephone's warning but recognized her sister didn't see the full extent of the difficulty. *There is a reason gentlemen do not fall in love with the furniture.* Though spoken with all the tact of a dreamy-eyed fifteen-year-old, the words had rung true in Daphne's mind ever since they were uttered.

A wish to recapture James's notice had first propelled her forward with this plan, but she found herself hoping even more that her new appearance would give her the measure of courage she'd been lacking of late.

"What the deuce is she wearing?" It was a forceful greeting even for Adam.

Persephone had only just led Daphne into Adam's book room to bid him farewell. Somehow Daphne had been convinced to go shopping for a new wardrobe.

"Take a deep breath, dearest," Persephone said. "Daphne looks lovely."

"She looks . . . grown up," he growled.

"She *is* grown up, you dolt." Persephone pulled her gloves on. "We are off on a shopping expedition. I thought I had better warn you before the bills begin arriving."

"What care I for bills? If you take her out looking like that, every unattached male in London will be following her about like imbeciles. You can't—" His fearsome brow furrowed further. "What have you done to her hair?"

"We cut it."

"I don't like it."

Persephone shot Daphne a grin. "What did I tell you? A triumph!"

For the first time since asking for Persephone's help to improve her appearance, Daphne began to feel more confident in the results.

"Have a good afternoon, my love." Persephone stretched up to kiss Adam's cheek. "We will be back with loads of boxes and a great many imbeciles in tow."

Adam stomped toward the door. "I am coming with you."

"Shopping?" Persephone sputtered.

"I will not have a repeat of Finley's behavior. No one will dare speak an ill word to either of you if I am there."

"An ill word?" Persephone moved to join him at the book room door. "No one will dare even breathe."

"All the better."

"No." Persephone spoke firmly. "London is already quaking in its collective boots having seen the black looks you've tossed about lately, not to mention the very detailed threats you've issued. I will not have you sending all of Society fleeing to the countryside."

"I care not where they flee to so long as they flee somewhere."

Artemis popped into the doorway. "If Adam is going shopping, I should get to go as well. You know I adore spending hours and hours at shops."

"Hours and hours, Adam," Persephone said. "*Hours.* Of clothing and bonnets. Do I really need to force you to turn that down?"

Adam's confused gaze moved to Daphne. "You agreed to this? You have never been interested in such frivolous things."

Embarrassment heated her cheeks. Though she loved Adam dearly, she was not about to admit the real reason for her sudden interest in being fashionable. She wanted to be something other than a silent wall-flower. She wanted to be noticed, a wish Adam would likely condemn.

"A necessary evil," she told him. "Besides, you once told me that appearing confident is often all one needs to be taken seriously. I believe it is time I looked like I belong in Society rather than giving the impression of desperately wanting their approval."

"Do not go begging for the approval of idiots, Daphne. They do not deserve to have that power over you." He crossed back to her and set his hands on her upper arms. "Promise me you are not doing this out of any misplaced desire to fit Society's definition of worth."

"I simply wish for my appearance to reflect the person I am: mature, capable, and worthy of notice."

He eyed her new hairstyle, his mouth turning down in disapproval. "What happened to that little girl who used to come sit with me in the afternoons?"

"I still sit with you," she reminded him. "I did just yesterday, in fact. And Persephone has agreed not to make morning calls tomorrow so I can sit with you then as well."

"Look at you. You grew up." He shook his head and sighed. "I don't like it."

Dear, sweet Adam. Daphne wrapped her arms around him, hugging him fiercely.

As expected, he objected immediately. "Do not grow maudlin." He disengaged himself from her embrace. "If you mean to empty my coffers at the shops, you had best get to it." He shooed her away but called out to her as she reached the door. "If you should see Mr. Finley while you are out, have the coachman shoot him, compliments of the Duke of Kielder."

"What if we should see Lord Techney?" Persephone asked.

"Same instructions." Adam dropped into his armchair. "I am in the mood to vicariously shoot people today."

Persephone laughed. "There's the Adam we know and love."

Chapter Fifteen

JAMES WALKED ARM IN ARM with his mother out to a chair set in the shade of an elm in the back gardens of the family's London home. Her health had grown evermore uncertain since her arrival in Town. She was noticeably paler and hardly ventured from her private sitting room. James worried a great deal about her.

"This will be just the thing, Mother, you'll see." He saw her comfortably seated, then tucked a light blanket around her legs and lap.

"Lawn bowls?" Mother asked weakly, the smallest glimmer of curiosity in her eyes.

"Ben and I found the old set in the attics and thought we'd enjoy playing a game or two."

"I am too ill to play," Mother insisted.

James patted her hand. "I know. But we might prove entertaining, at least. You're near enough to watch."

Mother smiled at him with such gratitude. "I knew you would think of the perfect diversion." She allowed the tiniest of heart-wrenching sighs. "I confess I have not at all enjoyed this trip to London. But I am trying to be optimistic, hoping you'll think of a way to fix all this."

"It is not so terrible as all that," he insisted. "Miss Lancaster is a lovely person."

"I can't say I know enough of her to decide one way or the other." Her earnest expression tugged at him. "I did not wish this for you, James. I know what it is to have that decision made by another. And I further know the unhappiness that comes of a marriage forced on two people who are not well suited. The late Lord Techney would hear no one's objections. Not mine. Not your father's. I had a dowry, and that was all that mattered at the time."

James was well aware that his parents' marriage had been arranged. He hadn't realized, however, that they had both objected to it. Father had been forced by his father in order to secure money for the estate. James was being pushed into a courtship for the sake of social standing.

Billingsley stepped into the garden. He addressed Mother, as was proper, but spoke loudly enough for James to overhear, which was their established pattern. Visitors and crises and any questions of household management were always seen to by him.

"The Duchess of Kielder, Miss Lancaster, and Miss Artemis Lancaster to see you, my lady," Billingsley announced.

James's mind jumped into frantic action at that announcement. Mother, by some miracle, hadn't lost her composure at the sudden arrival of the lady she believed had cost her son his happiness. James gave Ben a look meant to warn him to behave before nodding for the butler to show their guests in. He braced himself for the task ahead: keeping his family from making an already difficult situation even more so.

To his surprise, the ladies did not approach him. It seemed they had indeed come to see Mother. No one had called on her in the two weeks she'd been in Town. A visit from the Duchess of Kielder and her sisters would be a boon to anyone's social standing but particularly so for someone with no cachet to begin with.

"I hope you will not find our unexpected visit an impertinence," Miss Lancaster said to Mother. "Your health has been in my thoughts these past days. It is not unusual for a complaint of the throat to spread to the lungs as well, especially in the stale London air. Our apothecary here in Town swears by this particular species of mint for treating congestion of the lungs." She held a small fabric pouch in one hand, a slip of paper in the other. "And I wrote out instructions for preparing a very effective tea."

James stood closer to the duchess, near enough to send her a questioning look.

She answered quietly. "We called yesterday but were told Lady Techney was indisposed with a touch of congestion in her lungs. Daphne knows a great deal about medicinal herbs and brought a treatment she hopes will help."

The gesture surprised him, though it should not have. It was hardly the first time Miss Lancaster had offered her help and kindness upon hearing of the troubled state of Mother's health.

"Thank you, Miss Lancaster," he said. "That is very thoughtful of you."

"You are quite welcome." As if uncomfortable focusing on any one person, himself included, Miss Lancaster's eyes drifted about, not seeming to look at anything in particular.

What must that be like? James had never been timid. That Miss Lancaster continually participated in Society and managed conversations further elevated James's opinion of her.

He wished he knew how to set her more at ease. "That is a lovely shawl." Ladies usually appreciated when a gentleman admired their attire.

A tiny smile appeared. "It is my sister's." She made the admission almost as if expecting him to withdraw the compliment.

"Nonetheless, it looks very fine on you."

Her trademark blush made a reappearance but was accompanied by an actual smile. "Thank you."

Miss Lancaster seemed remarkably easy to please—a kind word, a simple compliment. He liked that about her.

She glanced just behind him. "We hadn't intended to interrupt your entire afternoon."

The irony of her concern struck him in the next moment. She worried she was interrupting his day. If a gentleman truly was courting a lady, her presence wouldn't be an interruption in the least. He was making a muddle of everything.

"Do you need to be on your way, or would you like to join us?" he asked.

She looked to her older sister and received a nod of encouragement. But even as he and Miss Lancaster walked toward the lawn game, she seemed unsure of her decision to stay. Was this more of her timidity, or had her hand been forced?

"If you do need to go, Miss Lancaster—"

But she shook her head. Her bonnet shifted about with the movement, and she straightened it with a quick nudge of her hand. "I am afraid I am often nervous with people I don't know well."

He had long since discovered that about her. "If it will put your mind at ease, my brother is about as threatening as a kitten. You've nothing to fear from him."

"I have found him to be pleasant company during our brief conversations. I do realize I needn't be nervous, but timidity is not always logical." She seemed to rally her courage. "I am happily surprised the weather is pleasant enough to proceed. Such a thing is hardly guaranteed this time of year."

James accepted her change of topic. "'Tis hardly guaranteed any time of year. England's weather is quite famous for its stubborn lack of predictability. The French have glory-starved emperors, and we have mercurial weather."

"And a wide assortment of lawn games."

James chuckled. "That is our national treasure, to be sure."

She smiled at his quip, just as he'd hoped she would.

"Has Lieutenant Lancaster arrived yet?" he asked.

"Sadly, no," she said. "Persephone is beside herself. One would think he was still the same eleven-year-old boy who left our home for a life in the navy instead of a seasoned sailor of twenty."

"And does the good lieutenant appreciate being babied by his sister, or does he merely endure it?"

She pondered his question a moment. "He does make quite a show of being put out by her fussing, but I have seen him shed tears when she embraces him. Outwardly he may be a grown man of the navy, but inwardly he is still her little Linus trying very hard to be brave."

James attempted to imagine being greeted with tears of joy rather than complaint. "You have a wonderful family, Miss Lancaster."

"That I do." They had reached Ben and the lawn bowls. "I should probably warn you, Lord Tilburn, that my sisters and I are particularly accomplished bowlers. We managed to convince Adam to convert a portion of the back garden at Falstone Castle into a green." She gave him a look of obviously feigned warning. He rather enjoyed the lightness it granted her countenance. "There is no fiercer opponent in bowls than one who has played the game in the shadow of a gibbet."

James leaned a touch closer and asked in a low voice, "Is there truly a gibbet at Falstone Castle? I have heard rumors, but one can never be sure which stories about the duke are exaggerated."

"There most certainly is." Miss Lancaster was rather pretty when she smiled, especially with that lone dimple drawing one's gaze. "A gibbet *and* stocks. And both have been used within the past decade. They are kept in very good repair, in fact."

"A gibbet and stocks on a bowling green?" James shook his head at the odd picture that formed in his mind.

"We take bowls very seriously."

He could feel a smile spread across his face. "Apparently. Perhaps I'd best secure you as my partner, then, lest I find myself in the unhappy position of being your opponent."

"That would be very wise." Her color rose, though she did not shy away from their friendly banter.

"Prepare yourself, Ben. Miss Lancaster and I mean to slaughter you."

Ben chuckled. "I shall simply have to find a slaughtering partner of my own. Tell me, Miss Lancaster, does your sister play?"

"They both do, though I do not believe the duchess is quite equal to it today. Artemis, however, will take up your offer with enthusiasm."

Ben returned to the chairs where Her Grace and Mother were speaking of something and Miss Artemis was doing little to hide her boredom.

"Ben is quite good at bowls," James warned his partner as their opponents returned, armed for battle.

"Then we must rise to the occasion," she said. "We cannot allow our younger siblings to best us so publicly."

James placed the first of Miss Lancaster's bowls in her hands. "Then I shall let you in on a well-held family secret." He attempted to look exceptionally serious. "Ben has an infuriating habit of knocking the kitty far to whichever side most of his opponent's bowls are not occupying."

Miss Lancaster tsked. "Then ought I to do my utmost to make that difficult for him?"

James nodded. "Obstacles always have impeded his aim."

"Ah. The benefits of familiarity." She adjusted the bowl, her eyes narrowing as she gazed down the lawn at the white ball awaiting her throw. "In exchange for that insight, I will inform you that Artemis is an unabashed and unrepentant cheat."

She made her toss, the bowl's arched path placing it a very tidy distance from the kitty.

"Another tidbit: Artemis sighs louder than any other person I know, particularly when she feels she is being bested."

James handed her a second bowl, which she placed at exactly the same distance from the kitty as the first, only on the opposite side. A third throw came to a stop very nearly in front of the kitty, though slightly off-center.

"Ah." James smiled. "I believe I see your strategy. To get closer than *your* bowls, one would have to throw around them, else risk simply knocking them closer."

Miss Lancaster looked up at him as he handed her the last bowl. She offered another dimpled smile, something he imagined few people ever saw. It was more than lovely. Natural and open in that moment, it was rather stunning. Something about her was decidedly different today, though he couldn't say just what. Something in her appearance, perhaps, or in her manner of carrying herself. Whatever it was, he found he liked it. She was still the same kindhearted person but with an added measure of confidence.

Only after Miss Artemis declared in a voice overflowing with sighs, "One cannot be expected to bowl with such a heartless sister as I have," did James realize he'd missed his partner's final throw. Her four bowls sat in near-perfect symmetry, a formidable guard around their treasure.

"A fine round," James said, feeling pleased that she'd done so well.

"Mark my words," she answered, her tone lighter than he ever remembered hearing it, "Artemis will find a way to undo what advantage we have."

The prospect didn't seem to overly alarm her. He was not expected to prevent the inevitable underhandedness nor find a means by which they could win. Miss Lancaster had, in her unspoken and calm way, given him leave to not worry for a moment—a luxury with which he had very little experience.

Miss Artemis began her turn with a truly dismal throw, followed by a very dramatic sigh.

James bit back a smile and saw out of the corner of his eye Miss Lancaster do the same.

"Sighing is one of her talents," she said.

"More than a talent, I would say. The girl is a prodigy." How they both maintained straight faces, James could not say. "Regardless, I do believe you have her beat."

"Lawn games are, perhaps, the only area in which I am remotely her equal," Miss Lancaster said.

"I take leave to doubt that." The honest comment earned James one more fleeting glimpse of her dimple.

Miss Artemis's remaining throws hardly improved. All James needed to do was place his own bowls in such a way as to make Ben's usual strategy extremely difficult to implement.

Miss Lancaster handed him his first bowl. "I believe we will slaughter them after all."

"I certainly hope so," he replied.

He lined up his first throw.

A high-pitched yipping sound was his only warning before a blur of fur and noise dashed onto the bowling green. Mother's latest adopted mutt had been banished to the stables for damaging the furniture in Mother's dressing room, but its natural exuberance apparently had not abated.

James moved swiftly toward the pup. "Leave those be, you scamp." His directives came decidedly too late. Not one of the bowls remained unmoved and the kitty resided in the fur ball's mouth.

The pup trotted over to him quite as if he were a hound bringing his master the prize catch of the hunt.

James squatted in front of the troublemaker. "That was not terribly sociable of you." A pair of enormous brown eyes watched him hopefully. "You've ruined the game, you realize." The pup dropped the now-wet white ball into James's outstretched hand.

Alarm pulled at Mother's features. She would worry over having the afternoon's activities ruined and the impression that would make on their guests. But what could he do? How was one expected to curb the enthusiasm of a puppy?

James heard someone approach from behind, the swish of skirts indicating a woman. He looked over his shoulder to find Miss Lancaster standing next to him.

"I am sorry about the game," he said. "We would most likely have won if not for this mongrel's interference." He could not think of a means of salvaging the game. Miss Lancaster would be disappointed.

"I told you my sister cheats."

He had not been expecting that reply.

Miss Lancaster shook her head. "No doubt she found some means of summoning her four-legged accomplice at the most opportune moment."

James rose, watching her in confusion. He tried to nudge the puppy away when it began snapping at the tassel on his left boot. That was all she had come over to say to him? No complaints? No demands? "You are not too disappointed about the game?"

She laid her hand lightly on his arm and once more offered her unaffected smile. "It is only a game. There is no real harm done."

"A level head in a crisis." James tossed the kitty back onto the lawn and wiped the puppy slobber off his hand with his handkerchief. "That is a pleasant change."

"Would a disrupted game of bowls generally be considered a crisis?" she asked.

He looked over at Mother still clutching her hands together in anticipation of something catastrophic. She could be very difficult when distraught. "In this house, everything is a crisis."

"And you are always expected to rescue the others?" Miss Lancaster asked.

That was more insightful than expected. He had a feeling a response was not at all necessary.

"Might I make a suggestion?" she asked.

She wanted to address *his* problem? James nodded, as curious as he was surprised.

"Allow your brother to sort out the mess this time."

He couldn't simply walk away. "This little scamp has quite upset things." As if to further prove his mischievous nature, the puppy continued nipping at James's tassels.

Miss Lancaster motioned toward the end of the bowling green where Ben had already gathered the scattered bowls and seemed to be setting up another game. "Mr. Tilburn appears capable enough."

"I should make good my escape, then?" The prospect was tempting.

Miss Lancaster nodded. "Allowing someone else to take on the responsibilities you usually undertake would probably be good for all concerned."

James had never walked away from a family difficulty, little or great. To leave the others to address a problem felt uncomfortably foreign. Yet Miss Lancaster watched him with patient anticipation.

The situation was not in the least dire. He might allow himself to see to his own amusement for just a moment. Surely that was not asking too much.

"I, for one," he said, "would very much like to know how this mutt will react to the sight of a shuttlecock." James felt remarkably light as he escorted Miss Lancaster to the basket of lawn games. There was something to be said for a smile he hadn't been required to earn.

Chapter Sixteen

BEING SOCIAL WAS EXHAUSTING. DAPHNE had talked and interacted with more people in the last few days than she generally did over the course of a month. The undertaking made her ever more grateful for those days when she had the pleasure of Adam's quiet company.

Today's afternoon appointment, however, was coming to an end. Adam had risen from his armchair.

"I do not know that Persephone will permit me to miss calls tomorrow," Daphne said.

"I will not be in London tomorrow." He set the book he'd been reading on his desk.

"You are traveling?"

He nodded, his expression less than enthusiastic. "I am for Shropshire, within the hour, in fact."

Daphne's heart froze on the instant. "Has something happened to Father?" His health had steadily declined during the years she and her sisters had lived with Adam and Persephone.

"His caretaker informs me his mental state has deteriorated further. I thought it best to see for myself how the land lies so I can give your brother a thorough explanation when he makes port."

Daphne nodded at the wisdom of that, though the timing struck her as decidedly convenient for a gentleman who despised London during the Season. "And you will miss a significant portion of the social whirl." She gave him a knowing look. "I am certain you are heartbroken about that."

"Keep your cheeky remarks to yourself," he muttered. "I take no delight in leaving my wife to fend for herself in this den of idiocy." He crossed to the sofa where she sat. An earnestness entered his eyes, and Daphne found she couldn't tease him further. "Neither can I be at ease abandoning her when she is not in the pink of health."

Daphne had noticed Persephone's flagging spirits, but no one had told her that her sister was truly ill. "If she needs to return home—"

Adam cut off her offer before she'd fully made it. "Persephone insists she is well enough to remain, and I have learned over the past seven years that arguing with her is as futile as explaining to the Regent the benefits of exercising economy."

"Or undertaking a reducing diet," Daphne offered.

Amusement entered his very somber expression. Daphne was glad of it. She didn't like seeing him so burdened.

"How long do you anticipate being gone?"

"The journey will not take overly long, but my sojourn there will depend entirely on what I find upon my arrival and how long your brother takes to arrive."

Daphne shifted a little to face him more fully. Adam was in his "methodical and conscientious overseer of the estate" mind-set. She'd learned long ago that he needed a listening ear more than anything else in these moments.

"And the entire thing will be endlessly complicated by the fact that I am taking Artemis with me." His annoyed tone spoke volumes.

"Why in heaven's name would you do that to yourself? You'll more than likely toss her out the carriage window halfway there."

The stern lines in Adam's face clearly indicated he was not anticipating the journey with any degree of equanimity. "At times like this, it is terribly inconvenient to be irrevocably in love with one's wife."

"You would do this for Persephone?"

He nodded. "I would do anything for her."

Artemis's dramatic enthusiasm grated on Adam; everyone in the family knew as much. Yet he was willing to endure her exclusive company and what would likely be a long string of complaints mingled with ridiculous daydreams in order to spare his wife the trouble of her. What must that be like? To have a man love her to the point of such selflessness?

"I have a few assignments for you." Adam moved straight to the heart of the matter. "First, do not allow Lord Techney to bully you, something he is infuriatingly fond of doing."

"I may be of a quiet nature, Adam, but when in the years I've been under your tutelage have you known anyone to *bully* me?"

He gave a crisp nod. "Next, keep an eye on that slippery fellow who purports to be courting you."

"Slippery fellow? *Purports* to be courting me?" She did not at all like his choice of words and hoped her tone told him as much. "You certainly take a skeptical view of things for one who has made himself exceedingly scarce in Society these past days."

"And yet," he said unrepentantly, "I have kept just as close an eye on Lord Tilburn as I did the day he took you for a ride in Hyde Park. The difference being this time I didn't choose to make my surveillance known."

A nervous flutter assaulted her stomach. "And what have you discovered with your spying?" She tried to sound less than concerned.

His gaze narrowed as he studied her a moment. "Likely nothing you haven't already noticed yourself but I'd wager have dismissed or explained away."

"Such as?" She couldn't entirely retain the surety she'd had in her tone a moment earlier. She had, in fact, noticed a few things that worried her.

Adam took up the topic with no obvious hesitation. "Lord Tilburn pays you the same amount and type of attention he gives his mother, his brother, and any number of his casual social acquaintances. He keeps surprisingly busy with estate, family, and political matters for one who is neither the lord of the manor, head of the family, nor holder of the seat in Lords. A gentleman undertaking a suit generally puts a great deal of effort into it."

Daphne swallowed down the small lump forming in her throat. "What is it you suspect him of?"

He shrugged. "Nothing in particular. I only think it odd that a man as thoughtful and meticulous as I have found him to be in the six years I've watched him would be so lackadaisical. His enthusiasm for any number of things is more pointed than it is for this courtship."

She'd seen with some alarm that his attentions hadn't grown more frequent, neither had they moved beyond the merest beginnings of a friendship. But this was *James Tilburn*. This was a dream coming to life. Despite her uncertainty, she wasn't willing to give up.

She set her gaze on the empty fireplace, not able to look at Adam while she spoke aloud her worries. "You think he has changed his mind regarding me?"

"No. I think he has yet to know his own mind where you are concerned. He strikes me as a man confused."

She felt his arm wrap around her shoulders. She pushed out a breath, days of worry and frustration escaping as she did. "What if he comes to the conclusion that I am not worth his time or energy?"

Adam gave her a squeeze. "I offered him only a single unobjected-to morning call. Yet he has come more than once. You predicted after the armed escort in the park that he would not return. Yet he has. Thus far, he has shown himself a gentleman of determination."

"But?" She looked up at him, sensing there was more.

"But I would ask that you be careful, Daphne. Use the intelligence God blessed you with. I have no wish to see you hurt."

She nodded. His words sobered her significantly. If he too had noted James's inattentiveness, she had not imagined it. If only she knew the reason.

"There is something else I need you to do for me while I am gone."

"Of course," she said, grateful for the turn in topic.

"Take care of Persephone. I would never countenance the idea of leaving her behind if you were not with her. I know I can trust your judgment explicitly, especially as concerns her health."

Daphne leaned her head against him. They'd sat in just that way many times over the last half dozen years, both in this book room and in his library at Falstone Castle. He was not quite the affectionate brother Evander had been, but he was far more the attentive father her own had failed to be. "I will see to it that she takes care of herself."

"And take care of yourself as well."

She promised she would.

"And"—an almost humorous degree of reluctant resignation entered his face and voice—"spend some time with that lordling you're so fond of. Part of me hopes my concerns are entirely unfounded."

Daphne smiled. "I hope they are as well. It would be nice to know you aren't the only gentleman of my acquaintance worth knowing."

"I will tell your brother your low opinion of him," Adam said, standing once more.

"Linus will simply laugh." She knew it to be true. "In fairness to him and to Harry, they both fit that mold as well."

"I imagine your father did also before his mind slipped away." Adam hadn't known Father during his more lucid years. Daphne herself had only a small number of memories from the time before he began shutting them all out.

She remembered little but snatches, moments frozen in time. One common thread ran through them all. She clearly recalled her father smiling—not smiling in general, smiling at *her*. He would sit at his desk, studying one Greek philosopher or another, and she would sit on his lap, pretending to read as well. He would often stop his studies to tell her about the gods and goddesses who had so wholly fascinated him all of his life.

She'd been too young to still remember the details of the stories he'd told her, but she recalled with perfect clarity the feeling of being held by him and the safety she'd found there. Her father had once been a source of love and reassurance in her life. But that had been long ago, before he had grown unreachably distant. Before Daphne's siblings had been consumed by the necessities of survival. Their departures, whether intentional or not, whether of a physical nature or an emotional one, had splintered her heart one crack at a time. Even now, despite years spent within the stable sphere of Adam's life and home, she never entirely escaped the anxious anticipation of yet another person she loved turning her away.

Chapter Seventeen

JAMES ENTERED LORD AND LADY Percival Farr's ballroom with a vast deal more confidence than he had felt since being made to undertake his courtship of Miss Lancaster. For one thing, all of London was abuzz with the news that the Duke of Kielder had left town for the wilds of Shropshire, lending an air of relief and relative safety to the various gatherings of the *ton*. Secondly, he had enjoyed Miss Lancaster's company enough during their previous encounters to find himself looking quite forward to her company once again.

"Tilburn."

James turned at the sound of Father's voice. He stood in a small group to one side of the ballroom, Miss Lancaster and the duchess included. Father beckoned him over.

"We have been discussing the issues of the day." Father held his head at that smug angle he always employed when finding himself the center of attention. Growing up seeing that stance, James had ever been careful not to mimic it.

"Politics, Father? At a ball?"

An iciness entered Father's expression, though probably apparent only to James. Father did not countenance being corrected, especially in the presence of others.

"I do not believe the topic offended anyone." Father glanced around the group.

Mr. and Mrs. Fillmore, who lived very near Techney Manor in Lancashire, recognized the cue, no doubt from their extensive familiarity with it. The Fillmores were more devoted to Father than the rambunctious mutt of Mother's was to James. Their place in Society did not equal that of an earl, even one of relatively minor importance, and thus they did not receive invitations to all the events Father did during the Season, but when they did find themselves in his company, they fawned on him. "Of course we weren't offended," Mrs. Fillmore offered quickly.

"'Twas fascinating." Mr. Fillmore nodded, apparently for emphasis, then added like a good hanger-on ought, "As always, my lord."

Father looked quite satisfied. "It seems the topic has not proven distasteful after all."

James held back the observation that both the duchess and Miss Lancaster had not offered their opinions.

"It seems to me a great many changes are needed in our nation just now," Father said.

As Father pontificated, James stepped closer to Miss Lancaster. "How long has he been holding court?" he whispered.

"Long enough for the majority of his audience to make covert exits."

"And you have remained because . . . ?"

"Because we were unwise enough to place ourselves too close for our departure to go unnoticed."

For some reason, James felt like smiling every time he caught the slightest glimpse of Miss Lancaster's dimple. It was not the only thing about her that captured his attention in that moment. Her hair was different, softer. It did not pull backward with the same tension as it once had. A few tendrils had even been left loose. That was likely an odd thing for a gentleman to notice, and he could not say with any certainty why he had.

"You've changed your hair," he said.

Her nod was small, uncertain, and an easily distinguishable question hung in her eyes.

"I like it very much," he said.

Her thank-you was quiet but sincere. She looked as though she was about to say something more, but Father interrupted. "And you, Miss Lancaster? Do you agree?"

"Agree with what, precisely, Lord Techney?" Her color heightened.

James lightly rested his hand on the back of her arm, hoping she recognized the gesture as the offer of support he intended it to be. Something about the contact proved comforting to him as well.

"We were discussing the need during these tumultuous times in our nation for greater responsibility amongst the citizenry," Father said.

"And amongst the government," Miss Lancaster added.

"How do you mean?" Father clearly hadn't been expecting anything beyond a blanket acceptance of his position.

Miss Lancaster only shook her head. She seemed to inch closer to James.

"Father—"

"I would like to hear what she means," Father cut across him. "Do you feel the government is being *irresponsible*, Miss Lancaster? Perhaps you are unaware of the many issues Parliament is even now addressing, the crucial votes which are being cast."

James inwardly winced at his father's condescending tone. The family was often the recipient of such treatment from Father, leaving Mother in tears, Ben in hurt silence, and James increasingly frustrated at his inability to shield those he cared for from Father's coldness.

Miss Lancaster spoke again, her voice no louder than before. "My ignorance, Lord Techney, is not so great that I do not realize those crucial decisions to which you refer are made only by those members of Parliament who bother to be present when the votes are being cast. Many are here in Town but feel their time is better spent on pleasure jaunts and social matters."

A palpable hit, to be sure. Father hadn't attended Lords in some weeks and not consistently before then. Many votes of importance were cast without him.

For once, Father seemed at a loss.

The duchess, however, appeared quite pleased. "Lord Tilburn," Her Grace said, "would you be so good as to escort my sister and I to those chairs on the other side of the drawing room? I feel the need to sit . . . over there."

"I would be honored to escort you both."

Her Grace allowed not the slightest hint of a smile. "How very *responsible* of you."

James was old enough to vaguely remember the gossip surrounding the Duke and Duchess of Kielder's marriage. Most of Society could not comprehend what had brought the two together. James could understand something of what His Grace saw in his wife—an intelligent, capable woman with an admirable degree of backbone.

"Will this do?" James asked when they reached a small cluster of chairs at the opposite end of the drawing room.

"Perfectly," the duchess replied. She sat, her posture ever so slightly slumped, as though she was particularly tired.

Miss Lancaster hesitated. "I hope I did not offend your father." She looked concerned. "I am accustomed to debating with Adam, who prefers directness to diplomacy."

"Allow me to worry about my father. I believe your sister would appreciate your attention."

The distress did not leave Miss Lancaster's expression. She turned enough to speak privately with him. "Persephone has seemed a touch unwell for a few days now. Without Adam here to look after her, I worry she will overtax herself."

"You need only tell me if she requires anything."

She smiled up at him. "Thank you."

He indicated she should take the seat beside her sister. "Has your prodigal brother made an appearance yet?" he asked.

"Sadly, no. Adam paid a call on the admiralty before leaving for Shropshire. We could hear the weeping all the way at Grosvenor Square."

"Weeping?" James took the empty seat beside Miss Lancaster. "I would never have guessed His Grace was the weeping type."

Both Miss Lancaster and her sister grinned at that.

James spoke to the duchess next. "I have heard a great deal about your absent lieutenant."

"If you happen to *see* a great deal of our lieutenant, or even a mere glimpse, do let me know," Her Grace answered. "He has me tied in absolute knots."

"I will keep a weather eye out, Your Grace. It sounds to me as though the duke has enlisted the highest of help."

The duchess smiled fondly. "Adam does know how to get things done."

They all looked up at the sound of approaching footsteps. James rose to his feet. "Good evening, Mrs. Bower, Miss Bower."

They offered curtsies and he the expected small bow. "Your Grace, are you acquainted with the Bowers?"

"I am," she replied. "A pleasure to see you both again."

James had first made the Bowers's acquaintance two Seasons earlier when the oldest Bower daughter had made her debut. Fortunately for him, she had set her sights on the younger son of a marquess and he'd not needed to maneuver his way out of the reach of her mother's ambitions. He didn't yet know the intentions of the younger Miss Bower.

"Our most sincere apologies, Your Grace," Mrs. Bower said, "but we have come in an attempt to deprive you of your company." She turned a bright smile on James. "Many of the other ladies have realized that you, Lord Tilburn, have not yet danced this evening."

She subtly inched her daughter farther forward. If Miss Bower shared at all her older sister's selfish nature or her mother's lack of social discernment, James meant to do all he could to make certain she did not rest her matrimonial hopes on him. "I have spent the last few sets speaking with my family and with the duchess and her sister," James said. "I believe that is time well spent."

"Well, yes. Yes, of course." Mrs. Bower gave her daughter another nudge, this one better understood.

Miss Bower smiled at him coyly. "You do mean to dance, though, do you not? This is a ball, after all."

"I do not wish to be rude." *Good heavens, how do I get out of this?*

"Then you will dance?" No one would ever accuse Mrs. Bower of being demure.

"I—There isn't—I—"

"Lord Tilburn is engaged for this next set," Miss Lancaster said quite without warning. "His good nature prevents him from refusing your invitation outright, but his integrity prevents him from not keeping his commitment. Can you not see what an impossible situation he finds himself in?"

The Bowers stared at her in surprise. For his part, James could have hugged her. She'd offered him the escape he'd not thought of on his own. A brilliant bit of counterstrategy.

"With whom are you dancing?" Miss Bower found her voice again quickly enough.

"I am promised to Miss Lancaster." He did not wish to force her into dancing with him if she chose not to. He had imposed upon her enough. "Whether we will join in the dancing or simply continue our very diverting conversation, I leave for her to decide. In either case, I am unavailable for the next set."

He held his arm out to Miss Lancaster, and she, sharp as always, slipped her arm through his as if about to take a turn about the room in anticipation of the beginning of a set.

"I do apologize," James added, not wishing to be rude despite the growing giddiness of having escaped the woman's very obvious machinations.

"Promise Cynthia the set after next, and all will be forgiven." Mrs. Bower's grin turned triumphant.

"Actually," the duchess spoke across whatever Mrs. Bower meant to add, "before your arrival, I had been on the verge of asking Lord Tilburn if he would be so good as to see that our carriage was called up. I am not feeling particularly well."

Miss Lancaster's attention turned immediately to her sister. She slipped her arm free of his to give the duchess a closer examination. Her Grace's coloring had dropped off noticeably.

"I will have your carriage brought around with all haste."

"It seems, Mrs. Bower," the duchess continued, "we are to deprive you of your company rather than the other way around. I hope you will forgive us."

"You will return and dance after calling the carriage, I hope." Mrs. Bower was not one to give up her cause easily. If she and Father ever joined forces, they could wreak havoc across continents. "Any number of young ladies are quite counting on you."

She motioned to a group gathered not many paces removed. Young ladies and their mothers, every last one of them. James had never wanted for willing dance partners at any ball, though he had never been particularly in the market for any.

Mrs. Bower smiled. Miss Bower smiled. The crowd nearby smiled. James, however, held his hand out to the Duchess of Kielder, helping her rise to her feet. He wove her arm through his. Miss Lancaster set her hand beneath her sister's other elbow.

"I am not an invalid," Her Grace objected.

Miss Lancaster dropped her hands away, leaving only James to assist the duchess. Their eyes met. He offered a smile, hoping her sister's rebuke, however quietly made, hadn't wounded her. She did look a bit disappointed but not truly hurt.

"I believe we should be on our way," Miss Lancaster said.

"Let it never be said I failed to recognize a damsel in distress," James said.

No sooner had they reached the anteroom than Her Grace spoke up. "While I will admit I am not feigning my current less-than-desirable state of health, I will say that I think it a bit much to deem me a damsel in distress, or Daphne, for that matter."

"You misunderstand, Your Grace. I was referring to myself."

She swatted at him playfully, if weakly.

He led her to a chair in the entryway, leaving Miss Lancaster at her side as he instructed Lord Percival's servants to call up the Kielder carriage.

"I am well aware that you hardly need me to do so," he said to the ladies, "but I would appreciate if you allowed me to accompany you home. It will set my mind at ease, especially knowing His Grace is not in residence."

"And also allow you to avoid doing the pretty at this ball," Miss Lancaster added with a laugh in her voice.

"Two birds, one stone."

"I will accept your offer most gratefully, Lord Tilburn," the duchess said. "And I thank you for it."

"You are most welcome, Your Grace." He was very seldom thanked for his efforts. He found the experience a wonderfully novel one.

Chapter Eighteen

By the time they reached home, Persephone appeared very nearly done in. Her complaints were of a vague nature: malaise, fatigue, a gnawing but not urgent hint of nausea. Not knowing the source of her sister's illness, Daphne struggled to recommend a tisane or tonic to ease her suffering. In the end, she instructed Cook to prepare a ginger tea to settle Persephone's stomach and charged Persephone's abigail with laying a rag ever so slightly damp with warm lavender water across Persephone's shoulders to help her relax and, Daphne hoped, sleep.

The next morning, by virtue of Artemis being in Shropshire, likely locked up in whatever makeshift version of a dungeon Adam had managed to scrounge up, and Persephone being yet asleep, thank the heavens, Daphne found herself walking about a small fenced square several blocks from their London residence, with only Fanny, the maid Adam always assigned to accompany his wife and his sisters-in-law on any and every excursion, along for company.

"You'll forgive me if I'm speaking out of turn, Miss," Fanny said but a few minutes into their sojourn at the park, "but that appears to be young Lord Tilburn up the path a bit."

It was indeed James. Techney House did not sit in this square, but young gentlemen often had rooms of their own away from the family home. Did he live near here, then?

I should go bid him good morning. Surely he would welcome my company.

Or was she simply being inexcusably presumptuous? Some of her most difficult memories were of dismissals like the one she feared awaited her up ahead.

"Must you always be underfoot, Daphne?" Persephone had more than once asked in tones of exasperation.

Athena had now and then rejected Daphne's attempts to offer help, insisting she was too little or simply making more trouble. In the years before he and Evander had left for the navy, Linus had often simply overlooked her.

Even as a very young child, she'd known her family hadn't meant to hurt her feelings, and most of their interactions were kind and loving, but those moments when she had felt so expendable resurfaced in her memory during times of doubt and worry. Though she had learned to guard herself against the possibility of dismissals by fading into the background, by being quiet and unobtrusive, she'd been trying a different approach of late, one she wanted to believe was better even if it was more of a gamble.

Being overlooked when one was hiding did not hurt nearly so much as being abandoned when one was asking to be loved.

"Do not fear, Little Sparrow," James's voice echoed across six years of hopeful recollections. *Do not fear.*

She took a fortifying breath. James had never been unkind nor outright dismissive. Surely he would not be now. But, then again, at times her own family did not always wish her nearby. Even her father, who had eventually come to shun her entirely, had not turned her away in her earliest years. Past kindness was not always a guarantee against future rejection.

His tiny mutt of a puppy, its coat a muddled mixture of browns and yellows, ran in between his feet, yelping excitedly. He didn't kick at it nor speak harshly but simply took pains not to step on its tiny paws as he continued his slow circuit of the park.

Daphne felt a smile spread across her face. This was her James Tilburn, with his puppies and his sparrows and his inherent compassion. She squared her shoulders as a small but appreciated surge of confidence took root in her. This was a gentleman worth the risk.

He saw her a moment before she reached him. "Good morning, Miss Lancaster." His surprise at her presence registered on his face, but she did not think he looked unhappy.

"Good morning." *Confidence,* she reminded herself. "It seems you have a little admirer." She indicated the puppy scampering about.

James gently nudged the animal with his boot. "He is certainly attached to me. I've not gone anywhere these past two days without him tagging along. He is actually my mother's, but his exuberance has frayed her nerves, and he has, out of necessity, come to live with me."

"And you are exercising him this morning?"

"I believe *he* is exercising *me*."

"I do not wish to interrupt your efforts, especially if you are trying to undertake training. That is no simple thing."

James smiled at her, and Daphne felt the tension in her begin to drain. "The interruption is a welcome one. Was there something in particular you needed?"

He would not be pleased to learn she had disrupted his morning for nothing more significant than a friendly conversation. "No. I merely wished to bid you good morning."

"Oh." James appeared genuinely surprised.

"Forgive me. I should have let you be." She stepped back. "Forgive me." Daphne turned quickly, escape her only thought.

"Wait, please."

She felt him lightly touch her arm and stopped at the tingle his fingers caused.

"Your maid is here to lend propriety, and the park is a very public location. There would be no impropriety in our walking together," he said. "Please, Daphne. Stay and walk with me a moment."

He had called her Daphne. She could not even breathe. She had imagined hearing "Little Sparrow" again but somehow had not realized the impact of hearing her actual name on his lips.

"I do not wish to make a nuisance of myself."

"You have not, and I doubt you ever could." He released his hold on her enough to move to her side and offer his arm. "Take a turn about the garden with me?"

"I would like that very much."

She hoped James didn't notice her hand trembling as she laid it on his arm. Faced with the prospect of spending time in his exclusive company— no matter that she'd desperately wished to—intimidated her. She wanted him to like her enough to begin to love her. She wanted it so deeply she must have absolutely radiated desperation.

"I hope you do not mind an addition to our party." James motioned to his side, where his faithful puppy trotted along looking quite pleased with itself.

"Not if you do not mind mine." She indicated Fanny, following at a close distance.

James dipped his head to the maid. "I remember Fanny well. She was with us the day His Grace sent out the cavalry to herd us through Hyde Park."

Fanny grinned.

James turned back to Daphne. "What brings you to this humble green? Falstone House is a good distance from this less-exalted part of town."

"Adam procured a key to the park some years ago, after I discovered that a very rare subspecies of thyme grows here, a variety that cannot even be found at the Chelsea Physic Garden." He had done so as a birthday present to her the year she'd turned thirteen. "I come here now and then to procure new cuttings of it."

"I am beginning to suspect your talent as an apothecary is greater than you've let on," James said. "Distinguishing between varieties of thyme is not something most people can claim to do. I, for one, am quite impressed."

"I did learn a vast deal about various herbs growing up. We had not the means to secure the services of an apothecary, and home remedies were often our only option."

"And you were given the role of healer? That seems rather weighty for a young child."

She had spoken to very few people of those early years of poverty. James, however, was an intent and kind listener. She appreciated that. "I was grateful to be of use," she said. "Being so young, I could do so little."

"The tonics you have provided my mother have done wonders. I know I mentioned it before but feel I must again," James said. "Though you seem determined to be humble about it, I am certain you worked very hard to learn as much as you have."

Daphne nodded, pleased at the praise. "I enjoy it enough that it never has felt like work." She smiled at the memory of her eager childhood self. "I used to save every coin I came across so I could buy herbs. My fondest dream at the time was to one day have myrrh."

"Why myrrh?"

"Myrrh has astounding healing properties, but it comes very dear. I never had the means of purchasing any."

They walked a moment in silence before he spoke again. "I suspect there is a great deal I do not know about you."

"We have not had much opportunity to know each other." She looked quickly up at him, hoping to gauge whether he'd taken her comment as overly forward.

"I shall have to badger you for information, then." He creased his forehead as if in thought. "Do you throw out spots when you eat berries or have heart palpitations when reading gothic novels?"

Daphne smiled. "No to the first question."

"And the second?"

"I have not ever read any of the offerings of the Minerva press, so I could not say how my heart would react."

James nodded with exaggerated thoughtfulness. The puppy ran off ahead only to return again, yelping as enthusiastically as ever. "I am very nearly certain you are not afraid of dogs."

Daphne laughed, something that pulled James's eyes to her at once. A smile spread slowly across his face. "Did you think this ferocious beast of yours would frighten me when I have lived the past six years in a forest inhabited by wolves?"

"Wolves?" A disbelieving chuckle colored James's tone. "There are no wolves in England."

"Oh, but there are." Artemis would have been proud of the theatricality of Daphne's response.

James looked doubtful but amused.

"To be completely accurate, the pack in Falstone Forest is descended from both wolves and feral dogs. But they look like wolves, they sound like wolves, and they hunt like wolves, so we think of them that way."

James made a noise of pondering. "It seems very fitting, does it not, that the Dangerous Duke should have a pack of wolves when no one else does?"

"Extremely fitting."

James's puppy ran several quick circles around her, its tail wagging happily. Daphne enjoyed watching it play, unaccountably pleased that the tiny animal liked her enough to include her in its excitement.

She was struck by how easy being with James could be. Some uncertainty about his feelings remained, but his company was not a drain on her. She didn't need to force herself to talk to him. Few people were like that.

"Now, let us see. What else can I ask you?" He maneuvered them both around a puddle left in the path from the light morning rain. "Other than concocting lifesaving tonics, what did you enjoy as a child?"

What had she enjoyed? Her childhood had been spent under the heavy weight of loss and poverty. Happier moments were not always easy to recall. "My brother Evander wrote to me while away at sea. I always enjoyed receiving his letters."

"Yes." James rested his hand over hers where it sat on his arm. "You have mentioned him before. I believe you were particularly close to him."

"I was." The subject did not bring with it the usual level of sadness, something she likely owed to James's comforting empathy. Still, she preferred a change of topic. "We also undertook the occasional picnic."

"A favorite pastime from my childhood as well," he said.

"Was it?" She liked knowing they had that in common.

"Ben and I discovered a meadow just far enough distant from the house to feel rather secluded. We would nip a few sweets from the kitchens and wile away a peaceful afternoon there."

"Our exploits were similar. Persephone and Athena packed a meal, and we escaped at a run. Those were amongst our happiest times. We seldom had picnics after the boys joined the navy. There was too much work to be done with fewer of us there to accomplish it."

"Have you had any at Falstone Castle?" he asked.

"We haven't." Daphne hadn't ever thought of the possibility. She had arrived at Adam and Persephone's home with those lighter times pushed far to the back of her memory.

"Would the duke allow it, do you think?"

"If Persephone wanted a picnic, he would let nothing prevent it. Schedules, inconveniences, not even the weather."

"Not even the weather?" She loved the way he chuckled at her humor.

"The skies would not dare rain when the Duke of Kielder wished them clear."

"And yet you describe him as a gentle and caring husband. To the rest of us, that seems an inarguable contradiction."

"He loves her," Daphne said. "That, I think, makes all the difference. Watching them, I have realized that contrary to popular belief, love is a rather essential ingredient in marriage."

"Yes . . . well . . . not everyone is blessed with that." James grew noticeably uncomfortable. "Some marriages begin on . . . on less than ideal ground."

Did he speak of his own parents' marriage? Daphne had noticed a marked lack of tenderness between Lord and Lady Techney.

"But not all marriages must *begin* with love," Daphne said. "So long as there is affection and mutual kindness. And, of course, trust."

"That, no doubt, is what you've always wanted in a marriage."

Her heart seemed to stop a moment when the significance of the topic sank in. They were discussing marriage. Not *their* marriage, but it still felt like a step in a more serious direction. "Yes," she said, knowing her voice had lost a great deal of its volume. "Affection and kindness are needed in any marriage. Trust, I think, is especially important. A marriage cannot last if it is based on dishonesty or deception. I have always thought that essential to any kind of happiness."

A moment passed before James spoke quietly into the silence. "So have I."

Chapter Nineteen

TRUST. JAMES WINCED AS THAT word echoed in his thoughts. He'd returned again and again to their conversation of that morning. How very telling that Daphne should mention that particular requirement. He too had always considered honesty a vital character trait, and yet he seemed to have lost his grasp on his own integrity of late. Desperate circumstances had driven him to take desperate measures. When Father had first backed James into this, Daphne had been little more than a name. She had in the last few weeks become much more than that. The faceless symbol of his father's tyranny had transformed into a feeling, caring human being. She had gone from the lifeless "Miss Lancaster" to the intelligent yet timid and softhearted Daphne. And when precisely had he begun thinking of her by her given name?

He pushed out a tense breath. Too many burdens were piling up, and he'd begun to sag under the weight.

James stepped inside his mother's bedchamber. She'd not come down for dinner. She sat in her four-poster bed, propped up by pillows. Her coloring was not good. Her eyes were closed.

"How is she?" he asked the abigail hovering nearby.

"She's in a bad way, my lord. Her throat has been ailing her, and His Lordship came in and upset her more."

Father very seldom acknowledged Mother, something which ought to have raised James's suspicions when Father had insisted his scheme was meant to benefit her. If he'd sought her out, there had to be a reason, and likely not a kindhearted one.

"May I ask what my father said to her?"

Mother's feeble voice answered. "He will not send for a physician, James."

He took hold of her hand. Her coloring had worsened just since he'd come inside.

"She is a touch feverish," the abigail said. "I'm worried for her."

"I truly do not feel well at all," Mother's throat sounded raw. "But your father said no one from the staff can be spared. He said not to even try, that he'd given strict instructions."

Father would deny her a physician's care because of the inconvenience? He had to know James would not allow such a thing. Was this meant to be a battle of wills, a chance to show James that he, Father, was the one with the power? Had James not already bowed to enough dictates for the family hierarchy to be painfully clear?

The abigail dabbed at Mother's flushed cheeks with a damp cloth. She needed a doctor's care. But the staff would never defy Lord Techney, even for James.

Daphne. Her name entered his thoughts like a bolt of lightning. She could help. Better still, he felt certain she *would* help.

"I know someone who is expert enough in the apothecary arts to help you feel better and rest until I can talk some sense into Father." He yet held her hand. "Only, please, Mother, be kind to her."

"You mean that Miss Lancaster?" Her pale features clearly registered her disapproval. "How can I when she has ruined—"

"No, Mother. You must not blame her for what you see as my loss of freedom. That is truly not the way of it. If I can convince her to offer her assistance, will you please show her the gratitude she deserves? Her tisane did make a difference for you."

All the fight drained from her in a moment. Her coloring disappeared but for the heat-induced flush in her cheeks. She nodded, though reluctantly.

James gently slipped her hand under her blanket. "I will be back as soon as I can," he quietly promised.

He moved quickly, arriving on horseback at Falstone House at an hour generally considered far too late for social calls. He could only hope Daphne and the duchess had not chosen to attend any functions that night.

Considering the vast disservice he was doing her in continuing his charade, his conscience could not be eased knowing he was about to ask more of her. But what else could be done? Mother was truly ill.

The door opened. "Are the ladies of the house in?" The request emerged rushed and, even to his own ears, a touch desperate. "I have an urgent matter I need to discuss with Miss Lancaster."

No show of surprise touched the butler's expression. He led James quite properly up the stairs to the small, informal sitting room. Daphne and her sister were both seated within.

Daphne looked surprised to see him there. And well she might be. Though she'd not changed into her night clothes, her hair had been let down, pulled back by a single ribbon.

"Forgive me," he said before he could second-guess his own audacity. "I would not under less urgent circumstances presume to be here at this hour."

Her shock changed immediately to concern. "What's happened? You look nearly done in."

"My mother is unwell and, for reasons that do not reflect well on my family, is not able to seek the help of our physician. I hoped you would be willing to see if there is anything you might do to ease her suffering."

"Of course." She spoke as though there were no question of her assisting. She turned to her sister.

"Take Fanny with you," Her Grace instructed. "And Willie, so he can bring back word if you need to remain longer than expected."

Daphne stood, turning to the butler still standing in the sitting room doorway. "Please have Eliza retrieve my trunk of herbs and give it to Fanny."

"Yes, Miss Lancaster."

Daphne stepped out of the sitting room and walked alongside him toward the front of the house. "What are her symptoms?"

"She seems to have developed an infection of the throat."

"Has her voice been affected?" The timidity that usually hovered over Daphne's was not at all evident. She spoke with authority and decisiveness.

"It has," James answered. "And she is feverish as well."

They reached the front entryway. Word had apparently already spread amongst the staff. A footman stood at the front door with his outercoat already on. Willie, no doubt.

"Is she sweating at all?" Daphne asked.

"Not that I noticed." His confidence in Daphne only grew as they climbed into the Kielder carriage, Fanny along for propriety. Daphne knew just what to ask and did so with an undeniable expertise. His worries eased simply having her there.

She did not hover at Mother's door when they reached it but walked inside and spoke to the abigail directly. "I understand your mistress is ill."

The abigail's chin quivered a bit. She needed to keep herself in one piece, but James feared she wouldn't manage it.

Daphne crossed to the distraught woman and placed a gentle hand on her shoulder. "If you will tell me all you have seen and observed of this sickness, I promise to do all I can to help her. I give you my solemn word."

The abigail rallied a bit. "She has lost most of her voice and finds even drinking water nearly too painful to endure."

Daphne nodded as she listened. She drew the abigail to Mother's bedside once more. "How long has she had this fever?"

"She was a touch warm when she woke this morning."

James didn't like how that admission drew Daphne's mouth into a solemn line. He stood but a few paces away, watching anxiously.

"The fever has not broken at all the entire day?" Daphne asked.

The abigail shook her head.

"Has she slept?"

"Only fitfully."

Daphne turned her full attention to Mother. "I wish to help if I can," she said, "but first I must know as much as possible about your illness. May I have permission to very gently feel your neck? I promise to be as light in my touch as I can be."

Mother opened her mouth to say something, but no sound emerged. Had she lost her voice entirely? James stepped closer, wishing he knew how to ease her pain.

Daphne waited patiently for an answer to her question.

"She can help, Mother," he said.

Mother at last nodded.

Daphne sat on the side of the bed and pressed her fingertips with utmost care along Mother's neck. James knew not what she hoped to feel or find but prayed she could do something. For a long moment, she moved her fingers about, feeling and watching Mother. She pressed the back of one hand to Mother's forehead, then her cheek.

"I am certain you find swallowing very painful." Daphne's voice alone was soothing, calming. "I do know of a very useful tonic for a painful throat, but you will have to swallow it. Can you do that?"

Mother nodded.

"Then I will see to it immediately." Daphne rose and nearly bumped into him, so close had he come to stand by her.

He might have apologized for getting in her way, but the concern he saw in her face silenced him.

"Will you walk with me a moment?" she whispered urgently.

He followed her to the far side of the room where Mother's writing desk sat.

"I will write out the recipe," Daphne said, keeping her voice low. "But, James, she needs a physician. Her throat is terribly swollen. Fever has clouded her eyes. She ought to be seen by a professional."

He paced away, then back again. "Father will not allow one to be sent for. He's given instructions to the staff not to, and I know they will not defy him on my account."

"Might your brother be sent?"

"Ben could go, but Father would likely refuse to pay the physician for his services."

Daphne's brow knit in thought. She'd wasted not a single breath, not a single moment in outrage at Father's edict nor expressing horror at the coldness of which his sire was capable. James was inexplicably grateful. Any other lady of his acquaintance would have washed her hands of his problems.

"If we both put our minds to it," she said, "I am certain we can think of something. We cannot simply allow her to be neglected when she is so ill."

She wrote in clear, concise lettering a recipe for her healing tisane. James checked on his mother once more. Her eyes were heavy with illness. Something had to be done. Father had to be dealt with.

A moment later, Daphne handed the recipe to Mother's abigail with strict instructions that were any of the herbs in the recipe not on hand, she was to be told at once so a suitable substitute could be found. The lady's maid rushed off, obviously anxious to help her mistress.

"Try not to worry, James." Daphne laid a hand on his arm. "I do not believe your mother is in imminent danger. We have time to think of a means of getting a physician here."

"I can only imagine what you must think of my family." He'd seldom felt more ashamed.

"Every family has its difficulties."

He pressed his hand to hers where it yet lay on his arm. "Thank you for all you've done."

That dimple of hers reappeared. "I am happy to be of help."

"Might I ask another favor of you, then? Will you stay here with my mother until her abigail returns?"

"I mean to stay until she is well again."

James took her hand in his and pressed a grateful kiss to her fingers. He'd come to her with a crisis, and she'd responded with a cool head and a giving heart.

"I will go see if I can talk some sense into my father. Wish me luck." He released her fingers and moved to the door.

James glanced back once only to find Daphne already engaged in cooling Mother's forehead. His heart tugged at the sight even as guilt twisted more painfully inside. She was so willing to give with no idea of how selfishly she was being used by them all.

Chapter Twenty

LADY TECHNEY WAS SLEEPING BUT not resting. The honey and licorice-root tea Daphne had instructed the cook to prepare had eased the lady's pain. Her fever, however, continued to rage.

Daphne dipped a cloth in the bowl of water and dabbed at Lady Techney's forehead and flushed cheeks. The water had warmed, so she'd sent the abigail to get ice from the ice cellar. She alone remained in the room with James's mother.

A debate raged in her mind. She knew several treatments to break a fever but hesitated to use them. A fever could at times be beneficial. She would feel more confident if she had a physician's assessment. If James could not convince his father to send for one, she would simply have to do her best.

That had always been the hardest part of being her family's only medical resource. She'd worried endlessly that she would make a mistake. She had borne that weight as a very young child, too young for such a responsibility, and felt it again in that moment. In the years she'd lived with Adam and Persephone, she had always been able to consult with a physician or surgeon or apothecary.

She gently dabbed Lady Techney's neck with the damp cloth, hoping to cool her as much as she could. Footsteps sounded from the doorway. Daphne breathed a sigh of relief. That would be the abigail returned with much-needed ice.

But it wasn't. Mr. Bennett Tilburn stepped inside, mouth pulled in worry.

"James said Mother was ill."

Daphne nodded. "She is sleeping now though."

Bennett's eyes did not leave his mother's face as he crossed to her bedside. He didn't reach out to touch her nor sit on the edge of her bed. Perhaps these were things sons did not do when their mothers were ill. She hardly knew if daughters did such things. Her mother died so long ago. She had no experience with mothers.

Daphne dipped the cloth in the water again and rang it out. How she wished the water were cooler. Where was the abigail?

"James sent me to see if there was anything I might do for you. He has some business with our father and said the matter was taking longer than expected."

That was not a promising turn of events. Perhaps James had been unable to arrange for the physician they needed.

"Would you take over for me here?" She indicated the cloth she was using to cool Lady Techney's brow. "I think she would benefit from a fever reducer, but I'll need to prepare that myself."

"You're an apothecary?" His tone was not doubtful, not quite teasing. He did take the cloth and the seat Daphne relinquished to him.

"I am something of an amateur apothecary, yes." She smiled in an attempt to hide her embarrassment. Few people had ever heard of her passion for herbs and responded with anything but dismissive amusement, as though she'd declared an undying interest in watching water boil.

Bennett nodded. "That explains James's lack of panic. He usually looks ready to burst with tension when Mother is ill."

"I hope I can live up to his confidence in me." A tiny bubble of pride grew inside. James had faith in her.

"Tell me how to do this." Bennett held the cloth with no degree of expertise. "I'm afraid I am a little useless in the sickroom."

That struck her as odd. "I thought I understood Lady Techney's health is often poor."

Bennett shrugged. "But James always does everything himself."

It was little wonder she seldom saw him. James's responsibilities stretched him far too thin.

"If you will dab gently at her forehead and cheeks and neck—anywhere that is flushed—the damp cloth will help cool her off until her fever can be brought down."

He nodded his understanding and followed her instructions. He could not have been more obviously unsure of his ministrations. His brow creased with concentration.

Daphne watched him a moment. "When the cloth grows too dry or too warm, dip it in the water again. But be certain to ring out as much moisture as you can so she's not soaked by it."

He silently nodded and kept at his efforts.

"Her abigail will return shortly with some ice to cool the water."

"And I should keep at this until then? After, even?"

"Until her fever breaks, we must make every effort to keep her cool." Daphne laid a reassuring hand on his shoulder. "Just continue as you are."

He gave her a quick smile and set back to work.

"I will return in a moment." She wasn't certain he heard her, but she left just the same.

Daphne stepped out into the corridor, hoping to catch sight of James. She followed the sound of tense, raised voices and found him and Lord Techney eyeing one another across a desk in what appeared to be a library.

"We are not a wealthy family, James. If I sent for a doctor every time that woman gets the sniffles, it would beggar me."

"This is no simple case of the sniffles," James returned. "She needs a doctor."

"She must learn not to be so dramatic."

Time to use the skills Adam taught you, Daphne. She rallied her courage. "If you two are quite finished, I would like to address the current difficulty." She kept her tone stiff and unyielding. Both gentlemen turned and faced her with matching expressions of shock. "Lord Techney, your wife is ill. Quite ill, in fact, and I mean that in the least *dramatic* way possible. If you will not send for a physician, I will and have the bill sent to my brother-in-law labeled 'services rendered on behalf of Lord Techney.' You can do what you feel necessary to settle your debt with the infamous duke, but I must warn you, he is not particularly fond of people who owe him money."

The thinly veiled threat sank in with all the force Daphne could have hoped for. Lord Techney swallowed audibly. "I hadn't meant to be cruel," he insisted in choked tones. "She is simply so often unwell."

"All the more reason for concern, sir. Am I to assume, then, a physician will be summoned?"

"Yes. Yes, of course."

Daphne gave a quick nod. "Very good. Now, Lord Tilburn"—she turned to James—"I believe your mother would appreciate your calming company."

"Of course." James moved without hesitation to the doorway where she stood.

To Lord Techney she offered a simple "Good day to you" before following James's path out of the room.

He was waiting for her when she stepped into the corridor.

"I am sorry if I offended you with my sharp words." She and James
made their way toward Lady Techney's bedchamber. "I could think of
no other way of getting through to your father."

He shook his head. "You were wondrous."

Relief surged through her. "Go sit with your mother," she instructed.
"Bennett is with her now, but she cannot help but be soothed by having
both of her sons at her side."

James disappeared into the bedchamber. Daphne remained behind in
Lady Techney's sitting area. She pulled out the small trunk she'd brought
with her in which she kept those herbs crucial enough to travel with. How
often she'd wished for a better means of organizing and storing them. They
sat in small boxes, cloth bags, and glass vials packed in protective straw. A
true apothecary would have the proper traveling trunk. She did not even
have an apothecary chest at Falstone Castle. The castle, along with Falstone
House, had a room for drying kitchen herbs and other plants, just as most
houses of any significance did. But an herb room was the domain of a
cook, perhaps an undergardener, and was a far cry from the space needed
for properly preparing more delicate medicinal herbs and for appropriately
storing and organizing the oils and mixtures she painstakingly created.

She took from her trunk those things she needed in that moment. Feverfew leaves. Black-elder flowers. She set both bags to the side. Her very own
mortar and pestle sat in a custom-made box, an extravagant purchase she'd
saved her pin money to buy several years earlier. She'd never regretted the
expenditure, especially in moments such as this.

She pulled out a small vial of lavender oil. A drop in the water used
to cool Lady Techney would help her rest.

Daphne tucked her supplies under her arms and returned to Lady
Techney's room. Everyone looked at her as she stepped inside. She nodded and motioned for them to continue their efforts.

After clearing the writing desk of papers and pens and inkwells, she set
out her things, then pulled out the stone mortar and pestle and prepared to
get to work. She waved over the abigail, who had returned with the ice. "We
will need a kettle of hot water, a teacup, and a tea strainer. Can you see to that?"

"Yes, miss." She dipped a quick curtsy and hurried off.

Daphne took a moment to add a single drop of lavender oil to the water Bennett used. "This will help her rest," she explained.

As she crossed back to the writing desk, James followed.

"I hope the footman sent to retrieve the physician can do so quickly," he said. "Mr. Cathcart is often away from home seeing to a sick patient."

Daphne knew in that moment she would do best to continue with her treatment. If the physician arrived quickly, so much the better.

"How does Mother seem to you?" James asked.

"Her fever worries me." Daphne opened the bag of dried feverfew leaves and added the right amount to her empty mortar.

"Another tea?" James asked.

Daphne added a generous pinch of dried black-elder flowers. "It is extremely helpful but tastes terrible. I only hope we can convince her to take it."

He stood mute at her side as she ground the herbs together. She'd learned over the years just how fine to make them. The crushing released necessary oils, but if she ground them too much, they would not steep properly to make the tea.

A kettle of boiling water, along with a cup and strainer, arrived in the next minutes. Daphne worked at the tea but looked a few times at James. His thoughts seemed miles away. Lines of tension creased his face.

"Perhaps you should sit a moment, James," she said. "You look ready to drop."

He shook himself. "I am tired is all. And worried."

"Your brother is doing a fine job of tending to Lady Techney. This tea will be ready shortly. And I have complete confidence in the timely arrival of your physician." That last bit was something of a stretch, but reassuring him seemed more crucial in that moment than blunt honesty.

"I will be more at ease if you can give me something useful to do."

Heavens but he looked near to bursting.

Daphne took his hands in hers. For just a moment, the feel of holding his hands paralyzed her. Though she'd dreamed of having his attention and affection, she'd not been truly prepared for this closeness. She pulled her thoughts together and led him to his mother's bedside, opposite Bennett. "Your assignment," she said, "is to sit here and think of a way to convince Lady Techney to drink the foul concoction I am about to bring over for her. Are you up for the challenge?"

He managed a halfhearted smile at her teasing. "I will put my mind to the puzzle."

He pulled off his jacket and hung it over the arm of his chair, clearly preparing to settle in. She'd not had to tell him the night would be a long one; he seemed to understand without words. How many such illnesses had he seen his mother through?

Lady Techney objected to the tea as much as Daphne had expected and as quietly, considering her lack of voice and energy. James spoke patiently and quietly to her, easing the steaming liquid past her lips a sip at a time.

Daphne stood out of the way, watching him. His kindness to her so many years earlier had not been an oddity, it seemed. He treated his mother with the same consideration. A woman would be fortunate indeed to win the devotion of such a man.

He looked back at her. "There is only a bit of dregs left in the bottom. Does she need to drink that?"

"No. Let her lie back and rest."

She took Bennett's place at Lady Techney's side, insisting he go get his sleep. James sat a bit limp in his chair, head resting in his upturned hand. He looked spent. Just how bad had his argument with Lord Techney been?

The feverfew tisane had not yet taken effect. Daphne would see to Lady Techney when it did. In the few minutes until that happened, she would do what she could for James.

She fetched a fresh cloth from the pile brought up by the maid. In a clean bowl, she poured some hot water from the teakettle, then added a chip of ice to cool it to pleasantly warm. She added a drop of her lavender oil and dipped the cloth in, then wrung it out. She folded the cloth in a long rectangle and crossed to where James sat.

"Lean forward a bit," she softly instructed. He looked confused for only a moment before complying.

His cravat had long since come loose, leaving his collar hanging limp.

She set the warm cloth against the back of his neck. The warmth combined with the lavender would relax him.

"Now sit back." She pulled a light blanket off a chair near the windows and brought it back to James, laying it over him.

"I cannot ask you to care for Mother alone," he objected.

"I will let you know if I need help. Rest assured, this is nothing I haven't undertaken before, and I am doing so now willingly."

He closed his eyes and leaned his head far back. "Thank you, Daphne," he said. "And I am sorry."

"What are you sorry for?"

A beat passed before he answered. "Too many things."

The poor man was obviously exhausted. "Rest a bit, James. You'll feel better if you do."

He must have taken the suggestion to heart; he was asleep within minutes. Lady Techney began to sweat shortly after that, a clear indication that the feverfew and black-elder tea were working as they should. Daphne sat at her side, dabbing Lady Techney's flushed cheeks.

She passed an hour in just that way before the physician at last arrived. He proved competent and efficient. They discussed symptoms and treatments employed thus far. After a moment of silent surprise at Daphne's abilities with herbs, the doctor declared himself impressed beyond words. He smelled the dregs left in Lady Techney's cup and his praise began anew.

"Precisely the aroma I would hope for. The blend, I would say, was expertly concocted."

She could tell his approval brought color to her face. If only she could find a way to control her blushes.

"Miss Lancaster has been indispensable." James had, it seemed, awoken. He shifted about and sat up straighter. The cloth she'd set on his neck slipped off as he stood. "How is Lady Techney?" he asked the doctor.

"The tea has begun to break her fever. She will be well given time and rest."

Daphne stepped back, intending to get out of the way. To her surprise, James moved to her side.

"How are *you?*" he asked, his eyes taking in every inch of her face.

Again her telltale blush surfaced. "I am holding up. A little tired," she admitted. "But nothing I cannot endure."

"You should rest. Everyone else has been permitted to." He motioned to the corner where the abigail dozed in a hard-backed chair.

Daphne was too tired to argue. "Why don't I take your chair, and you can sit up with your mother for a time."

The arrangements were made. James and the physician tended to Lady Techney. Daphne leaned back in the chair, the same warm blanket James had used tucked around her shoulders. She watched them as she sat there. A few times James looked in her direction and smiled.

She didn't think she had ever been more content. The dreams she'd formulated at twelve years of age were coming closer and closer to reality.

Chapter Twenty-One

MOTHER WAS ON THE MEND by that morning, something the family owed entirely to Daphne. In the quiet hours of night while this guardian angel of theirs had silently ministered to a woman she hardly knew, James's view of Daphne had undergone a material transformation. Though he'd not chosen to court her, he had come to realize that being permitted to do so was a gift he'd not fully valued. She was a wonder, a lady with a heart so deep and so giving as to put to shame every other person James had ever known. And he was fortunate enough to have the opportunity to know her better, to be her particular friend.

He pulled a chair up next to hers, where she sat keeping an eye on his mother's progress. "How is our patient this morning?"

"You'll be pleased to know she was alert enough for conversation earlier."

Oh heavens. "What did she speak about?" He hoped his nervousness didn't show.

"At first she simply said again and again how surprisingly good she felt." Daphne smiled the tiniest bit, her eyes heavy with weariness. "And I do not think she was at all prepared to find *me* at her bedside."

James didn't like the sound of that. "I hope she was not unkind to you."

"She accepted my presence after a time." Daphne rose and adjusted Mother's blankets. "Though she was upset that I wouldn't allow you to be awoken."

"I would happily have taken over for you."

"You were finally sleeping deeply. There was no need to disturb you." Daphne checked Mother's temperature with the back of her hand. She must have been satisfied; she returned to her seat once more. "Besides, tending the sick is a skill of mine, one I do not often get to use. I suppose that is something for which I should be grateful. Other than my father, I am blessed with a healthy family."

James nodded. That would be a blessing. "I have never known a time when Mother was not susceptible to illness. Father has no patience for it."

"You seem to have patience enough for the entire family."

They sat quietly, neither speaking nor moving. He'd discovered that about Daphne; she was not uncomfortable with silence.

"The physician was impressed to see that you travel with your own herbs and remedies," he said after another moment.

She pulled her legs up beside her in her chair. "Only those I need most often. I can generally find what I need in London, but these are taken from plants I cultivated myself. I know them better, know precisely how to use them."

"So you are an herbologist and a gardener?"

"The best apothecary is always *both*."

How she'd changed in the past weeks. He'd hardly had a word from her that first visit to Falstone House and only a handful more during their drive. They'd come far enough to speak easily.

"What first interested you in the apothecary arts?"

She didn't answer immediately. He saw in her face a debate, as though she wasn't sure she wished to answer his question.

He took her hand in his own, hoping to assure her that he could be trusted. He found, however, that he himself benefited from the connection. She soothed and calmed him every bit as much as her teas and tonics had Mother.

"My mother died when I was too young to have any real memories of her." She spoke in a quiet voice. "My father closed in on himself over the years since, pushing away everything and everyone. At first he was simply distant and hermit-like. I remember coming into his book room and asking to sit with him, something he allowed with less and less frequency. He would shoo me away or ask that I not disturb him." She seemed to think a moment. "He grew less reachable with each passing year. By the time I left home to live with Adam and Persephone, Father did not seem to be more than vaguely aware of the world around him."

What a difficult experience that must have been.

"Once, while his was still a purposeful isolation rather than an ailment of the mind, I asked Persephone what was wrong with him," Daphne continued.

"She told me his heart was broken. In my naivety, I assumed his *physical* heart was unwell. I knew enough to realize we could never afford to pay a man of medicine to cure him."

"So you sought out the cure yourself." He clasped her hand ever tighter, imagining in his thoughts a tiny girl with thick black hair and deep-brown eyes poring over books of medicines and concoctions in a desperate attempt to save her father.

She took a long breath, leaning against the back of her chair as she let the air out. "I finally asked the local apothecary where in the old book he'd given me I might find the treatment for a broken heart. He told me, 'There is no herb on earth can cure that.' I'd learned how to treat pain and fevers and infections but had to admit to myself that I could do nothing to get my father back."

"Has he been slipping away all these years?"

She nodded. "He is less aware of the world around him every time I see him."

James rubbed her hand with both of his. "I am so sorry. I cannot imagine watching a parent slip so slowly away."

"It is an agony I do not wish on anyone." Her head rested against his shoulder, though he didn't think she slept. While he hoped talking with him, sitting there with him, eased some of the pain he'd heard in her retelling, he found it lessened his burden as well. How was it that this remarkable young lady he'd not even known a month earlier could calm his mind by her very presence?

Guilt and relief made for an odd combination. He felt he'd learned enough of Daphne Lancaster to find a great deal of peace in the idea of courting her. She had a good heart. She was intelligent, well-spoken, selfless. Her dimple alone was reason enough to coax a smile from her. He could easily imagine himself being quite happy with her in his life, no matter the unfortunate way in which their courtship began. But knowing he had been, and out of necessity would continue to be, dishonest with her, if only by omission, nagged at him.

Her head grew heavy against his shoulder, her breathing steady and deep. He hoped she was sleeping. She'd spent the entire night tending to Mother. He adjusted his position enough to look down at her. She didn't even stir as he moved. Lud, she looked tired, even in her sleep.

"We have been unfair to her," a raspy and raw voice said.

How long had Mother been awake?

"*Life* has been unfair to her, I am discovering." He kept his voice low so as not to wake her. "She lost her parents as a child. As a young lady, she endured the rejection of Society simply because she is quiet."

"And we decided to hate her without even meeting her." Mother's pale features showed real remorse. "No one as sweet and kind as she could conspire the way I assumed she had."

"I fear everyone in the neighborhood will assume something of that nature should she eventually accept my suit. I believe most of London Society suspects something underhanded on someone's part." James gently rubbed Daphne's hand between his. "It is a shame no one is aware of her worth. Not even she seems to recognize it."

Mother tried for a moment to turn and look at him but, in the end, simply lay back, exhausted.

"Have you decided what you mean to do, James?" she asked. "Have you given up the idea of finding a wife of your own choosing?"

The question was certainly direct. He had spent the night firming his decision, yet it still pained him. "I have decided I must." He would not tell Mother of Father's threats and the subsequent agreement he'd made. She had suffered enough at the hands of her unfeeling husband.

A small tear appeared at the corner of Mother's eye. "You admire her and respect her. I can see that you do. That is a better start than your father and I had. And you are a better man than he."

He held back the *I should certainly hope so* that immediately sprang to his mind.

"Commit yourself to making her happy, James, and I think you will find your own happiness as well." Her eyes closed once, twice, and finally the oblivion of sleep took hold.

James stayed in his chair, holding Daphne's hand. She slept peacefully in the chair she'd occupied most of the night, her head still resting heavily against his shoulder.

Commit yourself to making her happy. He could do that. He'd learned a great deal about her already and could at least begin to guess at the things that would bring a smile to her face. He'd moved forward on the expectation of a cold rejection of the suit he'd been forced to undertake. In that quiet moment, having been given such a tender glimpse into the person she was, he found that outcome no longer suited him.

For the first time, he could almost imagine himself making a life with the remarkable woman seated beside him. If only a chasm of unspoken truths didn't stand between them.

Chapter Twenty-Two

James walked at Daphne's side in silence, carrying her trunk of herbs. She'd spent the late morning taking her breakfast and packing her herbs. He knew he had done a poor job of thanking her for the kindness she'd shown his mother. He was simply so unaccustomed to anyone helping him look after his family that the words refused to come.

Daphne did not seem overly concerned by the pause in conversation. She never did.

"A letter for you, Miss Lancaster." The butler held out a sealed missive. "A footman just delivered it from Falstone House."

She took the letter and thanked him. "It is from my brother-in-law," she said after a quick perusal of the address.

Did the Dangerous Duke object to Daphne's having spent the night at Techney House despite the presence of a maid for propriety? "How did he manage to get a letter from Shropshire so quickly?"

"Not *that* brother-in-law." How was it that her dimpled smile always forced a smile from him regardless of his distress? "This letter is from the harmless one."

James opted for an overblown show of relief. She might not realize how panicked he'd actually been for a moment. "There is a small sitting room just down this corridor a bit. If you'd like to read your letter there, I can gather what you need should you wish to pen a reply."

"I am happy to read it while I'm waiting for the carriage and during my ride home. But I thank you for the kind offer."

He could not say why her small expression of gratitude struck him with such force, but he realized in that moment that Daphne never failed to thank him for even the smallest things he did for her. Even gestures which were, in all honesty, insignificant never passed without an acknowledgment. Perhaps it was one of the reasons helping her never felt like a task he was required to do but rather a natural inclination.

Ben had only just stepped inside when James and Daphne reached the front entryway. "Miss Lancaster," he said, inclining his head. "Has James not allowed you to escape yet?"

"I am afraid he has kept me locked up in your dungeon all morning. It has been terrible, I assure you."

"In the dungeon?" Ben tsked and shook his head. "Sounds to me as though he is borrowing a page from your guardian."

"Adam does have a tendency to bring out the most sinister in people."

James had the oddest urge to brush his thumb along her cheek precisely where her dimple lay. It was adorable. Utterly adorable.

"I am pleased to have seen you before I left, Mr. Tilburn," Daphne said. "This letter is for you." She held out a missive folded smaller than standard and, if James was to hazard a guess, having arrived inside the letter she herself had just received. "From my brother-in-law, Mr. Windover."

"The one who raises sheep?" Ben asked, taking the letter with undisguised eagerness.

"The very one. He indicated in his letter to me that he hopes to have some sound advice for you."

"Then you told him about me?"

She looked immediately uncertain. "I hope you are not offended. He has learned a great deal over the past few years and is most willing to share his knowledge with others in situations similar to what his was."

"Offended?" Ben shook his head. "Not at all. I'm . . . flattered and . . . grateful. Thank you, Miss Lancaster."

Daphne turned a remarkable shade of red at Ben's effuse gratitude.

James knew she would far prefer an escape than to be the recipient of more attention. "I do believe we should allow Miss Lancaster to return home to recover from her long night," James said, giving his brother a pointed look.

"Of course." Ben's smile did not lessen. "Of course." He walked off in something of a daze, eyes continually dropping to his letter.

James held out his hand to her. She slipped her own in his as naturally as though they had done so many times. He had done nothing to earn her trust and felt infinitely more guilty realizing he had it and did not deserve it.

Seated across from her in the carriage, he took a moment to attempt an adequate expression of appreciation. "I am so touched by what you've done for Ben," he said. "His estate, dilapidated as it is, means the world to him. I have been at a loss as to how I might help him. You, in what I am discovering is simply your way, have hit at the very heart of the matter and addressed it quite perfectly."

"That is Adam's influence," she said. "He taught me long ago how to think through a situation and discover the actual problem, which is often quite different from what one first notices. Your brother, on the surface, seems to simply need funds, but his true problem is more long-term. He needs to know *how* to run an estate that is falling to pieces and how to build it over time. I happen to know someone who has done exactly that. Introducing the two to each other simply made sense."

Good heavens, she was a marvel. "But you not only realized the sensible solution; you made it happen too. In my experience, most people don't take that final step. Most can't be bothered."

"I think you have known the wrong sort of people."

Was it any wonder he'd come to like her so very much? She was intelligent, kind, calming. He reached across the carriage and took her hand in his, raising it to his lips and pressing a kiss to the back of her hand. "Has anyone ever told you, Daphne Lancaster, that you are amazing?"

"I can honestly say no one ever has."

He kept her hand in his, the simple gesture echoing as a flutter in his chest. "It sounds to me as though I am not the only one who has known the wrong sort of people."

Chapter Twenty-Three

FOR THREE DAYS, DAPHNE WALKED about Falstone House with a smile just beneath the surface. She could not remember a time when her heart had been lighter. James had come to call every day since Lady Techney's illness, and the previous evening at the ball, he'd even danced with her. And when engaged with others that night, he'd still looked over at her occasionally from across the room.

Daphne's smile could not help but peek through her usual reserve at the memory of those brief connections. She brushed her fingers across the tips of several flowers on a bush near the entrance to the small park where she knew James walked his small dog.

The gentleman she had fallen in love with during the past half dozen years was falling in love with her. She came remarkably close to squealing right there in a public green, an uncharacteristic urge she'd felt a remarkable number of times over the past few days.

Turning a corner, she spotted James just ahead. He tossed a stick, and the puppy he'd named Scamp rushed after it. Sitting on a stone bench nearby was Lady Techney.

James spotted Daphne in the next moment, smiling at her as always. He waved as they approached. "Good morning, Daphne."

"Good morning," she offered in return. "And to you, Lady Techney. You appear to be feeling well today."

"I am, and it is a very pleasant change." She fussed a moment with her lap blanket before resuming her stitching.

Daphne had learned during her long vigil at Lady Techney's bedside that James's mother was very fond of embroidery; she had mentioned it several times. Daphne's own mother had filled their home with stitchery during the short years of her life.

James walked with Daphne a few paces away, where Scamp was happily gnawing the already slobbery stick.

James took her hand in his as he'd done in the carriage a few days earlier. The gesture had so quickly become natural and easy between them. The feel of his touch momentarily robbed her of the ability to respond. She simply breathed and committed the moment to memory.

"I know my mother well enough to realize she is not likely to give you the thanks you deserve for the throat tonic you provided for her."

"Your cook has the recipe and can prepare it for her whenever she is in need of it." Daphne managed to get the words out whole despite the fact that James had not yet released her hand.

"I do believe you would put to shame any apothecary in the kingdom." He squeezed her fingers. "You've done wonders for Mother."

"I am so pleased she is feeling better."

He took up Scamp's stick with his free hand and tossed it away for the pup to chase. "Have you had word from Shropshire?"

"My father is quite ill, unfortunately. In mind as well as body."

"I am so sorry." He adjusted their position so her arm was threaded through his, pulling her closer to him. She accepted the thoughtful and supportive gesture and leaned a little against him. "Has your brother-in-law offered any specific information?"

"No." She sighed as he set his hand on hers where it rested on his arm. "But Father's situation is not at all hopeful."

"Do you and the duchess need to travel to Shropshire? I would be happy to help you make any arrangements."

She felt her telltale blush return but did not fight against it. By now, James knew her tendency to color and did not seem to mind. "We will wait to hear what Adam recommends."

"It seems, then, that you are in need of diversions," he said. "Anything you would like, Daphne. An afternoon carriage ride, a trip to Greenwich Park. Whatever you choose."

Anything she wanted. Would he think her odd or overly sentimental if she confessed to wanting nothing so much as an hour or two of his company? She had no desire to seem pathetic. A carriage ride about Hyde Park could be undertaken in relative privacy, but a longer trip to Greenwich Park would involve a great many servants, and Persephone would be required to attend for the sake of propriety.

"I am not sure," she said, trying to think of a third alternative.

"There must be something you want to do but haven't."

"I have been surprisingly happy here, James. Indeed, this Season is the first time I have ever come to Town when I haven't been desperate to escape."

"*Escape.*" A broad smile spread across his face. "You have given me the perfect idea."

"What is it?"

His excitement proved infectious. "Tomorrow afternoon you are going to have a picnic."

He had remembered that fleeting moment of conversation. She hadn't been on a picnic in ten years. The very thought rekindled long-forgotten memories of happy times and worry-free moments with her family, of shedding the weight of responsibility and hardship. "Oh, James, that would be wonderful."

"And I will personally make all the arrangements, so you need do nothing but attend and enjoy yourself."

"You are certain?" she asked.

James took her hand once more, raising it to his lips and brushing the lightest kiss on her fingers. "It will be my very real pleasure."

Long after she and Fanny returned to their carriage to make the drive back to Falstone House, Daphne held the back of her hand to her cheek, closing her eyes, shutting out every sensation but the memory of his kiss.

James discovered that doing a kindness for Daphne was both a privilege and a joy. He'd spent an enjoyable afternoon and morning planning the impromptu picnic. By means of a quick *tête-à-tête* with Her Grace at the Bowers' musicale the evening before, he'd discovered Daphne liked water-chestnut sandwiches, lemonade, and apple tarts. He'd also learned that the Lancasters had enjoyed only the most basic of accommodations when picnicking: a blanket, a basket of food, plates, and utensils. He meant to recreate those excursions.

Ben crossed his path as he made a circuit of the front entryway, awaiting Daphne's arrival. Inexplicably, his brother laughed almost on the instant.

"You find something entertaining?" James glanced out the windows at the sky, wanting further reassurance that the weather would cooperate.

"I find *you* entertaining. I haven't seen you this giddy since we were boys."

"I am not giddy."

Ben only laughed again. "Enthusiastic, then."

James shrugged. "I like picnics."

Ben motioned for James to walk with him toward the back terrace. "I have a feeling what you have come to like is Miss Lancaster."

"How could I not like her? She is intelligent and witty and a genuinely good person."

Ben raised an eyebrow even as he lowered his voice. "Am I to assume you are not so disgusted with your courtship of her as you were a few weeks ago?"

The reminder was a bit sobering. "I still cannot like how all this began. But I've had time to come to know Daphne better, and I have found reason to be optimistic."

"She's not the dragon you expected her to be?"

He had made a great many assumptions about her, none of which had proven accurate. "Better than that, even. The more I know of her, the more I believe we could make a good match of it."

Ben shook his head. "'A good match' is not the same as 'a love match.'"

Leave it to Ben to dampen the enthusiasm James had managed to find. "No. But it is better than what our parents have."

"You have resigned yourself to it?"

Resigned was far too harsh a word. "I like Miss Lancaster. Quite a lot, in fact."

Ben studied him a moment. "I've come to like her as well," he eventually said. "I don't care for the idea of her spending her life with a husband who regrets marrying her."

James pushed out a breath. The guilt he'd tried to assuage all week flooded over him again. He had spent far too much of the past weeks deceiving a good-hearted lady. He did like Daphne. She was a wonder and a pleasant surprise. He missed her when she was away and thought of her while they were apart. He might not have chosen her on his own, but he could be a good husband to her. "I didn't say I regretted courting her," he said.

"If you cannot go forward with this honestly," Ben said, "you really shouldn't go forward at all."

James shook his head. "It isn't that simple. This arrangement may have begun by force, but it does not feel that way any longer. Should I be fortunate enough to win her regard, I will do everything I can to make her happy."

"Everything except tell her the truth."

"The truth would only hurt her, Ben."

For the first time, his brother seemed to empathize with him. "An impossible situation, isn't it? Being honest means she would never trust you again, but withholding the truth is not the proper thing either."

"At times it feels completely impossible."

"But you do like her?" Ben pressed.

James nodded. "Quite a lot, actually."

"Well, that is a start, I suppose."

"Given time, I hope we can find something more than that." James was surprised at the strength of that hope. He wanted to find reason to believe their connection was based on more than lies and misplaced trust. He liked Daphne far more than he'd expected to. It confused him and pushed him forward all at once.

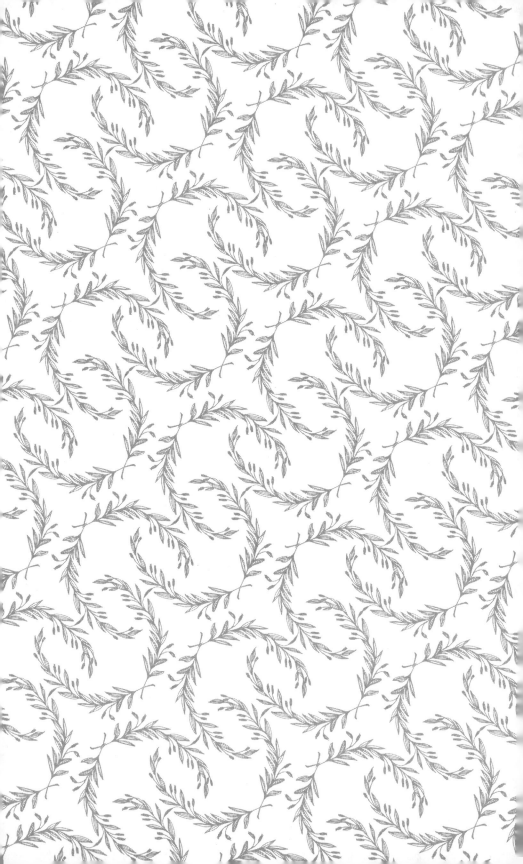

Chapter Twenty-Four

EVEN THE MOST TALENTED LANDSCAPE artist could not have captured the perfection of the meadow to which the Techney House butler led Daphne and Persephone. Though several other guests had been invited, Daphne knew James meant the picnic for her. She could not remember a time when something had been planned purely for her enjoyment.

"What do you suppose inspired Lord Tilburn to have a picnic?" Persephone glanced at Daphne, a teasing glint in her eye. "Perhaps merely a passing fancy?"

"I think it is a splendid idea." Daphne smiled, caring not at all that her cheeks glowed a revealing shade of red.

"I will say this, Daphne: Adam has his misgivings about this courtship, but I believe if he had been here to see the change in you these past few days, he would wholeheartedly support Lord Tilburn's suit."

"Once Adam has returned and we resume our afternoons together, I intend to tell him how wrong he was," Daphne said with a laugh. "The Dangerous Duke doesn't often find himself being fed humble pie."

Persephone's eyes shone with amusement. "I cannot say it is a dish he enjoys."

Daphne watched as James made his way to where they sat on large cushions beneath the cooling canopy of an ash tree. She hoped Adam really would come to see how wrong he had been about James. He was good and kind. Though his courtship had caught them off guard, his regard had proven sincere.

"Good afternoon," he greeted upon reaching them. "May I join you a moment?"

"Certainly."

He sat nearest her seemingly without hesitation. Daphne's heart fluttered frantically in her chest. The awkwardness of their earliest interactions had melted away over the course of the past week. A comfortable contentment had settled over her and a growing excitement. She had loved him for years, and finally, he had begun to feel the same for her.

"I believe your picnic is a success," Daphne said.

James smiled at her. She managed to hold back the delighted giggle that sight inspired in her. "This is *your* picnic, Daphne, despite the plethora of extra attendees. My father could not allow an opportunity for lording about to pass. He added significantly to the guest list. I hope that hasn't ruined it for you."

"Not at all. Everything is perfect."

He shook his head, though the gesture struck her as one of disbelief rather than negation. "Is she always this easy to please?" he asked Persephone.

"Daphne is, perhaps, the least demanding person I have ever known."

Why did Persephone's response not feel entirely like a compliment?

"I can see I have embarrassed you." James leaned closer, taking her hand in his, which had become a gesture he engaged in increasingly often of late. For her part, Daphne loved that he had adopted such a tender gesture.

"I blush very easily. You need not always assume I do so because you have embarrassed me."

"Have I though?" His gaze met hers.

Hearing herself being discussed had ever been an uncomfortable experience, and it *had*, in all honesty, been a little embarrassing. His words, however, were kind, unlike many conversations about herself that she'd overheard. Mrs. Hammond in the neighborhood where she'd grown up had always included in any reference to Daphne the phrase "the short, plain one." Mrs. Cole, from whom she'd collected the sewing they had taken in, had seemed particularly fond of the word *unpromising*.

"Daphne?" James's voice captured her attention once more. "Have I upset you?"

"Not at all. And the picnic truly is perfect, regardless of what my sister says of my complacent nature."

"I had not meant to imply that you are complacent," Persephone said. "You are certainly not that. You are sweet natured, a trait that is decidedly a good one."

"Hear, hear." James nodded firmly.

"The two of you will have me blushing furiously," Daphne warned. "And that would ruin this lovely picnic."

James's eyes focused off in the distance. "I fear it may soon be ruined anyway." A look of amused resignation crossed his face.

Daphne followed his gaze. Scamp darted about the gathered picnickers, most likely in search of a morsel or two. Several maids attempted to shoo him away from the table of food whilst guests did their best to avoid a confrontation with the enthusiastic mongrel.

"Perhaps I should rescue them," James said.

"Or rescue *him*—poor Scamp is outnumbered, after all."

"'Poor Scamp,' is it? I see he has managed to secure your sympathies." James's gaze shifted in the direction of his mother. "I do need to rein him in before he upsets too many people." By which he, of course, meant his mother.

He let out a whistle, then looked a bit chagrined as he apologized for not having warned Daphne and her sister. A moment later, Scamp trotted up next to his master looking as innocent as a lamb. James scratched him behind his ears, earning a very thorough licking of his hand.

"I can see who is in charge in this relationship," Daphne said.

"The mongrel is," James acknowledged. "I don't suppose the Falstone wolf pack has His Grace wrapped around their fingers, or paws, as it were."

"Hardly." Daphne stroked the soft fur on Scamp's back. "The wolves are afraid of Adam just like everyone else."

Scamp spun about, applying himself to offering Daphne the same affection he'd just bestowed upon his master. When she too scratched behind his ears, the pup leapt enthusiastically onto her lap.

James attempted to scoop up the puppy, but it scrambled from his grasp and went directly back to Daphne. "This scoundrel has absolutely no manners," he said.

Daphne allowed Scamp to set to work once more licking her hand from every imaginable angle. "But he likes me."

James smiled at her. "That is decidedly a point in his favor."

"Are you certain that doesn't make him dim-witted as well as badly behaved?"

"Not dim-witted at all."

He kissed her fingers—those on the hand not being accosted by Scamp— just as he had the day before. Perhaps someday that token of affection might give way to an actual kiss. Daphne had often dreamed of kissing James Tilburn. More frequently of late, in fact.

Scamp apparently found the loss of their mutual attention insupportable. He dashed off, weaving in and around clumps of people, yelping and jumping and generally causing increasing levels of chaos.

James sighed ruefully. "I'd best go gather him up."

"I think your guests would appreciate that."

He rose, assuring Daphne he would return shortly, and hurried off after his misbehaving pet.

"Yes," Persephone said into the silence he left behind. "I believe Adam would entirely approve of your Lord Tilburn."

"*My* Lord Tilburn," she repeated quietly, watching as James tried to catch up with his recalcitrant puppy. "He is wonderful."

"So I have noticed." An amused laugh touched Persephone's voice. "And he seems to think highly of you as well."

"Do you think he might love me?" Daphne asked, hoping Persephone would give the same answer she had given herself.

"I believe he is beginning to."

"So do I," Daphne whispered, her heart flipping over at the thought.

"I am so very happy for you, Daphne. I truly am."

Scamp returned in the next moment, sans James. Daphne scanned the gathered guests but did not spot him. Was he still trying to find the little mongrel? Several minutes passed without a sign of him.

"Shall I track down your master?" She rubbed the puppy's head. James would no doubt appreciate knowing his search for Scamp had been rendered futile. She rose, Scamp following on her heels as she walked amongst the guests. James was not among them.

Scamp abandoned her a moment later, running headlong into a cluster of trees not too far distant.

"Scamp!" Daphne followed its path. How absurd if she were to find James only after losing his dog. He no doubt would simply smile at her as he always did.

The puppy, as it turned out, was very fast. Daphne stepped into the trees, but Scamp was nowhere to be seen. Where had he gone?

"I am doing my very best."

Daphne stopped at the unexpected sound of James's voice. He too had come into the clump of trees. Perhaps the pup ran in sensing his master was there. If not, they could certainly find the mongrel easier if they worked together.

Together. Daphne silently sighed at the joy of that single word. She had so often battled with feelings of loneliness. Only in moments of hopeful daydreaming had she imagined that changing so entirely.

She moved in the direction of James's voice, spotting him just on the other side of a close cluster of narrow-trunked trees. He was not alone, which made sense when she thought about it—he obviously had been speaking to someone. That someone, it turned out, was his father. Their conversation appeared to be of a very serious nature.

Neither had noticed her arrival. She stepped back a little, hoping to get away before being caught eavesdropping, however unintentional.

"I give you full credit, son, for making a good show," Lord Techney said. "But there is something lacking in your efforts. Others have noticed that you do not seem appropriately eager."

"On the contrary," James said. "I have heard any number of onlookers make quite the opposite observation."

It was a decidedly odd conversation. Eager about what? A good show of *what?*

"Do not think I will sit idly by while you make halfhearted efforts to fulfill your end of this bargain," Lord Techney said. "You know well the consequences of refusing to follow through with this."

James's father had done something. Daphne thought back on the past few days, on the time she'd spent with James. He'd never mentioned any looming crisis. He would have told her. They had grown close, confiding in each other, to a degree, at least.

"I have not withdrawn from our bargain," James said. "I am fulfilling it. I expect you to do so as well."

She should not have kept listening but couldn't shake the feeling that whatever James and his father were discussing was of utmost importance.

"Do not assume, Tilburn, that I have not pieced together your counterstrategy. If Miss Lancaster rejects your suit, you intend to argue that you still kept your part of our bargain, that you had undertaken the courtship as agreed but can't be held accountable for her rejection."

Daphne's lungs tightened to the point of pain. Counterstrategy? One that involved his expectations of a rejected suit? His apparent hope for a rejection. From *her.*

She slowly shook her head, attempting to dislodge the unease that satu-rated her every thought. His attentions had been too pointed to have been anything other than an effort at courting her. All of Society knew his inten-tions and the happiness with which she had accepted them.

"The outcome of all this does not rest on my shoulders alone," he said. "You may have the power to threaten Mother and Ben and even me, but you cannot threaten her. You cannot force her hand as you have forced mine."

Forced his hand? No. He could not have meant that.

"I am not interested in her choices, James. Only in the outcome of yours." Lord Techney spoke with every bit as much firmness as James had a moment earlier. "This family needs the connection, needs the boost to our status. Your efforts here are meant to secure that. You will not fail me in this."

Say he is wrong, Daphne silently begged James. *You are courting me because you like me. Tell him. Tell him you are beginning to love me.*

But no correction was forthcoming.

Daphne's surroundings lost focus, her eyes refusing to sharpen the painful scene playing out before her. She leaned heavily against the tree, her breaths coming in near-silent gasps. James was being forced to court her.

She could make out their silhouettes and hear the vague sound of their voices still in quiet conversation, but nothing made sense in her spinning mind. Each breath she took required more effort than the last. Her throat seemed to be closing off as she looked away.

He was courting her to obtain social status for his family, to fulfill an agreement he'd made with his father. He did not pay her these attentions out of adoration or tenderness or any of the other reasons she, in her fool-ishness, had imagined. The gentleman she'd silently adored for six years had courted her just as she'd hoped but hadn't meant a moment of it.

And that meant he didn't love her.

Hot tears stung Daphne's eyes. She had believed him. She had naively embraced his lies.

She heard Scamp bark but did not look about for him. If anything, her surroundings had grown more indiscernible. A nauseating weakness over-took her. Daphne had never swooned in the course of her entire life yet felt dangerously close to sinking to the ground.

Long-past memories she'd forced herself not to think about rushed head-long to the surface. "Such a lovely looking family, the Lancasters. Except for that little Daphne. A little mouse of a thing. Has not a bit of her mother's beauty. She'll not amount to much." "Go, Daphne"—her father's voice—"I would far rather be alone."

The deep, pulsating wounds those comments and dozens like them had inflicted over the years ripped through her anew. She closed her eyes, pressing her hand to her chest the way she'd done since childhood. She'd always managed to push back the pain, ignore the sting of ridicule and rejection until time lessened its impact. But as she stood there alone in the small cluster of trees, the anguish refused to be silenced. For the first time, she could not discount those caustic evaluations. She had only ever warranted the notice of one gentleman, and he had fabricated it all.

"Daphne?"

She recognized James's voice but didn't open her eyes.

"What's happened?" he asked. "Are you unwell?"

Unwell? A less-apt word had likely never been spoken. Daphne forced herself to look at him, allowing herself the tiniest morsel of hope that she would see in his eyes something to refute the bitter truth she had stumbled upon.

His expression was precisely the same one she'd seen repeatedly over the weeks: concern, sympathy. A quarter of an hour earlier, that look would have melted her. Now she felt only cold.

She had wept for days after Evander's death. She had probably cried when her mother had died, though she'd been too young at the time to remember. Outside of those two moments, she had met the slightest threat of tears with fierce resistance. Standing there so entirely alone, forced to face the horridness of her situation, she did not hold back the rush of emotion.

"Good heavens, Daphne. You're crying."

She flinched at the soft brush of his fingers along her cheek. His hand stilled immediately.

"What has happened? Why are—" He laid his hands on her arms. She pulled back. "How long have you been standing here?"

"Please leave me be," Daphne whispered.

"You may have misunderstood something you heard. I—"

She pushed away from the tree, distancing herself from him. "Just leave me alone."

The panic-stricken look on his face told her what would come next. He would attempt to explain it all, to justify a month's worth of lies. She could not bear it. No one should be made to endure so much deceit.

Daphne turned and walked swiftly in the direction of the house, though avoiding the gathered guests at the picnic. She did not slow as she crossed back to the house.

She dropped onto the small bench set near the door, pressing her hand to her wounded heart. She could not stay—not now. Certainly Persephone would agree to leave forthwith. She likely would not even press Daphne for an explanation.

She only sank further at the thought of facing Adam. How certain she'd been that time would prove his doubts unfounded. How assured she'd felt of James's regard. But she'd been wrong. So very wrong.

Her fairy-tale courtship was nothing but a lie.

Chapter Twenty-Five

DAPHNE APPRECIATED BEYOND EXPRESSING THAT Persephone allowed her to pass the brief carriage ride back to Falstone House in complete silence. It was a merciful gesture. She knew she would not be permitted to escape the reality of her discovery long. And as the falling out between her and James became known, there would be questions. So many questions.

They stepped inside just as Artemis came bounding down the stairs. "London is ever so much more fun than Shropshire," she declared, rounding the corner and disappearing toward the back of the house.

"Is His Grace home, then?" Persephone asked the butler as they were divested of their outer coats in the front entryway.

"Yes, Your Grace. In his book room."

"Excellent." Persephone turned to Daphne. "I do not wish to abandon you, but—"

"Please, go greet him," Daphne said. "I know you've missed him."

Persephone made her way directly toward the stairs. For the first time since Adam's departure from London more than a week earlier, Daphne saw a genuine smile on her sister's face.

Daphne stood in uncomfortable indecision. Where ought she to go? How desperately she wished for her own room, her own bed to cry on. But Adam would demand a full accounting of her situation. She would rather not make that painful confession with her youngest sister listening in. Delaying the inevitable struck her as decidedly illogical, even if it was understandable from an emotional perspective.

"You have done quite enough thinking with your heart of late," she told herself. "It is high time you remembered how to lead with your head." Daphne nodded to herself, hoping to solidify her determination. She did not allow the slightest slump in her posture as she followed Persephone's path. She reached the book room door only a moment after her sister did.

Persephone lightly rapped on the door as she slowly opened it.

"I told you, Hampton, I did not wish to be disturbed today by anyone regardless of their business with me." Adam sounded thoroughly annoyed. That would make their coming interview all the more uncomfortable.

Persephone did not seem particularly put off by his tone. "Oh, but my business with you is of a most crucial nature," she said from the doorway.

Adam's head snapped up and turned in the direction of the door. "Persephone." He whispered the name almost as though it were a prayer. He abandoned his papers and desk and crossed the room. His intense gaze never left Persephone's face. "You"—he took her face in his hands—"are never again to remain behind when I leave Town. Ever."

Daphne stepped back into the corridor, uncomfortable for the first time with their poignant display of affection. She used to watch them and daydream of receiving the same tender regard. Those moments of wishful imaginings had been easier before James had made her believe those hopes could actually become reality.

She stood against the wall beside the book room door, taking long breaths and attempting to maintain her fragile calm. Tears served no purpose anymore. The time had come to be rational.

She could hear Persephone's voice once more. Adam had apparently concluded his greeting enough for her to speak. "I was not expecting you for several days yet."

"You were so busy leaping from one social event to the next, you were not even here when I arrived," Adam countered. "It does not seem to me that I was at all missed."

Daphne inched her way back into the doorway, her heart hurting a tiny bit more at the sight of her sister and brother-in-law quite happily in one another's arms.

"Would you like me to get back into the carriage and ride about a bit longer so you can fully appreciate my return?" Persephone's teasing tone would normally have brought a smile to Daphne's face. Adam brought out a side of Persephone's personality that was decidedly lighter than Daphne remembered seeing in all their growing-up years.

"If you so much as set one foot out of this house, I will have you locked up." Adam, of course, sounded entirely serious. His expressions of affection were usually grumbled and, to those who did not know him well, often sounded vaguely threatening.

"You are pleased, then, to have me home?"

"Infinitely. Though the staff indicated you would not be back for a few more hours. What brought about the early return?"

Daphne squared her shoulders. She would not force Persephone to make the explanation. She took a single step inside the book room, near enough to be heard but at a distance that hid her red-rimmed eyes. "I asked that we return early."

Adam looked away from Persephone, his gaze meeting Daphne's. "*You* asked? How strange. I was half convinced I would be required to pry you away from Techney House by sheer force, considering your Lord Tilburn was there."

She did not allow herself to so much as twinge at his excessively dry tone. Adam did not know how deeply she'd been hurt. Daphne did not intend to allow anyone to realize how desperately she'd wanted James to love her. The only thing more pathetic than a girl who had never been loved was one who wrongly thought she had been. She refused to spend the remainder of her life an object of pity. "As the purpose of my attending the various functions at Techney House these past weeks was to further explore the possibility of a match between myself and Lord Tilburn, my presence there no longer seemed necessary."

Adam stood beside Persephone with his arm comfortably around her waist. The two of them watched her with growing confusion and concern.

"You no longer welcome Lord Tilburn's suit?" Persephone asked.

"It seems we would not suit after all." She had often heard young ladies give just that explanation when a potential beau did not prove to be "the one."

"What utter rot." Anyone other than Adam would have rolled their eyes when using a tone of voice that so required the gesture. He never stooped to such a thing. "Though I had my misgivings, even a simpleton could see you two suit each other better than most courting couples." Adam's look of disbelief spoke volumes against Daphne's chances of escaping without being forced to provide a drawn-out explanation.

Still, she attempted to circumvent that unpleasant outcome. "As I said, we would not suit."

He shook his head. "That argument won't do. Try another one."

"We *really* would not suit."

Adam sat on the edge of his desk, keeping Persephone's hand in his. "This seems a rather drastic change."

A bit of redirection was more than called for. "I don't imagine she has told you, but Persephone has been quite ill during your brief absence from London."

"You were ill?" Adam was immediately consumed by this newest revelation, just as Daphne had known he would be. He cared about his sisters-in-law, but he treasured his wife. Her well-being would trump that of any other person's on earth. "How ill? Do I need to summon a physician?"

"I consulted with one several days ago."

That was news to Daphne. Why had she not been included? Her role in the family's health was long established. Yet she had not been told of this latest development, one serious enough to warrant the services of a physician.

"Why was I not sent for?" The concern in Adam's voice took some of the edge from his demanding tone.

"For the simple reason that my various complaints, while something of a misery, are not the least unusual for a woman who is soon to be a mother and need not cause concern in her husband"—her tone softened—"who is soon to be a father."

"A father?" His brow pulled deep, his eyes searching his wife's face. For once in all the years Daphne had known him, Adam appeared at a loss for words. "It has been seven years. I assumed—"

Persephone leaned her head against his chest. "So had I."

Adam pulled her into an embrace, his expression equal parts awe and affection. "We're to be parents?" he whispered.

"You are happy, then?" she asked from within the circle of his arms.

"Oh, Persephone." The two words emerged on a shaking, quiet breath.

Daphne slipped quietly from the room. She had intended only to provide a distraction by bringing up Persephone's illness. Instead, she had forced upon them a conversation her sister had likely hoped to undertake with more privacy.

They were to be parents. Though neither had told Daphne as much, she felt certain their hearts had broken over the past years worrying and wondering and wishing over the possibility of children. She was deeply happy for them both. Fate meant to be kind to at least some of the members of this family, and for that she was truly grateful.

She walked down the corridor to the drawing room, knowing it would be empty and therefore quiet. She took one step inside and realized she was wrong.

A young naval officer with golden curls and familiar green eyes stood near the window, smiling at her as she walked in. Her heart flipped about in her chest. Linus had arrived at last.

"I had hoped Adam wouldn't entirely monopolize your time," he said with a grin. "He is only a brother-*in-law*, after all. My claim on your attention is certainly greater."

"Good afternoon, Linus."

"*Good afternoon, Linus?* I have been away at sea for half a year, and all I am to expect is a halfhearted *Good afternoon, Linus?*" He tsked and shook his head, his trademark smile never slipping. "No doubt you would have had an embrace for Evander."

"Evander would not have teased me." Indeed, Evander would have embraced *her*.

"Guilty." Linus sighed. "Could you not spare me the slightest bit of sisterly affection—I am quite starved for it, I assure you."

"If you are in need of overt displays of adoration, I am certain Artemis would oblige you. Such things are far more her forte than mine."

Linus crossed closer to her. He had grown since she had last seen him, and not just in height. The navy, it seemed, did not produce scrawny men. She was absolutely dwarfed by him. "You have been crying," he said, his tone changing quickly to one of concern. "What has happened?"

"Nothing that an afternoon nap won't address." How easily the lie slipped off her tongue. She had no intention of telling all the world the true state of her heart.

"After all Adam's grumblings about you being 'so blasted cheerful' and having some lordling courting you, I fully expected to see you bouncing about the place, humming and dropping flower petals in your wake," Linus said.

"You expected to see me acting like an imbecile?"

He chucked her under the chin. "Are you feeling grumpy today, Little Daphne?"

She turned away. "Don't talk to me as though I were a child, Linus. I am eighteen years old. Just because I am small—"

He nimbly stepped around her, stopping directly in front of her. With an apologetic smile, he said, "I hadn't meant to hurt your feelings. And bear in mind, I have only seen you a handful of times since you were eight. I forget sometimes that you have quite grown up over the past decade."

She nodded. The mistake was understandable when looked at logically. "I am always surprised at how very much you change between visits."

"I grow handsomer each time, is that it?" He chuckled even as he tucked foppishly at his cuffs. Linus always did enjoy making others laugh. She liked that about him, though she acutely missed Evander's tender constancy.

"How long before you must return to sea?" she asked. "I daresay your leave will be cut short considering the situation with the former colonies."

"Actually, that is why I had hoped to intercept you." His jovial expression sobered once more.

"Has something happened?"

"Come sit with me a moment," Linus said, indicating the nearby sofa. When she obeyed, he followed and sat beside her. "I need your opinion on a matter of great importance."

His uncharacteristic gravity made her uneasy.

"You have always had a very good head on your shoulders and, even as a child, showed remarkably good judgment. I have found myself in a difficult situation and could use some advice."

"Of course." She would do anything to help her family. In that moment, she welcomed the distraction as much as the opportunity to be of assistance.

"Father's health has taken a decided turn for the worse," Linus said.

"Adam hinted at that. How bad is he?"

Linus took hold of her hand as if offering strength in the face of bad news. Daphne's heart crept into her throat.

"The physician does not expect him to live to the end of the year."

He is dying. She blinked hard. How often had she tried to help him, to heal him? It was all for naught.

"At the risk of sounding insensitive," Linus said, "the situation leaves me in a bind. I am Father's only heir. The estate and all the responsibilities that go with it fall to me. It is my duty to return to the family seat and take up my role there, but—"

"But you also feel an obligation to the navy," she said, thinking she understood.

"An obligation, yes, but a pull as well. I enjoy the sea. I enjoy the adventure and challenge. What would I do on land? It seems almost preposterous."

"You have spent nearly half your life at sea, Linus. Of course living on land is a daunting prospect, perhaps even an unwelcome one at the moment."

He sighed in audible relief. "Then I'm not merely a bad son?"

Daphne patted his hand. "Not at all. When you have spent years imagining your future one way, you cannot expect to let go of that without some resistance and—" Her stomach twisted at the painful realization that she might have been speaking about herself. "And regrets."

"I'm not sure I'm ready to end my naval career, but I also don't know if leaving the estate behind won't simply render me unable to focus enough to be of any use to the rest of the crew."

Determining the direction of one's future when one's present has fallen completely to shambles—Daphne knew very well the overwhelming nature of that dilemma. "Perhaps you need to give yourself time to decide. When does your ship put out to sea again?"

"Three weeks."

"And how long before its departure do you need to make your decision?"

Linus seemed to think a moment. "I could probably hold off on the decision up until two days before; that would allow for a very hasty trip to port if that is what I decide."

"You simply need to decide to be calm about it." Calm. Rational. "Think through what you want to do. Be logical."

Linus nodded, looking calmer already. "It would probably help to talk to Adam about the needs of the estate and what condition it is in. And I may write to my captain, ask for his opinion on how much I might be needed on board."

"Yes." Daphne spoke as much to herself as to her brother. "Find where you are needed and in what capacity you are most likely to be happy."

Linus wrapped an arm around her shoulders and gave her a very brotherly squeeze. "Evander always did say you had more wisdom than the whole family combined. Thank you for sharing a bit of it with me." He got to his feet, looking a little more himself but with a lingering hint of uncertainty in his eyes. "Now, one more nugget of knowledge, if you will. Where am I most likely to find Artemis?"

"She passed by just as Persephone and I reached home. I believe she was headed toward the back of the house, no doubt the garden."

He smiled mischievously. "I believe I will see if I can startle her enough to produce one of her famous feigned swoons." On that declaration, he made his way out of the room.

The day had begun on such a promising note, but then everything had fallen apart.

Father was dying. Though she'd not had his companionship for years, owing to the distance between them, both physical and mental, the thought of never seeing him again, never hearing his voice, drove a sharp shaft of pain deep into her heart.

What good were her remedies and tonics now? She would soon lose her father, and there was nothing she could do about it.

She closed her eyes against a flood of painful memories.

"Please drink it, Papa," her nine-year-old self pleaded. "You will feel better."

"I will be very quiet," she, with her voice that was younger still, promised. "Only let me stay with you."

Across a mere five years came her voice again. "Come live with us at Falstone Castle. Please. I cannot bear to leave you behind again."

His response had seldom varied. "Leave me be. I am happier on my own."

Her father preferred to not be with her. He was happier without her company. And he wasn't the only one to leave her behind. Evander had. Linus had just now left without a backward glance. Adam and Persephone had their own lives, of which she was only a cursory part.

And James. James had been playing a role from the beginning. How was so much heartache to be endured?

"Find where you are needed." She repeated her own advice.

But where was she needed? With Persephone consulting physicians without even a word of input from Daphne, something that in the past had generally always been done, her apothecary abilities didn't seem likely to give her purpose amongst them, at least not to the extent they once had.

Her afternoons with Adam had seemed helpful to him, giving him someone with whom he could discuss ideas and philosophies and issues of the day. She was needed in that respect. In time, the child he and Persephone were now anticipating would likely take her place in that. Adam would have his own child to raise and care for.

Her happiness for her sister and brother-in-law came with an unexpected surge of something very like mourning. Their own family was expanding, and she would not truly be part of it.

A maiden aunt could be appreciated and enjoyed, but she would not really be *needed*. She would be unessential again, just as she'd been when she was a child. Evander would not be there to make certain she was noticed.

Adam would be occupied with more personal concerns. Persephone, who had taken on the role of mother to Artemis when she was an infant, would take up that duty once more with her own child.

Daphne would have no place. She had learned as a child that usefulness went a long way to extending one's welcome. Perhaps a more in-depth study of her herbs would make her an asset to the community around Falstone Castle. If the local families and the vicar and even the staff at the castle benefited from her knowledge and skills, then she would serve a purpose among them. And she would stay busy. Endless occupation left a person with far less time for focusing on regrets.

Chapter Twenty-Six

FATHER WAS IN A RARE taking. He summoned James to the library the morning after the disastrous picnic. Only the obvious tension in Father's jaw belied his composed demeanor. James remained standing as he waited for the lecture. He knew precisely what Father would say and did not intend to drag out the interview.

"I understand Miss Lancaster left in quite a hurry yesterday," Father said.

"She and her sister chose to return to their London residence before the picnic began."

Father's gaze narrowed. "When do you intend to call on her again?"

"I do not, Father." James borrowed a page from Father's book, keeping his own expression confident and unruffled. "It seems we would not suit after all."

"You have ended your courtship?" Father gave him the look that always indicated his doubt in James's intelligence.

"No."

The slightest hint of relief entered Father's expression.

James kept his tone bland. "*She* ended the courtship. Quite unequivocally, in fact."

Father's gaze hardened. "What have you done?"

A question James had asked himself multiple times. He would not allow his father to see how upset he truly was over the previous day's events. "It seems you underestimated Miss Lancaster's intelligence—we both did. She discovered the true nature of this courtship and decided she deserved better."

Father remained silent, his expression frozen in a look of contemplation. He, no doubt, was composing some new plan or another. He would suggest a new strategy, an attempt to convince Daphne to trust him again. James wanted no part of it.

He spoke before his father could. "My conduct these past weeks does not bear scrutiny. I look back on the decisions I have made and the course I have taken, and I am—" He pushed out a tense breath. His self-evaluation had not been pleasant. "I am entirely ashamed of myself."

"Ashamed?" Father's scoffing tone left little doubt as to the state of *his* conscience.

"I acted dishonorably. Though the duke was the one to suggest the possibility of a courtship between Miss Lancaster and I, he would never have approved of me doing so insincerely. He watched me with such suspicion that I am relatively certain he had begun to see through the masquerade. And I, for my own well-being, simply tried that much harder to be convincing. I misled him and the duchess by word and deed. And my deliberately deceptive courtship of Miss Lancaster was absolutely inexcusable." James straightened his shoulders. "It is time I regained my hold on my own integrity."

"You intend to simply let her walk away?" Tension entered Father's tone. He so seldom allowed any emotion to color his words. James knew the interview would grow worse before he was permitted to leave.

"I intend to not impose upon her further."

Father leaned forward, pressing his forearms against his desk and meeting James's eyes with a look of warning. "You know the consequences of failure."

"I think, Father, you and I define *failure* a little differently."

Father didn't so much as flinch. "You will no longer receive your income from the estate. Neither will your brother."

"He is resilient." James knew the loss would be a burden to Ben, and he would do all he could to help.

"That is rather coldhearted for you, Tilburn." The comment was obviously meant as a mockery, an attempt to ruffle him.

"A trait, one could argue, I come by rightly."

Father seemed to recognize the barb, though he did not acknowledge it. "Can you view your mother's penury with so much indifference?"

"Not indifference, Father. Resignation. I know better than to expect you to act in a way that places any importance on the well-being of your family. I can do nothing to stop you from punishing any of us."

Father shifted again. If James hadn't spent a lifetime watching the man, he might have almost thought his father had grown uncomfortable. He knew better. Father was simply adjusting his attack.

"What of this family's standing?" Father asked. "We will never be able to hold our heads up in Society again."

"You know perfectly well that aborted courtships seldom reflect badly on the gentleman involved. This family stands at the mercy not of my actions but of Miss Lancaster's and, more daunting still, the Duke of Kielder. His Grace could destroy us with a word. I doubt he would hesitate at all to do so. He is the one you ought to be bargaining with, not me. You two formulated the original agreement after all."

Father paled noticeably. "The duke does not make bargains. Everyone knows that."

"Then perhaps you should go begging, on your knees, for mercy. Though it is my understanding he isn't overly fond of that either."

"No. That won't be necessary. I can fix this." Father nodded repeatedly. "I can fix this."

"How—?"

Father held a hand up to cut him off. "I can't fix it for *you*. But I can make things right for me and for this title you do not deserve to inherit. I need not be brought down by your idiocy."

James didn't dare even guess what Father was planning now. "Good-bye, Father. Go save your precious standing. I have far more crucial things to worry about." He turned on his heel and left the room, intending to put to rights the many things he'd done wrong of late. Refusing to allow Father to manipulate him into sacrificing his integrity once again was but one item on his list. Talking to Ben was another.

The butler approached James as he reached the foot of the stairs.

"You look concerned, Billingsley," James said.

"Cook has declared that she cannot prepare the venison her ladyship has requested," the butler explained. "The meat intended for this evening has gone off."

"Can she not obtain another cut? Or simply prepare a different dish?"

"I could not say, my lord," the butler replied. "She wished the matter settled by you."

"No one else in the family is capable of seeing to this?" Why had he even asked the question? No one was ever capable of handling anything.

"Lady Techney directed the issue to you."

Of course she did. "I will see to it."

The butler seemed satisfied and left to see to his other duties. On his way to the kitchen, James encountered the gardener, who spoke at length about an aphid infestation. Moments after directing the gardener to do his best in dealing with the pests, James addressed the coachman's concern over the need for a new axle on the traveling coach before the family returned to Lancashire. Then a footman gave James a letter from the gamekeeper at Techney Manor expressing concerns about poachers. This was Father's estate, deuce take it, yet everything fell on James's shoulders—James, who had been cut off by his father. James, who had been all but disinherited. He needed a respite, an ally. He'd had that for one brief moment, and he'd thrown it away. He'd lost Daphne's friendship as well as her unfailingly calm head in the midst of trouble, her support and encouragement.

He pushed back his regrets, something he'd done almost constantly since her departure, and set his mind to discovering his brother's very effective hiding place. After a moment's contemplation, the answer became clear. The only place a gentleman could have any hope of avoiding company was in his own bedchamber.

James knocked on Ben's door. His business with his brother held greater sway than the crises of the staff.

Ben opened the door, nodding to James.

"Ben, I—" James's eyes darted around the room, taking in the traveling trunk awaiting attention. "Are you leaving?"

Ben dropped a pair of cuff links into a drawstring bag and tossed it into a portmanteau. "In the morning."

An open traveling case sat half full on the floor. Several shirts lay strewn across the bed.

"When did you make this decision?" Had he offended his brother somehow?

Ben carefully folded a shirt—he hadn't the means to hire a valet to see to his clothing. "When I received the invitation from Mr. Windover."

Windover? "Miss Lancaster's brother-in-law?"

Ben nodded, his eyes wide with obvious anticipation. "We've been corresponding ever since Miss Lancaster wrote to tell him of my situation. I received an invitation this morning to be a guest at his home. He offered to show me around his land and talk about investments and changes that might help me begin to turn around my own estate."

Investments Ben would soon not have the income to undertake. James had decided the night before that he ought to have been up front with his brother from the beginning. Ben's income had been on the line, and he had deserved to know so he could prepare himself for the possibility of failure on James's part. Yet another well-meaning mistake he had made.

"I am afraid I have some bad news," James said, his stomach twisting. How did one tell one's brother that he had gambled away his inheritance?

"How bad?" Ben did not seem terribly concerned, his focus still on his packing.

"It involves Father."

Ben looked up at him. "That *is* bad. What did he do this time?"

No words came. Ben was going to lose everything. He couldn't think of any way to ease the impact of that revelation. All the effort Ben had gone to, the sacrifices he'd made over the past couple of years, his newfound correspondent would be for naught.

"James?"

James sat on the edge of the bed, reminding himself that Ben needed to know his situation before he committed to anything he could no longer afford. "My courtship with Miss Lancaster fell through."

"I noticed." Ben watched him in obvious curiosity, though not a great deal of worry.

"Father forced the courtship with threats I could not ignore." James took a deep breath. "One of those threats involved you."

Ben sat beside him, looking concerned for the first time. "What did he threaten to do?"

"With the match no longer a possibility, Father is going to cut off your income." There. It was out. "I'll do what I can to help you, but he's cutting me off as well. It—"

"James."

"—won't be much, but I'll come up with something."

"James."

"You won't—"

"Blast it, James. Stop talking and listen to me."

James nodded. Ben would be angry, and rightly so. But he deserved that. He would take whatever tongue-lashing his brother chose to inflict.

"You agreed to Father's scheme because he threatened to cut off my income from the estate?" Ben asked.

James nodded. "And Mother's pin money."

"And when he made these threats, did you check to make certain he had the ability to follow through with them?" Ben's tone was very nearly condescending.

"He controls all facets of the estate, Ben. He—"

"Cannot violate the terms of his and Mother's marriage settlement." Ben shifted enough to look James in the eye. "When I inherited my 'little bit of land,' as Father calls it, I had a solicitor look into my financial situation, including my quarterly allowance from the Techney estate. I wanted to know how much reliable income I had to work with." His gaze intensified, and he leaned a touch closer. "Father and Mother's marriage settlement set forth and guaranteed the amount any *younger* sons would receive from the estate."

"Then"—James's mind reeled as he pieced together what Ben was saying—"Father cannot cut you off?"

"No."

"It was an empty threat." The thought had never occurred to him.

"Incidentally," Ben said, "the marriage settlement also guarantees—"

"Mother's pin money." James knew the truth of it even as he spoke the words.

"I am afraid you have been duped, James."

James clenched his fists. Father had tricked him into compromising everything he stood for. It had all been a lie.

A string of unflattering assessments of both himself and his father issued forth with the fluency borne of years of silent cursings. He'd sold his integrity for a pack of lies. Like an utter imbecile, he hadn't even checked to see if Father had the ability to follow through.

A surge of bleakness tempered his anger. He had failed horribly.

Ben stood once more, a decidedly empathetic expression on his face. "I suppose, though, as the heir, you've never before had reason to wonder if you could be permanently cut off."

He had never worried about that. Father could not ultimately disinherit him. "It is rather ridiculous, then, that his threat to beggar me is the only one he has the power to see through. That is the one that did not work to begin with."

"The income of the heir was not specified in the marriage settlements," Ben said, empathy ringing deep in his tone.

"Lucky me," James muttered.

"What do you plan to do?"

James stood, an odd sense of numbness overtaking him. "I need to find someone to look after Mother—guard her from Father's coldness."

"A companion?" Ben asked.

James nodded. "A *fierce* companion, but one who will treat her with kindness."

"That likely should have been done years ago," Ben said.

James took a fortifying breath, his mind already listing the necessary steps to finding his mother a lady to keep her company and champion her. "I also need to find a source of income," he said as much to himself as his brother.

"Employment?"

He couldn't blame Ben for being shocked. Few members of the *ton* would lower themselves to seeking work. Most would live off their expectations or the generosity of their friends. "I've made enough selfish decisions lately. It's time I begin taking responsibility for myself."

Ben laid a hand on his shoulder. "Do you remember all those times we talked about finding the strength to choose our own paths? It is time you made good on those long-ago promises to yourself."

His own path. "That is a daunting prospect for a fellow who is at his lowest point and rather glaringly alone."

"You may have lost the devotion of a very remarkable lady, one who could probably navigate this maze with her eyes shut and her hands tied behind her back—"

James smiled a bit at the picture his brother painted. Daphne was, by all accounts, awe-inspiring. So capable and determined. He would never find another lady like her.

"—but you still have me," Ben finished. "I know poverty rather well. I'll show you how to live it in style."

"I look forward to your tutelage." James tried for a rueful smile, the effort feeling as though it fell decidedly short of the mark.

"Now get out so I can pack." Ben's smile took all the sting out of his words. But as quickly as it had appeared, his smile faded. "I wish all of this hadn't hurt Miss Lancaster."

"I made her cry, Ben." Regret solidified as a lump in his throat. "She deserves so much better than the way I've treated her."

"You said before that you thought the two of you could have been happy together. Was that just wishful thinking or . . . ?" Ben let the rest of the question dangle unspoken.

"I haven't stopped thinking about her since yesterday. Not just the regrets and the hating myself for what I did, but thinking about *her.* Where she is. How she's feeling. What it would take to see her again, and how impossible that hope is."

Ben set his hand on James's shoulder. "I am sorry . . . about everything."

"So am I," James said. "More sorry than I can even say."

"What comes next?" Ben asked.

"I need to talk to Mother." He only hoped she would hold up. Difficulties undid her easily.

He stepped inside his mother's bedchamber, coming face-to-face with the writing desk where Daphne had expertly concocted teas and tisanes to see Mother through that difficult night. He stood there a moment, mourning what might have been.

"James." Mother's characteristically quiet voice reached him from her place near the fire. She was out of bed. That was a good sign. "I am so pleased you've come. I had hoped we could visit before I returned to Lancashire."

He pulled up the ottoman and sat at her feet, as he'd often done as a child. "I was hoping for the same thing, as a matter of fact."

She gave him a look of something bordering on pity. "What happened with Miss Lancaster?"

He quickly explained how Daphne had overheard his conversation with Father and had learned of the real reason he had begun to court her. He could still remember so clearly the pain in her face, the devastation. She had cried. The sight haunted him.

"What did your father threaten to do if you refused?" Mother asked.

"Something I have come to find out he has not the authority to do," James answered.

"James." She lightly touched his hand, a hesitancy in the gesture that had never been there before. "I know you want to shield me from unpleasantness, the way you do everyone, but I would really like to know."

He couldn't immediately bring himself to burden her with the full extent of her husband's villainy. "He threatened you and Ben." He shifted uncomfortably at the idea of discussing this with her. She was too easily overwhelmed by difficulties. He offered what he hoped she interpreted as an apologetic look.

"If Miss Lancaster had asked you the details of a problem you were dealing with, no matter how difficult that problem might have been, would you have told *her*?"

James did not even have to ponder the question. He would have told her and without hesitation. Daphne would not only have remained collected during the conversation; she would have talked with him, helped him sort out the trouble.

"I watched you with her," Mother said. "She changed you. And though I was extremely reluctant to accept what was so obvious, feeling as though doing so was somehow betraying you, she changed you for the better. Do you know that it has been years since I have heard you laugh?"

Truly? He did not remember being so unhappy.

"Seeing you the day the two of you played lawn bowls was like watching a completely different person. The tension you always carry melted away, your"—her voice broke—"your *eyes* were smiling, James. I have not seen that since you were a tiny boy."

He had felt it too. For once, his responsibilities hadn't felt like burdens. He had truly enjoyed himself in a way he hadn't in years.

"I wanted to hate her for taking away your control over your own future, but the more I knew her, the more I found disliking her impossible."

He placed his hand over Mother's where it still rested on his arm and lightly squeezed her fingers. "Miss Lancaster is a remarkable person. I don't believe anyone could possibly dislike her."

"You would walk into a room," Mother said, "and your eyes would search the whole of it until you found her. A look of relief would cross your face, as though simply knowing she was nearby comforted you on the instant. *That* I could not explain away. Nor the fact that you turned to her so naturally when even the smallest difficulty arose or to make some witty observation or simply to talk to her. You are not one to open yourself up to people in that way."

Daphne had been an easy and natural confidante, something he hadn't expected.

"Do you love her, James?" Such a direct question was unlike Mother.

"Ben asked me the same thing."

"And what did you tell your brother?"

"Father's edict may have instigated this courtship, but the more I knew her, the more time I spent with her, the less I thought about the beginnings of all this. The courtship became real in my mind." It truly had. "I like her a great deal."

"You like the puppy a great deal, son," Mother said dryly. "Be honest with yourself, even if you cannot be fully honest with me."

"I suppose that is hard when I know there is no hope," James said. "I imposed upon her in a way I can never fully forgive myself. I am quite certain she never will. That is a difficult poison to swallow."

"How awful it is that my objections stemmed from wishing you to be happy with someone you loved." Mother's smile was infinitely sad. "In the end, you fell in love with her anyway, and now you are more unhappy than before."

You fell in love with her. He had, though he'd not before fully admitted it. He loved her, and she most likely hated him for what he'd done.

"Please do not fret over me," James said. "I am making the best of my situation. And I have not forgotten the difficulty with tonight's venison. I mean to suggest Cook make fish, as I know you like fish very much, and it should not be difficult to obtain."

She reached up and touched his face. "You always were such a wonderful, thoughtful boy. Growing up has not changed that."

His attempt at a change of topic had not worked. "I have not felt very wonderful or thoughtful of late. What gentleman could, knowing he had so poorly treated a lady he cared so much for?"

She held her arms open to him. Like the little boy he'd once been, he accepted her embrace gladly and with such need. He felt lost and alone and, in that moment, needed his mother.

"I love you, my dear James. And I have never lost faith in you."

Now, if only he could find reason to have faith in himself.

Chapter Twenty-Seven

JAMES STOOD, HAT IN HAND, in the entryway of Falstone House while the butler delivered his card to the Dangerous Duke. If ever a person had embarked on a fool's errand, he had. But this was something he could not leave undone.

The butler reappeared. "His Grace says you may join him in his book room, but he advises you not to."

Most any gentleman would take that warning and flee with all possible haste. James, however, had made his choice long before arriving here. The duke's temper was infamous, and James had to be absolutely certain Daphne had borne no blame for what he had done.

"I will join His Grace in the book room, thank you."

The butler's seemingly unbreakable mask of dignified professionalism slipped. "Truly?" he sputtered before recovering himself. "Very well, my lord." He turned and led the way up the stairs toward the first floor, no doubt still looking a touch shocked.

At the door to the book room, James paused long enough to firm his resolve. If His Grace's reputation was at all based in fact, James might find himself in need of assistance to simply leave the house.

The door to the book room stood slightly ajar. Pushing it open and stepping inside, the butler announced, "Lord Tilburn, Your Grace," in a voice entirely devoid of his earlier astonishment.

James stepped inside only to be met by the Duke of Kielder's glare as he stood not ten feet from the doorway.

"Only a fool would have come up after being warned not to," the duke said.

James nodded his understanding. "I believe that is one of the more accurate evaluations of myself I have heard lately."

An unfamiliar voice chimed in. "Methinks the fool speaks in riddles."

A single glance identified the third occupant of the room. He wore the uniform of the Royal Navy. His green eyes and golden curls immediately connected him to the youngest Lancaster sister.

"Linus," the Duke said, "you see before you the very definition of an imbecile."

"Ah."

"Tilburn, this is Lieutenant Lancaster."

James managed a creditable bow despite his growing apprehension. Confronting Daphne's violent-tempered guardian had been an intimidating enough prospect. Having her older brother present, he who had spent half his life training for battle, only made the situation worse. "I am pleased to meet you," he said.

"Odd," Lieutenant Lancaster replied. "I am not at all pleased to meet *you*."

"I deserve that."

The lieutenant's expression remained thoroughly displeased. "Oh, you deserve far more than that."

James nodded. "Agreed."

The duke seemed to abruptly lose patience with the exchange. He made his way to one side of the room and sat behind a large desk.

James turned to watch him, only then getting a good look at the desk where the duke now sat. The entire surface was covered with weaponry. Several dueling pistols rested beside a hunting rifle. *Who brings a hunting rifle to London?* A good portion of the desktop housed swords of varying lengths, and a particularly dangerous-looking dagger sat nearest the duke's right hand.

His gaze met the duke's. Never before had a single look chilled James to his very core. "In light of the fact that there are ladies present in the house, I opted to leave the more menacing weapons out of sight," the duke said. "Though several are still within reach."

James had a feeling he did not want to know what or where the hidden weapons were. "Yes, Your Grace." James's eyes swept the arsenal once more before shifting of their own accord to the lieutenant standing at the duke's shoulder, his hand resting ominously on the hilt of his uniform sword.

The duke picked up the dagger, casually spinning it about in his hand. "I assume you have come to plead your case. I suggest you do so quickly—that is my least favorite part of these encounters."

"His *most* favorite part involves the weaponry," the lieutenant said. "All of it."

He detected not an ounce of bravado in the declaration. "I have not come intent on defending myself, Your Grace. If I had only my own interests at heart, I would have fled to Lancashire or the Americas or someplace farther still."

"A much safer distance," the duke said, still handling the dagger with an alarming degree of finesse. "I did, after all, promise that if you hurt my Daphne, I would remove your vital organs with a blunt instrument."

James swallowed back a lump of apprehension. "I came because I have been concerned about Miss Lancaster."

"No doubt an oddly unfamiliar sensation," Lieutenant Lancaster observed dryly.

James had anticipated making his statement, enduring some kind of painful punishment, then limping away. The tongue lashing came as a surprise.

Perhaps a fast and detailed recounting of the truth of all that had occurred was best. The duke could not possibly think Miss Lancaster complicit if he knew the whole of it. That was James's first priority. "When my father first told me of your suggestion that I court your sister-in-law, I will admit I was hesitant. However—"

"I would never make such a harebrained suggestion." The duke's interruption was more growled than spoken.

For a moment, those words did not sort themselves into any degree of sense. "Shortly before Miss Lancaster's first at-home," James reminded him. "My father told me you approached him suggesting that I court your sister-in-law, beginning with calling on her."

"Calling on her was *all* I suggested."

Could that be true? Had Father lied? James's heart sank to his stomach. Of course Father had lied. He had done little but lie. "Calling on her was all I agreed to at first, along with offering a friendly greeting should I see her at balls or soirees."

The duke and lieutenant appeared wholly unimpressed with his original adherence to gentlemanly behavior.

"Under the influence of my father's threats and machinations, I allowed myself to be manipulated into pursuing a match with Miss Lancaster and did so by giving the impression of an eager and willing suitor and purporting a deeper affection than I felt."

"You lied to her." The duke's words were tight, angry.

"I did." He swallowed against the lump of regret and apprehension in his throat. "When your sister-in-law learned of my behavior, she put an end to our association, and rightly so. I am concerned that she will be blamed."

"She is a young lady who was actively and publicly courted," the duke said. "Every expectation was raised of a connection, and that courtship has ended. All of Society will blame her, and your perfidy will follow her, perhaps for years. My standing and influence will significantly lessen what she will endure, but even I cannot eliminate it entirely. She will suffer, and for that, Tilburn, I should run you through right here and now."

"But you do not blame her? You won't hold this debacle against her?" He cared too much for Daphne to allow her to be further injured if he could at all prevent it.

The duke pointed his dagger directly at James. "You risked your very life by confronting me in order to save her from mistreatment when you yourself are guilty of doing her an egregious injustice, of taking advantage of her good and kind heart, of subjecting her to the ridicule of an unforgiving Society?"

"Yes, Your Grace."

Far from improving the duke's opinion of him, James's declaration seemed to annoy his interrogator further. "And what do you hope to gain by this? Do you think I will plead your case to Daphne?"

"No, sir. Not at all."

The tension in His Grace's countenance emphasized the massive scarring that marred his face. The web of badly healed skin pulled James's attention despite himself.

Lieutenant Lancaster stepped around the desk, his gaze uncomfortably scrutinizing.

"I understand, Tilburn," His Grace said, "that you have arranged for your mother to have a companion. Your brother's financial position is relatively sound. Further, your father is withholding your income for the remainder of his pathetic life. Does that accurately sum up your situation?"

Surprised, James nodded once more. How had the duke come by such detailed information so quickly? He didn't think all of those things were common knowledge.

"Might I suggest"—more than a hint of condescension colored the duke's words—"when you are lord of your father's estate, you consider the possibility of hiring a new steward? The man I sent had only to buy the gum-flapper two pints at the local ale house before he knew everything there was to know about you and your family."

James sat in stunned silence. The duke's servant had plied the Techney man of business with ale in order to ask prying questions? What else was the duke willing to do to accomplish his ends?

His Grace showed no outward signs of a guilty conscience over something that most would consider more than a touch underhanded. "If any member of my staff so much as discussed my morning meal preferences, I would dismiss him forthwith." James would feel more at ease if he knew just what the duke's intentions were toward *him*.

"What do you intend to do about your current financial state?"

Likely the duke knew precisely James's plans, thanks to that drunkard of a servant. Honesty was decidedly the best approach. "I am looking to secure employment, perhaps as a gentleman's secretary. I do have some experience in the political arena and could likely make myself useful. I mean to give it my very best effort, at least." Lud, his voice hadn't cracked so much since his Harrow days.

The duke folded his arms across his chest and leveled James with a look that made his heart thud to a stop. He knew instinctively they'd reached the point in the interview where his answers would directly impact the duke's feelings about putting a painful period to James's existence. "Why not marry a girl with a large dowry like every other pinch-fisted, worthless worm of the *ton* would do?" The duke's scars grew more pronounced as his eyes narrowed and his mouth tightened. That did not bode well.

"Or better yet," the lieutenant jumped in again, "simply fall in line once more with your father's demands and hope he restores your income?"

The idea required no thought, no consideration. "I would rather be a pauper than puppet to a tyrant."

"How does your father feel about your decision?" The duke's tone had grown less mocking.

"My father's opinions no longer matter to me."

"Your father's opinions have never mattered to anyone of sense," the duke said. "You're not likely to secure many comforts on a secretary's salary." The duke's warning sounded decidedly halfhearted, as though he felt obligated to say something but would rather have seen James suffer unsuspectingly.

"If poverty is the price of integrity," James said, "I am willing to pay it."

"A very pretty speech." The lieutenant could hardly have looked less sincere. "What are your current intentions in regard to Daphne?"

Did his intentions really matter? It wasn't as though he had any options. "I do not mean to impose upon her. I only wished to make certain she was not blamed for this."

The lieutenant's eyes narrowed. "Then you had nothing to gain personally by coming here?"

They both studied him. The duke had not set down his dagger, and the lieutenant's hand continued to rest on his scabbard.

The duke broke the heavy silence. "None of us blames Daphne for your stupidity."

"Then she is well?" he asked, feeling his tension lessen.

The reassurance he expected did not come.

"She *is* well, isn't she?"

They offered no confirmation. Every ounce of anxiety returned. Something was wrong with Daphne.

"Is she ill? Has something happened?"

"We will look after Daphne," the duke said. He gestured with his dagger to the door. "Off with you."

Lieutenant Lancaster moved to James's side, obviously intent on seeing that he complied with the duke's dismissal.

James sidestepped him. "What is wrong with Daphne?" Panic surged through him. What had happened to her? Was she injured?

"You do not have the right to use her Christian name, Lord Tilburn," the lieutenant said, taking him firmly by the arm.

"What's happened? Please—"

A hard shove forced him to stumble to the doorway.

"Consider yourself fortunate that neither the duke nor I acted upon our first impulse to simply shoot you on sight." The lieutenant handed him over to a waiting footman. "Scurry off, Lord Tilburn. And forget you ever heard of Daphne Lancaster."

The book room doors snapped shut as the footman, joined by the starchy butler, escorted him down the corridor and out of the house.

"Please," he pled with the servants. "I only need to know that Miss Lancaster is well. Please."

The front door closed firmly. He stood there facing it, worry filling every part of him.

"Please," he continued pleading, though he stood there alone. "I need to know she is well. I need to."

No one answered because no one was listening.

Chapter Twenty-Eight

DAPHNE WAS DOING HER BEST to live her life as though nothing devastating had happened. She did not insist upon taking her meals on a tray in her room, neither did she seclude herself and refuse the company of her family. If she could pretend a degree of normalcy, eventually she might feel it.

She stepped into Adam's book room at the usual hour for their afternoon appointment a mere four days after the disastrous picnic. He had been occupied at Lords the previous two days, but he was home today.

Over the past six years, these near-daily meetings had served as a healing balm. Adam had shown her personal, tender regard at times when she'd desperately needed it. Now, with her heart fractured and her soul heavy, she needed his loving kindness more than ever.

"Good afternoon," she said from the doorway.

He glanced up from his desk. "Daphne."

She stepped inside. Some of the tension she'd carried these last four days dissipated. Here she would find comfort, if only she could keep him to safe topics. "What shall we discuss today?" she asked as she crossed to the sofa. "Parliament? Society? The weather?"

Adam's head turned toward the clock. "Is it that time again?" His was not the tone of enthusiasm she would have preferred.

"Yes. And you were not needed in Lords today."

He had not risen from his desk, nor set aside his paperwork. Still, he sometimes spent their afternoon together working on business matters while she read. She would not object to that today.

"I can select a book," she offered.

His next breath was loud and a touch impatient. "I don't truly have time for this today, Daphne. I am meant to meet with a man about refurbishing the nursery here after we've left for Northumberland. I wish it to be finished and ready by the time we return."

"You told me yesterday that you would set aside this time specifically for our afternoon together because it was the one day you didn't have to be at Lords."

He wrote something on the topmost paper on the stack before speaking again. "I cannot delay the start of this. The nursery is not at all ready for an infant. I will not risk having it unfinished when it is needed."

She searched about for a means of reconciling the conflicting needs. "Do you have to meet with him just now? Cannot you delay even an hour?"

"He will be here any moment," Adam said. "I thought, in fact, that he had arrived when you stepped in."

He had, it seemed, forgotten about her. She pushed that aside, telling herself there was a different, less discouraging explanation. "I can sit in the corner with my book while you have your interview. I won't disturb you."

He set his forearms on the desk, interweaving his fingers. "We'll have our afternoon discussion another day, Daphne. I need to see to the nursery. I have a responsibility to my child." He spoke the final word with the same tone and expression of anxious awe he'd had anytime Persephone's condition had been discussed the past few days.

"Of course. I would never ask you to neglect your obligations." She moved in the direction of the door once more. "Tomorrow, perhaps?"

"Persephone and I intend to begin interviewing nursemaids."

She pushed back her disappointment. "The day after?"

"I don't know." He offered a brief, apologetic smile.

"Another time, then."

He nodded, even as his attention returned to his pile of papers.

Daphne stepped out into the corridor, telling herself not to be selfish or maudlin. This was hardly the first time Adam had needed to cancel an afternoon with her, but it stung more acutely than it had in the past. He had sent her away when she needed him so much.

Though she felt sorely tempted to tuck herself away in her bedchamber, she knew if she gave in to the impulse, she might never convince herself to come back out. She made her way instead to the family sitting room and stepped inside with head held high.

Linus stood beside Artemis at the mirror. The two looked shockingly alike, even to Daphne, who had long-since grown used to the green eyes and golden curls of three of her siblings.

Artemis adjusted the bow on the bonnet she wore.

"The milliner told me it was a fashionable bonnet." Linus obviously wasn't entirely certain he'd been told correctly.

"Fashionable, yes." Artemis gave him a look of exasperation. "But is it *devastating*?"

"Devastating to whom?" The look of utter confusion on Linus's face brought a smile to Daphne's lips.

"To simply everyone." Artemis tipped her head slightly in one direction, then the other. "A bonnet is supposed to turn heads."

"It seems to be turning yours quite effortlessly," he observed.

She spun toward him, fists propped on her hips. "Would you stop being a *brother*, please?"

"But if I am not your brother, I cannot in all propriety purchase you a bonnet." He tsked and shook a finger at Artemis, his voice pitched precisely at the level a scolding dowager would use with a recalcitrant young lady. "A proper young lady would never allow a gentleman to purchase something so very personal for her unless he is a relative. Shameful, I say. Absolutely shameful! I shall simply have to toss it to the wolves."

"You are impossible." Artemis turned back to the mirror, obviously still deciding just how much she liked her brother's offering.

"I daresay you don't know a thing about bonnets." Artemis clearly intended the observation to be a sore slight on her brother's intelligence.

Linus chuckled lightly, earning a momentary glare from Artemis. "I am afraid I missed most of the bonnet classes onboard ship these past few years. I chose embroidery instead. Marvelous pastime."

"What do you think, Daphne?" Artemis turned to face her.

"I am not particularly fond of embroidery, myself." Daphne sat in a nearby chair. "Though Linus may very well be enamored of it."

"I meant the bonnet." Artemis shook her head. "This is far more enjoyable when Athena is here. She has absolutely impeccable taste."

Linus gave her a stern look, something he didn't often do. "Athena's taste in headgear may be second to none, but my manners are generally considered beyond reproach, and I will tell you that debating the merits of a bonnet your brother has given you out of the goodness of his heart while that brother is standing next to you, no less, is horribly rude."

Daphne could have predicted with remarkable accuracy what happened next. Artemis's lip began to quiver. Tears formed immediately. Her feelings had ever been easily wounded.

"Time to begin a very careful dance, brother," Daphne warned. "Artemis will be inconsolable otherwise."

Linus patted Artemis's hand. "I know you take bonnets very seriously, so I will take no offense at your very thorough evaluation of my offering."

Artemis sniffled but nodded what was likely meant to be an indication of forgiveness. Still, she glided toward the windows and settled herself in a posture of suffering and sorrow.

"Inconsolable over a scolding?" Linus shook his head. "Artemis weeps for being gently corrected, and you have not shed a single tear even though—"

"Did you not bring me a frilly present?" Daphne would not listen to yet another retelling of her dashed hopes and blighted future. Her spirits were low enough already. "I should have my opportunity to primp and preen in front of a looking glass as well."

Linus was undeterred. "Persephone said—"

"Only Artemis receives gifts now?" Daphne managed a sigh her sister would have been proud of. "You are a cruel brother indeed."

Linus studied her a moment, wearing the same expression she'd seen on all her family's faces again and again since she had fully retreated from the social whirl. Worry mingled with a sad kind of pity. Oh, how she wanted things back the way they had been. No one had expected her to be a raging success, but no one had seen her as an utter failure either.

"Your present is not frilly." Linus, it seemed, meant to not press the issue. He pulled a small box from the pocket of his coat and gave it to her. "I think you will like it just the same."

She couldn't begin to guess what it might be. The box was too small to hold a book. The only other thing she might have hoped for was herbs. But no one ever thought to give her that.

Daphne opened the package, curiosity displacing her momentary resurgence of heartache. In time, she hoped she would not need such constant distraction.

"Oh, Linus. It is lovely." She pulled a dainty hair comb from the box. The thin tines and body of the comb were made of a dark, lacquered wood. Ornamental leaves carved of a deep-green stone adorned the comb. She knew the leaves on sight. "Laurel."

"I know you have not always been fond of laurels, yet I can't help but think of you anytime I see them." He looked almost apologetic. "Father's love of mythology rubbed off on me, I daresay."

Daphne ran her thumb over the smooth stone leaves. Her namesake's myth had ever seemed a tragic one to her: an innocent girl pursued by one whose affections were not entirely honest transformed into a laurel tree to save her from her insincere suitor. What had once struck her as merely sad now seemed painfully fitting. Heavens, she was living her own myth.

"You don't like it." Linus's disappointment pricked her heart.

"I love it," she insisted. "It is so beautiful and unlike anything I've seen. Where did you find it? I've not come across anything like it in London."

Relief touched his features. "I saw it in a market in Africa."

"Africa?" That brought her gaze back to the comb.

"Yes, but the stone is jade, which comes from the Orient. The laurel motif, however, suggests it was carved in the Mediterranean."

She looked up at him once more. "Quite the world traveler, isn't it?"

He nodded and smiled at her. "The leaves made me think of you, but more than that even, I thought the bold colors would look very fine in your dark hair. Neither Artemis nor Athena could do justice to it."

The praise touched her, likely more than he realized. "It is not often I compare favorably to those two."

He put an arm around her shoulders and squeezed. "I think you'd be surprised."

She leaned her head against his shoulder. The ever-teasing, often-neglectful Linus seemed to disappear a little more every time she saw him. He was growing into a fine man, one she often felt she did not know at all. "I will cherish this," she said, meaning more than just the comb. "Thank you."

"You can thank me by wearing it and thinking of me when you do."

"I will think of you even when I am not wearing it. And I will miss you." Even if he resigned his commission and went to live in Shropshire, he would still be away, and she would be left behind. Loneliness had ever been her greatest struggle. She began to suspect it always would be.

She had pleaded with her father once, promising to be good and not disturb him if only he would allow her to sit with him in her office as he had once done. She had explained that she wished only to spend the day with him because she loved him. The sadness that had clouded his eyes hadn't lifted as he'd told her to go make herself useful to her sister. She had been only nine years old that last time she'd asked to be granted his company. Years of being told to go had finally convinced her she wasn't wanted. It was a feeling she continued to battle even now.

Persephone came in the room in the next moment. She'd been out making morning calls. Though she generally returned from her visits serene and rejuvenated, she looked just a touch harried. Her sweeping gaze took in the room and its occupants quickly and assessingly, a skill she'd perfected in her years as sole caregiver for her siblings. "That is a very fetching bonnet, Artemis," she said.

Artemis dropped into a chair, a look of utter despondency cast at them.

Linus grinned. To Persephone, he explained. "She had hoped the bonnet would be 'devastating.'"

Persephone looked her sister over once more before returning her attention to their brother. "She looks devastated, so I suppose that is a success."

"Not exactly how I'd envisioned my gift being received, but I'll take what I can."

"Have any of you seen Adam?"

Persephone's urgent tone fully captured Daphne's attention. "Last I saw him he was in his book room," she answered. "He was awaiting an important meeting with a tradesman."

Persephone crossed directly to the bell pull and tugged. Locating her husband seemed no unimportant thing.

"Is something the matter?" Daphne asked.

"Quite possibly."

Daphne felt the blood drain from her face. Had something happened? Had a complication arisen with Persephone's condition? Linus's thoughts must have traveled along the same path. He crossed directly to their oldest sister and took her arm in his, leading her to a nearby chair.

Persephone actually rolled her eyes. "There is nothing the matter with *me*."

But the entire family had known her too long and too well to feel at all confident in that declaration. She had always put herself and her own needs last.

A footman stepped inside.

"Will you please take a message to His Grace in the book room and ask him to step in here a moment?" Persephone asked.

She received a deep bow of agreement.

An awkward and heavy silence descended on the room. Persephone was clearly lost in her own thoughts. Daphne kept a close eye on her, evaluating everything she saw. Her color seemed fine, if a touch high. The warmth of the day could account for that. Persephone had thinned some in the last few weeks, owing, no doubt, to her lost appetite. That, Daphne's readings had assured her, would resolve itself in the weeks and months to come.

She exchanged looks with Linus. He appeared as confused and unsure of what to do as she was.

Several long minutes passed before Adam stepped into the room. His eyes fell on his wife, and the unmistakable look of love he always wore when first they found each other in a room slid across his face once more. But with it was a great deal of concern.

"What has happened?" he asked, sitting on the sofa beside her. "Are you unwell?"

Persephone shook her head. "Is everyone going to assume that for the next months?"

"Absolutely." How very unrepentant Adam sounded.

"Lovely," Persephone answered, her tone as dry as Adam's often was. "This has nothing to do with *me*."

"Then what is it?" Hopefully Adam would succeed in getting that question answered when no one else in the room had managed.

Persephone turned her head toward the windows. "Artemis, go put your bonnet away."

Artemis's mouth dropped open, her eyes wide with shocked horror. "Go put my bonnet away? Why can I not stay for your monumental confession? I want to know what the crisis is."

"There is no crisis," Persephone said. Then, cutting off the objections so clear on Artemis's face, Persephone added, "And neither is there anything to discuss that has the slightest bit to do with you. So, please, go put your bonnet away."

Artemis stood, jutting her chin out ominously, and pouted her way out of the room.

"Best of luck with that one, Adam," Linus muttered.

"I plan to auction her off at Tattersall's." His eyes hadn't left Persephone. "You, on the other hand, have me worried."

She brushed her fingertips along the deep scars on his face. "I am perfectly well. My health is fine." She lowered her a voice a bit. "This child seems perfectly fine as well."

Adam kissed her fingers. "Then tell me what has upset you."

"I had a very interesting visit with the Duchess of Hartley."

"She upset you?"

Daphne didn't believe that for a moment. The two duchesses got along famously.

"No," Persephone said. "And, before you ask, the duke is also not the reason I am upset. At least not directly." She took a breath, then squared a look at Adam. "His Grace has acquired a new secretary."

That earned her confused looks all around. Why did the duke's employee warrant such obvious displeasure on Persephone's part?

"I will move forward on the assumption there is more," Adam said.

"This new secretary just so happens to be a member of the aristocracy, one who by lucky chance met up with His Grace at their club yesterday afternoon." Persephone gave Adam a very pointed look. That look was exchanged by Adam and Linus next. It seemed everyone knew precisely who this mysterious gentleman was but Daphne. "He struck up a conversation with the young lordling, and upon hearing he is in need of an income, His Grace hired him on. Their Graces even went so far as to invite him to stay with them, owing to his current state of pennilessness. It seems he is quite the hardest working, least complaining, most grateful person Their Graces have ever encountered."

"Sounds . . . ideal," Adam muttered.

Persephone hmphed. "It was all I could do not to demand to know his reason for coming within fifty yards of this family. Milworth House is but two doors down from here, you know. And he is now living there."

Suddenly it all grew clear. James Tilburn was at the Duke of Hartley's London home. They might easily run into one another without even meaning to. Daphne slowly, mindlessly lowered herself into a nearby chair. Confusion jumbled her every thought.

"I fully intend to storm Milworth House," Persephone said in tones of utmost sincerity. "Broadswords, battle axes, crossbows, whichever weapon is nearest at hand. There will be bloodshed, Adam, and I will enjoy it."

"I have never been more attracted to you than I am in this moment." Adam's eyes fairly danced with excitement. "Nevertheless, I will not have you going on a holy crusade in your condition." Adam turned his attention to Linus. "Seems we underestimated the little termite."

Despite all James had done to her, hearing him belittled and mocked that way upset her. Daphne hated that he yet had such a hold on her sensibilities.

Linus's shoulders set in the determined and capable posture of a career navy man. "I will stand as your second, Adam, if that is what you mean to do."

Daphne found her voice on the instant. "You promised me, Adam. You promised no challenges would be issued." She'd pulled that promise from him within hours of her disappointment.

Adam assumed his ducal air. "I promised not to seek him out and demand satisfaction. He has come here, within sight of my home and my family. I made no promises on that score."

She ought to have encouraged the idea. Having James suffer even a fraction of what she had should have been cathartic. Yet the thought of anyone hurting James brought her no satisfaction. "I only wish the entire ordeal forgotten. The two of you breaking down the doors of the Duke of Hartley's home will be whispered all about Town. It would only further fuel the gossip and whispers."

"Really?" Linus sounded disappointed. "I've seen enough floggings during my career to know how to administer one."

Daphne had heard of the severity of floggings, of the horrific pain inflicted that way. She shook her head. "No floggings, no challenges. Both of you, please, just let it be."

She rose, making certain they saw in her determined expression that the subject was closed for discussion. No one objected until she'd reached the doorway.

"Can't we at least have a few of the Falstone wolves brought here to nibble on him a little?" Linus asked.

For that she could give him a small smile. "I will take it into consideration."

Once in the corridor, she stopped and leaned a moment against the wall, trying to regain her equilibrium. James was only two doors away. But why? Why would he abandon his own lodgings? His family home? And what was this about his needing employment, about his being penniless? Perhaps he had been in need of her dowry after all.

The others' voices continued in the sitting room, loud enough for Daphne to hear their words.

"She is too blasted calm about all this," Adam grumbled.

"A battle tactic you taught her, dear. And though I have not always agreed with you on that, the ability has served her well before. She has not crumbled when faced with Society, nor whispering gossips, and neither will she crumble now."

I will not crumble now. She was becoming quite adept at pushing away the sting of rejection and disappointment. She simply refused to allow thoughts to creep in, dismissed every surge of painful emotions, suppressed every feeling, and was learning to fiercely guard every vulnerability. In time, nothing would hurt her again.

Chapter Twenty-Nine

JAMES COULD NOT IMAGINE ANYTHING more ludicrous. He was hiding in the shadows of a terrace, peering in windows. Further, he was trespassing on land that belonged to the one man in England guaranteed to shoot an interloper on sight. Once the Dangerous Duke realized the identity of his uninvited guest, he would likely shoot him again just for good measure.

Had James not grown somewhat desperate the last two days, the idea of pretending to be a sneak-thief would never have occurred to him. But how was a gentleman supposed to check on the well-being of the lady he cared for if she never left her highly fortified London home?

The duke's family had finished their meal and retired to the sitting room. It was from that terrace that he watched them, watched *her*. She seemed well but not happy. The dimple he'd missed since they'd last met made not a single appearance. She seemed to listen politely to the conversations around her but never joined in. She didn't pout or sulk, but neither did she smile or laugh.

James couldn't determine simply by watching what might be the matter. The duke and the lieutenant had made quite clear something was wrong.

"What a pathetic lump you are," he quietly castigated himself. "Reduced to spying on a lady you no longer have the right to speak to."

Daphne rose from her seat and moved directly to the french doors. Had she seen him? Surely not. She would have told her brother-in-law or brother, and both men would have forcibly ejected him.

James kept to the dim corner of the terrace as Daphne stepped out. Perhaps she meant only to retreat for a bit of fresh air and would return none the wiser. But her steps rang of purpose. Her eyes searched the darkened terrace. He knew the moment she saw him there. Her posture grew stiff, her expression determined.

"Lord Tilburn," she said. The lack of feeling in her words spoke volumes of her contempt for him. "I only stepped out to tell you that you would be well-advised to leave." She turned swiftly toward the door.

In a panic, he grabbed her arm. An uncomfortable feeling flooded over him at that simple touch, not necessarily unpleasant but not soothing either. He had never reacted that way to her before—it was not the awkwardness of their earliest encounters nor the easy friendship of their last few days together but was a deep awareness of her presence there.

For the briefest moment, she seemed almost to relax. But then he felt her stiffen. He released her arm. He had no right to keep her there; he knew that. But he also knew he had only this one chance to say and see what he needed.

"May I have just a moment?" His words proved remarkably insufficient and sounded more than a little presumptuous.

Daphne stepped away from him.

"Please," he tried again. What would he do if she refused to stay? Infiltrate the kitchen staff? Take up residence beneath her bedchamber window? "Please."

Daphne paused just shy of the doorway. She did not turn around. He could see little beyond her outline contrasted against the light spilling out of the sitting room windows. She didn't speak a word but simply stood very still. Was she waiting for him to say his piece? Would she offer him no indication of how or what she was feeling?

He hadn't expected a warm welcome, by any means, but the chasm that separated them felt so foreign. She had always been easy to talk with and be near. Her presence had always been soothing.

"I—" What could he possibly say? *I heard you were ill? I'm sorry? I am an imbecile?* "How are you?" James winced, knowing instinctively the moment the words were said that he ought to have chosen something else.

Daphne didn't move in the slightest. "You have no right to ask me that," she whispered, more pain than anger in her voice.

He had not imagined he could feel more ashamed of himself than he had the last week. That simple sentence, said as it was in such a heartbreaking tone, proved him wrong. Would he ever manage to truly atone for his inexcusable behavior? She might never forgive him, but he needed to be certain she was well.

Daphne still had not walked away.

"I had heard you were ill," he said.

"I am fine." It was not at all convincing, coming in so small a voice.

"You do not sound fine." He stepped closer, telling himself that he wished only to make certain she was well. If he was being honest, though, he wanted to prolong the moment, to see if she would stay a little longer, perhaps talk with him the way she once had.

"You need not be concerned with my well-being." Daphne stepped closer to the wall, a little farther into the shadow.

"Not concerned?" He matched her movement, closing a little of the distance between them. "How could I not be? If you are truly—" For the first time since Daphne had stepped onto the terrace, James was able to truly see her. "You're pale." It seemed she really was ill.

A ghost of a smile hovered on her lips. "You say that as though being pale isn't one of my defining characteristics." Before she even finished speaking, the tiny hint of amusement in her countenance disappeared.

He stood close enough to reach out and touch her, something he found himself overwhelmingly compelled to do. "Daphne." He brushed his fingers along the top of her arm.

She closed her eyes. No smile touched her lips. The lines of strain on her face did not lessen. If anything, his touch seemed to upset her more. The look of misery on her face hurt more than a full-voiced diatribe would have. James let his hand drop back to his side.

"It was not my intention to impose on you further," he said. "I was concerned about you and wanted to be certain you were well."

She looked up at him then. "Adam will kill you if he sees you here, and Linus will happily assist him." He thought he detected the smallest bit of concern in her otherwise unreadable tone.

"I know."

She slipped through a separate door at the far end of the terrace.

Several long moments passed. He couldn't seem to pull himself away. He silently willed her to return, to speak to him again.

He hadn't truly apologized for what he'd done, hadn't made any semblance of peace with her. Though Daphne had insisted otherwise, James wasn't convinced she was truly well.

Far from finding closure, he only missed her more. Regaining her friendship seemed all but impossible. She didn't want him there—that much was clear. Likely, she wanted absolutely nothing to do with him.

Standing there in the shadows, James felt excruciatingly alone.

If Daphne knew one thing about gentlemen, it was that they were fundamentally confusing. She had pondered her brief and unusual conversation with James many times over the day and a half since their encounter on the terrace and still could not make heads nor tails of it.

He had been forced to court her, to feign interest in her. Why, then, would he knowingly place his life in peril simply to ascertain the state of her health? Such behavior served as rather convincing proof that women were not, in fact, the less logical of the sexes.

Realizing her thoughts had once again wandered to a subject upon which she had firmly told herself she would not waste further time, Daphne set herself to the task of making another turn about the small green in the shadow of Westminster. In an act of unforeseen underhandedness, Linus had enlisted Adam's support in all but forcing her to spend the evening out of doors by insisting she and her brother come to Parliament to fetch him at the end of his day there. Daphne would rather have remained at Falstone House with her herbs and books.

She glanced over at Linus hurrying to catch up with her. "You insisted on this turn about the grounds; the least you could do is keep up," she said.

The severe expression she kept up nearly slipped at his look of exasperation. The infuriating man deserved every ounce of trouble she was giving him.

"I've sailed on clippers that did not have your speed." Linus reached her side, though he seemed to have left his breath a few paces behind.

Daphne offered not the smallest bit of sympathy. "You were the one who suggested I needed a bit of exercise."

"The idea was Adam's. He should be the one sprinting after you."

"Would you like to tell him so?" She raised a questioning eyebrow in what she knew was a perfect mimic of Adam's well-known expression.

"Not on your life," Linus answered. "And not because I'm afraid of him, but because he is right. You spend too much time alone, and when you do join the rest of us, you are too quiet and withdrawn. I do not like seeing you this way."

"I have attempted to spend time with our formidable brother-in-law, but he is too busy. Persephone is quite distracted of late. Artemis never holds still long enough to serve as company to anyone of a more subdued disposition.

And you, dearest brother, have been quite preoccupied as well, attempting to sort out your own decisions." She would rather not hear another recounting of how very unhappy she must be and a moment-by-moment retelling of her "dashed hopes." Making a show of being in better spirits seemed a wise strategy. "I will admit, however, that I have been a bit dreary of late. If I can find a means of blaming Artemis for my gloominess, I have every intention of doing so. I simply haven't formulated a believable explanation yet."

Her show of humor did not appear to impress him. He watched her as though he expected her to dissolve into a puddle of tears at any moment.

"If it will put your mind at ease, I will tell you this much, though if you breathe a word of it to Adam, I'll skin you alive with a soup spoon."

Linus laughed out loud. "You have lived under the Dangerous Duke's roof far too long."

Daphne found she could smile at that. "He has had an influence on me, I will confess." They walked a moment in contented silence. "I am enjoying my rare moment outside, as Adam predicted I would."

"He is almost as intelligent as he is fearsome," Linus said.

"And he is coming this way." Daphne motioned toward the figure of their frightening brother-in-law walking in their direction with his usual air of barely concealed bloodthirstiness. "If you have other things needing attending, I am certain he will see to it I complete my day's exercise."

A look of relief slid over his features. "Excellent. I will leave you to it, then." He disappeared down the path before Daphne had a chance to say so much as one more word.

"Why is it that gentlemen can't seem to abandon me fast enough?" she asked no one in particular.

She had been doing better. Resignation had very nearly given way to something resembling contentment. But then James had made his sudden appearance—a few words, a kindly glance—and she once again found herself in a battle against her own heart. She would wonder for just a moment if perhaps James's most recent actions were indicative of some tender regard only to swiftly remind herself that she had misinterpreted his attentions in precisely that way before with disastrous results.

Self-pity had become a dangerous tendency of hers lately, one she would do well not to indulge. She rubbed a hand over the very spot on her arm where James had touched her two evenings before. That tiny contact had nearly brought her to tears.

She missed James. She missed the connection she'd thought they'd had, the tenderness she'd imagined in his eyes, the attentions she'd believed were sincere.

Adam arrived at her side in the next instant. "For all his show of being a rough-around-the-edges naval man, when it comes to dealing with the women of his family, Linus Lancaster is a blasted coward." Adam motioned her ahead. "Now. Two more circuits, if you don't mind."

"Are you walking with me?" It was not the same as being granted an afternoon in his book room, but it was better than being left out entirely.

"No one else in this family can win a battle of the minds with you, so I suppose your well-being falls to me." He motioned her ahead of him, back on the path that wove through the garden.

"Not even Persephone?"

"She *could*," Adam answered. "But being the ideal husband I am, I mean to spare her that task."

"How is she feeling?"

Adam shook his head. "None of your diversionary tactics. Persephone is not the topic at hand."

They passed a rosebush, its fragrance strong, almost being overpowering.

"I am growing exceptionally weary of discussing my dashed hopes, Adam."

He was unsympathetic. "*I* am growing weary of suffering through a daily tragedy of Shakespearean proportions."

She eyed him sidelong. "You are expecting me to stab myself in the family crypt?"

"I will stab *myself* in the family crypt if I have to endure your infuriatingly calm resignation one day more."

For all Daphne loved him, Adam was not always a comfort in one's time of need. "Resignation? You would rather I weep inconsolably?"

"Yes."

She smiled at the ridiculousness of that. "You wish me to turn into Artemis?"

Adam kept walking, his gaze decidedly not wandering in her direction. Daphne knew what came next. He always grew uncomfortable with personal conversations.

"You have retreated, Daphne. I find myself confronted once more with the little girl who came to live with me six years ago, who seldom spoke and rarely looked at anyone. I cannot like seeing this change in you."

The comparison pricked at her. She felt like that little girl again in many ways. The confidence she'd gained in the past half-dozen years had crumbled more than a bit, as had the assurance that her timidity and comparative plainness weren't the hindrance to happiness she'd once believed them to be. She was working very hard to keep the pain at bay.

A sudden commotion cut off whatever he meant to say next. People were rushing in and out of Westminster, voices raised in obvious panic.

"What the blazes is going on?" Adam muttered. He cupped her elbow with his hand and led her in that direction, eyeing the comings and goings. "Hartley." He called out to his fellow duke. "What is all this commotion?"

His Grace turned toward them, and Daphne knew on the instant that something truly terrible had happened. "Perceval's been shot in Commons."

Merciful heavens.

"Is the Prime Minister dead?" Adam asked.

"No one seems to know for sure." They were all moving very nearly at a run. "It is chaos. Utter chaos. Who knows how many others might be lying in wait with pistols at the ready."

Assassins in the halls of Parliament? Daphne forced herself to breathe normally and keep calm.

"We must not allow this government to come to a standstill at the hands of murderers." Adam twisted the handle of his walking stick a half turn in one direction followed by a full turn in the other and pulled an épée from within its wooden sheath. "Let's go clear the corridors."

"There might be any number of assassins inside, Adam." Daphne's stomach tied in knots.

"And I mean to see to it that number becomes zero." He turned to the Duke of Hartley. "Where's your man Tilburn?"

"Seeking information." They'd nearly reached the crowd pressing in and out of the entrance to Westminster. "Tilburn!" the duke shouted, waving.

The sudden return of James Tilburn amidst the turmoil of an assassination at Westminster surprisingly didn't fluster Daphne in the least. She felt more numb than anything else.

"I can't seem to get a consistent answer to anything, Your Grace." James addressed his employer. "All anyone can agree on is that Perceval was shot at close range."

"Tilburn, take Daphne home." Adam's words emerged clipped and quick. "Directly to Falstone House. No stops along the way."

"Of course, Your Grace."

"And remain there until I arrive," Adam added. "No matter the protests that house full of stubborn women will no doubt make, you stay there. Abandon them and I will scoop your brains from your skull with a ladle."

"I'll chain myself to the bannister if need be." That earned James a brief smile from the Duke of Hartley but no notable reaction from Adam.

"Daphne, show Tilburn where the carriage is and return home posthaste."

She nodded her agreement.

"And, James," the Duke of Hartley jumped in quickly, "have one of the Falstone House footmen send word to my wife that I am well but will not be home until the mess here is sorted."

"I will, Your Grace."

"Be safe, Adam," Daphne said.

"I always am."

The two dukes strode into the crowd. Daphne summoned the cool head Adam had long ago taught her to maintain and led the way toward the Kielder carriage. "To Falstone House," she instructed the coachman as James handed her inside.

Adam never employed anyone who wasn't the absolute best at what he or she did. His coachman was no exception. The crush of traffic on the London streets and the added chaos associated with the news spreading out of Westminster proved not the slightest hindrance. The coach wound at a quick pace down road after road on its way home.

"Your sister does not seem the type to give in to hysterics," James said, "but do you feel we ought to send for a physician?"

She shook her head. "Persephone is made of stronger stuff than that. We all are."

Another moment passed in silence. "I truly had not intended to force my company upon you again, Miss Lancaster. If you would prefer, I will keep to the corridor or entryway at Falstone House."

"As I said, Lord Tilburn, we are made of stronger stuff than that." Her calm came easily now, as if the well of her emotions had finally run dry. "I won't be bothered one way or the other."

Chapter Thirty

As Daphne had predicted, the duchess remained remarkably calm, though concern did touch her features as the evening wore on. Miss Artemis paced about, waving her hands dramatically and, no doubt, making silent predictions of doom. Daphne showed no emotions whatsoever. James didn't like it. The neutrality of her expression didn't fit her in the least.

She sat near the front windows, though she kept her gaze on her sewing. James leaned against the window frame. Daphne did not outwardly acknowledge his presence, though she must have noticed him there.

He had no idea where to begin, how to break through the barrier between them. Something had to be said, however mundane and idiotic it might sound. "The tonic you had made for Mother worked wonders," he said. "She was a vast deal more comfortable when she left for Lancashire."

"I am pleased to hear it." Still she kept her gaze elsewhere.

He inched closer. "Ben traveled to Northumberland. He is spending some time with your brother-in-law."

"Harry told us about your brother's visit in his last letter. He was quite looking forward to sharing all he has learned." She spoke with very little animation, her voice quiet, her tone politely conversational and nothing more.

James had no intention of giving up. He pressed on with the topic, all the while searching his mind for subject matter that might draw her from her seclusion. "Mr. Windover will have an eager student in Ben."

"I hope his time there will prove beneficial." She actually looked at him. James worked to keep his expression neutral. Instinct told him Daphne was far more jumpy than she let on. He feared any overt show of enthusiasm would only push her further away.

"I know your brother has been very concerned about his estate," she said.

"That concern has transformed into excitement since Mr. Windover's invitation arrived. I have been acutely relieved to see it."

She nodded slowly and without enthusiasm. The lady with whom he had shared his thoughts and worries had disappeared behind a stoic and impenetrable mask. He made no further attempts at conversation as the evening wore on. She clearly would not allow it.

Sounds of voices floated up from the entryway below not long after the ormolu clock on the mantel struck seven. The duchess was on her feet on the instant, her eyes glued to the door. Miss Artemis pressed her hand to her heart, watching the door as well. Daphne was clearly aware of the inevitability of someone's entrance but didn't seem anxious one way or the other. He was certain she was, but she didn't permit it to show.

The door flew open, and the Duke of Kielder swept inside, his formidable gaze ranging the expanse of the room. "Is everyone here in one piece?" He eyed them all and, apparently satisfied with what he saw, gave a firm nod. "Good. I'll be in my book room until dinner is ready."

"Adam," Her Grace said, stopping her husband in the instant before he turned back toward the still-open door.

He watched her in somewhat impatient anticipation. "I have to—"

"Adam Richard Boyce. You come over here this instant and assure me you are well and whole."

Something of her concern must have penetrated his obviously distracted mind. He crossed to her. "You aren't going to faint, are you?"

She took an audible breath and leaned in to him, wrapping her arms around him. He followed suit, holding his wife in a gentle embrace. James had never in all his life seen such a thing. His parents did their utmost to avoid each other's company.

"Do you know, Persephone," the duke said, "even after seven years of marriage, I am still shocked to realize you worry about me. No one else has ever bothered."

"I wasn't worried," she whispered, though the quiver in her voice belied her words. "You have set our dinner back, and I am hungry, that's all."

The duke did something James could never have imagined. He smiled. Not a broad, eye-twinkling smile, not even enough of a smile to turn up both sides of his mouth, but the tiniest twitch of his lips.

"Never let it be said that the Dangerous Duke allowed his duchess to go hungry." He pulled a little free of his wife's embrace and slid his hands to her face. "Have dinner set out. I'll join you and the girls just as soon as I've spoken with Tilburn." He pressed a kiss to his wife's forehead. "Will that wriggle me out of your black books?"

"For now," she answered, lightness returning to her voice.

The duke nodded his approval, then turned toward James. "You. My book room. Now."

James followed His Grace out of the sitting room and back to the very book room in which a selection of the Kielder armory had been laid out the last time he'd entered. The desktop on which it had lain was blessedly empty.

"Sit."

James sat in the seat facing him only to immediately discover how very uncomfortable and low to the ground the seat he had been offered truly was. His head only barely sat higher than the desktop.

The duke's expression remained stern. "Let me begin by saying that pressing you into service this evening is not to be taken as an indication of any level of approval on my part. Daphne needed to return home, and you were the most convenient means of accomplishing that."

What could he do but nod? He was absolutely certain a vocal response would be dangerously unwelcome. The duke didn't speak, neither did he look away. He simply watched James, eyes narrowed, mouth turned down.

The silence dragged on. Perhaps this was what was meant by the calm before the storm.

"Ah, Linus," the duke said without looking away from him. "Come in."

James watched the lieutenant's ominous approach.

"You were warned not to return." Lieutenant Lancaster spoke from a menacingly close distance, his eyes snapping with anger. "Onboard ship, we keelhaul men for ignoring orders."

"Stand down, Linus," the duke said, his voice as even as though he were attending to the well-being of a not particularly valuable horse. "You cannot keelhaul a man on dry land, and I will not tolerate idle threats."

The lieutenant did not back away in the slightest. Though the duke had the more apocalyptic reputation, the navy man's glare proved every bit as disconcerting. "It was not idle. I know a jaunty who'd be more than happy to oblige me."

"Save that favor for another time," the duke said. "I have asked Tilburn to be here. It is time, Linus, we did something about Daphne."

James looked from one of them to the other and back. He was worried about how withdrawn she'd become. Was there more the matter with Daphne than that?

"Are you certain about this, Adam?" Lieutenant Lancaster asked.

The duke nodded. "You can keelhaul him later if this proves a poor strategy."

"Do you promise?"

A ducal nod seemed to secure the lieutenant's faith in the plan. "How familiar are you, Lord Tilburn, with the story of Daphne from Greek mythology?" A decidedly odd question for the lieutenant to pose without preamble.

"Not very," James admitted. "Daphne was a nymph, and I believe someone turned her into a tree."

The lieutenant nodded. He lowered himself into a chair near the duke. "That is generally all anyone remembers. My father was a scholar of all things Greek. He once said Daphne's tale was the most tragic in all of mythology."

"Even more tragic than Perseph—?" A quick glance at the duke silenced James's question. His Grace would take any negative view of Persephone of old as a slight on his wife and likely himself. James reminded himself to keep his mouth shut.

Lieutenant Lancaster wove his fingers together, resting them in his lap. "My father believed Daphne's suffering was entirely self-imposed. Knowing cupid's arrow instigated Apollo's pursuit of her and not the natural dictates of his heart, Daphne did not trust Apollo's feelings for her."

Snippets of his education came back. "But I seem to remember that cupid's arrows created a permanent change," James said. "Though the beginning may have been forced, the outcome was not temporary." James could honestly say he'd never before discussed Greek philosophy outside of university.

The lieutenant nodded. "But history was decidedly against Apollo. Nymphs were beautiful and desirable, but demigods did not pursue them with long-term intentions. They were generally viewed as expendable and inherently unimportant. A nymph, after all, is not a goddess."

He watched the two men, uncertain of the exact purpose of this discussion, knowing only that it had to do with Daphne.

"So Daphne of myth ran from Apollo, not because she despised him but because she anticipated his eventual defection," Lieutenant Lancaster said. "She felt certain he would hurt her, would wound her heart with his false declarations of love. She begged the river god to save her from what she feared most. In general, people view the river god's solution as unnecessarily cruel."

"He turned her into a tree," James said. "That does seem rather drastic."

"He gave her precisely what she wanted," the lieutenant countered. "Daphne pleaded to be saved from pain and heartache. But suffering is part of being human. She could only truly escape it by feeling nothing at all." Lieutenant Lancaster's voice took on a pointed quality as undeniable as his glare. "As my father said, hers was tragic, self-imposed suffering. What might have happened, he used to muse, if, instead of running, instead of cutting herself off so entirely, she had turned around and allowed the possibility of love to give her courage as she faced her fears?"

"Or," the duke spoke for the first time since his brother-in-law had taken up the unexpected tale, his tone strangely accusatory, "if Apollo hadn't been so blasted bacon-brained in the first place."

"In the Lancaster family," the lieutenant continued, "our lives have the uncanny tendency to resemble those of our ancient counterparts. I, for one, am hoping to *not* be strangled with my own lyre. If I possessed the smallest degree of intelligence, I would have chosen a different instrument, though at thirteen, it had seemed rather too comical a choice to turn down." He shrugged, something of a mischievous smile hovering on his lips. Did all the Lancasters know how to produce just such a look? James had even seen Daphne's face light with mischief on occasion.

The lieutenant continued. "How likely is it, do you think, Lord Tilburn, that our Daphne will find herself transformed into a tree?"

"A tree?" Was the man in earnest? "Not likely, I would venture."

"On that, sir, I must beg to differ." The lieutenant offered no further explanation.

"I place the blame entirely on Apollo," the duke said. "If he'd been a man of purpose and determination, he not only would have wooed her with some degree of capability but would also have caught up with the stubborn girl before things got so blasted out of hand."

James knew something about unsuccessful courtships and felt more than a bit of sympathy for Apollo. "Perhaps he realized too late what he would lose if he did not redouble his efforts. Perhaps he never was given the second chance he needed."

"Perhaps," the duke ventured, "he was a thick-witted buffoon."

"But the river god might have given Apollo an opportunity to make things right before turning the poor girl into a tree," James insisted.

Of a sudden, both men were looking directly at him, their expressions quite serious. The duke spoke, though obviously on both their behalves. "Had he—reluctantly, mind you—postponed the transformation long enough for Apollo to try his hand under very, very close scrutiny—"

"*Armed* scrutiny," the lieutenant amended.

"—and only out of love for the nymph, not any degree of empathy for the bird-brained Apollo, would the addlepated man have made a mull of it, do you think? Would he have only made things worse? Made more promises only to break them?"

James understood now the reason for the story. He was cast in the role of Apollo to his modern-day Daphne. "If given the opportunity, he would have tried again. And again and again if need be."

"The river god might still have whisked Daphne away, feeling Apollo was not good for her or good *enough* for her," the duke warned.

"At least they could have discovered as much." James's pulse pounded in his neck. They were going to give him a chance. Daphne might still reject him, might want nothing to do with him, but he had a chance. "If nothing else, she might not have hidden herself away. Her loss of vibrancy was the true tragedy, not Apollo's lost opportunity. She deserved better. She still does."

"That," the duke said, rising to his feet, "is exactly what I needed to hear."

James rose as well. His Grace and the lieutenant walked away from the desk, pausing a few steps from the doorway. He looked back at James. "Come on, then. Time for dinner."

"Dinner?"

"You do eat, do you not?"

"I do." What was the duke getting at?

"You'll be taking your evening meal here tonight." His Grace pushed open the doors.

James took several quick steps in order to catch up with his apparent host for the evening. "I doubt I will be welcomed by the rest of your family. They were hardly happy to see me this evening whilst waiting for your return."

"That is also not required." His Grace motioned James into the drawing room. "If they wish to carve you alongside the braised beef, so be it. But if your presence here will help Daphne come back to us, then it is worth trying."

"I will do whatever I can," he promised. "I hate seeing her so withdrawn."

"In case you are wondering," the duke said, "you will be permitted to speak to her, look at her, be in the same room as she, but"—His Grace moved closer, eyes boring into James's, his expression growing more ominous—"under no circumstances will you be permitted to touch her. One finger, Tilburn—you lay one finger on her, and I will break that finger and all its companions one at a time with a hot fire poker."

"And *I* will drop you in the Thames with an anchor tied to your neck," the lieutenant added.

"I understand." James accepted the limits placed on him. He hadn't expected to be permitted anything.

The Lancaster sisters were all in the sitting room when James and his would-be torturers stepped inside.

"Is Lord Tilburn staying for dinner?" Her Grace asked, clearly not too pleased by the prospect. "I hadn't expected a guest."

"Lord Tilburn is here as my prisoner," the duke explained.

"Oh, how wonderfully horrid!" Miss Artemis sounded delighted. "I just knew you could be a dastardly, bloodthirsty guardian, Adam, if only you would put your mind to it. Prisoners! How wonderful!"

James's attention was on Daphne. Physically, she appeared whole. But her eyes were different. The spark had disappeared. The look of forced serenity on her face slipped momentarily into surprise when her eyes fell on James. She stood stiffly, brows drawn together, lips turned downward. James stepped forward, alarmed, as the color in her face drained by degrees.

She held up her hand. He stopped a few steps from her, knowing what the gesture meant. Daphne's eyes darted in the duke's direction, then returned to James's face almost immediately. She did not look at all happy to see him.

"Why have you remained?" she asked in an urgent whisper.

"Your brother-in-law invited me to take my evening meal here."

Daphne shook her head. "The Dangerous Duke does not issue invitations. He threatened you."

"I wanted to stay, and he is allowing me to." It was something of a twist to the actual facts but true, just the same.

She only looked more confused. The life still hadn't reentered her eyes, but at least there was a hint of animation in her face. "Well, then, welcome, Lord Tilburn."

So formal. So impersonal. He bowed in response. "A pleasure, Miss Lancaster."

She was not particularly talkative with her family, he noticed as the evening wore on. Aside from the occasional nod or quietly offered response, Daphne kept to herself throughout the meal. James had seen her with her family before and did not remember her ever being so distanced from them.

After dinner, Daphne took a seat near the window while the rest of her family sat in a more intimate grouping around the empty fireplace. No one seemed surprised by the distance she placed between herself and her family members. How commonplace had this become?

He had hoped in time to achieve some degree of absolution from the lady he'd harmed. But his goal changed entirely over the course of that single evening. He swore to himself he would do whatever he must to see her happy again, whether or not she ever forgave him. *His* Daphne would not meet the same fate as her namesake.

Chapter Thirty-One

DANGEROUS DUKE OR NOT, ADAM Boyce was going to die a slow and painful death. Daphne had spent the previous night in shock owing to James's "invitation" to dinner. Adam, quite conveniently, was away from home nearly all the next day. Daphne walked directly to his desk shortly after his return that evening fully intending to demand the explanation he owed her.

He looked up at her only briefly, nothing in his demeanor seeming at all concerned at the fierce look she flung at him. "Do not attack me with glares, Daphne. You know I am quite immune to them."

"How could you?" she asked.

"Grow immune to glares? I could not help it. The talent developed naturally."

She had no patience for jests. "You forced Lord Tilburn to have dinner with us last night."

"The poor boy was starving to death." Adam flipped over a page in the stack of papers he was reading. "Hartley hasn't been feeding him."

Why could he not simply give her a direct answer? "Lord Tilburn is not starving to death. The duchess would never allow such a thing."

"That shows how little you know of the matter, Miss Daphne." Adam only ever called her "Miss Daphne" when he meant to tease her, something the *ton* likely thought him incapable of. "The recently impoverished Lord Tilburn has accepted employment but is just stubborn enough not to accept a single morsel more than he feels he has earned. Some of those morsels go to feed a tiny mongrel who is overly fond of him, meaning there is a puppy living in the Hartley's back gardens that is growing fat while its master goes hungry. I believe that qualifies the lad as a miserable wretch in need of a free meal."

"What do you mean by 'newly impoverished'?" Persephone had said as much when she'd first revealed James's residence at the Milworth House.

Adam set down the quill in his hand. The slightest of sighs tinged a bit with impatience escaped as he looked at her once more. "Generally the phrase indicates that a person has very little money at his disposal and that the situation has come about only recently."

"I know what the phrase means." Why must he be so infuriatingly difficult? "What I do not understand is why you have applied it to him."

"Because he has very little money, and the situation has come about only recently—"

"Adam, do be serious for one minute."

The Duke of Kielder adopted a truly jesting mood only on the rarest of occasions—fewer than two or three times a year. Why must he do so at precisely this moment?

"Please stop speaking in riddles and talk to me." Daphne could feel herself growing more upended by the moment. She had fully expected to confront Adam, receive some ridiculous explanation of his motivations, offer him a stinging set down, and then leave with head held high, having bested the most feared man in the kingdom. He was being maddeningly uncooperative.

Adam leaned back in his chair and crossed his arms in front of his chest. When she realized his stance exactly mimicked her own, Daphne dropped her arms to her side. She couldn't be entirely certain he wasn't needling her. She would normally have called him on it, insisted he take her seriously. Her feelings had been pricked far too often of late, however, and she knew herself unequal to the task of enduring mockery.

"*Now* you wish for me to talk? *Now* you want conversation?" Adam allowed a single, dry, unamused chuckle. "Have you finally decided to break your seemingly impregnable silence without being marched about the gardens of Westminster by force?"

In the six years she had lived in Adam's home, he had never once ridiculed her, but in the little more than two weeks since the disastrous picnic, he had done so on more than one occasion. She felt all the bravado and indignation she'd built up in order to sustain her through this confrontation slip away.

Daphne whispered, "Could you not simply say 'You are an idiot, Daphne' and leave it at that?" She knew she had mere minutes before the tears she'd fiercely held at bay would break past all her barriers.

Adam stood and reached her side so swiftly she hardly realized he'd moved. "Daphne," he said, his tone softer than it had been but still firm and a touch exasperated. "Come sit with me."

"No, thank you," she answered.

"There was no question mark adorning the end of that sentence." With one hand at her back, Adam guided her gently but forcibly to the sofa where they had spent many a pleasant interval the past half dozen years. Those enjoyable interludes seemed ages ago.

"Allow me to answer the various questions you have posed," Adam said.

Daphne kept her gaze on her folded hands, attempting to regain control over her emotions. Tears were useless, and she refused to indulge in them. She'd not cried during their walk in the garden. She'd not grown teary during dinner the night before. Where had this emotional upheaval come from?

"The Techney estate is solvent and in no particular financial danger," Adam said. "Lord Tilburn, however, is in quite the opposite state, having been cut off by his father in light of what is viewed by that man as his son's recent failure."

Daphne stiffened. Was that why James had returned to her life? To have another go at courting her in hopes of reconciling with his father's pocketbook? "Then he truly came here last night because he's impoverished?"

Adam rested his heels on the ottoman in front of him, legs crossed at the ankles. "He came because I told him to, and he remained because I insisted upon it."

Her heart dropped. James hadn't come in order to see her specifically. That came as more of a blow than she would have expected.

"Lord Tilburn may be a lot of things," Adam said, "but he is not an imbecile. Had I not required his presence last night, he would not have been here."

Daphne nodded, the misery of understanding rushing over her. She had hoped at least part of James's motivation had come from missing her the way she missed him in spite of everything. Obviously her heart wasn't as guarded as she thought.

"Wipe the tortured-puppy look off your face," Adam instructed. "That was not intended to serve as an unflattering assessment of *you*."

How could she possibly take it otherwise? Harry had more or less been forbidden to court Athena, but that hadn't kept him away. When Persephone and Adam had been separated in the early days of their marriage, Adam had crossed several counties despite his intense dislike of leaving home in order to be with her again. James came to dinner only because he was forced to, just like he'd been forced to feign interest in her in the first place.

"Though I do not particularly like Lord Tilburn and certainly don't entirely trust him," Adam said, "I think he stayed away in order to avoid upsetting you further than he has."

"Stayed away? He's been living two doors down."

"And has not yet attempted to beat down the door. That shows both sense and self-control."

Daphne rose, confused. "If his presence upsets me, why did you make him stay?"

"*Does* his presence upset you?"

"Of course it does. How could it not? After everything he did, after everything I have endured, his presence most certainly upsets me." The impulse to shout in frustration proved nearly as unshakable as the need to cry out all her pain. "This is supposed to be a safe haven, Adam. I am supposed to be safe here, safe from him and from the tabbies of the *ton* and from . . . from . . . everything."

Adam said nothing for the space of several uncomfortable moments. Daphne glanced back at him. He wore the expression that always indicated he was sorting out something complicated. Daphne had no desire to be dissected and evaluated.

"Daphne."

She waited for whatever final assessment he meant to offer.

"There is a vast difference between a safe haven and a hiding place," he said. "One brings a person peace, the other unending loneliness. I refuse to watch you dwindle away in fear."

She faced him, attempting to look determined and confident despite the unnerving ring of truth to his words. "I am not afraid."

"You are terrified." The declaration came without pity or question. "Terrified of being brushed aside and forgotten."

"Adam—"

"I've hired Lord Tilburn away from Hartley. He will be staying here for the remainder of the Season."

"You *what?*" Daphne felt her eyes widen even as her stomach dropped to her toes. "Are you mad?"

"I am tired, is what I am. Tired of waiting for you to pull yourself out of this hole you've dug for yourself." His expression was stern, unrelenting. "No more sulking, Daphne. No more hiding."

She could feel herself closing in at the prospect of facing James every day, of reliving all the pain he'd caused her. "I cannot do this, Adam. Though you no doubt see it as a weakness and a failing, I cannot so easily dismiss ridicule and censure and heartache. Those barbs may bounce off you, but they pierce me. They pierce me every time."

The look of disappointment that entered Adam's eyes came as a blow. "Life is never entirely painless, Daphne. But you cannot have the happiness without passing through the sorrow, and doing so makes you stronger. Hiding from it only makes you a coward."

She flinched at the declaration. While Adam had at times been stern with her, he had never spoken so harshly.

He left her standing there in the doorway. Without another look in her direction, he sat at his desk and took up his paperwork once more. A single set of tears pooled in her eyes, followed closely by another. For the first time in years, she made no attempt to stem the tide of emotion.

She slowly made her way to her bedchamber. Curled in a ball on her bed, she allowed a lifetime of heartache to escape. The tiny child desperate for her father's affection wept alongside the young lady in love with a gentleman who did not love her in return.

Chapter Thirty-Two

DAPHNE TUGGED AT ONE KID glove as she descended the stairs. Uncertainty slowed her steps, but determination pushed her forward. A nearly sleepless night spent in contemplation and internal debate had finally solidified her decision in the quietest, darkest hours of early morning. Though she felt almost overwhelmingly nervous, she refused to go back into hiding. She may have been a plain and uninteresting nymph, but she was not a coward.

Artemis stood in the entryway, her open palm pressed to her heart. The look she gave Persephone dripped with dramatic suffering. "I shall waste away to a mere waif if made to pass another hour in the confines of my dungeon."

"Your bedchamber is hardly a dungeon," Persephone said. "And you have not been confined to that room. You have the entire house and the back grounds at your disposal, and you have made any number of excursions out into London."

"A free spirit must go about in the world without restrictions, Persephone." At this, Artemis's eyes turned heavenward, creating the perfect picture of longing and heartbreaking agony. "Walls and gates stifle and suffocate a heart meant to fly beyond the bounds of—"

"I am sorry for your suffocating heart, my dear, but you cannot venture out into Town unaccompanied by your family, no matter its appeal."

"I wish only to go out into the park. I can see it from my window, calling out to me, just out of reach." She clutched her hands together before her as though a condemned prisoner at once pleading for mercy and praying for the welfare of her soul. "And I solemnly vow to give any criminals—though you realize meeting an *actual* criminal would be wonderfully exciting—a very wide berth."

"Adam's insistence on storming the halls of Westminster only moments after the Prime Minister was murdered is the closest any member of this family will be permitted to come to the criminal element," Persephone insisted. "I will not allow you to go searching for one—and do not argue that you won't go looking. I know you."

Daphne took a fortifying breath. She had anticipated this contretemps and recognized the opportunity to put her newfound determination to the test. "I will walk about the park with her," she offered with more assurance than she felt.

Her sisters turned toward her in perfect synchrony. Their looks of surprise would have been identical if not for the hint of triumph that touched Artemis's face.

She reached her sisters' sides and acted as though she didn't notice how very shocked they were. A turn about the park was hardly reason for such amazement. She didn't think she had been that withdrawn.

Persephone skewered Artemis with a scolding look. "Even with Daphne keeping you company, you are not to venture outside the walls."

Artemis enthusiastically linked her arm with Daphne's. "We will be pattern cards of decorum," she promised.

Persephone gave her a look of patent disbelief. "All I ask is that you do not run amok amongst the flowerbeds."

Artemis wrinkled up her nose. "That was five years ago, Persephone. I am far more dignified now."

Daphne bit back a smile and saw Persephone do the same. *Dignified* and *Artemis* rarely found their way into the same sentence.

"We shan't be gone long," Daphne told her oldest sister.

"Take a leisurely stroll," she was instructed in return.

Daphne firmed her shoulders and stepped outside arm in arm with Artemis. Though clouds covered a great deal of the sky, the air outside proved less chill than one might expect. Summer was quickly arriving. Town would soon grow unbearably warm, and Society would flee to the countryside. The slightest breeze stirred the shrubbery lining the front path that led to the door, but the temperature was pleasant.

Artemis sighed. "Oh, I had wished for a positively leaden sky. To walk about under threat of rain is far more heartrending, don't you think?"

"Receiving a thorough drenching would not be particularly welcome though," Daphne answered. "Perhaps you could consider our partially cloudy skies a happy compromise." Bless Artemis for choosing a topic as benign as the weather. Daphne had feared she would delve directly into love and loss and unending heartache.

"But don't you see, Daphne, I have decided something quite, quite important." Artemis pulled her by the hand into the central garden. "My decision is so important, in fact, that I capitalized the word *important* when I wrote in my diary about it."

Oh dear. "What is this important-with-a-capital-*I* decision?" Daphne asked warily.

"I am going to fall in love in a park, or at the very least in a place that is green and alive. Further, I have concluded that there absolutely must be water." Artemis grinned at her, eyes overflowing with excitement. "Is that not simply divine?"

"I confess I do not understand the necessity of water, let alone a park."

Artemis groaned in a fashion Daphne knew all too well. She could have spoken her sister's next words along with her, so familiar was the response. "Daphne, you have absolutely no romantic sensibilities."

"I know I am a sore trial to you," Daphne said dryly. She steered them along the tree-lined path, a pleasant place to spend a morning, even with one's exhausting younger sister.

"If you had shown a bit more feeling, maybe Lord Tilburn would not have—" Artemis clamped her hand over her mouth but too late.

With effort, Daphne kept the pain of Artemis's unfinished declaration from registering in her expression.

"This park is nice, but I have always loved Persephone's little garden at the castle. It is so green, with so many flowers and so much grass." The words rushed out of Artemis in an unmistakable attempt to cover her blunder. "And a great many flowers. Oh. I already mentioned the flowers, didn't I?" She looked utterly miserable.

Daphne supposed she ought to take pity on her sister. The poor girl's mouth did have a tendency to run away with her. A few uncomfortable moments of alarm might help teach her to think before she spoke though. Daphne kept her peace, allowing the sounds of nature to hang in the air between them. The breeze rustled leaves. Somewhere, a lone bird called out for its missing companions. A canine yelp full of enthusiasm and energy joined the cacophony.

A great deal of uncertainty slipped away as she continued to walk. Daphne knew she had made only the smallest of strides by leaving the house without being forced but felt remarkably proud of herself. Adam would certainly recognize the step for what it was. A tendril of hope began to weave its way around her heart. Her future began to look a touch less lonely. She need not thrust herself into Society but, in time, might not feel the urge to hide from it.

They had traversed nearly half the distance around the park when a flash of brown fur darted in front of Daphne, circling about her legs and barking with marked excitement. The merest glimpse identified the tiny pup, and in an instant, her heart lodged firmly in her throat.

"Hello, Scamp." Her voice trembled a bit. She lowered herself enough to stroke the pup's head with shaking fingers. Scamp's presence all but guaranteed the presence of his master.

James arrived at her side in the next moment, his look both amused and apologetic. "I let him off his lead for only a moment, and he immediately darted in your direction."

She straightened, reminding herself of her newly acquired measure of courage. "I did not realize Scamp had stayed in London after your mother returned home." Though, thinking on it, she believed Adam may have mentioned something on that score.

For some reason, her innocuous observation made him shift uneasily. "I had thought—He would not have been—" James cleared his throat, apparently struggling to reply. An almost embarrassed smile touched his lips. "I grew rather attached to him and couldn't bring myself to send him away."

"Has he caused you a great deal of trouble?" Perhaps if she kept to the topic of ill-mannered puppies, she could prevent herself from falling to pieces. His reluctant admission of tenderness toward the ramshackle mutt tugged at her heart in a worrisome way. She would not allow herself to fall for him once more. Bravery was one thing. Stupidity was another altogether.

"His trouble stems only from youthful spirits and a dislike of confinement," James answered.

Artemis broke into the conversation. "Would you care to walk with us, Lord Tilburn?"

"Speaking of youthful spirits and a dislike of confinement," Daphne said under her breath.

James bit back a smile as if they'd just shared a very personal joke. They used to do that a lot, back when she still trusted him.

"I would enjoy walking with you," James said. "Let me see if Scamp will allow me to put him back on his lead."

While James fussed with the uncooperative pup, Artemis whispered urgently, her eyes wide with excitement. "Daphne, he must have been most desperate to see you again. Why else would he come to work for someone as horribly terrifying as Adam, staying right here at Falstone House, even with Adam and Linus both carrying their sidearms about with them in warning? How very promising!"

"Keep your voice lowered." How she hoped James had not overheard. She kept her own voice to a barely audible whisper.

James seemed to have accomplished his task. Faced with the difficulty of holding Scamp's lead in one hand and walking with two ladies, he asked Artemis if she would be terribly offended if he offered his free arm to Daphne.

"Certainly not, Lord Tilburn." Artemis seemed positively gleeful. "For I am working quite tirelessly at making the perfect picture of sorrow and suffering. The sky has been horridly uncooperative, but walking in apparent loneliness would be quite a nice touch, do you not think?"

James's brows knit together and, after a moment of hesitation, he nodded. Daphne slipped her arm through his when he offered it. The feel of his arm beneath her hand still affected her as much as it ever had. Her heart beat louder, her cheeks felt warmer. They slowly retook the path she and Artemis had been walking before James and Scamp's arrival.

"I am not at all certain just what your sister meant by all she said." James kept a firm grip and a close eye on Scamp, though he glanced over at Daphne as they walked. "Does her sense of the dramatic never taper off?"

"Not ever." How she wanted to ask him how he felt about staying at Falstone House. She feared the answers too much to ask. Her bravery did not yet extend that far.

"Let us hope her desire for sorrow and suffering cannot be fulfilled vicariously. If she tells your brother-in-law that I walked with your arm through mine, he will likely amputate mine." Most people quaked when speaking of Adam's threats. James, though clearly acknowledging the reality of Adam's fierceness, was not quelled by it.

Artemis kept to the promise she'd made Persephone and did not wander off nor trample the flowers, though her face took on the dreamy expression that indicated her thoughts had flown quite far afield.

"How much longer will Lieutenant Lancaster be ashore?" James asked.

"That is not yet firmly decided. Our father is quite ill, and Linus is torn between returning to our family home and returning to sea."

"I am sorry to hear your father's health is poor." James's eyes met hers, and she saw real concern in their depths. "Can anything be done for him?"

"I am afraid his decline is irreversible."

James pressed her arm to his side, a squeeze she instinctively knew was meant to comfort her. Beyond allowing her to read the letters sent by Father's caregiver, no one in the family had truly reached out to her. As Artemis was wont to point out, Daphne did not allow herself to be openly emotional. Most people would not think to comfort someone who did not look in need of it. But James had done exactly that.

"A difficult position for your brother," James said. "He no doubt feels his responsibility to his fellow seamen yet cannot deny his family duty either."

"We do not know yet what he will decide."

James watched her a moment as they walked. "If I do not mistake the matter, you hope he will choose to remain."

How had he seen that? She had worked hard at keeping her opinions hidden lest Linus be unduly influenced by them. "I worry less when he is on dry land."

"You have already lost one brother." James understood what she had never voiced out loud.

"And both of my parents," Daphne added quietly. Though death had not yet claimed her father, she knew full well she had lost him years ago.

James slipped his arm back enough to entwine his fingers with hers. "Please tell me if I might do anything for you. Anything at all."

"Thank you." How she managed the response, she could not say. Her eyes were fixed on her hand still held in his.

A moment later, they were once more arm in arm like any promenading couple. That flicker of hope she'd felt upon first leaving the house grew a little brighter. She did not know yet if she could trust its light, but she clung to it for that one beautiful moment.

Then that moment died.

Mrs. Bower and her daughter came around the corner and directly toward them. There would be no avoiding the encounter.

"Why, Lord Tilburn." Mrs. Bower rushed over, her daughter swift on her heels. "This is fortuitous."

Miss Bower's attention shifted too quickly to Daphne. "Miss Lancaster. What a surprise."

"Indeed," her mother said. "I had understood you and Lord Tilburn were no longer on friendly terms."

James spoke before Daphne could think of a response. "I cannot imagine why anyone would think that. Clearly Miss Lancaster and I are quite fond of one another." He indicated their current friendly position.

"You are walking here alone?" Miss Bower's words held a note of censure.

Daphne decided it was time she joined in her own defense. "My sister Artemis is with us, as I am certain you can see."

"Artemis." Mrs. Bower tapped her finger against her lips. "Are all of the Lancaster sisters named for goddesses?"

"No, Mother. Daphne, you will recall, was only a nymph."

That distinction had pained and bewildered Daphne all her life. She had always been the nymph among the goddesses.

"Daphne wasn't merely a nymph," James said. "She was the daughter of the river god. Apollo mourned her tragic loss eternally. There was and is nothing 'mere' about her."

The praise was as buoying as it was unexpected. And yet, there he stood, his chin held at a defiant angle as if daring the Bowers to contradict him.

"At least her name isn't 'Cynthia,'" Artemis said, her offhand observation punctuated by some indefinable thrust. "I'd hide away in a turret tower if I were burdened with such an insignificant and dull name as that."

Daphne's champions had quite effectively silenced the Bowers.

"If you will excuse us," James said. "I should very much like to continue my pleasant sojourn with my lovely companions."

"We will see you at the Kirkham's ball at the end of the week?" Mrs. Bower asked.

"If I attend, I will do so as a member of Their Graces's party and, therefore, cannot say whether or not our circles will overlap." As far as set downs went, it was a gracefully and pointedly executed one.

The Bowers understood the message. Their upward aspirations would not be accomplished on James's coattails. They continued on their way, heads pressed together, plotting already.

"Lord Lampton will no doubt be at the Kirkham's ball," Mrs. Bower told her daughter. "He is of higher standing than the Tilburns will ever be. We must set our sights a touch higher."

"But Lord Lampton is so odd," Miss Bower objected.

"He is an earl, Cynthia. He is allowed to be odd." It was the last thing Daphne overheard before the ladies were too distant for their words to be distinguishable.

A moment of silence passed between Daphne, James, and Artemis. The others were no doubt waiting for her to fall to pieces. She didn't intend to. "Artemis, I didn't realize you disliked the name Cynthia so much."

"I don't dislike it at all; it is a lovely name." Artemis glided past them. "I simply dislike *her*." She looked back over her shoulder. "No one speaks to my sister that way. Not anyone. Not ever."

Daphne was touched more than she felt equal to expressing. She didn't think Artemis had ever come so close to saying that she cared about her.

"The Bowers are insufferable," James said. "I hope you don't mean to give heed to anything they said or implied."

She squared her shoulders. She had, after all, decided just that morning to be strong and courageous even in the face of her own lingering doubts. "I am determined, Lord Tilburn, that no one will ever be permitted to hurt me again."

Chapter Thirty-Three

JAMES DISCOVERED FIRSTHAND THE DUKE of Kielder's capacity for battle strategy. No matter the enormity of tasks he was assigned every day, James still found himself crossing paths with Daphne several times, even if only in passing. Though she still hadn't smiled at him, she seemed a bit less jumpy in his presence.

They'd walked about the park with Scamp that morning, as they had each of the past few mornings. Afternoon had come, and James found himself looking for her again. The Falstone House staff was every bit as loyal as His Grace had insisted during their weapons-punctuated interview. Not a soul would tell James outright where Daphne was to be found.

A perusal of the family and public rooms yielded no success. He didn't dare attempt to infiltrate the kitchen. No doubt the cook had instructions to toss him in her soup pot if she felt so inclined. He walked along the back of the house, hoping to spy Daphne taking a turn around the back gardens.

He heard movement just inside a door on the east end of the house. Perhaps whoever was inside would be willing to point him in Daphne's direction. He knew before even stepping inside that he'd found the herb room. The aromas wafting out were as strong as they were varied.

He stepped inside and nearly laughed at what he found. All his searching, and there Daphne was tying up bundles of some plant or another.

"You seem very hard at work." He realized the moment the words left his mouth just how inelegant a greeting it was.

She didn't seem to mind but simply kept at her efforts. "I was meant to spend the afternoon with my brother-in-law, but he is occupied with matters relating to the impending arrival of the newest member of the Boyce family."

Boyce was the duke's surname, though few people thought of him by anything other than his very intimidating title.

"So you have chosen this undertaking to fill your afternoon instead?" James stepped farther inside. "Does Falstone House not have enough staff for this?"

"I enjoy working with the herbs," she said. "I think Adam knows he would have to sleep with one eye open if he ever took this task away from me."

James smiled a bit at the absurdity of that threat. Daphne was a gentle soul; he knew that without a doubt. "You not only know how to use and grow the herbs but how to preserve them as well?"

She tied off the twine wrapped securely around a bundle of bright-green herbs and snipped the end. "The more I know about the plants I use, the better able I am to use them most efficaciously."

"Can I assist you at all? I haven't your knowledge, but I am very good at following directions." He winced, knowing his recent history reflected unflatteringly on his tendency to do what he was told. Daphne didn't seem to take his remark badly.

"How are you at hanging things on high hooks?" She glanced up at the myriad hooks adorning the ceiling. "I always have to use a step stool."

James smiled. "I received very high marks in herb hanging at Harrow."

"Top of your class, were you?" He heard a smile in her words, though one had not appeared on her face.

"No one could compete with me," he said. "Fortunately for you, my skills are entirely at your disposal just now."

She held her bundle out to him. "The hook just behind you, near the other bundles like this."

He pointed to the one he thought she meant.

Daphne nodded.

"What plant is this?" he asked as he hung it on its hook.

"Marjoram."

"And what is it used for?" By the time he turned back from his task, she had already begun tying another bundle.

"It is a soothing herb, used to treat pain and anxiety and internal discomfort." She spoke as she selected green-leafed herbs from a basket.

James stepped up to the table where she worked. "That plant appears to be a different one."

She discarded a stem she apparently found lacking. "This is sage."

He could see Daphne had a great deal of experience with preparing herbs for drying. She worked without the slightest hesitation, creating perfect bundles with no visible effort.

"What is sage used for?" he asked both out of a desire to keep her talking and an unexpected curiosity.

She looked up from her neat pile of leaves. "Don't you know anything, Lord Tilburn?" Her shock was too theatrical to be real. "Sage"—she held a sprig of sage up, pointing it directly at him—"is used to ward off evil spirits."

He smiled at that. "I'm very pleased to know that. I have had the most unimaginably bad luck with evil spirits of late."

A smile touched her eyes. With a little more teasing, might her dimple make an appearance as well?

"The throat tonics I recommended for your mother had sage as one of their primary ingredients."

"Ah." James watched her wind her bundle with twine. "Am I to hang that one alongside the marjoram?"

She shook her head. "I mean to give sage its own little corner. The other herbs are afraid of it, you see."

James nodded soberly. "Very sage of you."

She groaned. "Horrible, Lord Tilburn. Horrible."

He hung his head. "My lowest marks were in puns."

Daphne began another bundle of sage. If the size of her basket was any indication, she'd be working with the herbs for some time. James looked around the room as she worked.

"There must be a dozen varieties in here."

"Twelve, exactly." She looked up from her work, a light in her eyes James hadn't seen since their falling out. "There are twice that many to prepare at the castle. I am hoping Adam will allow us to return earlier than expected so I won't run out of time before the cold comes."

"You enjoy this."

Daphne nodded, an actual smile beginning on her face. James enjoyed seeing it.

"Do you have a favorite of those twenty-four?"

"Catmint," she said. "It is used to treat infectious fevers."

"Why is it your favorite?"

"It is so useful, an essential part of any herbalist's collection. Yet few people have any idea what it is." Here was the animation James had missed seeing in her. "And being in the mint family, it has such a wonderful fragrance if a person gets close enough to experience it. When it flowers, the blooms are so quietly beautiful, simple, and elegant."

"Will you tell me about the others?"

She looked surprised at the request. "What? All of them?"

James nodded. He truly wished to hear more. She was happier talking about herbs than she'd been since his arrival at Falstone House.

"Let us start with—" He looked around a moment before settling on a prickly looking bundle hanging on the opposite side of the room. He held a hand out to her. Daphne's attention was fixed on the various hanging herbs, her brows knit in thought. She accepted his hand, though he doubted she realized what she'd done. He led her to the herb he meant to start with. "This one."

She kept her hand in his. "Rosemary. Very efficacious in treating headaches. And this"—she indicated another bundle nearby—"is soapwort. Excellent for treating boils." She reached with her free hand for a jar nearby, filled with a collection of something horn shaped. "Comfrey root," she said. "It is also called knit-bone. It's used to treat injuries."

He walked about the herb room with her, listening to her vast store of knowledge. She knew the herbs and oils and dried roots on sight. She could list their uses and, he fully suspected, knew precisely how to prepare any tisane or poultice called for.

"You amaze me." He meant every word. "Is there anything you don't know?"

A very becoming touch of color pinked her cheeks. Next to a fleeting glimpse of her dimple, he enjoyed seeing her color above almost anything. Not that he wanted to embarrass her. It was simply such a sincere reaction. Too many people of his acquaintance weren't genuine. He had liked that about her from the beginning.

"What else can I do for you?" He truly wished to be of service in whatever way he could. Her happiness and well-being had become essential to his own.

"You needn't actually stay if you've other things to attend to," she said, settling herself at the worktable once more. "I'll only be tying up herbs."

James took his previous position as well. He missed the feel of her hand in his and wondered if she'd even noticed the gesture. "I have a hanging talent I need to put to use."

She smiled at him then, a small one but a smile just the same. James would hang herbs with her all day for a fleeting glimpse of that dimple of hers.

It was a shame, really, that the *ton* couldn't see her in that moment. She was so capable, so confident. Her passion for these herbs and the obvious years of study she'd invested lit her up in a way no one ever saw. No gentleman seeing the sparkle in her eyes as she worked could resist falling at least a little in love with her. It was little wonder he was finding himself in precisely that position.

He loved Daphne a little more every time he was with her. And he knew with utter certainty that he wouldn't be the only one to fall under her spell. She was slowly but surely shedding the paralyzing timidity that had kept her hidden from Society's view. She would likely always be quiet and subdued, but she wouldn't go unnoticed.

Gentlemen would begin courting and wooing her, and one of them would succeed in earning her love in return. That someone, however, would not likely be him. For he was Apollo, the one man she could never trust again.

Chapter Thirty-Four

DAPHNE COULD NOT MAKE HEADS nor tails of James Tilburn. He had become surprisingly attentive. They had regained something of their previous affinity, but questions lurked in her mind.

Why had he suddenly renewed his interest? What were his intentions? Did his tender treatment of her indicate deeper feelings, or did he merely feel sorry for her or guilty about his previous behavior?

"I confess I had no idea Africa had been so intricately divided," James said, holding up a particularly odd-shaped puzzle piece.

"The continent rather begged to be made into a jigsaw puzzle, did it not?" Daphne stringently kept to the most neutral of topics. She enjoyed conversations with him but felt far too vulnerable to delve into anything of a personal nature.

"We had a puzzle very like this as children." James tried to fit his piece in, but it wouldn't go. "It was of Europe, however, and not nearly so difficult. Your geography lessons must have been brutal."

She couldn't hold back a smile at his exaggerated tone. "Artemis was the only one of us subjected to this puzzle during her lessons. Linus brought it home with him during a visit."

A brief moment passed as they continued unhurriedly working at the complicated pieces. Persephone sat nearer the sitting room windows, applying herself to a bit of embroidery. Artemis had taken full possession of the room's fainting sofa in order to practice death scenes, having declared her previous efforts "sadly lacking in elegance."

"Has your brother decided whether he means to leave the navy or continue on?"

The inquiry was a natural one but pricked her heart just the same. "He announced this morning that he had made his choice."

James's eyes immediately flew to hers. The briefest of seconds passed. "Oh, Daphne." Those two words were saturated in compassionate understanding. "How soon does he return to his ship?"

Without a single word of explanation from her, he knew what had happened and precisely how she felt. No other person she'd known had ever been able to do that. His kindness coupled with her own shaky emotions nearly undid her. "He will be here less than one more week." The words did not emerge entirely steady. "The *Triumphant* is due to sail in six days."

"This must have come as a blow."

She nodded. "Part of me clung to the hope that he would choose to resign his post, but he is a man of conviction, and we are, after all, a country at war. By all accounts, that war will spread to two fronts in the weeks ahead, the situation with the former colonies being what it is. I think I suspected all along he would return to fight."

James turned the puzzle piece about in his hand, but his eyes never left her face. "If his principles dictate he return, then certainly he must. But I know how much you worry about him."

Those were precisely her feelings. "I cannot fault him for his decision, but I am—"

"Concerned." He smiled kindly. "I have ever admired your compassionate nature. In my experience, that is a far too rare quality."

Heat stained her cheeks. *Admired* was a decidedly pleasant word coming from him—perhaps not the exact word she wished most to hear but encouraging, just the same. She felt rather like a fledgling chick inching closer to the edge of the nest, uncertain of what came next but not yet ready to brave the possibilities.

"My tendency to fret over people is nothing worthy of such praise."

His brow furrowed. "Do you really think the compliment insincere?"

"Not insincere, merely . . . exaggerated." She judiciously applied herself to the puzzle, finding this new topic as disquieting as their previous. Why could they not go back to discussing the continents or the weather? Her footing was much surer in those arenas.

James apparently did not intend to let the matter rest. "And if I were to tell you that in addition to your kind heart, you have a remarkable wit?"

She shook her head, keeping her gaze firmly fixed on the puzzle in which she had long since lost interest. "I am no comedienne, sir."

"I suppose you also discount your admirable intelligence."

"As my company is very seldom required by anyone, I have always had ample time for reading. It is not intelligence so much as years' worth of lonely hours in need of filling with something. Anything." She shrugged a little. "What good have my stores of trivial knowledge truly done me, after all?"

He offered no rebuttal, no further inquiries after her nonexistent charms. When the silence grew overly long, she hazarded a glance at him, half expecting a look of dismissal or an eagerness to be about his business. But his gaze appeared riveted on her face.

"Good gracious, you actually believe that." He sounded entirely shocked.

The blush she'd felt begin moments before intensified. "I know what I am," she said quietly. "And I have long since accepted the truth."

James stood abruptly. "Miss Lancaster. Would you be so good as to take a short excursion with me?"

She didn't immediately comply, trying to ascertain his intentions.

"Please?" he added, his voice quiet but firm.

Reminding herself that she had decided to be brave, she rose. He did not offer his arm as she had expected him to but instead took hold of her hand, entwining their fingers, then led her directly to the drawing room doors and out into the corridor. She had not at all sorted out his reasons for their sudden 'excursion' but was too lost in the wonderful feel of her hand in his to think overly much about it—until they reached their destination: the large gilded mirror hanging near the entryway.

James released her hand and turned her to face the looking glass hanging at a level just right for viewing nearly all of oneself. He stood directly behind her, ever so slightly to the left. Their eyes met in the mirror.

"Tell me what you see," he said.

An odd request, to be sure. "You and I and the corridor."

"No. I mean, when you look at yourself, tell me what you see."

She dropped her gaze to the floor, mortification sweeping over her. How could he ask such a thing?

No sooner had her head lowered than she felt his fingers lightly press her chin upward once more.

"Tell me what you see." He made the request once more, speaking with greater emphasis.

She stood very still. What did she see? A person should never be made to admit such a thing. "I am not very tall," she answered tentatively, picking her most innocuous feature. "I know I am a bit plain, but that is preferable to being homely, I suppose." Tears stung the backs of her eyes. She blinked several times to keep them at bay. She took a wavering breath but pressed on. "I do like to read, so I would consider myself well informed. I did not particularly take this Season, but I am welcomed by all the *ton's* matrons, which is something of an accomplishment, I suppose."

James watched her, his expression unreadable.

She diverted her gaze and lowered her voice to a level just hovering above a whisper. "That was likely not what you meant. One cannot 'see' those things."

James laid his hands on her upper arms, moving close enough that she heard his very quiet words. "Would you like to know what I see?"

Would she? Surely he would not make the offer if his impressions were unflattering. Calling once more on her determination to be courageous, Daphne nodded, though she could not bring herself to look at him.

"You have the thickest hair I think I have ever seen on a lady and of such a pure shade of brown. I am certain that many of the ladies in Society are secretly quite envious of it. Likewise, not a soul who is privileged enough to see it could fail to notice your lovely smile, though I truly hope *I* am the only one who finds that one lone dimple so distractingly fascinating."

Daphne looked up at the mirror. He stood very close, his eyes fixed on her reflection.

"But it is your eyes, Daphne, that draw one in. They glow with unmistakable intelligence, especially when you speak of your herbs, and you have the remarkable ability to see the world for what it truly is, even if you do not see yourself quite so clearly."

He moved closer still, his breath rustling her hair as he spoke. Never in the course of their acquaintance had he stood so near. She dared not look up at him lest he see more in her eyes than she was yet ready for him to know. That she still loved him, she could no longer deny. Trusting him, however, was coming by inches, and slowly at that. A part of her knew that were he to stand so breathtakingly close to her on a regular basis, she would forgive him almost anything.

"Society is rife with empty-headed misses," he said. "A gentleman with any sense whatsoever wishes for so much more than that. He wants that rare combination of goodness and intelligence. He counts himself most fortunate if those essential qualities accompany a pretty face. That, my dear," he lowered his voice to a whisper, "is what *I* see."

Only when he brushed moisture from her cheek with the pad of his thumb did she realize a tear had escaped her eyes. He tucked a loose tendril of hair behind her ear.

"Why don't you see that, Daphne?"

She closed her eyes against the pain of that question. "Because that isn't me. I am just Daphne, the plain, unnecessary sister. The nymph among the goddesses. The one who is forgotten in a heartbeat."

"I assure you, that is not true in the least, for I tried valiantly. A great many heartbeats passed after the disastrous picnic, and I found myself entirely unable to forget you."

Daphne opened her eyes, though she did not look up at him nor at his reflection before her. "You forgot me within moments of our first meeting. Given time, you would easily do so again."

"Would I have returned after that first tea if I had immediately forgotten you?"

"Of course you would have," she said, pain piercing her anew. "You were required to return. You were forced to remember me."

"Things may have begun that way," he said, "but as I came to know you better, I continued my courtship, not because I was required to but because I wished to. I returned eagerly, willingly."

"But not honestly." She was not certain he was being entirely honest with her now.

"I can make no justification for my lack of integrity," he said, "nor will I try. I might have been cajoled into that first meeting, but I was not coerced into all of them."

Into all of them. That was not at all comforting; neither was the realization that he had no recollection of a moment that had altered her life. "The call you paid at our at-home all those weeks ago was not our first meeting." She saw confusion in his eyes. Confession seemed the best course of action. "We first met six years ago," she told him. "I was hiding on the terrace during my sister's come-out ball, spying on the festivities through the windows. You caught me there but kept my secret. Your kindness to a terribly timid little girl stayed with me long after that night. But on the few occasions afterward when our paths crossed, the complete lack of recognition in your expression told me as nothing else could that you had utterly forgotten me, just as everyone else does. Just as everyone *always* does."

What had possessed her to confess so much to him? Daphne had told no one of her encounter with James Tilburn on the Falstone House terrace.

If James did not already think her entirely pathetic, he most certainly would after hearing her history.

It was not pity, however, that she saw enter his eyes. His gaze as it reflected back at her from the mirror appeared very nearly amazed. "Your hair hung in two long braids, and you wore the frilliest nightdress I could possibly have imagined."

Daphne's breathing came to a sudden halt. Did he actually remember?

"You were a study in contradictions." James watched her intently. "You were so tiny, no larger, I thought at the time, than a girl of eight or nine, yet you acted older despite your timidity. You seemed terrified to so much as speak, yet you were defying the Dangerous Duke's demands in order to snatch a peek at the ball."

Good heavens, he *did* remember.

"I never could be entirely sure of your age, which is likely one reason I did not recognize you in the light of day, but I assure you I recall that meeting. I told my brother about you, and I thought of that little girl often over the years."

"You did?" Her amazement rendered the question almost breathless.

He nodded. "I never learned your name or your exact connection to His Grace. None of the duchess's sisters appeared to be the right age. I assumed that little girl was a distant cousin and never did inquire further." The confession brought a crease of worry to his brow. "The only excuse I can make for myself is that I was young and still a little too flighty and preoccupied with my own worries. But I told Ben of a little girl who reminded me of a determined little sparrow who sought her freedom even in the face of oppression."

Daphne's breath caught in her lungs. *Little Sparrow.* How she had longed to hear him say that again.

He shifted beside her. Daphne's gaze remained glued to him. Was he leaving?

James stepped in front of her and brushed his hand along her cheek. Daphne very nearly held her breath, the touch unexpected and pleasantly unsettling.

"All these years," James said, still standing near her but no longer touching her face. "I've wondered what happened to that little girl. I ought to have realized. You have the same brown eyes. More to the point, you have the same bravery—something both my brother and I envied in that quiet child."

"I have never been very brave," Daphne said. Had not Adam told her himself she had acted unforgivably fainthearted?

James took her face in his hands. "You taught me how to be courageous, both then and now." A curious trembling began in her middle at the feel of his hands on her face. His words somehow penetrated her increasingly fuzzy thoughts. "And you have shown me how to be kind, how to care for my family without being taken advantage of. You have shown me what it means to be good and worthy. Though I most certainly do not deserve your regard, I intend to try to win it."

"You did not actually want my regard but were forced into pursuing it." It pained her to bring the topic up once more, but she was so confused. She had no idea what to think or believe.

"As I was reminded recently, Apollo was a thick-witted buffoon." His hands slipped from her face to her shoulders, though his eyes didn't leave hers. "*His* Daphne never did know the sincerity of his regard, but I am determined that *my* Daphne will."

Her breath caught, the unexpelled air pulsing in rhythm with her pounding heart. "*Your* Daphne?"

"The duke would likely chain me up in the attics for being so presumptuous." He made as if to pull away.

Daphne took hold of the sleeve of his frock coat. "*Your* Daphne?"

He stepped in close once more, his voice low and intimate. "I mean to do all I can, dearest Daphne, to prove myself worthy of being yours and of calling you mine."

Fear warred with hope. "You are asking a lot of me, James," she whispered.

A sigh of relief escaped his lips. "You called me James."

She bit down a smile. "Have you missed that?"

"I have missed *you*."

"I am here now," she said.

She heard his thick swallow, then his shaky breath. "Daphne." Her name was a plea on his lips. "Tell me I am to have another chance."

"I do not trust easily," she warned.

He nodded. "And you have ample reason to doubt me." He looked so worried, so heartbroken.

She reached out and touched his forlorn face. "But you are also giving me reason to believe, however tentatively."

He closed his eyes. His shoulders rose and fell with a deep breath. "I will not squander this opportunity," he vowed.

"Neither will I." An unexpected surge of bravery overtook her. She rose on her toes and pressed a kiss to his cheek. His arms wrapped around her on the instant. His hands splayed on her back, holding her close to him. She turned her head the tiniest bit, facing him directly. A scant breath separated them.

He bent slowly toward her. All thoughts fled but one: James Tilburn was going to kiss her.

The lightest touch of his lips on hers sent her pulse racing. She clung to him, not wanting the moment to end.

But she heard the front door open just out of sight of where they stood. James must have noticed the sound as well. He stepped away from her a bit.

Very purposeful footfalls preceded the arrival of both Adam and Linus, neither looking particularly pleased.

Adam's gaze settled on James. "Tilburn."

"Your Grace," James acknowledged, the smallest bit of worry in his tone.

"We"—Adam indicated Linus with a slight lift of his head—"have just had a most interesting conversation."

Adam did tend toward cryptic explanations in favor of useful ones, especially when he was displeased. Daphne turned to Linus, hoping for more information.

He did not disappoint. To James he said, "Your father is a parasite."

Chapter Thirty-Five

With effort, James assembled his muddled thoughts. Fear that the duke and lieutenant had come to skewer him for the frustratingly brief kiss he'd shared with Daphne dissipated with the realization that Father was making trouble. Again.

"I will move forward on the assumption that I find myself in a position of apologizing for my father's behavior."

"A good assumption," Lieutenant Lancaster muttered.

"What has he done?" James knew without a doubt he wouldn't like the answer.

"I refuse to gossip in the corridor," the duke said. "To the book room."

The Dangerous Duke and the young lieutenant made a very intimidating picture as they strode purposefully in the direction of the stairs. Watching them, James wondered how he'd managed to summon the fortitude to face the fearsome duo after his mistreatment of Daphne. They felt almost like allies now.

He turned toward Daphne and held out his hand.

"You wish for me to join you?" she asked.

If she doubted something as basic as his desire for her presence—his *need* for it—even after their tender moment of affection, then he had more work ahead of him than he realized. "I discovered quite early in our association that you are a godsend, Daphne. If you are willing to help me through yet another disaster of my family's making, I would consider myself even further in your debt."

She shook her head, color stealing across her face. She blushed adorably, though James knew better than to tell her so. She took the hand he held out to her. Progress had been made, certainly, but he still felt her hesitation. He needed only time and opportunity. She would eventually see that he could be trusted despite his less-than-stalwart history.

"What do you think your father has done?" she asked as they walked together down the corridor.

"I cannot even begin to guess."

"Could he—" Her question ended as abruptly as it had begun. She pressed her lips together, her eyes darting away from him.

James had learned to recognize that expression. She was holding back. "You must never worry about telling me anything, Daphne."

She studied him a moment, gauging his sincerity. He must have appeared at least momentarily trustworthy. "Do you suppose your father has decided upon another young lady to whom he will demand you pay your addresses?"

"He can demand until he's blue in the face, for all the good it will do him," James said.

Still, she looked unsure. "He might offer to return your income if you do."

"There is not enough money in all the world," he insisted.

"*All* the world? Are you certain? That seems like a great deal of money to me." He heard the smile in her voice and, better yet, saw that her expression matched her tone.

They stepped into His Grace's book room. The duke and the lieutenant occupied the precise positions they had upon James's first encounter with the formidable gentlemen. The air, however, was not thick with the feeling of impending doom, nor were a full dozen weapons laid out for emphasis. Much had changed in a short couple of weeks.

He saw Daphne seated comfortably in a chair near the desk, though not the one he knew from experience to be ridiculously lower than the others.

"Your father has learned of your employment here," the duke said without preamble.

"I haven't exactly kept it a secret," James said.

"I believe Techney rather wishes you had." The duke leaned back casually in his chair. "Does the phrase 'blot on the family name that is best forgotten' sound familiar to you?"

"It is practically my second given name."

"Signing contracts must leave you with muscle cramps," Daphne said quietly.

James bit down a smile. To his surprise, the duke and lieutenant did the same.

"Your father waxed surprisingly eloquent at the club this afternoon about his worthless son and how desperately he wishes the young whelp didn't continually give him reason to . . . What were the words he used, Linus? He painted such a precise picture."

The lieutenant didn't waste a single moment. "He bemoaned that he was burdened with a son who was a ne'er-do-well drunkard with a thirst for gambling so insatiable that he needs to seek employment simply to keep the sharks from tearing him to bits."

That was drastic, even for Father. "What utter—"

His Grace held up a hand and cut off the rest of James's protests. "Sadly, I was not done with my retelling."

"There is more?" James asked. Though he should not have been surprised, he was.

"Apparently unconvinced he had maligned you thoroughly enough, your loving father told everyone who would listen that you are an unrepentant rake who continually pretends to court unsuspecting young ladies as a matter of sport." What little humor had been in the duke's tone disappeared entirely. "He has warned all who will listen that you have set a goal to run the gamut of innocent young ladies in London."

James dropped into the low-lying chair across the table from the duke. Father was ripping him up before all of Society. "I am assuming that since you have not shipped my mangled remains to your Northumberland gibbet, you do not put a great deal of store by my father's declarations."

"As I have told you many times, Tilburn, your father is an idiot."

James slumped lower. "An idiot working very hard to denounce me."

"What are you willing to do to salvage your good name?" The duke pierced him with a challenging look.

James found he could not entirely rise to the occasion. "What can I possibly do?"

"You?" His Grace very nearly laughed. "You can do nothing. *I*, however, could do a great deal if I were so inclined."

"Considering my history with your family, Your Grace, I do not in the least warrant your support."

"No, you don't." The duke's stern gaze remained fixed on James. "To contradict your father would be to stake my own reputation on your trustworthiness. Whether or not you are a man of honor has been a topic of very unfavorable debate in this household."

James nodded. "Understandably so."

"Well, Daphne." The duke looked away from James for the first time. "What is your opinion on this matter? Does Lord Tilburn warrant my declaration of trust?"

James's heart dropped to his boots. While he had promised mere moments earlier that he would work to regain her trust, he knew full well he did not yet have it. The duke and the lieutenant had turned their attention to her. Seeing for himself the denial on her face would be too much. He kept his gaze on the desk.

"I have seen the care he takes of his mother and brother. He works very hard to keep Techney House running smoothly. I cannot imagine he is any less responsible with his family's Lancashire estate," Daphne said, though with a hint of hesitation. "You know as well as I do that he has worked very hard as your secretary and without complaint. I am certain the Duke of Hartley would concur."

It was, when one considered it, a very glowing evaluation of his work ethic. James had not expected that. Yet somehow, the compliments felt hollow.

"That is not what I asked, Daphne," the duke said. "I want to know if *you* trust him."

With that clarification, His Grace hit upon precisely what had been missing from Daphne's response. Nothing in her recommendation had been in the least personal.

She studied her clasped hands a moment before lifting her eyes to her brother-in-law.

James held his breath.

"I would trust him with my own estate if I had one," she said simply.

If ever a man had been humbled by an undeserved show of support, James was in that moment. She would trust him with her own land and home. He did not warrant Daphne's support but somehow had it.

"Linus," the duke said, "I believe that is endorsement enough to go through with our plan."

They had already formulated a plan?

Lieutenant Lancaster stepped forward, his posture stern and unyielding. In a crisp, authoritative voice, he addressed James. "Let me preface this by saying in no uncertain terms that I make this offer because of my unwavering faith in my sister's judgment, not because I have decided to fully trust you."

James nodded his understanding.

"Your father will destroy you if he continues this campaign of his," the lieutenant continued. "Even if his efforts were thwarted forthwith, some damage has already been done. There is just enough of a hint of truth to make people wonder. If your name is to be salvaged, all of his accusations must be addressed."

It made sense but hardly seemed likely.

"Whilst I have been serving in the navy," the lieutenant said, "the duke has overseen our family estate, allowing his man of business to undertake whatever efforts were necessary. My father is still living but not mentally capable of . . . well, of anything. Being of age and more able to see to my family's affairs, I have all but taken over the helm now. Knowing I will be at sea once more, I had intended to hire an estate manager of my own."

James nodded, though he wasn't certain where this was headed.

"Here is our proposition for you, Lord Tilburn. Your father's efforts have made it imperative that you not, in fact, earn your living lest Society see this as confirmation of his lies."

"I have nothing to live on if I do not—"

The lieutenant cut him off with a look. "In the eyes of the *ton*, you must not be seen to be working for your keep. The actual truth of the matter could, in fact, be quite the opposite. In deference to my sister's declaration of trust, I am offering you the position of estate manager on my family estate in Shropshire."

James could only stare. Without references, without an interview, he had been given a position? An income?

"It would not be presented as such, however," the lieutenant said. "We would put it about that the estate needed greater supervision, and the Duke of Kielder, knowing you to be competent, has asked that you oversee it. He has much greater cachet in Society than I do. Were he seen to be showing trust in you, that would go a long way toward establishing your honorable nature. You would have use of the manor house, its upkeep being provided through the estate. In lieu of a specific income, you would receive a percentage of the estate's profits. Such is an acceptable arrangement for a gentleman in the eyes of Society."

"I do not know how to even begin thanking you." Overwhelming gratitude rendered his words nearly unintelligible.

"You can thank me by not running the estate into the ground." The smallest hint of humor entered the lieutenant's tone. James had a feeling the naval man was not usually as stern as he had known him to be. Obviously he loved his sister a great deal and understandably struggled to forgive the man who had hurt her.

"I will run it with as much care as I would my own lands," James said.

The lieutenant nodded, apparently satisfied.

His Grace once more took control of the discussion. "That should address the issue of your pennilessness and should do much to quiet the speculation about your gambling debts and general lack of responsibility. We still, however, must address your father's comments about your treatment of innocent ladies."

"You've done so much already, I could not possibly—"

"This family does nothing halfway," His Grace insisted. "If Daphne has not tossed you out on your head yet, we are willing to stand by you."

His shock only continued to grow. He had never in all his life experienced such a show of support, especially from a family to which he had no claim and whom he had wronged so entirely. "Again, I thank you."

The duke leaned back in his chair, a contemplative expression on his face. "If your father were to receive an invitation to join us here at Falstone House, do you think he would be of a mind to accept?"

Father, turn down an invitation from Society's elite? No chance of that. "He would accept without hesitation."

"Perfect." The duke smiled in unholy triumph, and James felt the slightest twinge of apprehension on Father's behalf.

"What are you two planning?" Daphne sounded more intrigued than concerned.

"Let us just say," the duke replied, "that this is one performance Harry will never forgive himself for missing."

"Oh dear." Daphne's laugh brought a smile to James's face.

"Now, out, both of you," the duke ordered. "Linus and I have a few details to work out."

In the face of such a pointed dismissal, there was nothing to do but leave. James stepped into the corridor behind Daphne and walked beside her as she moved away from the book room. He owed her such an enormous debt of gratitude that he felt entirely unable to express himself.

She spoke first. "I know the look I just saw on my brother-in-law's face. It is precisely the expression he wears when his least favorite cousin comes to stay. Your father is to be woefully mistreated, it seems."

"Would you think me a black-hearted villain if I said I hope that proves true?"

"Adam will not disappoint you on that score." Lud, he loved her smile.

"I know full well that he would not be supporting me without your vote of confidence—a gesture on your part that I neither expected nor deserve. I cannot begin to tell you how humbled and indebted I am."

She did not look at him, though he could see a bit of color touch her cheeks. "I certainly hope I am not so shortsighted as to refuse to acknowledge your virtues simply because you did not conveniently fall top-over-tail in love with me."

Her attempt at an unaffected expression fell noticeably short of the mark. He could see the lingering pain in her eyes that his one-time disregard had caused.

"Daphne, I—"

"My family and I put every ounce of strength we had into our home during our years of poverty," she rushed on, cutting across his words. "The land and tenants deserve to be cared for and cared about."

"I promise to do my very best for them, but—"

"I am certain you will be given a great many tasks to prepare for your father's arrival. I won't keep you from it." Daphne quickened her pace, throwing a glance back over her shoulder as she reached the stairs leading up to the family's quarters. "Good day."

He watched her disappear up the steps. "Good day," he quietly replied.

Despite his awkward leave-taking and her conviction that he did not care for her, some progress had been made. She trusted him, at least a little. And somehow, he'd begrudgingly won the support of her brother and brother-in-law.

Beyond that, she had let him hold her, even kiss her. It had been brief, almost to the point of nonexistence, but it was, without question, reason enough to hope.

Chapter Thirty-Six

THE NEXT EVENING, FANNY MOTIONED James aside in the corridor. She was the chambermaid who had accompanied James and Daphne on their memorable ride through Hyde Park. She held an impressive handful of deepest-red roses.

"Miss Daphne prefers the red roses," Fanny whispered, her eyes darting about the corridor as if she were sharing a great national secret and feared being found out. "These're the reddest we have, I'd wager."

Fanny had taken a great interest in his rather pathetic romantic endeavors, asking after his success whenever they crossed paths. She had a crookedly endearing smile and an infectious enthusiasm James had grown quickly fond of.

Though the flowers were beautiful, their fragrance filling the air, James couldn't like the idea of Fanny's getting in trouble for taking them. "Will you be scolded for this?" he asked.

She shook her head confidently. "M' uncle is the groundskeeper here at the London house. He knows all about you courting our Miss Daphne. We're all cheering for you, in fact. Such a quiet, sweet thing, Miss Daphne. She deserves a good man who loves her."

James took the bouquet with a smile of gratitude. "Perhaps if the rest of the staff would rally behind me and drop a few kind words in Miss Lancaster's ear about how worthy and good I am."

Fanny laughed, her smile turning evermore lopsided. "We'll do that, Lord Tilburn."

He smiled, touched by her support. "Wish me luck."

"I'll do even better," she said. "I'll pray."

As he reached the corridor that led to the drawing room, James decided Fanny must have been praying for all she was worth. The lady who had occupied his every waking thought stood at the head of the enormous grand staircase. She smiled when she saw him.

"You look exceptionally happy this evening," he said.

"This promises to be an enjoyable evening." Her eyes strayed repeatedly during the brief reply to the small bouquet in his hand. James recognized a hopeful expression when he saw one.

He offered her the flowers with as much gallantry as he could without being ridiculous.

"I know these roses. You've been pilfering the grounds?"

Ah, that lovely dimple of hers! "It seems the groundskeeper likes me. He allowed me to bring these to you."

They walked beside one another, neither speaking, though the silence was not awkward. A natural, easy smile touched Daphne's lips as she breathed deep the roses' fragrance. James simply watched her, pleased that she appeared less somber than she so often did. If mere flowers could have such a happy effect, he told himself he'd find a way to bring her an offering regularly.

James slipped his hand around hers and lifted her hand to his lips. "I have missed you," he whispered.

She looked quite convinced he was teasing her. "Since breakfast this morning?"

"Is it so strange to miss someone after such a short separation?" he asked.

"If that someone is me, yes."

James held up his index finger in warning. "Daphne. Do I need to pull you in front of a mirror again?"

"I have thought back on that conversation."

He could not tell by her expression whether those recollections had been pleasant ones.

"Did you mean what you said about continuing your courtship because you wished to and not merely because you were forced?"

His Daphne was standing on the proverbial riverbank, debating whether to accept the river god's escape or turn and attempt to trust her Apollo. Theirs was a tenuous connection, the thinnest, most fragile of threads.

"I meant it with utmost sincerity," he told her. "I liked you from the first, and that liking grew to affection. Soon that affection deepened to a tenderness I have never felt for another person in all my life. In time, my dearest Daphne, I hope you can come to trust the truth of that."

They reached the doors to the drawing room, and James released her hand and motioned for her to precede him.

Daphne looked at him with uncertainty as she passed. Beneath that bewilderment, however, was a reassuring hint of hope.

Miss Artemis's voice rang through the drawing room. "Are you absolutely certain I cannot pretend to die?" she asked with something akin to desperation. "Or at least swoon? I am particularly adept at feigning a swoon."

"No such display will be required this evening," the duchess said.

James happened to meet the duke's eyes in that moment and caught in them a look of amusement that would not have seemed so foreign on any other gentleman. He had always suspected the duke cared a great deal for Daphne but, until that moment, hadn't realized he had a fondness for his youngest sister-in-law as well.

"Your father accepted our invitation almost before we issued it," His Grace said with a twist of his mouth.

"I do not find that particularly surprising." Father had likely nearly swooned himself at the prospect of being a guest at Falstone House.

"It is absolutely essential that you do not appear particularly surprised by anything that might be said or done this night." The duke gave him a penetrating look, emphasizing the importance of his words.

"I will do my best, Your Grace, though I cannot guarantee my acting abilities."

"Your best is all we ask."

"Is there anything I might do to aid your effort, Your Grace?"

"You can begin by not 'Your Grace'-ing me all the time. Your father must be made to see that you are an accepted part of this family."

But was he? James fervently wished it were true, though he could not quite convince himself. "What do you want me to call you?" He was not about to hazard a guess.

The duke did not pause to ponder or debate with himself. Apparently he had thought out this part of the plan ahead of time. "Kielder will do. Though my family members call me Adam, I think it wise not to give your Father any reason to find you impertinent."

"And the duchess? How am I to address her?" He seemed to have hit upon an unexpected question.

The lieutenant, standing in the drawing room doorway, gave the decisive opinion. "The privilege of Christian names is rarely given between any gentleman and lady unless they are inarguably related. I believe Persephone must be 'Your Grace'-ed and 'ma'am'-ed throughout the evening. And Artemis had best remain Miss Artemis"—he threw his youngest sister an impish smile—"though it lends her an air of maturity that could never ring entirely true."

Miss Artemis clasped her palm to her heart. "Your cruelty has slain me!" she declared in tones that rang with drama as she sank to the ground in an excessively graceful manner.

Not a single member of her family rushed to her inert form, nor looked the least bit concerned. Their countenances registered a mixture of amusement and exasperation. James found himself smiling, something that seemed to occur far more often than not of late.

A moment after melting into a heap on the floor, Miss Artemis regained her feet. "Was that not quite convincing?" she asked, obviously certain her swoon had struck fear into their hearts for her well-being. "I am certain Lord Techney could not help but be moved by such a sight."

Their Graces merely shook their heads, turning to each other for a private conversation.

Lieutenant Lancaster came to Miss Artemis's side. "Should a swoon prove necessary, we will be certain to inform you."

"Excellent." Miss Artemis could scarcely have looked more satisfied. "We must concoct a secret sign of some kind, a word or a gesture by which I will know I need to have a convenient fit of the vapors."

James leaned a touch closer to Daphne. "Miss Artemis must keep everyone's days lively."

Her eyes smiled up into his. "If there is one thing I can say for my family, it is that life amongst us is never dull."

He laughed at that. "Life with *my* family is hardly dull, but it is an entirely different kind of interesting."

Her expression clouded with concern. "How is your mother?"

"She is well," James said. "And tells anyone who will listen that your teas are nothing short of miraculous."

"I am so pleased she is feeling better." To his utter astonishment, Daphne slipped her hand into his. "I have always admired how deeply you care about her. You are a good son, though I have my suspicions no one ever tells you as much."

He lightly touched her face with his free hand, a shiver of awareness passing down his arm and through his body. She affected him more every time he was in her company.

He knew her blush was one of pleasure. He brushed his thumb along her cheek. Given time and a little encouragement, she might come to trust him with more than just a hypothetical estate. One day she might allow him to care for *her*.

Something hit James squarely on the temple—too small and soft to cause injury but solid enough to get his attention. At his feet, a wrapped candy rolled to a slow stop. That, no doubt, was what he'd felt hit his face. But who had lobbed it at him?

Lieutenant Lancaster, standing beside Miss Artemis, who appeared to be fighting a veritable fit of laughter, tossed an identical candy repeatedly in the air, catching it without taking his gaze off James. He mouthed the words "hands off" with a look of warning.

James complied but reluctantly. He had no desire to antagonize Daphne's brother, though the prospect of continuing to keep her close to him was remarkably tempting.

An upstairs maid poked her head into the room. "Lord Techney's carriage has just pulled up, Your Grace."

"I ought to have him placed in the holding cupboard," the duke said. "Alas, the evening calls for a bit more subtlety, more's the pity."

"The holding cupboard?" James asked Daphne. "I am dying of curiosity."

"It is a very large closet," she explained, "one large enough to seem like a small, windowless room. Adam considers it a somewhat acceptable stand-in for his beloved gibbet and stocks while he is in London. He only recently resigned himself to the fact that Persephone will not be persuaded to permit the installation of a rack."

"Father is to be tortured, then?" He likely should have felt more sorry for his sire than he did.

"Subtly tortured," Daphne said.

The lieutenant, who had been watching at the door, leaned back inside the room. "He has just been let inside by the butler."

The duke turned to his family. "You all know your parts."

James's was, apparently, to follow the lead of everyone else. He wondered just how difficult that might prove to be.

Miss Artemis crossed the room and stood with James and Daphne. She quite deliberately arranged herself in a pose of utter innocence, turning her face up toward him with a look of sweet adoration—not unlike a very young girl might give an idolized older brother.

"That is doing it a bit brown, Artemis," Daphne said, something of a laugh underlying her words. "You are only supposed to make it clear that you like Lord Tilburn. Looking at him as though you were his ever-loyal puppy pushes the display nearly past believing."

Artemis sighed, a sound filled with martyrdom and suffering. "You know nothing of theatricality. If one is to play a role, one must do so entirely." Her posturing never slipped for a moment.

She rather did remind James of the looks he often received from Scamp. He was hard-pressed to keep from laughing. Maintaining his countenance with the whole family undertaking such overblown performances might very well prove impossible.

"Lord Techney," the butler announced.

James stepped toward the door, intending to greet his father and make any introductions. A swift look from Lieutenant Lancaster, however, kept him in his place. For some unspoken reason, James was meant to keep back.

For a moment, Father hovered in the doorway, obviously thrown off by the lack of notice his entrance had created. Even the butler had already disappeared.

Almost as if it were an afterthought, the duke turned toward the new arrival. "Ah, Lord Techney."

That was the extent of Father's welcome. Not a single "Pleased to see you" or "Good of you to join us" seemed forthcoming. James held back the confusion he felt, knowing his one assignment was to appear entirely composed during the evening's performance. Father looked confused enough for the both of them.

The duchess took pity on him, going so far as to invite him to step into the room and informing him that dinner would be served soon.

Father made his way inside, though with obvious uncertainty. James could not recall a time when his father had looked anything but utterly confident. The sight proved both disconcerting and oddly enjoyable.

"So you are James's father," Lieutenant Lancaster said when Father came near where he stood.

The lieutenant had never referred to James by his Christian name—the young gentleman likely *thought* of him by several names unfit for company.

"I am." Still, Father appeared unsure of himself. How had they upended him so quickly? No one had been outright rude, nor insulting. They simply appeared to not particularly care for what consequence he might be in a position to claim.

"You must be very proud," the lieutenant said. "He is quite well thought of."

"Is he?" The genuine surprise on Father's face was particularly lowering. "I have heard any number of unflattering things about him lately."

The lieutenant appeared momentarily taken aback, though something of a twinkle passed quickly through his eyes. He spoke next in a tone of conciliatory explanation, as though he'd hit upon the reason for Father's ignorance. "I can only assume such unfounded gossip is circulating exclusively in less exalted circles than those in which this family walks."

A direct hit, to be sure. Father had quite neatly been reminded that though he might lord it over his family and toadying admirers, his current company held positions decidedly above his touch.

"Is this truly your father, Lord Tilburn?" Miss Artemis asked with an air of absolute believable ignorance. Were such a thing not entirely beyond the pale, she might very well have made a name for herself on the stage. "I have wished to make his acquaintance."

"Shall I make you known to him?" James hoped his acting abilities were sufficient to disguise the question as a mere social nicety when he'd actually asked for the sake of determining what was expected of him.

"Yes, please."

James undertook the introduction, then figuratively stepped back to watch what would unfold.

"Our father is a scholar," Miss Artemis told James's father. "He has many times been quite in demand by the dons of Oxford and Cambridge, and many of his papers on ancient Greece have been published to accolades and widespread acclaim. What do *you* study, Lord Techney?"

Father? Study? James managed to keep his expression neutral, but only just.

"I have never really been of an academic bent," Father answered, his tone clearly indicating his disapproval of those who were.

Miss Artemis gave him a look of utter commiseration. "We had a neighbor who said that a lot." She lowered her voice to a conspiratorial whisper. "He was terribly slow and not at all bright."

To say Father looked startled would be a gross understatement. If not for the look of sweet innocence on Miss Artemis's face, he likely would have taken immediate umbrage at the insinuation that he was himself unintelligent.

"If you do not tend toward academics, you must have some other accomplishments. Do you travel? My brother"—she glanced briefly at Lieutenant Lancaster—"has seen nearly all the world. He has stepped foot on five continents. To how many continents have you traveled?"

"I had my Grand Tour as a youth." Father had always been quite proud of having undertaken that rite of passage.

"Oh, pish." Miss Artemis waved off this tidbit as though it held no weight whatsoever. "Europe hardly counts. We have *tenants* who have been to Europe. Surely you've seen other parts of the world."

"I am not a traveler."

She instantly looked sympathetic. "Linus did say some of their very young sailors do not travel well either. They haven't the constitution for it, poor things."

Father had been compared to a lackwit, a tenant, and a lower-class cabin boy. One thing James would say for the evening's entertainment: it was thorough. A beat of silence just long enough to grow quite uncomfortable passed. Father actually tugged at his cravat. James had never seen his father so thoroughly bested, and by a fifteen-year-old girl, nonetheless. What else did this formidable family have planned?

Into the thick silence, the Falstone House butler announced dinner. The duke entered with his wife, their air of aristocratic superiority one the prince himself would have struggled to emulate. Humble pie seemed the menu item of the evening.

Lieutenant Lancaster accompanied Daphne, and James walked into the dining room with Miss Artemis on his arm. She kept up her role nearly flawlessly, only once betraying herself by grinning up at James. He kept his own smile in check by clenching his jaw.

The dinner conversation passed in much the same vein as the premeal discussion. James sat near enough the duchess to overhear her ask Father about individuals who stood so far above him in consequence that he could not possibly have any personal acquaintance with them. The lieutenant, seated on Father's other side, brought up matters of state only to interrupt himself and apologize for having forgotten that Lord Techney had not been embracing his Parliamentary duties. Miss Artemis continually glanced at their guest with a look of mingled pity and disappointment. His Grace more or less ignored him. Daphne kept her eyes on her plate, though James could not say if this came about because of her timidity or because of a need to hide her amusement.

Father looked thoroughly relieved when the ladies rose and left the gentlemen. James thought the reaction terribly precipitous. As for himself, he had no doubt the evening was far from over.

Chapter Thirty-Seven

THE DUKE NODDED TO HIS butler, an indication that the man ought to bring in the usual after-dinner fare. He returned, however, without a single decanter or glass, instead carrying a silver salver on which lay a box any gentleman would recognize as containing a pair of Manton's dueling pistols. The duke lifted the cherrywood box and set it on the table.

James reminded himself forcefully of his instructions to appear unsurprised. Fortunately, Father's attention was so riveted on the unexpected sight, he paid James not a whit of attention.

The duke silently pulled an immaculate pistol from its box. He examined it thoughtfully. "I understand you have been quite talkative these past few days."

Father must have sensed the question was aimed at him. "I am not sure what you mean."

"Rumor has it you have told anyone who will listen that your son is a profligate, worthless, and irresponsible young man. Yet I have placed my confidence in him this past week or more while my secretary is on holiday. Tell me"—the duke's tone had turned decidedly cold—"which of us is mistaken in his character? You?" His Grace pinned Father with a look so black James shuddered despite not being its recipient. "Or I?"

"I . . . uh . . ." Father's eyes darted between the pistol held so confidently in the duke's hand and a deadly looking dagger at the ready near the duke's side.

"It is also widely discussed that you claim your son is an inveterate gambler, without morals or self-control, that he has no regard for your fortune or good name. Lord Tilburn has been a guest in this house in the company of members of my family, and we have seen not a hint of what you claim. Again I ask you: Who is the idiot? You? Or every member of this family?"

Father paled noticeably. "I may have exaggerated a little."

"And that in itself is another falsehood," the duke said. "If there is one thing I cannot abide it is a jackanapes with the gall to lie to me while he is sitting at my table."

Not an ounce of color remained in Father's face. James could hardly fault him for his fear. The Dangerous Duke was so called for good reason.

"Your son has found a place in this family, not because of your efforts but because of his character. If you malign him, you malign this family, and that I will not tolerate. Lest it has slipped your notice, I am the Duke of Kielder."

His Grace set his pistol on the table but kept one hand on it. The duke, the lieutenant, even the butler glared at the quivering Earl of Techney. James very much feared his father would suffer the swoon Miss Artemis had offered to feign.

"I hold greater sway than the Royal Family," the duke said firmly. "Society dares not contradict me in anything. A single word from me, a look, and you would find yourself irrevocably and universally shunned."

The duke, then, understood Father's only weakness—his desire for prestige and importance. James never could threaten him in that way, so every attempt he made to undermine his father's bullying proved fruitless.

"You would ruin me?" Father's voice actually broke.

"Ruining people is for the unimaginative," the duke said.

Father's belabored attempt to swallow was likely heard as far afield as Ireland. "I believe I understand your message."

"How surprisingly astute," the duke drawled. Without a word, he rose and left the room, obviously intending to join the ladies in the drawing room. His companions did the same.

"I cannot imagine what you have done to earn yourself such fierce defenders," Father said under his breath, walking at James's side. The remark carried less censure than his comments usually did.

"I chose to be honest with them," James replied. "In return, I learned to put the feelings of others above my own—a lesson, I assure you, I was not taught at home."

"I have had quite enough set downs for one day, Tilburn." Father kept his voice low, but his tone snapped. "You humiliated our family and now have chosen to see me threatened for attempting to pick up the pieces of our reputation."

They stepped into the drawing room on the heels of the duke and Lieutenant Lancaster. Father's expression immediately became one of meek acceptance, all the fight James had heard in his tone but a split second before evaporating.

James did not dwell overly long on the change. As always, when he knew Daphne to be nearby, his eyes immediately sought her out. She sat near the fireplace, watching him with a questioning look and a concern he found infinitely touching.

She rose as he reached her side. "Adam would not tell me what he and Linus planned to do," she said. "I hope he has not caused you difficulties."

"Not at all." He hoped his smile was reassuring. "They may have done the impossible and convinced my father to, for lack of a better expression, stop talking so much."

"I hope you are right." Her eyes focused over his shoulder, and an unmistakable aura of uncertainty settled around her.

James turned in the direction of her gaze and watched his father approach them. A surge of protectiveness swept over him. He would not allow Father to injure Daphne's tender feelings any further. He moved closer to her, knowing he likely appeared very proprietary but hoping the stance would prove a warning.

"Miss Lancaster," Father said.

James resisted the urge to wrap his arm around her shoulders. The lieutenant might very well have him keelhauled were he to step so far out of the bounds of propriety. Still, he kept close to her side, prepared to resort to fisticuffs with his own father in a drawing room if necessary to protect Daphne from the man's vitriol.

"Yes, Lord Techney?" Daphne trembled slightly as she spoke, yet her voice held an admirable note of determination.

Hang propriety, he inwardly declared. He took gentle hold of her arm and stepped the slightest bit in front of her, conveying without words that Father was not to mistreat her.

Father's eyes darted quickly in the direction of the duke and lieutenant. His countenance paled a little. "My wife has spoken of little beyond the efficacy of your throat tonics. I felt to express her . . . *our* gratitude."

Daphne dipped her head ever so slightly. "I was pleased to be of assistance, something she seemed to receive little enough of."

James saw his father's jaw tighten in response to that well-placed verbal thrust.

"I will endure a set down from the Duke of Kielder but not from an overlooked debutante who—"

"That is quite enough, Father." James spoke through clenched teeth.

"Boy, do not—"

Across the room, the duke cleared his throat loudly. The lieutenant unsubtly moved his sword hand to his scabbard.

Daphne drew the smallest bit closer to James. He kept his hand on the back of her arm, allowing his thumb to lightly stroke it in what he hoped she interpreted as a gesture of support. If Father uttered another disparaging word to her, James would fillet him and leave the duke to deal with the remains.

Father offered something of a bow and stepped away, finding a seat somewhat removed from the rest of the company. James remained at Daphne's side, still thrown off by the odd sight of his father cowed.

Miss Artemis dove into a rather heart-wrenching recitation of *The Rime of the Ancient Mariner.*

James led Daphne to a sofa, taking his seat beside her.

"You must think me the worst sort of coward," she whispered too softly for anyone else to overhear.

"Why on earth would I think that?" he replied in the same low tone.

"I ought not to have shrunk away from your father. I ought to have been confident and unshaken." Her face fell. "Instead I stood there shaking, waiting for him to say something cutting."

Miss Artemis's performance completely held the attention of the others in the room. James cupped Daphne's chin with his hand and turned her face up toward his before pressing a light kiss on her forehead. He lingered, fighting the temptation to actually, truly kiss her.

A man might expect a lot of different reactions after tenderly kissing a lady with whom he'd fallen in love. James, however, hadn't anticipated her face crumbling, a sheen of tears in her eyes, and a swift, silent flight from the room.

Running from the drawing room hadn't been part of the night's planned entertainment, but Daphne hadn't known what else to do. He'd held her so tenderly. He'd defended her to his father. She could feel her defenses crumbling entirely, and it terrified her.

James appeared in the empty sitting room only a moment after she arrived.

She tightened her clasped hands, tension radiating through every muscle in her body.

"I am sorry," James said. "I should not have kissed you as I did, especially in front of so many people."

I should not have kissed you. This most recent kiss was far less personal than the one they'd shared in front of the mirror. Did he regret that as well?

She tried to step away, but he took her hand, holding her near him. Gently, he brought her back to his side.

"What would it take, my Little Sparrow, to keep you from flying away again?"

The long-treasured endearment seized her heart and rendered her momentarily unable to speak.

"Ours was a difficult beginning," he said, "but I swear to you, my affection for you is deep and real."

"I do want to believe you," she whispered. "But I have been hurt too many times."

"Mark my words. I will find a way to prove myself." He leaned toward her and lightly kissed the tip of her nose. A shiver tiptoed down her spine and echoed through her arms and legs. He stood so close she could smell his shaving soap and feel his warmth.

He leaned his forehead against hers long enough to say again, "I *will* find a way."

Chapter Thirty-Eight

"WHY DO I HAVE THE feeling you are not attending to me in the least, Til-burn?" Lieutenant Lancaster's amused comment broke through James's abstraction. He had, in fact, been woolgathering, a seemingly constant state for him of late.

"My apologies," he said. "I am afraid my thoughts were wandering."

He had far too much to think on to entirely prevent such a thing. The rumors his father had started seemed to be dissipating. Society eyed him with greater respect and acceptance. He would leave in only a day's time to begin his new "job" in Shropshire. And yet Daphne weighed more heavily on his mind than anything else.

I do want to believe you. But I have been hurt too many times. Those words hung in his mind, an unshakeable reminder that he had caused her pain and that those wounds continued undermining his efforts to win her regard. He didn't know how to overcome that obstacle.

The lieutenant handed him a folder of papers regarding the Shrop-shire estate they'd been discussing for the better part of two hours. "We've covered most everything, I think. Adam's man of business can answer any further questions you might have after I've left port."

What must the gentleman think of his newly acquired steward if he could not focus for the space of a single interview? "I appreciate your for-bearance and assure you I am not usually so easily distracted."

Lieutenant Lancaster merely smiled. "I would not have hired you if I thought otherwise. You see, the protective older brother in me is deter-mined to hate you for the rest of your life." A light chuckle took the bite out of his words. "However, the fair-minded gentleman I would like to think I am beneath all that recognized long since that you are surprisingly trustworthy."

James pushed out a breath as he slumped back in his chair. "If I can convince you of that, why can't I seem to persuade your sister to believe as much?"

"Lud, man. Why do you think?" The lieutenant shook his head in exasperation. "She has far more to lose should she be wrong."

James rubbed his forehead with the tips of his fingers. He'd been scrutinizing the situation night and day without coming to any sort of conclusion. Securing Daphne's trust felt impossible, yet he knew he couldn't live without her. What could he possibly do?

Lieutenant Lancaster muttered something unintelligible, then said, "I am going to shed the avenging brother role for a moment and give you some advice."

James locked eyes with him. "I would be greatly indebted for any insights you'd share with me."

"Daphne does not trust easily nor often. Life has taught her not to." An obvious measure of sadness entered the lieutenant's expression. "Our father began his mental decline nearly the moment our mother died. Daphne was three years old. *Three*. She was too young to realize the distance he placed between himself and his family had nothing to do with her. She had just lost her mother, then her father essentially abandoned her. The infant who had miraculously survived the ordeal that claimed her mother required so much attention that the rest of the family had no time for the little girl who was so lost and afraid. We could not afford to keep servants, so there was not so much as a nursemaid to offer hugs and reassurances and the most basic attention."

James could see Daphne as a tiny girl, lonely and hurting. The image caused a sharp, throbbing ache inside. A little girl with Daphne's expressive eyes, silently pleading for someone, anyone, to love her again. It was that vulnerable, abandoned soul he so often encountered now, the one who struggled to believe his professions of affection for fear that doing so would simply result in further suffering.

"None of us saw her pain; we were too busy trying to survive. But Evander did." The lieutenant did not manage to hide his lingering feeling of loss. "He attempted to be older brother and friend and father figure, but he was only a child himself, really. When finances required us to leave home, Daphne grew extremely quiet—even for her. He worried about her, not in an offhand, occasional-thought sort of way but a nagging, soul-wrenching anxiety. At times when we were lying down for the night on ship, he would wonder aloud if she was well, if anyone in the family remembered to talk to her, or if she'd begun to disappear like she tended to do."

James watched as his conversational companion visibly clamped down his rising emotion, something he'd also seen Daphne do.

The lieutenant continued. "I generally told him to quit jawing me dead and get some sleep. But his constant worry rang in my mind. He prayed for her—I heard him. And he wrote to her with fevered dedication. When he died, his last words were a plea for me to look after her."

All words stopped as the usually composed officer, bedecked in the intimidating uniform of the Royal Navy, fought back a tear that hung at the corner of one eye. Life had dealt the Lancaster family far too many heavy blows. The realization made James want to hold Daphne near him all the more.

"Adam proved an invaluable ally," Lieutenant Lancaster said, having regained most of his composure. "But his first loyalty has always been to Persephone, as it should be. And next in line will be his own children. Daphne knows as much, and with the arrival of the first of those children now on the horizon, she is feeling the anticipatory pain of abandonment already. She expects people to brush her aside, to forget her in a heartbeat. She sees it as evidence of her own worthlessness. Having seen her internalize so many losses, is it any wonder that when I heard of your conduct, I wanted nothing so much as to hunt you down and shoot you myself?"

James knew he would not hesitate to do so should anyone cause Daphne such pain. "I am surprised you didn't," he said.

"I would have," came the calm answer. "But for one reason." He leaned forward a bit, his gaze intensifying. "You came back. Not to make excuses, not to justify yourself or further your own interests. You came back and faced two gentlemen who would as soon run you through as listen to you because you were worried about *her.* And while I still loathed and despised you, I waited and watched. For the first time in Daphne's life, someone had refused to abandon her, however unavoidable many of the previous desertions had been. If there was any chance you could be trusted, you might very well prove precisely what she needed—someone who wouldn't walk out on her."

"I wouldn't." James heard the edge of frustration in his voice. He never seemed able to convince anyone of that. What could possibly prove it true besides time? And how much of that did he have, really?

"There has never been any real security in her life, though she has had more of it with Adam," the lieutenant said. "Daphne is not the sort of young lady for whom baubles and trinkets serve as proof that she is valued and treasured. She needs to feel safe, to feel she can depend on someone. Show her that you understand and that you value her. And whatever you do, don't give up."

"I hadn't intended to."

"Then perhaps in time, I might decide I like you, Tilburn." A smile touched the lieutenant's face once more, pulling an answering one to James's.

"You might even come to call me James."

"I wouldn't bet on it." But Lieutenant Lancaster chuckled.

She needs to feel safe. Show her you value her. He wanted her to feel safe and valued and secure. He wanted her to know she could depend on him. But how? What did he know, after all, of building healthy relationships? He'd certainly never seen any before coming to know the Duke of Kielder and the Lancaster family. He dared not hope to convince Daphne of anything beyond his sincere intention to try.

Chapter Thirty-Nine

MISERABLE DID NOT BEGIN TO describe Daphne's state over the fortnight since James's departure. She felt excruciatingly alone, abandoned, and uncertain. Though she missed Linus and worried about his safety, she did not feel his absence as acutely as she did James's.

But she, along with her sisters, was now traveling to Shropshire to visit their family home and look in on their father, and James was there, seeing to his new duties as estate manager.

Did he miss her? He told her he would, but he hadn't written. Persephone must have realized Daphne hoped for a letter—no doubt she'd noticed how dejected Daphne felt each time the post had arrived without a missive from him.

"Without a formal understanding between you, he cannot write to you," Persephone had reminded her after a full week of disappointment. "Lord Tilburn is commendably careful of your reputation. I do not doubt he would write if he were in a position to do so."

"Do you really think so?"

"Do you really doubt it?" Persephone's half-scolding, half-empathetic look remained fresh in her memory even a week later as the countryside passed outside the carriage windows.

Persephone was likely correct—James would have written if not for the dim view Society would take on such a thing. It had been quite some time since she'd truly questioned his sincerity. Their past was not without difficulties. For the present, his dedication to her was real. But what did the future hold?

If her family noticed her preoccupation during their journey, they did not speak of it. Persephone still felt and looked a bit green about the gills.

Adam fussed over her comfort and well-being. Artemis kept up a constant stream of chatter they only vaguely attended to until Adam commanded her to immerse herself in a "lousy novel" and "cease abusing our ears." She took it in stride and promptly produced a gothic offering from her over-large reticule.

A flood of conflicting emotions washed over Daphne as the carriage turned up the gravel drive that led to their home. Happy memories mixed with painful ones. Her father's repeated dismissive gestures fought for precedence in her thoughts with her siblings' cheerful laughter during rare outings to their favorite picnicking spot. And mingled amidst all of it were thoughts of James. He was there somewhere.

The butler greeted them upon their arrival. He informed Adam in an aside Daphne strained to overhear that Lord Tilburn was with a tenant that morning, seeing to an urgent bit of business, and wished them to know he regretted not being on hand to greet them.

Daphne could not say which she felt more: grateful for the reprieve or disappointed at not seeing him.

Everyone made their way to their various bedchambers with the casualness borne of familiarity.

Which of the tenants had James been called upon to see to? She knew all of them. Her heart ached at the thought of any of those hardworking families struggling. Was it a minor crisis or something more pressing? She shook off the worry. James was more than capable of seeing to the business of an estate, and he would do so with unwavering dedication.

Daphne untied the ribbons of her bonnet as she reached her bedchamber, her thoughts flying in hundreds of directions at once. Only after she stepped fully inside did her surroundings at all register. She stood, mouth slightly agape, bonnet dangling on its ribbons held distractedly in her hand.

Her bedchamber had been entirely transformed. Poverty had rendered most of their home austere and practical over the years they'd lived there. Though she'd had the means and the permission to change it since Adam and Persephone's marriage, Daphne had never done so. Her rooms at Falstone Castle in Northumberland and Falstone House in London were all that was comfortable and pleasing, yet she hadn't personalized those spaces overly much either.

This bedchamber, though, the only one she had ever truly felt was hers, did not look at all the way it once had. Gone were the drab and worn window hangings, replaced by sheer white draperies billowing in a light breeze slipping in through the open window. The quilt made from discarded scraps no longer lay stretched across the bed, a coverlet of vibrant greens and browns in its place, gorgeous pillows complementing its splendor. Fresh flowers sat in a vase on the bedside table, alongside a miniature Daphne did not immediately recognize.

She picked up the tiny portrait. Tears started to her eyes. Though she had never seen that particular miniature, she knew its subject instantly: her mother. How she wished she'd known her, that she had any memories of her that had not come secondhand.

Her eyes lighted next on an armchair, faded and nicked, set comfortably close to the small fireplace across the room. She pushed back the lump of emotion that instantly rose at the sight of the very chair in which she had spent her earliest remembered days on her father's lap, listening to his stories. Her only happy memories with him were tied to that battered bit of furniture. But who had placed it there? Who could possibly have realized the connection?

She ran her fingers over the still-familiar contours of its back and arms, desperately searching her memory for the sound of her father's voice, the laughter and happiness she'd once heard in it. She hoped that in a day or two she would find the courage to sit in it and think back on the man her father had once been and the carefree child she could almost remember being.

She pulled herself away, returning her mother's miniature to its place on the bedside table, then crossed to a tall chest she'd never before seen though knew precisely its function. From her countless visits to the local apothecary, she'd learned to recognize an apothecary cabinet; she'd wished for one ever since.

The two dozen drawers, beautifully inlaid and charmingly worn, still bore their labels. Fennel. Catnip. Feverfew. So many herbs she'd scrimped and saved to purchase as a child and learned to use out of a desperate worry that something would happen to her family and she would lose them all.

One particular drawer captured her attention: myrrh. Other young girls likely dreamed of dolls or beautiful dresses. She used to promise herself that if she ever came into a fortune, she'd buy myrrh. She never had.

Daphne pulled the drawer open only to gasp aloud at what she saw. Myrrh. She had myrrh. Every other drawer also held the items its labels

indicated. Here before her was what would have amounted to a vast treasure during her years of struggle.

On the very top of the cabinet, she could see the corner of a book and
reached up to pull it down. An apothecary's guide to herbs and medicines.
She thumbed through the pages, not stopping to read any of the entries. As
she did so, a folded piece of parchment fell out and drifted to the floor.

She picked it up and unfolded the paper. It proved to be a short
note written in an unfamiliar hand, addressed to her.

Miss Lancaster,

*I understand from Lord Tilburn that you have an interest in and an
aptitude for herbal healing. I have reached an age where continuing my practice is no longer practical. Knowing this cabinet and its contents will be in
worthy hands sets my mind considerably at ease.*

The missive was signed "M. Hapstead," a name she had never before
heard, though she guessed him to be an apothecary of advancing years. She
could not imagine he would simply give her the cabinet, not to mention
all its contents—the collection was far too valuable. Someone must have
purchased it. James had been mentioned, but Daphne knew him to be
entirely without funds. Adam, though he cared for her just as he would his
own sister, had he one, would not have understood how much such a thing
would mean to her.

She turned around, examining again the change in her room. To her
knowledge, her family members seldom came in there. She did not venture
into the others' chambers either. They were private domains. No one would
have thought to engineer such a change, nor realize one was long overdue.

The housekeeper would not have undertaken a redecoration; such
did not fall under her jurisdiction.

Daphne sat, dazed, on her nearly unrecognizable bed. As the shock
began to wear off, she came to the indisputable realization that she loved her
new bedchamber—adored it. The room felt so serene. Even the colors were
precisely what she would wish for, earthy and calming. And though she'd
never seen so many decorative pillows on a bed in her life, the touch was
charming rather than excessive. One even had tiny embroidered decorations:
delicate flowers and—she leaned closer—birds. Her heart hammered. Not
merely birds; they were sparrows.

James. Only he would think to add that.

Her eyes stole around the room once more. No. She could not imagine a gentleman ever thinking to alter the appearance of a room. Yet somehow it seemed almost possible.

Daphne pulled the sparrow-adorned pillow into her arms, clinging to it as her brain struggled to make sense of everything. She realized then that she had missed a letter partially hidden beneath the pillow she now held.

The handwriting was Linus's. The family received a general missive from him now and again, assuring them he was well and informing them of his activities, though they all suspected he skipped over the more difficult parts of all he experienced. He had never written specifically to her.

Daphne slipped off her half boots and pulled her legs up onto the bed. She leaned back against the soft mountain of pillows and broke the seal on Linus's letter.

Dearest Daphne,

You know me well enough to realize I am not one for writing letters. I have come to understand, however, that I have done you a disservice in not sharing with you something I ought to have years ago. The memory is difficult, and I have very seldom spoken of it.

I remember well your heartbreak when Evander and I left for sea. Even the ignorance of youth did not hide that fact from me. He took a great deal of ribbing from our shipmates for the multitude of letters he sent you. We never reached a port but he had a missive, often more than one, ready to send home. I wonder sometimes if you realize how much he adored you.

No one in the family ever talked about Evander. Sometimes it felt like he'd never existed.

I miss him. Heavens, I miss him.

She took a shaky breath, so many emotions gripping her. She returned to the letter, pulled to it by some unseen force.

I do not mean to inflict further pain on you, for I care far too much to want to see you hurt. I hope you will understand that I mean only to show you that you were never forgotten. I was with our brother when he passed. He spoke of you, Daphne. Even in those final moments, you were never far from his mind. In the years since, you have often been in my thoughts as well. And I confess myself relieved when I saw that Adam had come to cherish you as Evander did and as I have learned to do.

Such sentiments probably should have been delivered in person, but emotional discussions never come easy for me. Please know that I am sincere, however clumsy I may be at expressing myself.

   Yours sincerely,
   Linus

She did not know how long she spent rereading the letter, her arms yet wrapped around her pillow. Thoughts of her late brother brought the usual feelings of grief and loss. But something changed as she sat there. A sense of peace began to penetrate the sadness.

All was quiet other than the light rustling of the new draperies. She glanced at the portrait of her mother, then across to her father's chair, then at the apothecary cabinet. The room could not have felt more tranquil, more perfect.

She knew that somehow James had a hand in all of it. This was the kindhearted and gentle young man she had treasured from the first moment they'd met, the gentleman she had loved through all the heartache and pain of the past few months.

He held her very heart in his hands, and she intended to find the courage to trust him with it.

Chapter Forty

JAMES PACED NERVOUSLY OUTSIDE THE door to Daphne's bedchamber. He knew she had arrived and felt certain she was inside. Did she approve of all he'd done in there? Had he presumed too much? Made a mull of the entire thing?

He'd come upon an embroidered pillow in a shop window in Coventry during his journey from London. The sparrows had made him think of her. He hadn't intended to do anything beyond leave it in her bedchamber, thinking perhaps it would bring a smile to her face when she arrived.

His first day in Shropshire, he'd slipped into Daphne's room and stopped dead in his tracks. He'd seen servants' quarters and tenant houses that surpassed the refinement of her bedchamber. Afraid his work in Shropshire would prove more arduous than he'd been led to expect, James had peeked inside all of the family rooms.

The rest of the house proved unexceptional—elegance mingled with practicality, modernity alongside the traditional. Only Daphne's private quarters still bore the mark of aching poverty. Why had the room never been refurbished? How could her family have allowed such a thing?

As he'd stood there surveying the badly worn furniture and threadbare linens in her room, he had experienced a moment of pure inspiration. Her brother had insisted she didn't feel safe or secure or valued. What lady would, living in surroundings so starkly inferior to that of her family members', a constant reminder of years of struggle?

"Please, don't let her hate it," he whispered, hoping the heavens were listening. Divine intervention seemed his only chance of winning Daphne's heart. "Or if she does hate it, let her not hate *me*." He opted to cover all possibilities, lest providence prove mischievous. "And if the bedchamber itself comes up short, at least let the apothecary cabinet meet with her approval."

He'd gladly sold his watch and diamond stickpin to pay for the cabinet, knowing on sight it would mean the world to his beloved. He only hoped he hadn't been misled, that it truly was the fortuitous find he thought it was.

The doorknob turned. James attempted to project an air of casualness. How ridiculous he would seem hovering around her door. He watched it open, his nerves on edge.

The sight of his Daphne after two weeks' separation fairly stole his breath. Her quiet beauty might escape the notice of Society, its fascination set on all things gaudy and loud, but he could not imagine any lady's loveliness striking him with greater force.

His appearance seemed to cause more surprise for her than anything else. "James."

Questions flitted through her eyes, though she did not speak any of them aloud. If she were too shy to ask about the room outright and he lacked the gumption to broach the subject himself, they might very well remain in the corridor indefinitely, discussing inane topics and fretting uncomfortably.

He simply needed to draw himself up, quit acting like a child yet in leading strings, and jump in. "Daphne—"

His words ended abruptly just as her head snapped in the direction of a hacking, rasping cough. James had come to know that sound well during his short time in Shropshire.

Daphne looked back at him, worry and pain written all over her face. "That is my father, isn't it?"

James nodded.

She looked again in the direction of her father's bedchamber even as another cough echoed from within its walls. Her brow knit with worry, grief filling her posture. "My papa is really going to die."

He could not be blamed for what he did next—any gentleman with half a heart would have been powerless to do anything else. He took her in his arms, silently and gently holding her.

He could offer no words to contradict her assertion. Mr. Lancaster was indeed going to die. Even to James's untrained eye that much was obvious. The local physician doubted he would last the remainder of the summer.

James had made a point of visiting the ailing man a few times each day. Though he doubted anything he said penetrated the fog that shrouded Mr.

Lancaster's mind, James kept him informed of his work and efforts around the estate. He meant it as a show of respect for the father of the lady he loved and a gesture of recognition of the capable person the man had once been.

In the midst of Mr. Lancaster's often indecipherable mutterings, James had learned some invaluable things. He'd heard snippets of Mr. Lancaster's childhood visits to the Shropshire estate, a small, unentailed property his father had eventually left him. The recounting gave James a better understanding of the land's history and prior uses. Far more valuable, though, was the insight he'd gained into the father who had unknowingly broken his little girl's heart. What he'd learned had softened James's feelings toward the man.

"Would you like to go see him?" he whispered to Daphne, still safe in the circle of his arms.

He felt her shake her head even before he heard her refusal. "I'll go with the others. Later. I don't—I'll wait."

"I think you should look in on him, Daphne."

"He won't even remember me." The slightest catch in her voice revealed the pain she felt.

"He will not *recognize* you," James said, "but I promise he does remember you."

She looked up at him. "He did not remember me even when I lived here, before his senility grew so pointed."

James gently cupped her face in his hand. The heartbreak he heard in her words caused a matching twinge in his own chest. How lonely she must have been growing up. "You should see him, my dear."

"I do not think I could bear it." Her face momentarily crumpled.

"I will come with you," he said. "You don't need to face this alone."

"Will you hold my hand?"

Was this even a question? "Of course."

With the cloak of bravery he had come to associate with her wrapped firmly around her once more, Daphne took a breath and walked in the direction of her father's chamber, her shaking hand held firmly in James's.

He pushed the door open. Daphne's grip grew tighter as they stepped inside. The room was kept somewhat dim, though not overly so. The nurse who looked after Mr. Lancaster was a capable and hardworking woman who kept the room tidy and well aired. Unlike far too many sickrooms, the stench of illness did not hang heavy and stale about them. Mr. Lancaster's valet took pains with the man's appearance, though his employer could not possibly realize nor value the service. Still, the efforts at maintaining the gentleman's dignity spoke volumes of the two servants' human kindness.

"Good afternoon, Mrs. Ashton," James greeted the nurse, who had turned from her tidying at the sound of their entrance. "Miss Lancaster has come to look in on her father."

Mrs. Ashton nodded and smiled, the look one of approval and empathy. She no doubt realized better than anyone how little time remained for such visits.

"I do not know if I can do this," Daphne whispered, pulling so close to him their arms brushed.

"I will be right here with you, dear." How different being her support and defender felt from every other time he'd been required to play that role. She did not demand it of him, and yet her sincere gratitude could not be doubted.

Daphne was silent as they reached the bed in which her father had spent every moment of the past few months. James squeezed her hand, hoping to remind her that she did not face this ordeal alone.

"Good afternoon," James said upon realizing Mr. Lancaster was awake.

His thin face turned in their direction. Every breath wheezed out of him slowly and painstakingly. Daphne did not visibly react, though James felt certain her father's deteriorated condition affected her.

Mr. Lancaster's eyes narrowed, a look of momentary confusion in their depths. Then he nodded a greeting. "Good day to you, Robert." He pulled in a rattling breath.

"Robert?" Daphne whispered.

James leaned a bit closer to her and explained in a low voice. "I understand that is his brother's name."

Her eyes met his, worried and sad. "He thinks you are my Uncle Robert?"

"He often thinks Mrs. Ashton is his mother." James wanted Daphne to understand that any lack of recognition had nothing to do with her or her father's valuation of her but with the state of his mind.

"Thought I'd go riding today." Mr. Lancaster's raspy voice brought their attention back to him.

"Do you mind if I introduce you to a pretty young lady before you head to the stables?" James asked. He'd learned during his first visits to Mr.

Lancaster that it was best to go along with whatever mental wanderings seized the gentleman.

"Always time for a pretty girl." Mr. Lancaster's declaration preceded a bout of deep, continual coughing.

The usually stalwart Daphne stood in obvious distress, her eyes bleak. James rubbed her upper back with his free hand.

After sipping from the cup Mrs. Ashton pressed to his lips and muttering a very childlike "Thank you, Mama," Mr. Lancaster turned his attention back to James and Daphne. "Halloo, Robert," he said, having forgotten he'd addressed him already. "Didn't hear you come in."

James didn't reply. Mr. Lancaster's attention was fixed on his daughter, though he likely had no idea who she really was.

"She looks like my Daphne," Mr. Lancaster said in an offhand manner.

"Does she now?" James shifted his hand to Daphne's far shoulder, as near to an embrace as he'd allow himself in company.

"A smart girl, my Daphne." Mr. Lancaster's words came out breathy as he struggled to fill his lungs once more. "Just a little thing, with quite a good head on her shoulders."

"I've heard that about her," James answered. Beside him, Daphne had grown pale, her eyes fixed on her father.

"Just like her mother." Mr. Lancaster nodded slowly, gaze wandering about. "Pretty but quick, with wit and brains." His voice grew ever quieter. "Like her mother."

"No doubt she'll make a good match one day," James said.

Mr. Lancaster looked at him then, brow drawn in obvious irritation. "Already married. To me, you bounder." He followed that declaration with several epithets Daphne ought not to have been privy to.

James whispered an apology. "He does not recollect himself enough to hold his tongue." To Mr. Lancaster he said, "I meant Daphne."

"I have a girl named Daphne." Mr. Lancaster drew in several difficult breaths. "Cute little thing. Likes to sit on my lap. Asks the smartest questions."

When he dissolved into coughs, Mrs. Ashton provided his glass of water once more. She looked across at James, communicating without words that perhaps they ought to draw the visit to a conclusion. He knew the gentleman's endurance was all but nonexistent.

He nodded his understanding. "We should let him rest," he whispered to Daphne.

She remained entirely mute as he led her by the hand from the room. James closed the door behind them. The corridor was blessedly empty, providing him with a moment to gauge how overset she might be.

"I hope that was not too upsetting, Daphne."

She fought with her composure. He could not very well leave her in the corridor battling emotions for anyone to see. She would be mortified.

He wrapped an arm around her shoulders and led her to the small sitting room nearby. It was empty, so he left the door ajar.

Daphne leaned her head against his shoulder when he sat beside her on the sofa. She sighed. James took her hand in his.

"I understand what you meant now when you said my father remembered me but did not recognize me."

"He has spoken about all of you at one time or another," James said. "Though he shifts unpredictably between believing himself a child and speaking of his own children."

"He remembers us, then?"

"All of you except Artemis. He does not seem to have any recollection of her. Mrs. Ashton believes he remembers his family as it was before his wife's death but has shut out any memory afterward."

"He was rarely with us afterward," Daphne said. "Actually, that is not entirely accurate either. He spoke at times with the boys and quite a lot with Persephone. But not often with Athena. He never really acknowledged Artemis."

"And what of you, Daphne? How was he with you?"

She did not answer immediately. James gently rubbed her hand with both of his, knowing the memories she had were not always happy.

"He told me once, when I was no more than seven, that he had no use for me, that he would much rather be alone than in my company."

James winced. Was it any wonder she'd learned to guard herself against anticipated rejection? "Your father speaks more of you than of anyone else. And I assure you it is not to disparage your company. There is an abundance of pride and adoration in his recollections."

"Then why would he have sent me away?" Heartache permeated every word, something in her tone putting him firmly in mind of a pained and frightened little girl.

James shifted enough to very nearly face her, though it necessitated breaking the contact between them. She must have sensed his gaze because she turned her eyes up toward him. "I know you have been through an ordeal this afternoon, but have you the endurance to hear a bit more, something which will probably prove likewise tumultuous?"

"Is it something awful?"

"No."

She nodded, and James took it as permission to proceed. He hoped he was doing the right thing.

"Your father told me—or whomever he thought me to be during that visit—that though his wife was an acclaimed beauty, what had captured his interest and heart was her wit and intelligence and goodness. Those qualities, he said, were what continually drew him back to her." Daphne seemed to be holding up, so he continued. "During another visit, he told me that his second daughter looked the most like his wife."

Daphne nodded.

"But," James pressed forward, "that of all his children, 'little Daphne' had the largest measure of her mother in her. He said that spending time with you was like being in company with a miniature version of his wife."

"He never said anything like that to me," she whispered.

"I think that is why he spent so much time with you when you were very small, because you reminded him of her. Those same qualities he treasured in her, he treasured in you."

"But then he didn't want me anymore." Her eyes had taken on that pleading quality that tugged so fiercely at James's heart.

"I honestly believe, Daphne, that he couldn't bear it. You reminded him so much of the lady he had lost and missed acutely, and the pain pushed him beyond his limit. It does not excuse what he did, nor make it right. But you must understand that his neglect came not from any shortcomings on your part nor a lack of love on his but from a misguided attempt to save himself from the agony of his grief. And I believe that by the time the pain would naturally have abated to the point where he might have returned to normal life, his mind had already begun to deteriorate and he no longer truly realized what he was about."

She looked away from him, not in anger or pique but with an expression of contemplation. "You have certainly given me a lot to think about."

"I hope that you will," he said. "Life has placed far too many burdens on you. This is one you need not carry." James brushed a loose brown tendril away from her face. "You look positively done in," he said, guilt pricking him at the realization.

"I am rather worn to the bone."

"You should go rest, perhaps even have a dinner tray brought to you."
"I might just do that." She rose, and James followed suit.

Not two steps from him, she turned back. "I meant to ask you," she said hesitantly, "did you have a hand in . . . that is . . . did you have my bedchamber redone?"

James's stomach knotted. He'd forgotten about that bit of presumptuousness. "I did," he confessed. Suddenly nervous, he rushed through his excuses. "It was so dreary. I could not imagine you being remotely happy in there. I only meant to make the smallest of changes, but the project seemed to grow entirely out of proportion. I hope you are not upset with me, that it is at least a little to your liking."

She stepped back to where he stood waiting for her condemnation. Her delicate hand lightly touched his face. Daphne rose on her toes and pressed the lightest of kisses on his cheek. "It is perfect," she whispered.

So shocked was he by her salute that he did not so much as blink. He only remembered to breathe after she had already slipped from the room.

He was so close to securing her regard. He could sense it within his reach. The walls she had erected to protect her battered heart had begun to crumble, and he needed only to find his way in.

Chapter Forty-One

A NOTE FROM JAMES ARRIVED with Daphne's cup of chocolate the next morning, asking her to take a walk with him about the grounds near lunchtime. She didn't have to even ponder the invitation. Accepting was automatic.

She saw him before he saw her, his attention claimed at the moment she stepped outside by something in the opposite direction. The breeze ruffled his hair, giving him a very natural at-ease look. The tension he'd constantly worn during those first weeks of the London Season had disappeared. Freedom from the tyranny of his father had done James a world of good.

He smiled broadly the moment his eyes fell on her. Daphne's heart warmed at the pleasure in his expression. No one ever seemed as happy to see her as James did.

"Good day, Daphne," he greeted her, taking her hand in his. He did not hold himself to the more formal salute of kissing the air above her hand but pressed his lips to it directly. "I hope you have no other engagements this afternoon."

She shook her head, reminding herself to breathe. "Do you?"

"None but this one." He pulled her arm through his, and they walked for a moment in silence. "I have come to truly like your childhood home, Daphne." James wore a look of quiet contentment.

"It is very beautiful," she said. "Though you did not see it in its more ramshackle days. Without the means of keeping it up, the land and house grew too neglected, I fear. Adam's attentions have rectified that over the past seven years."

"I did not mean merely its appearance," James said. "I'm not sure precisely how to explain what I mean. It is the feel of the place I've grown to value most. It is peaceful. My childhood home was anything but. I did not realize until I came here how much I felt that lack growing up."

Peaceful. Daphne nodded to herself. The estate always had felt that way, even if the feeling hadn't entirely freed her of worries and upheavals. "I remember during our picnics I would lie back on the blanket and watch the clouds pass above me and simply soak in the quietness of it all."

"That sounds absolutely perfect," James said.

He continually surprised her, understanding the things she valued without having to ask. "We had a particular spot we loved most." She relived the memories even as she spoke of them. "It sat just far enough from the house that we could forget for a time the pull of responsibilities and worries. We were permitted to be carefree children for the hour or so we lingered there."

"It was a happy place for you, then?"

She sighed. "Very."

They turned down a path that led along the side of a copse of trees. A light breeze rustled the leaves and created ripples in the ankle-high grass just beyond the narrow path. Daphne leaned her head against his upper arm, discovering that doing so felt entirely natural.

"I was concerned about you last night," he said. "You were very quiet."

"I have had a lot on my mind."

"Sometimes it helps to talk with someone," James said.

She turned her face up to him. "You always have been quite willing to listen to me. And you even manage not to appear annoyed that I am taking up your time."

"Perhaps that is because I am not annoyed."

"Not at all?" She doubted he found recountings of her difficulties a pleasing way to pass an afternoon.

"I find I very much enjoy talking with you," he said. "You are not empty-headed or demanding. Better yet, you are not a shrew."

"A shrew?" Daphne chuckled at that. "I should hope not."

He stopped walking, necessitating her own halt. James released her arm. Just as her heart began to drop, he stepped in front of her, taking her hands in his and smiling. "I have missed your laugh. It is far too rare a sound."

Warmth stole across her face.

He stood silently watching her, his eyes continually drifting toward her mouth. Daphne's heart pounded in her throat. He swallowed, still silent and intent on her face.

James pushed out a breath. "You'd best put that dimple away, Miss Lancaster. I swore quite faithfully to your sister that I would behave with utmost decorum."

Somehow, that only made her smile wider.

He shook his head, a twinkle of amusement in his eyes. "See, now this is precisely why I had to decide against a picnic." He began down the path once more.

Daphne quickly caught up to him. "A picnic?" She had yet to go on a picnic. The one in London hardly counted, having ended in such monumental disaster.

"I even inquired after your family's traditional picnicking spot," James said, his step very nearly jaunty. "It proved far too isolated, especially considering your unwillingness to keep your dimple out of sight." He smiled at her as though he would rather be there with her than anywhere else in the world.

"What have you planned instead?"

He assumed a very serious demeanor, one belied by the lingering amusement that tugged at his mouth. "A most proper walk around the grounds, Miss Lancaster."

"And there is no chance we might have a picnic?"

"Your sister and brother-in-law would decidedly disapprove. And though I am rather fond of picnics, I am also rather fond of being left alive."

His teasing tone proved infectious. "I suppose your life would be a very steep price to pay for a single picnic."

"I am pleased that you think so," he said. She loved seeing him smile so freely. He rarely had before breaking with his father. "I am likewise pleased that you have agreed to such a lackluster activity as taking a turn with me. Strolling with a rather ordinary fellow cannot be nearly as enjoyable an excursion for a beautiful lady."

A beautiful lady. To hide her furious blush, Daphne offered a light comment. "I do believe you are flirting with me."

"I most certainly am," he replied.

An excited yelping cut off whatever he intended to say next.

James turned in the direction of the sound. "Blast it," he muttered under his breath. "That pup manages to ruin more moments . . ."

She slipped her hand from his and began leisurely walking back toward the house. "I'll leave the two of you alone, then."

He called after her, his voice nearly begging, "Please, don't leave."

The words reverberated in her mind, echoing in her own voice again and again, the sound reminiscent of the very little girl she'd once been, through her growing up years, and as recently as the silent pleas she'd held back during Linus's departure. "Please, don't leave" had ever been her words. So many times she had begged using that precise phrase, but never had it been directed at her.

She turned back just as James reached her. His was a look of near panic. Had he truly been so upset at the possibility of her walking away?

"Daphne," he breathed out her name, relief filling the single word to near bursting. "I hadn't meant to make such a mull of things. I have been racking my brain trying to think of the right way to go about all this, but romance and courtship are hardly my forte."

"Romance?" The word emerged so quietly he likely hadn't heard.

"You deserve all of that, but I'm such a muttonhead about it all. I will try. I swear I will. Only, please, Daphne." He took hold of her hand, the gesture almost frantic. "Please, don't leave me."

Her heart pounded, her thoughts swirling around.

"I realize life has not taught you to trust easily. My own history with you has only added to that. But I swear to you, I will not walk out on you. So, please, do not walk out on me."

Good heavens, he looked very nearly desperate, worried to the point of utter agitation.

"Why is it so important for me to stay?" she asked, praying his answer was the one she longed most to hear.

He gently took her face in his hands. Stepping closer to her and bending so they stood nearly eye to eye, he whispered, "Because I cannot live without you." He closed his eyes, anguish radiating from him. "Because if you ever left me, I'd be broken. Just like Apollo mourned his Daphne the rest of his life. Just as your father still grieves for his wife. I'd be lost without you, Daphne."

"Oh, James." Emotion broke her words even as hope surged within her.

He leaned his forehead against hers, eyes still closed. "I love you," he said quietly. "I love you."

Words she thought never to hear, though she'd dreamed of him saying them since she was twelve years old. "I was not leaving, James."

He opened his eyes and pulled back only enough to look at her. "Not now? Or not ever?" he pressed as though he depended on that answer to go on.

The implications of his question struck her with such force she required a moment to catch her breath. He wanted her with him always. He loved her. "I'll not ever leave you, James."

He kissed her gently, holding her with a tender earnestness, as though she were a very fragile treasure. He broke the seal of their lips but immediately thought better of it and kissed her once more.

"We should return to the house," he said after a moment. "Else your brother-in-law will likely make good on his threats and murder me at last."

"I won't let him."

He kept an arm around her waist as they walked up the path once more. "He *is* the Dangerous Duke," he reminded her.

"Yes, but I am not afraid of him."

James pressed a kiss to the top of her head. "You do not fear the Duke of Kielder. You were not intimidated by my father nor crushed by the unkindness of the Bowers, and by some miracle, you have begun to forgive me for my many trespasses against you."

"I have had a very busy Season."

He laughed and pulled her ever closer. "You are remarkable, my dear."

She very much feared she would wake up at any moment to discover this all was little more than a glorious dream.

Chapter Forty-Two

"Please drink it, Papa." Daphne held a cup of steaming tea near her father's mouth. "You need your rest, and this will help you sleep."

He didn't object. Daphne had tended to her father over the past week, her devotion to him evident in every tender ministration. James had declared her remarkable, but he was finding the word insufficient.

"Has he drunk it all, Miss Lancaster?" Mrs. Ashton slipped past James and into the room. Daphne's attentions to her father had allowed the nurse a moment to herself now and then, something for which she'd praised the heavens. "I'd like to see him resting more peacefully."

"As would I." Daphne rose, though her concerned gaze didn't leave her father's face. "He does seem a little improved this past week."

"That's your tonic's doing." Mrs. Ashton took Daphne's vacated chair. "Now you just leave Mr. Lancaster to my care. His lordship's anxious for your company, I daresay."

Daphne looked over at James, giving him that secret smile she only ever offered him. "You've been very patient."

He dismissed the apology he heard in her words. "It is always a pleasure to watch you healing."

She slipped her hand in his without hesitation, without worry. How far they'd come in so short a time. He was quite possibly the luckiest man in all the world.

Artemis stood in the corridor, just to the side of Mr. Lancaster's bedchamber door.

"Papa is awake if you wish to see him," Daphne told her sister.

Artemis shrugged a single shoulder. "I was only passing by."

"But you haven't looked in on him even once this past week." Daphne set her hand on Artemis's arm.

Artemis pulled free. "*He* hasn't mentioned *me* once these past fifteen years. He doesn't miss me, and I don't miss him." She flipped her hair as she walked away, chin held defiantly high.

James didn't believe the show of indifference. Daphne likely didn't either.

"It seems your entire family has been wounded in one way or another by your father's decline."

Daphne nodded, her eyes still trained on Artemis's retreating form. "We will all have to make our peace with it in our own way."

He heard tears in her voice. "Darling?"

"I worry about her, is all. And Linus. And Athena. And Persephone." She turned a tremulous smile up to him. "Now you'll likely tell me I worry too much."

"You care, Daphne. I love that about you." He ran his finger along her suddenly rosy cheek. "And I love the way you blush."

"How fortunate for you, then, that I blush so easily."

He took her hand once more and walked with her toward the back of the house. "How soon does your family mean to leave for Northumberland?"

"In only a fortnight or so. Persephone and Adam wish to begin preparing the Falstone Castle nursery and interviewing for a local nursemaid."

Only two weeks. "I suppose you'll have to go with them."

She rested her head against his shoulder as they stepped outside. "I can't very well stay. Father is hardly an acceptable chaperone."

"No, he is not." It was an unfortunate thing for many reasons. "This house will be so empty without you."

"I have always been the one who was left behind," she said. "I'm not at all accustomed to being the one doing the leaving."

James's heart lodged in his throat. He forced his next words out despite the impediment. "You could stay. I wish you would, in fact."

"I can't. We aren't family."

He pressed forward while his courage held out. "I'd like us to be, my dearest Daphne." He stopped and turned to face her, taking her hands in his. "I know I have a great deal yet to atone for, and I do not yet deserve your full trust, but someday, someday soon, I hope—I pray that I will have proven myself worthy of your love and affection."

She kissed his cheek, something she did more and more often of late. "You have it already, James."

"But do I have enough of it to hope that one day we'll never have to be apart?"

Her eyes flew to his face. "What is it you're asking of me?"

He lifted her hands one at a time to his lips. "I am asking if you . . . Will you marry me, Daphne?"

Her smile blossomed on the instant, though she didn't answer his hastily posed question.

"My dear?" he pressed nervously.

"Of course my answer is yes. A thousand times yes."

Relief rushed over him. He pulled her into his arms, pressing light kisses to her hair and face. "I will do everything in my power to secure your happiness," he said between kisses. "I swear it."

A yelp followed that sounded strikingly like agreement.

He ceased his show of affection long enough to cast his meddlesome puppy a disapproving but amused glare. "Have you been eavesdropping this entire time, you unmannered mongrel?"

"The little scamp," Daphne added.

James chuckled. Then, wrapping his arms around her once more, lifted her from the ground and spun her about in a show of unabashed celebration, their laughter echoing through the trees around them.

Chapter Forty-Three

THE DUKE OF KIELDER REALLY ought to be given full rein of everything in the kingdom. The man regularly accomplished the impossible. Only ten days had passed since James had sought formal permission from the gentleman to marry Daphne, and there they were, married and ready to embark on an abbreviated wedding trip he'd not been required to plan or finance.

"I cannot abide the sight of newlyweds," His Grace had said when James had objected. "I am paying you to get out of my sight—a wedding gift *to myself.* Say another word against the idea, and I'll toss you off the roof."

So James had graciously conceded the point and opted not to bring up the fact that the duke had obtained and paid for the special license that had allowed them to marry in such short order. He also kept mum about the miraculous arrival of his mother in Shropshire. Except for her short and somewhat dismal trip to London, that lady had not left the immediate grounds of Techney Manor in twenty years. Ben made the journey from Northumberland, bringing with him the regrets of the Windover family that Mrs. Windover's fast-approaching confinement did not allow them to attend.

Perhaps the most miraculous occurrence of all was Father's presence. His attitude shocked both James and his brother into near incoherence. He did not once attempt to bully or threaten or intimidate them. He spoke to Daphne with utmost gentility and respect. He mostly ignored his wife, something for which they were all immensely grateful. The only person with whom his interactions were not outwardly unexceptional was the duke. James did not know what precisely had passed between the two gentlemen beyond what he'd seen at the memorable family dinner several weeks earlier, but he knew without a doubt that his usually blustery father was utterly terrified of his son's new brother-in-law.

James stood near the entryway, waiting. Three hours had passed since the wedding. A seemingly endless meal celebrating the marriage had finally reached its conclusion, and any moment now, his new bride would join him, and they could begin their journey. A smile tugged at his mouth. *His new bride.* Not a month ago, he'd been plagued with doubts, wondering what miracle would be required to finally win her heart and her trust. Now he had a lifetime in which to prove himself worthy of it.

"A word with you." The duke spoke as he strode to where James stood. The man would likely always be intimidating, though James found he did not feel quite so nervous in his presence as he once had.

"Certainly, Your Grace."

The duke gave him a look of complete annoyance. "I will not be 'Your Grace'-ed by my own family—at least not those on the Lancaster side. Like it or not, you're included in that number."

"I find I like it very much," James said. Daphne always smiled when her brother-in-law grumbled in that irritated manner. James had not yet reached that level of familiarity but almost felt a bubble of amusement.

"The relations I can tolerate call me Adam," he said but not in a way that would naturally invite familial regard. Somehow, though, the invitation did not feel begrudgingly made.

"I will attempt to do so," James said, "though I admit it will not come naturally."

"Of course it won't. You are not a presumptuous mushroom. Work on it—you'll get it eventually."

"I will."

The duke's expression shifted quickly from annoyance to threat. James took an involuntary step backward.

"I believe it is customary," the duke said, his tone low and a bit ominous, "for a guardian to spout vague threats to his ward's new husband should that husband bring any harm to his new wife."

James nodded, glancing quickly at the duke's right boot, where he'd learned a dagger was always sheathed.

"I, however, do not make *vague* threats." The duke's eyes narrowed. "Should you show yourself in any way less than worthy of the trust Daphne has placed in you, you will find yourself swinging from the gibbet at Falstone Castle, taken down regularly to be beaten, then locked in irons in the dungeon and placed in the room I refer to as the Rat's Nest, where the vermin will be delighted to make your better acquaintance. You will next be invited to join me in my vast, dense forest, where I will leave you for the wolves to chew on."

That threat was about as far from vague as possible. "I understand, Your Grace."

"You don't look worried." The pronouncement seemed to simultaneously annoy and please the duke.

"I have no intention of ever mistreating Daphne," James said. "She is far too precious to me. If I appear unconcerned by your very thorough description of torture, it is only because I know I will never do anything that will warrant such treatment."

The duke glanced around them, obviously checking to be sure they were alone. He lowered his voice and, in a tone that spoke of discomfort, said, "I realize I am likely not supposed to play favorites, but Daphne is just that. She came to me a broken and lost little girl." No one in the *ton* would have believed the sudden emotion in the Dangerous Duke's voice. "Though she has grown into a lady of self-possession and wit, she is still fragile in so many ways. She is important to me. Her happiness is important to me."

"Then it seems we have something in common, Your—Adam. Lud, that feels dangerously impertinent."

His Grace actually smiled. Though the action accentuated the duke's scarred visage, James found him far more human and approachable in that moment.

"Daphne is inexpressibly important to me," James continued. "I love her more than I have ever imagined loving another person. And I will cherish her every day for the rest of my life."

His Grace nodded firmly. "See to it that you do. And see to it you are back here again in a fortnight as you promised. My wife is anxious to return home, and when she is uneasy, I am uneasy."

The sound of footsteps alerted them to the arrival of the ladies of the household. James watched Daphne's approach with a feeling of utter contentment. He counted himself fortunate for the miracles that had brought him to that point.

A flurry of activity erupted as they approached the door. The carriage was all but ready to go. The family all seemed to be bidding their farewells at once, raising a chaotic noise of voices. James clamped down his own frustration at still finding himself several people separated from his wife.

"Hold." The duke's booming voice cut through the madness, and everything in the entryway came to an immediate stop. He looked over his gathered relations and staff. To the maids, he said, "Take Lady Tilburn's bandboxes to the carriage." As they scurried away, he addressed the footman hovering nearby, "Go make yourself useful elsewhere."

Having dismissed the staff, he turned his attention to his relations. "I am certain you ladies made plenty of good-byes and exchanged well-wishes before joining us. It is, therefore, the gentlemen's turn to do so."

The duchess smiled at her husband, her expression empathetic. "Of course." She kissed her departing sister's cheek affectionately and, taking Miss Artemis by the hand, stepped back.

His Grace locked gazes with Daphne. No words were immediately forthcoming. They simply watched each other, similar emotions crossing their faces: tenderness, affection, and a hint of sadness. Then the duke opened his arms, and Daphne stepped into his brotherly embrace. Still neither spoke. Once or twice, His Grace appeared on the verge of saying something but didn't.

After several long moments, he pulled back a space. He gave Daphne a very serious look. "Don't forget I taught you how to use a pistol." He motioned with his head in James's direction.

Daphne smiled up at him and nodded.

The duke did not release his sister-in-law yet. Again, a look crossed his face, clearly indicating he wanted to speak but couldn't bring himself to do so. "Take care of yourself," he finally whispered.

"I will," she answered, her words watery.

He stepped abruptly away. "Don't keep the horses standing." The words came out as a command and a reprimand, though with the slightest break. Who in Society would ever guess that underneath the Duke of Kielder's imposing iron exterior beat a heart not entirely made of stone?

Daphne crossed to James's side. She allowed him to take her arm and walk with her out the door to the waiting carriage. He handed her inside before stepping up himself and sitting beside her. The carriage lurched to a start.

He expected Daphne to watch out the windows longingly as her childhood home disappeared from view. She looked instead at him and smiled ruefully. "I know we are returning in only two weeks and that this will be home to us for some time, but—" Emotion cut off her words.

He handed her a handkerchief.

"I had not realized," she said as she dabbed at her eyes, "how difficult it is to be the one doing the leaving."

James slipped his arm behind her, pulling her to him in a one-armed embrace. He held her thus as her emotions settled and was most pleased to feel her lean into him.

After several minutes, Daphne broke the silence between them. "Could you have possibly imagined when you were being so kind to a tiny little twelve-year-old girl on a terrace that you would actually one day marry her?"

James chuckled. "That would be a decidedly odd thing for an almost grown man to imagine about a twelve-year-old child."

"But not the other way around," Daphne answered. "I decided there and then that I would very much like to marry someone just like you."

James slid his arm so it wrapped around her waist rather than her shoulder and joined his other arm with it, truly embracing her. She snuggled up to him, a posture so trusting and natural that his heart became ever more hers in that moment. "In all honesty, my dear, I thought many times over the years since that fortuitous encounter that were I to find a young lady—one grown, mind you, but with the same courage and sweetness— that I would marry her in a heartbeat if she would have me."

She laid her hand on his chest and gazed up at him, her smile entirely devoid of the sadness that had far too often marred it. "You'll keep me, then?"

He pressed a lingering kiss to her forehead, then her cheek. He hovered just above her lips and whispered, "Always, my Little Sparrow," then sealed the declaration with a heartfelt kiss.

About the Author

SARAH M. EDEN IS A *USA Today* best-selling author of witty and charming award-winning historical romances. Combining her obsession with history and her affinity for tender love stories, Sarah loves crafting witty characters and heartfelt romances set against rich historical backdrops. She holds a bachelor's degree in research and happily spends hours perusing the reference shelves of her local library. She lives with her husband, kids, and mischievous dog in the shadow of a snow-capped mountain she has never attempted to ski.